VARIATIONS on NIGHT and DAY

VARIATIONS

on NIGHT and DAY

Abdelrahman Munif

TRANSLATED FROM THE ARABIC BY PETER THEROUX

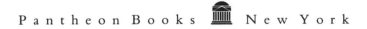

Pantheon Books   New York

All rights reserved under International and Pan-American
Copyright Conventions. Published in the United States by
Pantheon Books, a division of Random House, Inc., New
York, and simultaneously in Canada by Random House of
Canada Limited, Toronto.
Originally published in Lebanon as *Taqāsim al-Layl wa al-
Nahr* by Arab Institute for Research and Publishing, Beirut,
in 1989. Copyright © 1989 by Abdelrahman Munif.

Library of Congress Cataloging-in-Publication Data

Munīf, 'Abd al-Raḥmān.
[Taqāsīm al-layl wa al-nahr. English]
Variations on night and day / Abdelrahman Munif ; trans-
lated from the Arabic by Peter Theroux.
"The third volume in the *Cities of Salt* trilogy."
I. Title.
PJ7850.U514T3613 1993
892'.736—dc20   92-50786
ISBN 0-394-57673-X

Manufactured in the United States of America
First American Edition
9 8 7 6 5 4 3 2 1

That cloud brought this rain.

—BEDOUIN SAYING

The time has come! Something great is coming toward us; there is a huge, cleansing storm brewing, a storm that will sweep away all the laziness, apathy, idle dreams and corrupt hostility from society . . .

CHEKHOV, *The Three Sisters*

We won't share that life, but we are living for it today. We work and suffer in creating it. This alone is the purpose of our existence, and, if you will, our happiness. That which we imagine might be, sometimes, a glimmer of the possible, and it is in probing the possible that the power and possibilities of the future lie.

—ANAïS NIN

Mathematicians say:
  If . . .
  and . . .
  then . . .

An era of defeat, and in places of exile, soothing talk of history, or the illusion of history.

VARIATIONS on NIGHT and DAY

1

Dawn of the century—the opening decades.

The world, the whole world, in that quaking era, so full of anticipation and possibilities, looked around, as slow as a tortoise, as swift as a bolt of lightning, to question, to listen carefully for distant thunder, watching with dread for the approaching morrow.

Then, everything was open to reevaluation, to reapportionment: ideas, regions, countries, even kings, sultans and little princes. New states rose suddenly, and others vanished. Continents were divided along their latitudes and longitudes.

Regions and peoples divided and united as powerful decision-makers willed, according to their interests and their capacity for breaking treaties and promises.

Kings and sultans, and with them their courtiers, contrived ways of taking over at a moment's notice, or were sentenced to exile in distant islands, there to die forgotten and in silence.

This was the world at the dawn of this century. In Mooran, that desert buried in sand and oblivion, its hundred princely emirs fought over their shares as eagles fight. Their "states" expanded and shrank, and sometimes disappeared, on the whim of rainfall and locusts, of raids and plagues reaching this desolate place along with visitors. But as Mooran survived these calamities, and its sons composed and recited poems, and horse races were run again, and young girls went out unmolested to the brooks, and the people were contented, the hundred emirs undertook to transform it into an inferno. They were afflicted by a very special sort of madness, a madness which recurred every several years, which came on suddenly and ceased with equal suddenness; but which, while it lasted, left behind victims, hatreds, vendettas enough to make life continually fearful, and unending scores to settle.

Mirkhan bin Hadib, who was the emir of Mooran and the surrounding area for two days' journey in every direction, was ruined by one of the locust invasions. His princely neighbors envied him, and exploited his weakness and his emirate's flowing brooks within one year of the flying locusts' arrival by sending their flocks to the water. Their soldiers followed the flocks, and since two emirs could not occupy one brook, a humbled and unwilling Mirkhan bin Hadib was coerced into banishment in addition to his defeat.

When she heard the news of Mirkhan's flight, Najma al-Mithqal, the fortune-teller of al-Hadra and its environs, said that "a brook cannot sustain two, especially in these days." She added, ironically: "If the flood had come and gone, there would have been nothing to say about it. I believe Mirkhan will not be back—he is gone for good."

When Mirkhan contacted Najma from his exile to seek word of the days to come, she answered, "If there is any power in the flood, it will come and slake; it will rise and flood and foam, flow over, and wind down the slope." When he required more clarification, she said, "If the flood weeps, its tears will dry, but will gush forth again by and by."

When Najma al-Mithqal's relatives asked her whether it was likely that Mirkhan would return, she told them, "He has gone, and gone for good, but God may yet send a successor to do what he can, so let the stars look down and watch . . . we shall see."

As to how Mirkhan bin Hadib had survived and been able to escape, the most reliable story had it that Muflih ibn Mayyah had protected him and helped him flee. When a messenger from the Bani Suhaim came and asked him to join them against Mirkhan, Ibn Mayyah's long-remembered and often-quoted answer was: "If you drink from a well, you don't throw rocks into it. Mirkhan and I—God is my witness—had our differences, but I won't lift my sword against him, or cause him any harm. Leave him to God. If anything more befalls, you and I will all be one people until Judgment Day."

The Bani Suhaim were in dire need, at that time, of Ibn Mayyah's silence; their need was far greater than any hope they had of winning him over, so they looked the other way as Mirkhan crossed the desert, and let him go. And that is how he got away.

Because the vanquished princes were prisoners of the past, and their future was behind them, as a wise man once said, Mirkhan al-Hadib, who had cursed and threatened, and made the most sacred oaths to revenge himself against the Bani Suhaim, did not try to do anything, nor did he allow anyone else, least of all of his own men or family, to try either. He absorbed himself in defeat, and, later on, in prayer.

He prayed hundreds of times each day, and between each prostration and new prayer, he turned his face toward Mooran and wept. He raised his imploring, tear-stained face to Heaven, asking God to bring down punishment on the Bani Suhaim, to wipe out their livelihoods and exterminate them and their descendants. But his frustration ran so deep, and his prayers were so slow to reach their destination, that he was crushed with despair; and it was said that he went mad.

Khureybit was Mirkhan's second son. He prayed behind his father, but Mooran, or their return to Mooran, interested him much more than the prayers. His longing was brought on by the tales told at night, songs of home, dreams of his childhood, and that fertility engendered by the union of the sea and the shore. In daytime, the busy encampment of the emir of the Farhuds, in that era of noise and second thoughts, made him dream even more, especially since he took the sober, deadly paralyzing advice repeated in his own father's council every Thursday evening, and every day, in the council of the emir of the Farhuds, Thamer al-Farhud, as an unceasing provocation for him to act.

"We don't need legions and banners to take Muzhir bin Suhaim's head," Khureybit said to his uncle Dahaim one day. "What we need is the dark of night and one rifle shot; a hot ember becomes ash by evening, and we'd be back here, as if he had never been."

His uncle Dahaim nodded, and whispered, "It's true what you say, nephew, but we may pay for the bullet every day. It could be the mistake of a lifetime, one without parallel. If you don't kill, you'll get killed, and all to no purpose."

The uncle turned his face toward the spot where Mirkhan was praying; reassured that he was absorbed in prayer, he continued, "The best thing, nephew, is for us to prepare, and when we are ready, we won't let anyone know what we're up to. When we're sure, we'll slip in on some moonless night. Whichever of us dies will have a grave there in our own land, and if we win . . ."

Dahaim could not imagine victory. His face clouded over and he sighed, "But it will be days and years before we get to that task!"

A few months more passed, and Khureybit could wait no longer. His father and older brother prayed, and every Thursday evening they cursed Muzhir and reminisced, but he and his younger brother, Ayed, and Uncle Dahaim, their dreams fed by Thamer al-Farhud's words, "Time is like a sword—strike it, or it strikes you," and the noise that sounded over the beaches, whose echoes reached even the hundred quarreling princes—they and a band of men slipped out, one pitch-black night, and headed across the desert toward Mooran. A month later they arrived. On a night as dark as the one on which he'd set out, Khureybit and his men threw up ropes, scaled the walls of Muzhir bin Suhaim's fortress and hid until dawn. At the first light of day, as Muzhir was inspecting his horses before morning prayers, the concealed men came out and killed him. With his murder, the Bani Suhaim were defeated, and the Hadib clan came back again.

That was the official story as Khureybit's historians later recorded it, though most of the eyewitnesses had left this life for the next, and there was no trace of proof left from those times.

According to one story not recorded by the historians, though it was told by the people at the time, a woman had helped Khureybit and his men to get into the fortress and hide, whether out of love or for money, or both. It was said that Thamer al-Farhud had bribed a number of Muzhir's men months before Khureybit's arrival, and that it was they who had been Khureybit's means of entry, concealment and ultimate success.

With the murder of Muzhir bin Suhaim, his "state" collapsed, for states, in those times, were bound to their emirs: as long as the emirs were alive and strong, the "states" prevailed and even grew and expanded, according to the emir's power and alliances, but when emirs were defeated or killed, their states were wiped out, at least until the sons of the defeated emirs could try and "recover" the dominion of their fathers and grandfathers, to begin an endless cycle of attack and retreat and, inevitably, revenge.

As Khureybit returned, this time, the world was passing through an era of great convulsions and transformations; to be on this or that side could mean total victory or sweeping defeat. To be with the winners meant getting something. To be with the other side meant losing everything; it meant joining the refugees' caravan bound for oblivion, silence and death—that is, if one had not been killed at the outset, as had happened to hundreds, to thousands, of those seeking the dominion of their fathers and grandfathers.

Was this shrewdness? Chance? Destiny? None of these words meant anything, for the meanings and implications varied according to whether the victor or the vanquished spoke them. Since Khureybit had triumphed, and at this particular time, Mooran, this forgotten little town, in this remote desert, grew and expanded, to the point where its borders were no longer known!

Najma al-Mithqal, the fortune-teller of al-Hadra and its environs, said, when an envoy of the Bani Suhaim came to ask how she saw the days to come, "The world is a wheel—one day up, and tomorrow at the bottom."

When he pressed her to tell more, she said, "What may have lasted for others won't last as long for these."

When he insisted on knowing more, she looked around and replied sharply, "Now the Pleiades are not enough—we must seek out another star to appeal to, and we'll see. You'll go back in safety, but not this year or next; you'll go back when Scorpio is in Canopus and the Little Dipper!"

2

MUZHIR BIN SUHAIM'S HEAD MIGHT WELL HAVE stayed on his shoulders for quite some time longer, and might even have become a venerable head, adorned with honor and old age, had he not played that most dangerous of games: interfering with the allies of Britain, and seeking help and backing from their enemies. For no sooner had Muzhir sent bands of his men to expel Mirkhan al-Hadib than he ran into Thamer al-Farhud, and the two men quarreled. The rift between them began when Thamer refused to turn over Mirkhan, and grew with mutual threats. When Muzhir sought the support of the Turks to help him confront the Farhuds and the English, he sentenced himself to a course with only two possible outcomes: victory or death.

Why did Muzhir commit that fatal error? Was it intelligence that moved Khureybit to choose the outsiders?

The very words shimmer with the ambiguous harlotry of meaning. Intelligence, courage, reading the wind and stars, asking the guidance of old men, fathers, grandfathers and grandmothers, even reading history and knowledge of the Arabs' history—none of these explained the two men's choices, even taking into consideration the place Mirkhan had "chosen," which compelled Khureybit to be there as opposed to any other place.

The great states that had, in the past, tolerantly pretended to know nothing and see nothing when smaller powers quarreled over water and grazing land, and allowed them to go on killing one another, tolerating their loud noise and at times their recklessness, were no longer able to allow or tolerate anything.

No sooner did Muzhir go to Britain's enemies, at that time, than he was himself seen as an enemy and had to be destroyed. When Khureybit killed him, it was taken as a sign that he was a friend who could be relied upon, particularly since Thamer al-Farhud had not forgotten him for a single moment. He sent him gifts and numbers of men, including some of his friends, to assist Khureybit and stay close to him.

Because the great powers did not, at that time, have the time to deal with this huge number of small emirs and sheikhs or to prevent the movement of princes from one side to the other as in the past, Britain, perhaps as a result of a lottery, or on the recommendation of one of its dreamers who loved moonlight, the desert and the hobby of king-making, selected Khureybit. They put him in charge of the small emirs and protecting the caravan roads, and asked him to keep a watchful eye on the neighbors, the Turks and the eastern coast.

Khureybit had not imagined or aspired to more than returning home to Mooran, to be emir of the town and the surrounding oases and brooks; if its borders reached a two-day journey in every direction, he would have recovered all his father's and grandfather's domains and been gratified, able to sleep securely. Once he was chosen as the chief and representative of the lesser emirs, however, some madness stirred within him: he must have the whole desert, for it alone could protect him from enemies and time: the perfidy of passing days.

So Mooran began to expand. Khureybit was extremely tall, his body was tough and strong, and he was young, too, so he saw things other men did not see, and heard things that others did not hear; riches found their way to him that were unavailable to the others, and with the riches arms and advisers. Because he retained his rough clothes and stayed with his soldiers, and thought nothing, at times, of making generous gifts, he appeared in the eyes of many a man unlike the other emirs. He remembered his father's prayers and supplications, how people nodded obediently, out of fear and humility, and one day he observed to his uncle that "you can't deal with the bedouin, the bastards, except just three ways: gold, the sword, or 'the eternal garden underneath which rivers flow.'"

Uncle Dahaim nodded, convinced, and utterly delighted that his brother's son had grown up in this short time.

"What you say is true, nephew, and there's no denying it. It's not just true of the bedouin, but of everyone else, too." He added, in a different tone of voice, "This Mooran is treacherous—it will take advantage of you and ruin you. You have to be very wary, very careful, and sleep as lightly as a wolf."

Within a few years Mooran gave Khureybit its loyalty and obedience, channeled its alms to him and furnished soldiers, prayed behind the imams he dispatched everywhere; it even became a "great power" in this vast sandy ocean which had never before known a formula for existence that satisfied him or his friends.

In al-Hadra, Najma al-Mithqal heard only garbled and contradictory versions of the news, but in time learned that Khureybit bin Mirkhan had captured the fortress and killed Muzhir bin Suhaim. She said in surprise, "Who marches by night plunders, he doesn't gallop, and Ibn Mirkhan's fall will be the fall of a fugitive. Look who's behind him: are they Muzhir's children, giants' children or Farhud's?" She added, to herself, "True, anyone bitten by a snake is wary even of a rope, but the things he does are things only a fugitive or a madman or a daredevil would do."

She twisted around to look up at the sky and said stolidly, "The stars are stones in the sky; the falling one shows what you say; the runner has a head and tails. The Pleiades turn from the throne to the Dippers . . . if Mirkhan comes and rules, I'll cut off my hands and feed them to the dogs!"

It made no difference what Najma al-Mithqal said, because the people remembered only what they wished to, and heard only what they wanted to hear. Thus Khureybit filled their lives, their days and their nights, with noise, preparations for war and the expectation of Paradise.

Thamer al-Farhud was the beginning, and as Khureybit advanced in years, he continued his conquest of the surrounding regions, which grew year after year, outstripping all the Farhuds. Soon Butler, the British military chief of the whole region, paid a visit to Mooran.

"We and the Farhuds are cousins," Khureybit told him. "We take after them, they take after us, and we will never forget their favors to us, but you know, God keep you, those bedouin—their heads are harder than stones, they won't accept any but one of their own. Be sure to send us one of your brothers who can sit here and come to terms with us."

The British were not long in sending a team of advisers and reliable men, not only in marksmanship, be it of cannons or machine guns, but in other things as well, and they were careful to send money and gifts as well.

It was clear, from the bustle and noise, from the crowding of sheikhs into Mooran, that something was in preparation, something that would soon become evident.

Khureybit, who seemed to be the prince of Mooran, differing little from the other princes, changed with the expansion of the emirate and the growth of his own power. At Butler's suggestion, he proclaimed himself Sultan of Mooran. In this way he was different not only from the other emirs, but from other sultans as well: he wanted to become a tribe of one, not "a flock with a guide," as one historian had written of his father Mirkhan's flight, with his small family, to Thamer al-Farhud.

The men closest to Khureybit remembered that he got married the day after the murder of Muzhir bin Suhaim; it was his second marriage after the wife he left back with his father. Thereafter, in order to strengthen his relationships with the tribes, and the various regions, and in order to create his own tribe, within five years he married as many times as he was years old, as Sheikha Zahwa claimed proudly. Once he was rich and settled, it was impossible to count his wives or children, especially his daughters.

Khureybit grew more powerful with every passing year, and the ranks of his wives and children grew, too. Much as the neighboring lands aroused his appetite, and tempted him to annex them, he was able, for a long time, to resist mobilizing his forces in order to seize and subdue them, though there were two things he did incessantly: he talked about the need to conquer these countries, since he was the only one able to govern them, and he sent bands of armed men on raids here and there, to cut roads, plunder caravans and sabotage the borders. These bands of course, were always loyal to or dispatched by his enemies, thereby harming his interests, endangering him, and forcing him to put a stop to them.

When events had reached a certain point, a convenient point, he banished those who had prevented him from raiding one of these countries. The advisers vanished or left town, some of them reverting to pastimes that had occupied them at a certain time, for which they had come to Mooran in the first place. They went exploring for ancient ruins, studied the strata of the earth, went hunting or studying the flora and fauna of the desert. Khureybit launched a new campaign with the aim of enlarging the Sultanate, levying the charity tax and dispatching imams to institute worship according to the true faith in the territories he had subdued.

Such was the course of most of Khureybit's campaigns; and because he wanted to create a new tribe, and a sultanate different from anything else in this desert, he wanted his sons to grow up fast, so that they might share the building of the new domain; to be, like him, devoted to it; and to be capable of winning it back should fate turn against them and take it away. He put special effort into raising them, and assigned a group of men he trusted to indoctrinate and prepare them for the arduous days to come. The greatest attention was focused on Mansour, Khazael and Fanar, as they were the oldest of all the brothers, so that when Mansour's death in battle caused his father a grief that would never be forgotten, he turned to Khazael and Fanar in hopes that one or both of them would become his true legacy on this earth.

3

ONE OF SULTAN KHUREYBIT'S FAVORITE PAS-
times, one of which he never tired, was edu-
cating his children. He often spent all
morning on Monday, which was the day he had appointed for his
children to be with him so that he might check on their well-being,
see what requests they had and sort out their mothers' problems.
After he had given his orders and had Irfan al-Hijris record them so
that action might be taken, he would start a discussion with one question or comment in order to teach the children history, war, ethics or
philosophy. Their talks began in a general, abstract manner but before
long became very specific: how he had acted to establish the Sultanate,
who had been with him and who against him, and what each man had
done; what sort of foes he had faced, how they fought and how he
finally beat them.

He loved to talk, casually and at great length, and at times even
reenacted the whole scene as if it were happening again. The awe-

struck children followed it all raptly, according to their respective ages
and mental powers; it delighted them to make him pause at the wonderful or incredible parts. The Sultan obliged, and retold the events
with extra details, watching the effect of his words in the eyes of his
children, the guards and other listeners. The more enraptured they
were, and the more plainly they showed it, the happier he was to tell
more stories.

He used to tell Talleh al-Oreifan, one of the palace functionaries,
with special responsibility for the children when the Sultan was absent: "Children, Talleh, are like horses, they never get tame unless you
shout in their ears, and never come to water unless you whistle for
them. Time after time, they understand and respond, but if you leave
them and don't teach them, you'll just lose them—they'll only be a
misery to you."

The Sultan's sons, who prepared for this day by putting on their
best clothes and perfuming themselves, were made to repeat after
their mothers certain ambiguous expressions, which were messages
directed to His Majesty. The Sultan knew the meaning of these messages in advance—most of them conveyed longing and a desire to be
with him—but never gave clear replies, much to the confusion of both
the children and the mothers. When the muddled messengers reported on what they had conveyed and what the reply had been, there
were ructions between the bearers of the messages and the senders,
compelling the mothers to send more explicit messages in the weeks
following. Between the mothers' incessant emphasis on the necessity
of transmitting the messages accurately, and on bringing home even
more exact word-for-word answers, and the Sultan's insistence that
they learn their lessons, the children did not know what to do or
to say.

"If he weren't a veritable camel, how could he ever bear these burdens, Nahi?" Talleh asked his assistant, Nahi al-Farhan, one Monday.
When Nahi said nothing, he added, "These women are never satisfied;
they never rest or let anyone else rest!"

Although Nahi knew who he was talking about and what he was
alluding to, he asked simplemindedly, "You talk as the bedouin pray,
Abu Jazi: a quick genuflection and prostration, and no one can understand a single word!" He laughed. "If you have something to say, say
it, Jazi."

"Ibn Hijris scribbles on a few scraps of paper, saying, 'To whom it may concern, kindly take action.' And Dughaim al-Sarhud takes his green pen and writes, 'Received and read.' And what with al-Hijris and al-Sarhud, and His Majesty's new babies and new wives, we're lost, Nahi. Now we need a fortune-teller to see our way forward."

"Abu Jazi," answered Nahi cynically, "he's a total madman, but if no one asks and no one says anything, the wives stay away."

"But women are insatiable, and they can't keep quiet, my friend."

"Let them dizzy our royal master."

"He has no one but us—right, Talleh? 'What have you done about this business or that affair?' We're never through unless they keep quiet or he goes traveling."

"I counsel patience, Abu Jazi."

"How are we supposed to have patience with fools and women?"

"Just be patient and everything will turn out fine."

The same stories were told and retold, and the demands of the wives and children mounted steeply with the growing number of children flocking to the Monday meetings. Irfan al-Hijris recorded as much as his slow hand allowed him to write, after wetting the pen on his lips, and made three copies of each request, one for His Majesty's files for safekeeping, the second for his files for his own reference, and the third for Dughaim al-Sarhud, who adorned it with his seal and signature and the unvarying formula, "Received and read—take action." The document was then forwarded back to Irfan, who kept it among his papers, so as to collect all three copies again; he sent them on to Talleh for further action only if the requests were urgent, and as a rule reviewed each several more times.

Since everyone who resided at the palace had requests as befitted their rank or degree of closeness to the Sultan, and so many were about equal in rank or relation to the Sultan, or pretended to be—a pretension shared by their people who followed up on their requests, demanding immediate action, before any other request—the noise and insistence overwhelmed the energies of the palace supervisors and administrators. The result was chaos, delays and sometimes quarrels. As soon as complaints reached the more senior authorities and the Sultan's ears, everything changed: action on all requests came to a halt and a new staff of administrators was brought in to replace the old one, at the predictable cost of many threats and grudges.

The petitioners and their demands and vehement nagging were a great irritation and annoyance to the palace administrators, who wondered why they were never satisfied and never grew tired of complaining, but the people who did not make demands or send messages, and those whose requests were infrequent or humble, were regarded with just as much surprise and wonderment.

Fanar was the only one, or more precisely one of the very few, who made no demands and carried no messages. He sat before his father, listening closely, and when he gazed around, it was at the small faces which stammeringly conveyed the messages, generally in the form of proverbs or verses of poetry which they barely understood. Some handed over slips of paper that had passed through many hands before coming to rest in the Sultan's hand, which contained in most cases their mothers' needs and demands. Fanar watched these scenes at first with surprise, then out of curiosity and, still later, love of learning.

"My good man, he's all eyes and ears," Talleh al-Oreifan once told Fanar's uncle Omair. "He takes it all in and stores it away, and you don't hear a breath out of him. He's not like the rest—he has no greed, no demands. When His Majesty asks him if he has any request, he starts, and says, 'Only your well-being, Your Majesty.'" When he saw how pleased Omair was at this praise, he went on carefully. "And Ain Fadda didn't teach him only religion, it taught him more than that—morals and manners!" He added in a whisper, "And manliness, too."

The Sultan, who loved making a show of his power and having others feel the importance and gravity of every decision he made, and by extension the mental powers that had gone into that decision, recollected stories that the others knew just as well as he did, perhaps even better, but he wanted to extract lessons from them, and wanted his children to have a perfect grasp of everything he said.

Khureybit spoke to Dahaim a few months later, when he felt sure that Fanar was the eagerest of his sons to listen to his stories and the most able to grasp them.

"You know, old man, that coddling just corrupts children. None of these women has anything on her mind but her child—they pamper and spoil them. If the boys never know hardship, if they don't know heat and cold, if they never know danger, they'll never grow up into reliable men."

Dahaim smiled. "We've seen things no one will ever see again, Abu

Mansour—the kind of hardship we knew doesn't exist anymore. Those days are gone—these are different times now."

"But we have to train and teach them, Uncle, and pray for them."

"But not endanger them, Abu Mansour."

"Adversity is a thing of the past, Uncle—now it's all talk, drinking coffee, and hunting, combing their beards and waving sticks. When the music stops, things will change, though."

"That's the truth, Abu Mansour."

"And that's not all, Uncle. A boy has to be disciplined even if his mother doesn't like it, because a boy without discipline, without war and hardship, will lose his way—you'll lose him."

"That's the truth, Abu Mansour. But as the Syrians say, 'Once on a steed, they'd stop a stampede'; because those boys are still infants."

"They've grown up, Uncle, they're men. When a boy's grown, treat him that way."

The two men were silent for a time. They were reminiscing, remembering when they were boys: the way of life then, the hardships they faced, and how different the old days were from the present.

"What's gone is gone, Abu Mansour," said Dahaim in a deep, throaty voice, "and now we have to fear what's coming. I feel afraid, really—my fear is of dying afraid. No one around us these days knows the hardships we've seen . . ." He shook his head several times. "Now they get whatever they want without even asking for it."

Khureybit chanted sadly:

"Who knows longing, but who has endured it
Or passion, other than its victims?"

He added, a moment later, "It's true that we've prepared for anything that can happen, but we have to be strict with them so that they can carry this burden."

"God willing, we won't see Our Lord's face until we've done all we have to do, Abu Mansour."

"Don't worry, Uncle," laughed the Sultan. "We're still young and strong."

This talk was accompanied by muffled rumors in the Rawdh Palace, which, since they involved the Sultan, were circulated warily and behind closed doors. Some said that Fadda had left the palace in a rage;

others said that the Sultan was angry with her and had kicked her out. There were attempts to intercede, to please and persuade her, but all failed, which became obvious when her sojourn with her family lengthened, and the Sultan seemed depressed and irritable—unusual for him.

Everyone in the palace had his or her own views on Fadda's anger and expulsion from the palace, and on Fadda herself; two of the Sultan's wives swore that the Sheikha, Ummi Zahwa, had spoken abusively to Fadda, and one of the wives said she had slapped her, too, and demanded that she leave the palace. The Sultan's oldest daughter said that he had said he never wanted to see her face again. Watfa, whose rank was enhanced by her having given birth to a baby boy, smiled broadly and said nothing when asked about the affair, but her manner left the impression that she had become the Sultan's favorite, and that Fadda no longer meant anything to him, which had led her to quit the palace in anger.

Moza always went with her mistress and remained a frequent visitor to the palace, and even slept there one night. It was not clear why she spent the night or why indeed she came at all; nor was anyone able to pry a single word out of her. Fadda's detractors said that Moza had come to carry off her mistress's gold, and when the Sultan left Fadda, they were sure. Those who sympathized with the lady and the slave girl said that Moza's return had something to do with readying the palace, particularly Fadda's bedroom, because she would be coming back in just a few days. Still others said that the Sultan himself had asked Moza to stay, had spent considerable time alone with her, had given her a letter and gifts for Fadda, and had asked her to try and conciliate with her so that she would come home.

One of Moza's woman friends said that Moza had been in a state of profound depression for two months, crying constantly and unable to endure anyone's company. She could not eat a thing. People could scarcely believe that this was really she: her color was gone, her eyes bulged out, and she looked far older than her age. This friend added that when she got Moza alone and asked her what was wrong, she answered only, "My master and mistress . . ." and fell silent, only shaking her head in grief. This was taken to explain Fadda's departure and long absence from the Rawdh Palace as well as the moodiness that marked the Sultan and his own actions.

Watfa's servant Lulua confided in a few trusted friends that the palace midwife, Warida, had admitted to her mistress three days after the birth of the new prince, Mufarrih, that Fadda had shown her a large amount of money and begged her to strangle that infant to death when she learned it was a boy. When the midwife refused to do it, Fadda threatened to expel her from the palace and punish her. Lulua said that her mistress told the Sultan, who was skeptical and summoned the midwife, who told him everything. And surely that was at the bottom of what went on later!

Tahany, the Sheikha's slave, said that the wager between the Sultan and Fadda over the third pregnancy was the real cause of what went on. The Sultan, who had forgotten the wager, or had ignored it, a short time after the birth of the third child no longer remembered it, and wanted no one to remind him, unlike Fadda, who had not forgotten the wager for a single day. It was said that she had told her family about the matter, and her family spread news of the Sultan's consent, saying that he would announce it publicly soon, and this angered him and led to the subsequent events. What lent credence to this story was the Sultan's new marriage within a few days of Fadda's departure from the Rawdh Palace, and the fact that he took his new wife along with him on a hunting trip—before, he had always taken Fadda.

Tahany told the story with a smile and a look at her listeners' faces so that each might sense that Ummi Zahwa was behind the affair, that she alone made all the decisions in the palace.

Talleh al-Oreifan, who as a rule did not like idle gossip, and who hardly ever uttered a word of it except under duress, and then only to close friends, told Nahi al-Farhan, when he heard the stories and rumors: "Fadda's family, Nahi, are impossible—they're like people riding behind you, they never ride without putting their hand out. They still have never heard a single word without their dividing things up: 'This is ours, and that is ours, and His Majesty will see this and hear all about it.' And if His Majesty doesn't put them in their place, that's no tragedy, he'll keep an eye on their daughter, and tell them: 'Look sharp and draw your borders, friends!'"

"I'm afraid it's going to be like so many stories before it, Abu Jazi, and tomorrow or the day after when she gives him a fourth boy, she'll go back to where she was before and her family will ride again."

"It's got nothing to do with us, Nahi. As they used to say, 'Whoever marries our mother is our stepfather.'"

"Abu Jazi, let's wait and see how the story comes out."

Just a few weeks later something completely unforeseen happened, when the Sultan married yet again, a girl from the al-Mudalji clan this time.

During the days of wedding preparations the palace was rife with whispers and rumors, this time plainly and in louder voices: "His Majesty chose her from the al-Mudalji clan to prove to Fadda that the Mudaljis are with him, not with her, and that he can do anything." One of Fadda's servants, widely suspected of informing his mistress of everything that went on in the Rawdh Palace, insisted that "it was my lady that chose her—you'll soon see it with your own eyes." Tahany's comment was vague: "In the Rawdh Palace only the Sultan rules." And others said yet other things.

Watfa still denied reports of a new marriage, and her servant Lulua said that the Sultan had demanded the return of his children whom Fadda had taken with her, and that they would be back any day now, without their mother.

Moza's surprise visit, and the commotion it caused, changed much of what was being said: she went into her mistress's wing of the palace and took up her position there, and while she pretended not to hear the questions people asked her, clear, wordless answers could be read in her eyes. The Sultan summoned her, which fueled rumors and anxiety; she spent a full hour in his wing, and two servants reported that they had seen her laugh in his presence, and he ordered tea for her. Two or three hours later, shortly before sundown, she left the palace in a three-car motorcade.

When Nahi al-Farhan heard the news, and saw things with his own eyes, he rushed to see Talleh and told him, making no secret of his unease: "God help us, Abu Jazi—didn't we put our hearts into these problems? When people are through with the Sultan, they'll go for the Mudalji—they've already said everything that can be said against her. There are a lot of good men, and God knows they've done everything they can."

"There's nothing for us to do. We haven't heard or said a thing." Then, after a moment, as if remembering his innate caution: "That's the truth, Nahi. They used to say, 'If you talk at night, lower your voice; if you talk in daytime, beware.' But people never learn, except at their own expense."

Then events took a completely unforeseen course: Alanoud bint

Salem al-Mudalji arrived at the Rawdh Palace with a crowd of ladies, among them Moza. She was given a whole wing of the main palace building to herself; it was beside Fadda's wing. The wedding formalities were swiftly celebrated. Three days later Fadda returned to the palace, and while she seemed plumper, she was otherwise unchanged; nor, indeed, had her position in the palace changed. The people looked at one another and wondered what was happening.

4

HALIMA, WHO GAVE KHUREYBIT TWO CHIL-
dren, Mudi and Fanar, and passed from the
scene rather quickly, left an ineradicable in-
fluence on the personalities of her two offspring. The two felt that
they were of a strain apart from the lineages of the other mothers; to
their father, they were distant and forgotten. Khureybit spoke of them
as one would speak of an old friend or some lost object. When he
summoned them from Ain Fadda to spend a few days in Mooran, he
always asked them about "the little dervish," as he was fond of calling
their grandfather, Sheikh Awad. To the young boy and girl, however,
the old sheikh's fame filled the eyes and ears of the whole world, despite the kindness and simplicity that made him the very model of
self-effacing humility. They were constantly visiting Ain Fadda to
seek his guidance in religious matters.

Sheikh Awad never discussed the ancientness or prominence of the
family line in the way lineage was discussed in Khureybit's councils

and encampments, though the women of Ain Fadda, especially the elderly ones, and the young men on the verge of manhood, talked about little else but the sheikh's ancient and venerable ancestry, and the role his family had played in supporting Khureybit and establishing his rule. This talk reached shouting pitch whenever they heard reports that Khureybit had married yet another woman or that another of his wives had given birth to a son. They talked and looked at Fanar and remembered Halima, who had borne only him and Mudi. If Sheikh Awad heard their talk, or someone came to interrupt his praying, to tell him of Khureybit's latest marriages or the sons born to him, he would say, a sad smile playing around his lips, " 'All such are transitory, but to your Lord's face belongs all honor and majesty.' " If they spoke on or pressed him, he would speak, after a long, silent pause, as if to himself. "Muhammad was an orphan, and was alone, but God made him strong and gifted." If they pressed him further, he would say, "Our grandfather was an orphan, and was alone, but look how he turned out."

Sheikh Awad loved ants, cats and little lambs, and protected them; he allowed no one to step on them or throw stones at them. He kept the lambs safe from greedy knives, especially of the younger men. He also loved children, and they loved him back.

If Fanar remembered anyone in Ain Fadda, it was the image of his grandfather. The first grief he ever felt was when one of the women carried him, smelling and kissing him and repeating, "Where are your eyes to see this, Halima?" The first time he ever felt proud was when the youths of Ain Fadda dressed him in clothes such as the adults wore, and they turned him this way and that, looking him over admiringly and talking among themselves more than to him directly. He looked like a king, they said, and they told him more than once to hold his head up and keep his back straight, to look strong and grown-up.

Mudi listened to the women's talk, and loved the boys' games. Now she had no one in this world but Fanar. Her childhood ended swiftly, and she became a girl older than her age: she looked after her brother, she prepared his meals and made his bed, and never stopped telling the stories she had heard from old and young about Fanar the prince. Fanar the prince was lost in his gaudy robes, and behaved as an adult, and used some of the words he had heard from his grandfather.

In Ain Fadda he truly felt like a prince, and an adult. The open spaces, the palm trees and the brooks were the witnesses to his actions and all his behavior.

In Mooran, during the visits he was forced to make at his father's request, in the immense crush of young princes, servants, guards and visitors, he felt even smaller than the ants that crawled around Ain Fadda; at least the ants there had someone to protect them. Here he was lost in the crowd, the noise, and the mad rush to carry out the wishes of the sole Sultan: Khureybit. If anyone spoke to him, it was to ask who he was and why he was wearing those silly clothes, and he did not know whether to respond to the questions or to the questioner's suspicious and mocking eyes.

He was unhappy in Mooran. He did not like the place and did not see how people could live there. Since his father had forgotten him, he did not hesitate to ask his retainer, Nassar, for permission to go back to Ain Fadda. His grandfather before him had advised Nassar to seize the first chance, after securing the Sultan's leave, to go back home. Muzna told him the same thing. Mudi kissed Nassar's hands and pleaded with him not to delay.

His mother's sister Muzna said, "Mudi has been insane since the moment Fanar left Ain Fadda—her mind just isn't there. She can't eat, she can't drink, she can't sleep until he's back. If he stays away, she'll sicken and die. Day and night, all she does is cry out, 'Where have they taken him? What's happened to him?' We're at the end of our wits. We tell her, 'Dear girl, Fanar is with his father, he's a guest there, they're taking excellent care of him, don't worry, now stop shouting.' But she shouts instead of sleeping. I don't have the patience to last until he comes back. Mudi is just going to be the madwoman of the house, of all Ain Fadda, until he comes back!"

So he came back, a few weeks later, amid all the noise and fanfare with which Ain Fadda welcomed home an honored and loved guest. His uncle Omair insisted on marking the occasion with parties that lasted for days, and on slaughtering a number of sheep over the protests of Sheikh Awad, claiming it was only right that Ain Fadda remember Fanar's homecoming better than it remembered his absence.

There was a constant exchange of stories, news items and questions between Ain Fadda and Mooran, followed by whispers, comments and yet newer stories, until life slowly returned to its pleasant state, almost as if at the beginning of time. Sheikh Awad's prayers rang out in the summer nights, as did the young men's songs on the outskirts of the village, the same old stories were told over and over again, and the people laughed and carried on as if hearing them for the first time.

When Fanar turned twelve, during one of his father's visits to Ain Fadda, Khureybit looked at him differently than he ever had before. He told him, and his grandfather, who was absorbed in his prayers, and Uncle Omair, and a number of standing and seated observers that "from now on Fanar's place is in Mooran; he must be near us, to assist us. If anyone wants Fanar, they'll know where to find him—you are all most welcome in Mooran!"

Because the Sultan spent three days in and around Ain Fadda, Sheikh Awad got no sleep for three days. He wanted to be alone with the Sultan, to ask him, even to beg him, to leave Fanar behind, but the Sultan was never once alone during those days, nor was he ready to consult privately with Sheikh Awad, since he was certain that the sheikh had nothing to say, and so instead of talking to Khureybit the sheikh prayed.

His grandmother was more perceptive, perhaps because she was more loving, and after talking to herself aloud, and saying the unsayable for everyone to hear, she shouted at the grandfather, at Muzna and Mudi and everyone else around her, "This is their child, you people, and if they don't take him today, they'll take him tomorrow or the next day. Think about it! If you want the best for Fanar, his place is there!"

His uncle Omair was a practical man, in spite of the fantasies and delusions that passed through his head some nights. He wanted Ain Fadda to remain, to grow, to become important. He remembered when Mooran had been even smaller than Ain Fadda; it would still have been tiny and backward had Khureybit not lived there and made it a capital city. And while Omair slaughtered a large number of sheep in order to help Ain Fadda grow, and in spite of the parties he had given to welcome Fanar and other important family members, and though his father never stopped praying for a single day, Ain Fadda continued to shrink in size and importance: the town's young men were tired of singing and had wearied of waiting, and saw emigration as their only gateway to a better life.

When Omair saw the Sultan, he wanted to gather his children

around, as he used to call up his army. "We may be able to fight from
Mooran," he said to himself, and so he was satisfied and cooperative
with regard to Fanar's leaving. He wondered what would become of
Fanar there. How would he live, where would he stay, what kind of
people would be around him?

"And according to your orders, Your Majesty," he told the Sultan
on the third day, as he was preparing to depart, "Mudi will remain
with the prince."

"Yes, yes," answered the Sultan, turning around.

"And in order that they not trouble anyone, Your Majesty, I'll go
with them, and with your consent we'll arrange everything."

That was how Fanar and Mudi moved to Mooran, and with them
Uncle Omair.

Their grandmother was impassive, almost severe, as she bid them
goodbye. She said she would come to visit them in Mooran, and that
Mooran was like Ain Fadda. She gave each of them an Ottoman Ra-
shadi coin, and as she pressed the one into Mudi's hand, she whispered, "What I need to tell you, Mudi, is that you're his sister and his
mother, and you can depend on him." The children's grandfather was
absent from this leave-taking, and they looked all over for him; at last
they found that he had spent most of the time in the small room on
the roof of the house, beseeching God to make Khureybit forget to
take the children. When he heard Khureybit's loud laughter and saw
the people streaming out of the encampment, led by Fanar in his
gaudy robes, it seemed to him that God would not answer his prayers
in time, so he left the upper room and ran after the moving motorcade. Alaiwi, a servant who was watching everything carefully, said
that tears coursed down the old man's face as he waved to Fanar and
Mudi.

Aunt Muzna, who stayed silently by her mother, and tried to occupy herself, feeling assured that she would catch up with them as
soon as they got settled in Mooran, then said aloud, "When you get
your tents up and your coffeepots all ready, send for me and I'll come,
if not the next day then the day after that!"

The motorcade moved off from Ain Fadda to Mooran. Fanar and
Mudi sat in the second car from the front, behind the Sultan's.

5

IN THE RAWDH PALACE, AMONG THAT FABU-
lous throng of old and young, amid the car-
nival of languages and skin colors unlike any
other in the world, Fanar and Mudi were lost. Had it not been for
some of the old palace attendants, they would never have found a
place to sleep or in which to keep the few things they had brought
with them from Ain Fadda.

The palace was something of a marvel: dozens of wings and suites
opening on to one another. Along the sides were the guards' and servants' quarters. In the center stood the two-story main building, occupied by the Sultan and his three closest wives, with balconies
overlooking the great hall on one side, and the contiguous buildings,
most of them recently built, on the other two sides. Most of these had
been put up recently. The fourth, southern side, overlooked the horse
stables.

No one knew exactly who controlled the palace or how it was run, for in spite of its great number of officers and administrators, the palace's main features were its noise, commotion and chaos. The oldest palace residents had first choice of accommodations, furniture and even food, not because of any formal decision or agreement, but because this way imposed itself through habit and precedent. The same distinction held for the short-term guests in the east wings, which were divided from the interior by a high wall. Newcomers who came to live in the palace met with no end of trouble, for in spite of the Sultan's orders, which were generally indirect anyway, by way of Dughaim al-Sarhud or one of the Sultan's servants or guards, a newcomer had no idea what to do or where to turn. If he were offered a place—which usually did not happen—in most cases it had been wrested from some other person who had been occupying it, or not, with a great deal of ill will and refusal. Sometimes the servants or guards would lock up the rooms and leave the palace, or lose the keys, so obtaining furniture and other necessities could be atrociously difficult. The storehouses were jammed with old and useless things, since any shipment of new furniture meant the automatic disposal, within a very few days, of the old furniture, and the substitution of the new. These matters were guided by orders from the princes and princesses, servants and guards, so that the old always got mixed with the new, with no one clearly aware of who had taken or returned what, and with the possessions stacked in this way it was impossible for anyone to know what exactly was there and what was not.

Once these difficulties were surmounted and this problem dealt with, which usually took several days of complications, feuds and the intervention of higher authorities, there was the matter of relations between the residents and the visitors: any visitor, no matter how old or socially prominent, was considered fair game for dozens of hunters, opportunists and lurkers. With the exception of the Sultan's uncles and brothers, who often spent extended periods at the Rawdh Palace, with news of their arrival always coming before them, every newcomer was subjected to a number of inspections and virtual attacks: it began with the guards exchanging looks, then asking innumerable questions about various matters and people, in order that each side obtain ample information about the other: how close they were to the Sultan, and how socially prominent they were. This information was weighed against the number of horses or automobiles, guards and other entourage, their clothing and weapons and comportment. When this part was completed, and no further information was required, there were other inspections to ascertain other points, such as the preparedness of the guest. These inspections were carried out with extreme artifice and cunning, and dealt with the most precise facts about the new arrival: why he had come, how long he would stay, and dozens of other questions, all put spontaneously as if they were part of a general conversation held in total candor, but each side knew how to answer, and how to deceive, in order to mislead the other or give erroneous ideas, which led to each side reevaluating the other.

The information and assessments were immediately conveyed to the rear stations, which were arranged by rank. It was usual to proceed indirectly, so that one of the seated men, who as a rule had not taken part in the questioning and inspection, might suggest that the newcomer leave at once; or a servant might show up, in a manner not lacking skill, to ask that someone might come, by way of those offered firsthand information so that an assessment of what had been said and done might be given, in order that it might be determined whether or not a higher authority in the chain of command need be involved, to sort out the guest's level of intimacy or importance; to see whether this kind of procedure need be followed, or abandoned in favor of something else. All this went on in an atmosphere of jokes, small services being offered, and the advice of bystanders.

The goal of the inspections, services and arguments was to establish the status of the newcomer, his rank among the many rival ranks within the palace. The newcomer would inevitably become part of one of the disputatious powers, in one of the camps, to be an appendage of one of the power blocs. To be sure, this did not happen that quickly or clearly, but in the new arrival's first hours and days, most probabilities were settled, and left their long-lasting mark.

Although the chief aim was to establish the newcomer's status, or to win him over, there were many complex side effects, some of them funny. The errors, the lies, the swindles to which old and young alike resorted were the subject of discussion and were passed around from place to place, in different versions. Sometimes they even reached the Sultan, with all the exaggeration and provocation and incident, which generally led to real battles that began in the women's quarters and spread to the whole palace, even at times requiring the intervention of the Sultan or one of his representatives to restore calm. Sometimes new administrators had to be brought in and residents and guests moved far away; sometimes new wings had to be built on to the palace—all this to quell the feuds, to put barriers or distances between the antagonists.

It was impossible for anyone in the Rawdh Palace to remain neutral or unaffected. The daily incidents and stories that circulated made everyone a participant. Even the visitors and functionaries and the men who delivered groceries became, in one way or another, part of the palace's problems and concerns.

While the men's contests and skirmishes took place in the open, in the shadows of the walls or below the palm trees, with shows of jocularity and the pretense of friendship, the women's battles raged behind closed doors, in secrecy, and took extremely cunning and injurious forms, for every woman who set foot in the palace turned it upside down and changed the rules, especially the rank of the people within. Everyone recalled what had happened when Fadda, the Sultan's favorite wife, arrived. No sooner had she settled in the central building than everything in the palace changed, and the Sultan, who spent months of each year on the move from place to place, fighting and raiding, or else settling feuds among the tribes that supported him, now gave up his travels, or at least limited them as much as possible. He delegated his sons to make these trips on his behalf, with the help of their uncles or his own uncles. He did so that he might spend time with Fadda. No one said so out loud at first, but when the central building was enlarged and part of the servant quarters cleared out—more precisely, two of the Sultan's other wives were cleared out—the whispers became open criticism, and the murmurs became accusations circulated by the servants to the public. But the Sultan's presence in the palace, and the fact that the matter related directly to him, meant that nothing could come of the stories. His presence generated fear, as several times he had punished servants and the storage-house workers, even having three of them executed for minor infractions as well as for repeating slanders about him, which he might have spoken himself. Fear was not his only deterrent: he also made overtures in the form of gifts, small compensations and pay raises. These also on occasion were a form of excuse, which his angry wives accepted with a sort of equanimity, or so the huffy wife put it about via her servants or relatives, with ever-mounting boasts of the expensive gifts that came along with the Sultan's visit, though her exaggerations might meet with plain disbelief.

If it had nothing to do with the Sultan or one of his close wives, though the degree of closeness was generally not spelled out, whether in terms of seniority or blood or the number of sons she had given him, sometimes for reasons that no one was aware of, it remained a secret between the Sultan and that woman—otherwise, the war that broke out, especially among powerful women, might rage on uncontrolled, with no one knowing where it would lead. It began with whispers from one bedchamber to another, from one wing of the palace to another, then took the form of coldness in relations followed by a breaking off of relations, until it escalated to the exchange of accusations, until at times one of them was dead.

There were many instances when servants in the Rawdh Palace were killed; such instances even recurred frequently, but usually occurred—more precisely, always occurred—in the Sultan's absence. When servants were killed, it was usually because they were a direct instrument of the ongoing war, for it was they who delivered messages and spread rumors and accusations, and they who ran in this direction or that to provoke trouble. Some of them even pursued battles more zealously than the combatants, and in some cases they knew more than they ought to have, which was considered reason enough to kill them.

It was customary for men to resort to arms, either in an outburst of anger or because of the embarrassing, minutely detailed stories originating in that "forbidden zone" which led them to do away with one of the message-bearers. The opposing side's slaves or guards would not be slow to strike back with similar murders by night, with the excuse that the crimes had been a mistake, or an accident while cleaning their guns.

That is how men were killed. Women were usually dispatched with poison or through childbirth. Several times, though not very often, women were found to have thrown themselves down the wells in the palace, or died of suffocation late at night in the North Bath, not far from the main building. And three of the Sultan's women "died of grief," in the words of Watfa, the Sultan's fourth wife. More than that were found hanged in their rooms—the servants swore that the rooms had been locked from the inside.

It was true that there were rather few murders, as compared to ru-

mors, beatings or expulsions from the palace; chases, gunfights, escapes and disappearances. The jokes, anecdotes and rumors that circulated, and the ridicule of the opposing side, were clearly favorite
pastimes of the women, and not a few of the men as well. Odes that
were composed to praise or deride a given person were on everyone's
lips, and the servants learned them by heart and recited them with
gusto, as if venting anger or taking revenge. Some private guards who
had spent much time in the palace affirmed that these odes reached the
Sultan, who sometimes smiled and sometimes grew angry; and sometimes, they said, he repeated them, asked questions and asked for interpretations. As a rule, nothing came of his interest, especially when
time passed, or the creator of the ode was not known, or the palace
was relatively tranquil.

When there was no battle raging in the palace, it was usually because one had just ended and another was being prepared. At times
there were no battles at all, or they were muffled by the unexpected
return of the Sultan or some other exceptional circumstance such as
his marriage to a new wife from one of the powerful or hostile tribes.
In such cases the Sultan craved special parties and the lavish giving of
gifts, firing of guns, and especially festivals for his horses and the new
horses he was receiving. This concern, whether directly from him or
generated at his suggestion, was not merely an expression of joy but
an assertion of power, tantamount to actual messages to the relevant
parties at home and abroad.

New events inevitably convulsed the status quo, altering the con-
stellation of alliances and feuds, with yesterday's foes becoming
friends, and yesterday's battles becoming new friendships and alliances. The rumors and accusations, the stories and anecdotes, were
quickly forgotten—as if they had never been. The transition, of
course, took place indirectly and rather quietly, but it was usually
speedy, with apologies, banquets and the mandatory exile of many
servants, advisers and guards on both sides, and those who'd had
a hand in some of the insults and incidents. Their banishment was
usually temporary, on the pretext of mistrust, or because there was
some other need for their services. It frequently happened that some
of those exiled died in mysterious circumstances. And a number of
them, after what they judged to be a sufficient period, sent word via
their friends or family to the party that had quarreled with them to
declare their readiness to disclose some of the scandalous things they

knew about—things they had actually witnessed or taken part in—which information and implications could be put to great use.

Children and youths in the Rawdh Palace were quick to imitate the grown men and women. At first they did so at the goading of the servants, or because of the kind of talk and atmosphere that surrounded them, but quickly they went further than anyone. Their alliances and feuds, formed by their emerging leaders, instigators and abettors, so expert at ridicule, cruelty and warfare, made no distinction between who their family liked and who their enemies were. The important thing was to be skillful, and to deploy this skill so that their families would notice.

There was not a child in the Rawdh Palace who did not have a pistol or rifle, and with so many guns around, and so much talk of battles and heroism, and because weapons were a father's first gift to his sons, it was very common to find guns in children's hands. The adults cautioned the little ones, gave them ammunition, and told the servants to keep their eyes open, but nothing was simpler than getting around all this.

Not only fixed objects but animals were targets for the children's bullets. They chased the dogs and cats and competed in killing them, or pretending to. The animals were often permanently crippled, and in that case, as soon as they could be caught, they were kept tied up to make easier targets. Some horses, too, were found dead, on one occasion one of the Sultan's horses, Ad'aj, or Blackeye. The stablemen had no choice but to make up excuses to offer the Sultan. They said the horse had fallen ill, that a scorpion had stung him, and finally that they had allowed him to graze in a certain field where he had eaten a poison plant, and when they went out searching, they found him at the edge of the pasture, swollen and dead.

Slaves and servants, too, provided target practice, especially when times were hard, though as a rule their killers were never made known. The action taken in such cases was not the apprehension and punishment of the killer, but vengeance wrought against the animals, slaves and servants of likely perpetrators, carefully and secretly, so that morning sometimes brought the discovery of a dead horse or a sudden outbreak of fire in one of the wings of the palace. There were several instances of slaves found murdered beside the palace, in the walled palm-tree garden or near the stables. There was no respite, not even temporarily, until the palace officials turned tough, announcing loudly that they had told the Sultan everything; he would be arriving any day now. At this point the elders and wisest men intervened to put an end to the frivolities. "We know who's doing these things," they declared, "and when His Majesty comes, we are going to tell him every small detail—and then let everyone watch out!"

With this, things calmed down. There were secret negotiations, marred by pressure and haggling, initiated by the women in the beginning, if the dispute were between the men, and when some possible sort of agreement had been reached, followed up by some of the older men until conciliation had been effected. The disputes were formally ended with visits and banquets, usually hosted by the friends and relations of the former antagonists.

In times of quiet and content, especially when the Sultan was in residence at the royal court, the palace was, with the exception of the main building and men's council, a hive of activity night and day, with the bustle of children, servants, women and eunuchs. Visits were exchanged, gifts were sent back and forth to show off what had been given, stories were told, servants were ordered around—all this and much more transformed the palace into a veritable beehive. With nightfall, impudent pranks began, along with the tense, fearful traffic of securing nighttime assignations—rarely with innocent intent.

What enlivened the palace more than anything else, and dissipated the overpowering monotony, particularly in the quarters of the abandoned wives, aunts from both sides of the family and lady visitors, numbered most days in the hundreds, were the innocent pranks and tricks that were played on most nights. The women had become experts at this. There were uncounted nights in which sleepers' faces were daubed with paint—they tried this with most visitors. Every night the younger children frightened the women with horrible screeching, or by switching off all the lights. Sometimes a maidservant would dress up as a man and suddenly barge in—the hostess staged this trick to amuse her visitors. Dozens of similar pranks involved food and drink, and the unending hilarity, laughter and shrieking could be heard in the men's quarters.

Somewhat crueler tricks were played on the servants and slaves with even more surpassing skill. Men joined in, set contests and made bets, and the servants, or some of them, took part, whether for fun or out of a very injudicious simplicity.

6

THE SULTAN HAD BEEN MARRIED TO FADDA FOR slightly more than four years at the time Fanar and Mudi arrived at the Rawdh Palace to stay for good. In that time she had given him two sons and was already near the end of her third pregnancy, which was why the Sultan cut short a number of his trips to head home to Mooran early. It was not only because he longed for Fadda and loved her more than his other wives, but because of the bet they had made. Moza, the palace midwife, had been right both times before, and smilingly made a bet with the Sultan himself: "You can chop my head off, Your Majesty, if my lady doesn't give birth to a boy." This time she was even more certain, and ready to make an even bigger bet. The Sultan longed for and expected a third boy from Fadda as a special sign to himself, and to his other wives as well, that Fadda was different from other women: she was never late, and she only bore sons!

When Moza said that the baby would be a boy, Fadda stretched her hand out to the Sultan, smiled and declared firmly, "I'm with Moza—there's my hand on it. We have a bet!"

The Sultan laughed. He wanted the bet, even if he lost, and he said, "There's my hand. I say it will be a girl!"

Their bet was made. Every night the amount of the wager grew higher and its conditions were made more severe. This went on in an atmosphere of pleasantries and secret misgivings—the Sultan had been consumed by this matter for as long as he had known of Fadda's pregnancy. Even in his travels he pondered and waited and hoped.

As he made his homeward journey, with all its demands, cares and fears, he was the center of everyone's concern, though his only concerns were Fadda and the expected baby. He had completely forgotten Fanar, or at least paid far less attention to him than he had on previous trips. The Sultan repaired to his suite early to rest, and left Dughaim to look after the other arriving travelers, which caused a certain amount of embarrassment: no one knew whether the situation called for temporary measures or a permanent solution—if Fanar had come to stay, then the thinking was to put him behind the wall, in back of the men's diwan, which required a great many decisions and changes in keeping with the importance of this new visitor, since he was different from the others. Nor was it known whether it would be fitting or necessary for Mudi to be with him, or to have a place of her own.

Nothing was settled for days, during which period Dughaim al-Sarhud was unable to speak privately to the Sultan to get clear and specific instructions. The result was that Fanar and Mudi were moved from one suite to another almost every night, until at last two of the palace's elderly ladies intervened to obtain a suitable place for the two new guests.

The prince was not spared the pranks that had befallen almost everyone else who had stayed at the palace. He was not the direct target of the prank, since he spent most of his time in the men's diwan, at his father's request, even at his order, but his guard Nassar did not escape it. On the third day of their stay his rifle was stolen, and all his attempts to recover it or locate the thief were in vain. Qatma, Mudi's servant, had to endure practical jokes for two nights in a row, and on the fourth night, while she was sleeping in the room next to Mudi's, someone crept in and daubed her face with soot. The next day she was the object of much amusement and curious looks. One of the maidservants was so bold as to say rather loudly, "If a person doesn't feel someone putting soot on her face, who knows what else they might do without her feeling it!" Qatma was frightened, angry and embarrassed, because she had always been proud of being able to detect the sound of a cat's footfall even in her deepest sleep, as she put it. She answered the stares and smiles by saying that she had been dead tired from the journey and all the activity since arriving.

Mudi found a dead rat in her room the following night, which occasioned much terror and screaming. Dughaim heard about it and was quick to seek other accommodations for the new arrivals, after battling for hours to meet with the Sultan to discuss the matter.

The ruler of the palace, Princess Fadda, was too busy with the Sultan and her pregnancy for more than a brief visit with the newcomers. During the private lunch the Sultan hosted for them in his private suite, after giving a very large lunch party the previous day, the Sultan announced, as they spoke before the meal, that Fanar had come to Mooran to stay.

"And within a few years," smiled the Sultan, gazing at Fanar, "we hope to be celebrating his marriage!"

Fanar, lost in his gaudy clothes, and lost even more desperately in sweat and embarrassment, did not know what to do, not here in the diwan nor later on when they ate.

The Sultan gave much thought to how he would welcome Fadda's third son—he had never been so excited. More parties were given in the palace, more sheep were slaughtered, and more gifts and favors distributed than ever before.

A number of family elders spoke to the Sultan one night after the fuss died down. "You know, Your Majesty," they said, "that Almighty God is the Giver. It is He who makes of seed a male or a female. He is all-powerful."

The Sultan saw there was something they wanted to say. To encourage them he laughed and said loudly, "There's no arguing with what you say, my good men, but I see something else in your faces."

"Abu Mansour," said Dahaim, who was the Sultan's oldest paternal uncle, "we are with you. We want you to have as many offspring as there are grains of sand. We want you to celebrate every one of them, but you must know that a boy comes from his father's loins, and as long as the father is one, as long as you are the father of these children, you must treat them as equals. You shouldn't say that this one is such and such a woman's son. All of them are your children, the older before the younger, the one who is present before the one who is traveling. We see that you do not discriminate between one and the other."

He said this, provoked by the rumors circulating in the palace, having moved in whispers from the women's quarters to the men's, originating in Moza's reports of the bet between Fadda and the Sultan over whether the baby would be a boy. It was said that the Sultan had conceded to name one of Fadda's sons Sultan after him. Along with this rumor were increasing reports about the Sultan's anger with Khazael. Two of Dahaim's personal guards reported that they had overheard the Sultan tell Khazael angrily to "keep out of my way—I don't want to see your face again." And indeed Khazael did leave, with a number of friends and guards. No one knew where he went or how long he would be gone. Other things were said, but the guards did not catch them.

This is what led the family elders to speak up. The Sultan listened carefully, smiling broadly, and made his reply.

"Whoever has been talking to you, my friends, has not been telling you the truth. You know that a man grows a new heart every day. There is no limit. If we paid attention to every little thing that people said for and against us, one person saying one thing and another person saying something else, we would not know what to do. You know as well as I do, or better than I do: when two shepherds quarrel, or become too friendly, the sheep are lost!"

He nodded several times, when suddenly Khazael's image and departure glimmered in his mind's eye.

"We sent Khazael away on an errand," he added by way of explanation. "We gave him a job to do. We told him, 'Settle this and come home as soon as possible.' If you've heard anything besides this, it's not true!" His tone changed. "When we went to Ain Fadda, we told Fanar, 'This is where you belong, Fanar, and you must be with us.' We took him with us and came. A few days ago my men saw him and said he's brilliant, there's no one like him. You all know that he has to be near me so that he can learn. God willing, he and his brothers will yet assume our burden. Have no fear, my friends. Trust in God. You know that saying: 'Don't advise a striver.' And, God willing, with your advice and your own striving, and by your very presence, everything will turn out fine."

The Sultan's words had the desired effect, especially because he remembered to mention Fanar, who had been ill. The doctors treating him said that it was merely a matter of containment and a change of climate—he would certainly regain his health if he were surrounded by an atmosphere of love and solicitude, as he had been in Ain Fadda.

"You see, my friends," said Dahaim in a deep voice, with the image of Fanar, so different from the rest of the brothers, in his mind's eye, "an orphan's tear can rend rock!"

They all thought of Fanar's mother, and maintained a sad silence.

The Sultan knew much of what people had heard, by way of the women and servants he had assigned to tell him everything they heard, and was worried lest events get out of hand, making it hard to regain control over them, to eliminate the doubts which were said to have spread even into the desert, specifically to Khazael's uncles, and to some of his other wives' tribes. He showed tolerance toward a number of his wives and relatives instead of alienation. He did not hesitate to arrange a new marriage for himself that same winter, and took his new wife along with him on a hunting trip that lasted more than twenty days. Word reached him that Watfa, the wife he had taken before Fadda, and who had borne him two girls, had given birth to a third child, a boy. When he heard that she had given him a male child and named him Mufarrih, he gave parties no less grand than those celebrating the arrival of Fadda's third son. Ummi Zahwa, who got wind of what the women were saying, commented that "Abu Mansour's children are like the teeth of a comb, like the seeds of a pomegranate—there's no distinguishing between them. Well, some are different colors. But the mothers are never satisfied, day or night!"

That was not all. The Sultan visited two of the wives that had given him daughters, and it was reported that he carried the two girls around, played with them, and lavished gifts upon the mothers—something he had never been known to do before. People were more than ready to spread the news. Even the ruler of the palace, Fadda, made no secret of her displeasure at that, but did mask it with sarcasm. There was a party given to show off her third son—whose public presentation was delayed, as he, unlike his brothers before him, had been very sickly—and at which a large number of women were present. She smiled as she spoke.

"I was afraid, when they circumcised him—I screamed, and said to myself that I wish it had been a girl, to be spared all the torture." When this was greeted with clucks of surprise and dismay, she glanced around, focusing a special smile on certain faces. "These days, what's the difference between a girl and a boy, unless of course the mother is a horror, who has girls."

"No, my lady," said Moza, who was bolder than all of them, "there is a difference—about this long." She showed how long with her thumb and index finger.

"Isn't that a little long, Moza?" smiled one of the ladies.

"Don't worry, my girl," laughed Moza. "They grow, and grow— God help the women of the world!"

There was more. For the Sultan, who always received an adversary's surrender in person, or at least made sure to be present to assure himself of the defeat, to give orders to pardon or execute, who delighted in giving lessons in the art of war and courage, in ethics and dignity, so that his enemies might hear it from himself so that they could retell the story, had for the first time delegated these duties to Khazael.

"The men with you, Khazael," he told the youth before a gathering of family elders, "are each worth a hundred other men. They've been tested, and you can put them to any test, and as for the leaders, their reputation has gone before them. There is no one like them in Mooran or anywhere else. I want you to make us proud of you, Khazael, and come back to us safe and sound, with that bastard's head on a spear and the rest of him scattered for the vultures."

He took a deep breath to fill his chest and addressed the old men while watching Khazael.

"We have invested great hope in you, Khazael, and this is my opinion and everyone else's. Don't be slow to give us some good news. As we say: The right artisan never disappoints in his craft. Victory and success are from God alone, and may He bless you."

The task entrusted to Khazael involved no more than the disciplining of a small tribe whose camps were located near the frontiers, open to many influences; the tribe's loyalties had changed several times as pressures were exercised on it. It was whispered, in the Rawdh Palace, that the Sultan's plan was for Khazael to be killed in the operation, but the rumors dwindled and died with the news, confirmed as fact by most people, that Khazael had actually gone hunting and not to battle after all.

It was also said that the Sultan had sent his uncle less than a week after Khazael's departure, and told him to take charge of everything himself, out of fear that there might be errors time would render unsolvable, especially with regard to the tribal chief, whom he wanted taken alive for several reasons. He wanted the chief to be an asset of his own at the frontier rather than an instrument in his enemies' hands, and so that people who said that Khureybit knew nothing but killing would now see that he understood mercy and kindliness, too. Khureybit's surmise proved correct: his uncle did his job well, and Khazael returned victorious, saying that he had truly become a man.

Before the year was out, Sultan Khureybit sent Fanar on an official visit to Britain, at the suggestion of his adviser, who told the Sultan that the British royal family raised its children to bear responsibility and to go on missions to foreign countries, so that they might get to know the countries and learn from them and so that foreign kings and presidents would get to know them.

7

DESPITE THE YEARS FANAR SPENT IN THE RAWDH Palace, he always remained a stranger there. He was unable to become part of the palace, or to join the hidden powers that fascinated and influenced him. His father did include him, and was more impressed with Fanar with every passing month, but he was worried about the influence of Uncle Omair on the boy, particularly the fact that since Omair's arrival in Mooran the man never gave his mouth a rest, as the Sultan put it.

Not only that, the Sultan was told that when Omair left the Rawdh Palace he would immediately call on other gatherings, one after another: "This and that goes on, and this is permissible but that isn't." The Sultan shook his head in rage at what he heard, and said to himself, "We've done everything to get along with them, to please them and shut them up, but we're no sooner rid of one than along comes another—we get rid of the little dervish and along comes Omair. Well, so what!" When the Sultan met with him, he asked how his father was, and whether Ain Fadda was getting any rain—this was his way of insinuating that Omair should go back home. Omair gave him vague, disjointed replies, with a broad smile that expressed his happiness and comfort at being in Mooran. When Fanar fell ill, Omair had a strong pretext for staying. One day he told the Sultan that he felt compelled by necessity to remain in Mooran.

"As you can plainly see, Your Majesty, the child is tired and sickly, and I'm afraid he'll worsen if I leave him."

"Trust in God, my good man, everyone is giving Fanar the very best of care, and doting on him."

"But an uncle's care is special, Your Majesty."

"Too much care will spoil him, Omair."

"That's the truth, Your Majesty; only until he has recovered and put on a little weight."

"Healing comes from God, my man, and as you know: healthy birds are never too fat."

They had this conversation two or three times. Omair always pretended not to understand; he had come here with the intention of staying, of being near Fanar, to play a part in his upbringing and education. The Sultan regretted leaving his son in Ain Fadda all those years, and knew how close Fanar was to his uncles; he wanted to test his ability to wrest the boy from that world and those thoughts without resorting to cruelty or force, especially since the doctors treating Fanar swore that there was no illness to which they could ascribe his condition. "He needs a change of climate," they said. Constipation, they said. They would have to monitor his mental state, and to try and make him flourish in new surroundings.

Fanar was like a delicate plant which sickens from getting too little water, or too much. He fell ill for no reason, and suffered arbitrarily. His wide eyes followed the Sultan wherever he went, wherever he turned, and his ears took in every word he spoke. The Sultan was bewildered.

"If I look at him," he told his uncle Dahaim, "all I see are his watchful eyes. He listens with his eyes, ears and heart, and that dim-witted Omair persists in filling his head with nothing but stories of the afterlife."

"As soon as he's better, he should take up hunting."

"That's the truth, Uncle, and along with the hunting he'll get a

military carbine, so that he can deal with some of these people here
and there who are giving us headaches."

Soon thereafter, the Sultan took Fanar along on one of his campaigns. Before setting out, he had a word with the boy's uncle Omair.

"So Ain Fadda is such a fine place—when we return we will expect
to see you there, Omair."

Mahyoub, chief of the Sultan's personal bodyguard, remembered
that particular campaign for years to come:

"It was a good year—there was a lot of rain, and people were
happy. All they had to do was earn their living. His Majesty's orders
were clear: 'We have to fight, Mahyoub, if not here then somewhere
else.' And we looked around, we tried to understand, but we didn't
see anyone. Such and such a tribe was at its winter camps. Another
tribe was off somewhere else. No one was thinking of war. One day
we were in Khubra Sanida and some bedouin came along and told us,
'The merchants are robbing us.' We charged off to find who was robbing them, but God sent us a different group of people, including a
wanted man. As soon as His Majesty saw them, he gave the orders:
'Shoot them.' There were seven of them. I swear to God, we lined
them up, Fanar before the rest of us, and when His Majesty said 'Fire,'
we fired. We killed them all, and buried them and went our own way."

Mahyoub shook his head, smiling sadly, and continued in a different tone of voice. "His Majesty said: 'This is nothing—we have to let
the boy fight with his hands and taste fear. Three or four days later, at
night, late at night, we told twenty of our men, 'Go off a good distance, and shoot around us, but not at us.' We gave them enough bullets for all of mankind and devils, too, and told them to fire, but high,
above our heads. 'Be very careful!' We would fire back. We told them,
wait an hour and go. And that's what happened, but caution is no
match for power. We were hundreds strong, all armed, and we didn't
tell our men where to shoot, because we were afraid of giving away
the ruse, even if it meant a few of the others getting killed. Anyway,
as they say, real tragedies don't happen until nighttime. The bullets all
missed us, but a spent shell, falling from the sky, hit Fanar, wounding
him on the arm near the shoulder. His Majesty was afraid, but when
he saw the scar, he laughed and said, 'That's your diploma, my boy,
don't worry.' Seven or eight of the party we sent out were killed, and
we had three wounded and one killed. We don't know who fired the
bullet."

The following winter, the Sultan told his uncle Dahaim, who had accompanied him on a hunting trip with a number of the Sultan's sons, "After that night, Uncle, his heart was like flint." He laughed, looking on as Fanar readied his falcons for the hunt. "He was afraid when we killed those bedouin. I confronted him, but when I saw him, I said to myself, 'We've made a mistake,' but you know, Uncle, there was no turning back from there. I said to myself, 'We'll trust in God,' and we set off. A few days later we came upon that group we told them about, and this time I saw him: No, by God: he was eager, and led the way, and with my own ears I heard him shout, 'The winds of Paradise are blowing, let's go!' "

"Only the first time is hard, Abu Mansour," smiled Dahaim, "in that as in everything else. Everything that comes after is much easier."

That night much of the Rawdh Palace was awakened by the sound of crying and lamentation. Those who were roused from their sleep later said that "it was before dawn broke, and everyone was in their deepest sleep, and then came that sound that frightened even the bravest among us. No one knew whether to believe their ears or not—everyone asked themselves, 'Is the palace on fire? Is someone dead? Is there a flood—are we going to die?' After the first sound came another sound, and this one was nearby. Everyone ran after it, here and there, until they came to Prince Fanar's suite. 'Tell us, people, what on earth is going on here!' Qatma just stared at everyone and screeched, and from within we could hear Mudi screaming and carrying on. 'Tell us what horror this is!' No one answered or spoke at all. The women went in to Mudi and found her half-dead, her hand on her shoulder, screaming, 'Fanar's hurt, Fanar's killed!' They told her, 'Trust in God, girl, Fanar is with the Sultan, no one can hurt Fanar, he's out hunting, not fighting.' But still: 'Fanar's hurt, Fanar's killed.' She didn't calm down until morning, so no one else could either. By daybreak Ibn Sarhud had sent several messengers out, telling each of them, 'Get to His Majesty, get his news, and come back here.' Only then did Mudi rest a little—she was tired, and stretched out, but she didn't lift her hand from her shoulder, and she didn't stop crying for three days. On the third day a messenger came back and swore a thousand and one oaths that he was telling the truth—it was the Sheikha that made him swear—then he said that Fanar's wound was a mere scratch, as if he had been singed by an ember; the boy was fine, walking around and talking. The messenger added, with another oath, that 'the Sultan himself had heated a cloth to cauterize Fanar, and it worked perfectly.'"

Mudi was ill the first week. She touched no food, in spite of urging from old and young alike, except for some liquids they compelled her to drink, and refused everything else, until people were more worried about her than they were about Fanar. Their concern mounted when she met privately with the first messenger, then the next one, so that she could assure herself that the information was true—that his wound was minor, and that he was completely healed.

The second week, Mudi consented to eat some light meals, though she was still mournful and weepy and stayed in her room. Qatma assured the visitors that her mistress was on the way to recovery and asked them not to bother her, since she needed her rest, sleep and medication, on the orders of the English lady doctor. The visitors hesitated, wishing to check Mudi's improving condition for themselves, to look in her face and read in her eyes the penetrating power of her intuition—to see for themselves whether Fanar was stricken.

Mudi recovered her health in the third week. She left her room for the balcony several times and received a few visitors, though her uneasiness had not entirely left her. She was visibly wan, inspiring sorrow and pity, until the Sultan returned.

Fanar came back to Mooran, to the Rawdh Palace, and at last to the suite he shared with Mudi, where he saw and heard everything that had befallen his sister. Mudi followed his every gesture and word, and asked how he had been wounded, where, and at what time, nodding confidently all the while. Surprise was evident on the faces that surrounded them, and in the looks exchanged by their listeners: everyone was amazed at what had happened, Fanar no less than the rest of them.

Tahany, who had nursed Mudi in her illness, was neither frightened nor unsettled. She said that as a girl she had been just like Mudi, often intuiting events which had yet to happen. But with the passage of time, her "thoughts clouded up," she claimed, "so that I hardly know Friday from Thursday." She comforted everyone who asked her about Mudi, and forced Mudi to drink more liquids that she had prepared herself, which greatly speeded up her recovery.

As to the grandmother who had recently come to Mooran to visit "her only darlings—Mudi, Fanar and Omair," especially since no news whatever of Omair had reached Ain Fadda, she had no idea what had happened. When she arrived at the palace and was told of Fanar's trip and Mudi's illness, she told Qatma, who tried to comfort her and smooth things over, "If only I'd come earlier, everything would have been fine—now, my poor heart—can I stand it?"

After she saw Mudi, who was sleeping, she said, "This news is no omen of yours but of Satan's, you poor thing." She shook her head wrathfully. "When are they coming back?"

"You know as much as I do, my dear lady."

"God bless you, now whom do we have to flatter, where should we turn?" She went on, to herself, "After Ain Fadda all happiness passed away, and now we see our children dying and being butchered and there is nothing we can do about it." She spoke softly but with rage: "May God punish tyrants and all the pitiless."

The grandmother regained her composure and strength as Mudi's health improved and Fanar came home, though there were many who expected her to die quickly. Omair, who had stayed on in Mooran for a few days after the Sultan's trip, now left suddenly, telling no one where he was going or for how long he would be gone. Nor was it known whether he would be coming back to Mooran or Ain Fadda.

This news got everyone in the Rawdh Palace excited and was retold in countless different versions. The women, for example, said that the spot Mudi kept clutching, by her shoulder, was not just the place where Fanar had been wounded, but—three or four of the women claimed, with the rest silent on the point—that she had a blue mark there resembling the actual healed wound. Lulua went further, telling her mistress that she had seen the mark with her own eyes, when it first appeared, with blood trickling from it!

That piece of news might have been on everyone's mind had not subsequent palace events virtually banished it from memory.

For during the Sultan's trip back to Mooran, during a rest stop in Ajira to give his slaves time to surround an area famous for its abundance of gazelles, there arrived a sudden guest: Sahib, or Hamilton.

Hamilton, whom the Sultan called Sahib, or "Friend"—at Hamilton's suggestion, it was said—was on his way back from a journey with a number of the Sultan's slaves and bodyguards. He had been out identifying likely sites for sinking wells for water and mapping the northern border region. His fellow travelers said that Sahib had spent a long time digging at Tel Deeb, not far from his encampment, and

that he unearthed many idols, which they said he carried away on
three camels.

It was a very cordial reunion, celebrated by hastily arranged festivities, for the Sultan had not expected to meet Sahib in this place or at
this time—he was completely taken by surprise. To show his friendship and power, he instructed his men "not to leave out a single art or
sport for Sahib to see," so there were camel races, target shooting,
gazelle hunting, singing and dancing. The weather was mild, so all
the festivities were held in daytime in the open air, rather than at dawn
or sundown, which lent them a special air of delight, and Sahib did
not hide his enthusiasm.

"Such an encounter with Your Majesty," he told the Sultan, surrounded by some of his men, "makes a man forget his troubles—
makes one wish he could stay here forever!"

The Sultan ignored this praise; he was intent on persuading Sahib
to stay. He said, hiding his joy, "God keep you, we need your help,
and the help of good people like you—and with God's help we will be
able to repay you."

They talked of many other things, but Hamilton was meeting
Fanar for the first time, and after watching him carefully, and listening
to what his friends had to say about the Sultan's campaign, found great
pleasure in talking to the prince. As he had done years before on first
arriving in Mooran, when he'd spent several days hunting with Khazael, and it was said that he had competed with him at sharpshooting,
he now gazed at Fanar and followed all his movements. He also asked
some of the men how Fanar had received his wound and where; he did
not want to bother Fanar himself with these questions, or to burden
the Sultan.

On the last night before the return journey, there was a full moon
and a refreshing spring breeze. Hamilton told the Sultan, "This East,
Your Majesty, is the cradle of revelation and the natural habitat of
prophecy—no one can understand it without living here."

The Sultan nodded, in the moonlight, like a lizard, and replied in
his deep voice, "That is the truth, Sahib, and it seems you have decided to live among us and work with us."

"I've given it a lot of thought, Your Majesty, and it has been my
aim, after finishing my maps of the northern borders of your country,
to ask Your Majesty's permission to leave." He smiled as he looked

into the Sultan's eyes. "But I cannot go against Your Majesty's wishes—especially given the irresistible charm of this land!"

The Sultan was as pleased as a child, feeling assured at that moment that he had realized many important goals on this trip. He stroked his beard and recalled the effort he had put into trying to make Sahib stay. He thought to himself, "A coincidence is better than a promise."

8

HAMILTON WAS NOT AN INDIVIDUAL, BUT MANY in one, a throng of persons in one, and in proportion to the harmony that united them was hostility that often led to feuding and disunion. He was a lover who could not hide his love, and an almost malefic hater, serene most of the time but capable of becoming, in a moment, a savage, wolfish beast with an unquenchable thirst for blood, even for the sight of it. He had a powerful, insatiable love of knowledge and discovery. When he was beset by questions, he felt confused and useless. Christian and atheist, he thought nothing of experimenting with other religions. He was loyal to the Empire but detested it. Money to him was a mere means of doing business, a means of entry, an autonomous power in itself. He wished he were a king people never tired of gazing upon, and yet longed to be an anonymous and unknown man. He said to himself, in moments of candor, that "the more powerful and knowledgeable a man becomes, the more lost and weak and stupid he is."

When people asked him why he always kept so busy, why he wore himself out, he said that "a man's worth is in knowledge and serving others—one should never stop learning or helping others for a single moment, because in these things lies the true source of pleasure, and the one reason a man is on this earth."

When he was on camelback under the sun's burning blaze, with the desert sand below him rolling on like the leaves of a book, he felt that he was the only man capable of this mission; that an awesome power had been entrusted to him. When he reached his destination, he felt lost and benighted—how had he been so stupid as to come to Mooran to pursue such a stupid pastime?

He could see himself as an impossible imbecile for coming to this accursed desert, and in the next moment imagine himself a prophet for Mooran and the region. He was propagating the faith of the West, and wanted it to spread everywhere—something only he was capable of doing. At night he was filled with the conviction that England had sent him here to get rid of him for good. In daylight he was convinced that the overwhelming power that had moved him to come here was all he needed to erase—not only for the Empire but for the whole West—the old religions; without that power he would never enable them to hold any faith at all. The Arabs, to him, were the living proof of the origins of ancient man, the very image of the possibility of humankind remaining in its early state. His own people were a race of recently made creatures who had no future except to the extent to which they were able to spread their roots into the past. Among the Arabs, and only with them—though they were so evil and disgusting—could there be a new faith: the old faith in new hands.

How had Hamilton gotten like this—why was he like this? He could give no satisfactory answer, though he had given it much thought. He sometimes attributed it to nature; had he been born in one of the imperial colonies and become familiar with the smells and sunlight of the East, surrounded on all sides by black and brown faces, he might have seen Britain, the whole continent, and indeed the New World, as an artificial thing, as a plaything.

He could not stand to be a mere functionary in a system where he had no importance other than in making rules or levying taxes. Neither could he see himself as a mere soldier, with only a rank and a serial number, fighting for a cause he did not share.

He was filled with longing for light and shade that struggled and intermingled, only to engender something stronger and less yielding, a man more intelligent and high-minded, if perhaps a little madder. The school that tore him away from the remotest East, to make of him a valued student in London, in the view of those teachers with their spectacles perched on the tips of their noses, cramming his memory with forgettable facts, filled him with the desire to find a culture without teachers or spectacles, outside university walls, a culture formed by the senses, more profound and less refined.

He decided to study Near Eastern languages, and told his father that "one cannot know the West without knowing the East, and one cannot learn modern languages without knowing the ancient ones."

His father still had a certain affection for the East, and wished in his heart that his son would be an extension of himself, with no need for these justifications. Hamilton would always have a clear memory of what his father said.

"The East was made to be an arena for our horses and our knights."

Hamilton would say: "Father pronounced that last word with relish—it carried the weight of all his ancestors. And I was proud, because by choosing the languages I had, I had chosen the East. I knew that I had been created for a great mission, and that I would succeed in it."

"The East," he came to repeat, "is not only a geographical place, or mere religions and rituals and incense—it is a mass of uniquely blended elements, combined with and perhaps dominated by the element of chance, so that it subverts any effort at easy or early understanding. The East is the cradle of life and perhaps its grave, when you consider the profuse joy that fills its days, and how it is the depository of all man's pain and care and sorrow. It is mankind's memory, and the homeland of all life's contradictions. The East, serene and contented though it may look, carries in its depths the force and madness of volcanoes. Mankind's infancy and senility both, like brothers, remind one of an old man holding his grandson by the hand, trying to show and teach him the secret of life."

At times he repeated it even to himself, though he was not persuaded, "because their modern language," he thought perplexedly, "seems so supple, so tender, yet so unable to define or comprehend an idea, even though language is the only possible means of putting things in context, to define and understand them. Never mind—we remain in a constant state of such intense alertness that we fall into the traps that our weak minds, so accustomed to laziness and laxity, set for us. Our minds are inclined to ease and simplicity, to avoid whatever is dark, difficult or harsh. It is the hardest test man faces in this life, and rarely does anyone pass it except for those strong men dedicated to remaking history, though they pay a price, a great price for performing that service, if indeed they do succeed at it."

Hamilton did not stop at this comparison, but told himself that "a man born in the East is born for life—for trial and death. In the West, he is born with a constant longing to forget, and so he resorts to anger in order to gain increased powers of memory, or to perish. If his anger slumbers, he resorts to drums and shows to restore joy to his being, but faces a new oblivion."

"Orientals aren't contemptuous; they see themselves as part of nature, an extension of it—one of its phenomena. They see life and death differently than westerners do. They see death as the other side of life. Just as a man cannot put the rain back where it came from, or veil the sun, they are not inclined, they are not apt, to see themselves as needing to resist or challenge nature. They live in harmony with it. Their first step is to understand it, to unite with it so that it becomes part of them and they become a part of it. The greatest, the most frivolous mistake of non-Orientals, is their silly insistence on resisting nature, rather than trying to understand it and adapt to it. Orientals— I am not speaking solely of those now living—are more realistic, far-sighted and sensitive because they look at nature with respect and work with it lovingly. Even if they seek to corrupt nature, they do it humbly, entreatingly, just as a child behaves when his mother is angry at him; despite the difference in their ages and their different way of seeing things, there is a great deal of understanding and affection, arising from the profound sense of belonging, of continuity between the two."

Hamilton said none of this aloud, or in front of anyone, because he was not sure about the strength or soundness of the ideas that occurred to him or persisted in their orbit in his mind. They mocked him and attracted him mysteriously, especially as he rode long distances on his camel, or lay quietly on the sand gazing at the sky, at the stars suspended like lamps: shining, close, even warm.

But suddenly the dream page turned to reveal another that had no connection with what had come before. When he agreed, with apparent reluctance, to stay in Mooran, by the Sultan's side, he put aside the burning questions that had bothered him, having become sure that in his new work he would not appoint a king, but he would found a new kind of kingdom, for this East that so wearied and yet so enchanted him swarmed with little kings, and he thought little of replacing one of them with another. He wanted something different, and thought that he may have stumbled across traces of it in Khureybit, and later on in Fanar.

Images from history flashed through his mind's eye, along with images of the present, and he hastened to begin, noting to himself that "aging kings need someone to tell them how to act, how to govern; young kings only need to be told what to do."

He was like Khureybit's shadow; he never left him except when the Sultan approached the little gate in the mud wall that led to the women's quarters. Khureybit could not believe that Sahib had consented to stay, to be so close to him. In his past journeys, with others, Sahib had spent only a few days, then had departed—only to go, as Khureybit knew, to his rivals and sometimes even his enemy, though he was unable to discuss it or ask questions. Now Hamilton was putting all his time, ingenuity and contacts at the Sultan's disposal; more than that, he seemed to be the only friend he could trust and get help from in every way, at every time.

Since Hamilton had read much about the desert and its people, he now wanted to do something no one else could do, and so one of the things he did was to cross the wild, uncharted desert from east to west, and he was planning to cross it again from north to south. This was a source of great pride to him. He had spent long months in bedouin camps, listening to them, eating with them, and even dressing as they did.

When he first put on Arab clothes, they seemed to him outdated rags, but he soon discovered that they were just right for him and for the desert. He thought back sadly on a colleague of his who preceded him to Mooran, and how detested and feared he was because he would not adapt to this clothing, and how that friend was killed in a battle he had plunged into zealously, only to prove to the bedouin that he was courageous.

Hamilton, on the other hand, was addicted to Arab clothes; he

could not give them up. When he was compelled to wear his own
clothes, to board a plane or travel, he felt disguised. He smiled and
laughed when he caught sight of himself in the mirror—this was the
thing his friends did when they saw him in European clothes: they
smiled.

"The desert, like a woman, looks serene, simple, supple and beautiful. It requires understanding and affection—it has numberless faces.
When angry or wild it seems to be a different creature altogether. At
night it is a different thing than it was in the day. In winter it isn't as it
was in the summer or any other season. It is the same thing but bears
no resemblance to itself. It changes in a moment and re-forms in a
moment—a world in the never-ending process of creation."

So Hamilton said to himself, so as to remain constantly watchful
and alert, and not to resort to false, final convictions. The images and
concepts that had filled his head before had now all been shaken and
altered, so that even he ridiculed them; he considered them vain myths
dreamed up by so-called vagabonds, the product of their weakened
minds and bodies—they were too beaten down to advance, to give
themselves to the real desert. They were content to record a few
thoughts, mostly lies drawn from their dizzy, opium-poisoned fantasies, or old tales stolen from the back alleys of old cities, from the lips
of catamites and whores, especially the whores of the coastal cities,
where they spent most of their time exploring the desert!

The men of the desert were the true fruit of this habitat, one of its
phenomena, its revelations. Despite their total simplicity and candor,
there were deep layers of tough, dead scales undetectable by a fleeting
glance, or by a relationship based on flattery. It was true that they
listened, but they thought long over what they heard and finally
understood it as they chose. They were full of suspicion, they did not
trust easily, and when they fell out, they did it with harshness and
finality. When they gave, they gave generously, and while they gave
little at first, they never stopped giving.

Now that he had traveled even to the remotest corners of Mooran,
and knew its land and people, and monitored its contending wolves,
he wrote to his employers that "Khureybit is the likeliest of the con-
tenders, since he appreciates the favor we have done him; he is also the
cleverest and best-prepared of them all. The powers that support him,
which he can deploy, blaze with unique religious fervor, and this is not
the case with any of his rivals, but could make all the difference in

Mooran if correctly and profitably handled." His employers were quick to support his views.

In the daytime councils, Hamilton curled up like a cat not far from the Sultan, listening and nodding in understanding and agreement as Khureybit's discourse flooded on, strengthening his men's morale and preparing them for the next battle. To show Hamilton he possessed enough power and ability to make everything easy, all he needed to do was persuade "Sahib and the boys," as the Sultan never tired of repeating.

When Hamilton did speak, it was rarely to do more than ask a question or make a comment. Although there were many who did not speak in the presence of the Sultan unless they were asked to, or unless they had something urgent to say, their silence was different from his. They thought of themselves as one bloc, in such a way that any one of them spoke for all, so that no one was harmed whether one or any other of them spoke. But this stranger, this outsider, made them uneasier with his silence than with his speech; his stares moved among all their faces, leaving a bitter curiosity: Why had he come? What did he want? Their curiosity never left their hearts, however, to reach their tongues, because the Sultan's trust confused and silenced them.

Hamilton was a different person at night, when their councils stretched on until late.

". . . And you know, Your Majesty, that His Britannic Majesty's government must consider conditions in the region, and local reaction. While the government offers you its unreserved support, as is made clear by their aid, and by my presence here among you as well, you may not actually provoke others, or turn them into Britain's enemies. Thus the government privately and tacitly agrees to take measures to eliminate your rivals; all we need to do is find a covert and acceptable means."

Hamilton pronounced these words belatedly, and after doing some careful checking. The Sultan, who had been waiting for this consent, wasted no time.

With every step the Sultan grew more inclined to listen to what Hamilton said: "If it is possible to annex this region peacefully, by enriching the tribes and sheikhs, that would be preferable to annexing it by force. If we can do that secretly, or noiselessly, that would be preferable to doing it openly, or by stirring up others."

Month after month, year after year, they were not two persons, but Siamese twins, one body with two heads. While they did part late at night, the whole daytime and early evening sufficed them to talk about everything: How Britain thought and how people of the desert thought. What Britain wanted, now and in the future, and what the Sultan wanted. The rest of the time they talked about horses, history, tribal genealogy and the battles of yesteryear, and when they were weary of talking, then those who were waiting talked. There were many of them, they had a great deal to say, and they were ready to say it. When they spoke, surprise was evident on Hamilton's face, then he looked overjoyed and awed: "These simple, forgotten, uneducated people—how did they get such fertile minds, such matchless wit?"

When Hamilton thought about it, he attributed it to the contemplation and hardship of their lives, then to that hidden heritage, passed on from fathers to sons, from grandmothers to grandchildren. Their gift of memorization was the result of their climate, their environment, he reasoned, since without memorizing places and things in this cruel desert, a man was exposed to peril and perdition.

Hamilton shook his head in wonderment, and added to himself: "The desert night, with its moon and stars, the waiting for new seasons and rains, for caravans, keep their eyes and ears, and even their noses, ever open to detect anything new. They learn quickly, but very much in their own way."

He recalled how one Arab he knew, Najm, had come to "know" English through his close relationship with Edward Hearst, who had come from Britain to set up telegraph bureaus: within a few months he could understand it. His English was humble and required gestures, but it was good enough; Hearst, who had spent three years in Mooran, had learned fewer than ten words of Arabic. He pronounced even those as a child might, provoking more laughter than understanding.

When the Sultan captured al-Huweiza years later, Hamilton said to him, "I've read in books, Your Majesty, that whoever wishes to acquire new territories, and keep them, must always keep in mind two crucially important facts: to get rid of the former ruling family, and to reject any fundamental changes in the laws or taxes of those territories."

The Sultan nodded, delighted with his victory, and began to apply, instinctively, Hamilton's advice, without having read any of it in a book or heard it from anyone else. Much later Hamilton learned that the orders the Sultan gave to do away with the ruler of al-Huweiza and most of his family had been given early on!

Fanar hardly ever left his father's council. For day after day he was the focus of Hamilton's attention and care. The Sultan watched developments carefully and seemed delighted by their closeness, but when he remembered Omair, he said to himself, "The day will come to settle accounts . . . we shall see."

9

R EARING A HUMAN CREATURE, ESPECIALLY ONE
partly grown and matured, is more difficult
than taming a wild beast," is what Hamilton
said when the Sultan asked him to look after Fanar and to keep him
away from Omair, and Omair's thoughts away from him.

"No matter what his experience or how well read he may be, no
man is like any other. And there's always the degree of readiness and
desire on the part of the other." When he considered Fanar's assiduity
and closeness to him, Sahib said to himself, "It would be impossible
to remark the change taking place if he were close to me. Proximity
makes it harder to see, to judge changes between yesterday and
today."

As he was trying to think of the best means he might use, he said
laughingly that "if rearing depends on books and theories, then there's
a greater chance of failure than of success! Especially if we start the
books at page one."

The game looked baffling to Hamilton, and continued to seem so
the better he came to know Fanar. For he was no ordinary boy by any
means. Nor could the training he needed be ordinary: it involved the
shaping of a king or sultan. If the rearing of kings or their children
were a tedious or difficult undertaking even in royal courts, so bound
by their restrictive traditions, then rearing kings in the open desert,
exposed to the four winds, was a terrifying adventure, loaded with
risks. Not only that: the wary boy, almost as timid or fearful as an
elderly bedouin encountering a new world, with his immense store of
prayer, incense and magic, and that vision he found so many ways of
hiding, all stemming from his solitude, sorrow, meditation and sickness, which bred his feelings of pain and aversion, made Hamilton feel
that he was making a certain losing bet. But he was ready to undertake
the mission, almost as if to punish himself, to flee from some hidden
thing; and he did not want to acknowledge his defeat too soon.

It took a long time and an infinity of schemes to work at making
Fanar talk, almost as a psychologist might do, about what his life in
Ain Fadda had been like, what his likes and dislikes were, and dozens
of other seemingly innocent, spontaneous questions. Often the response was silence, or a boy's sly smile, or, on rare occasions, a few
words that only confused Hamilton more.

The Englishman did not admit defeat.

As to separating him from Uncle Omair, as he had promised the
boy's father he'd do, he may have taken a good step toward victory.
When the Sultan sent a messenger to Omair, telling him that his presence in Mooran was not required, and that it was in his interest to go
back to Ain Fadda, Omair took the news at first with incomprehen-
sion and then ignored it. When the Sultan sent further, more explicit
messages, Omair nodded willingly and told Talleh al-Oreifan, the
Sultan's latest messenger, that "I'll happily obey His Majesty's order,
Talleh, but the boy is not going to stay among a lot of infidels and
eunuchs."

When the Sultan asked Talleh when Omair was leaving, he gave
him a different answer, his eyes downcast: "He said, Your Majesty,
that he would happily obey His Majesty's order, if someone will set
his mind at rest concerning Fanar." He paused, and looked at the Sultan, and added, "I think, Your Majesty, that Omair feels offended."

"Boys aren't raised by prayer and raising hands to Heaven, Talleh.
The boy has to get to know the world, and people. He has to fight

with his hands and his teeth. Fanar is a sultan's son, not the son of the sheikh of a mosque."

Fanar's grandmother wasted no time coming to Mooran, and it looked as though she had come to stay. Fanar was delighted to spend nearly all of his time with her. When she was compelled, some months later, to go back home and tend to her ailing husband, she sent Fanar's aunt Muzna to take her place in Mooran.

Even Omair, who has been gone a long time and was nearly forgotten by everyone, had become active in camel-trading, which forced him, as he said, to visit Mooran every now and then, and to spend months there getting to know the market.

Fanar's uncle and his maternal relatives may have been absent at times, but Mudi was always there. There may have been things his grandmother or Muzna forgot to tell him, or report to him, but Mudi forgot nothing. Her aunt once joked with her that "no one would ever believe that you know all these things!"

"Those and a lot more besides, Aunt," was Mudi's reply. She knew that she was fighting on familiar ground, against undisguised enemies.

"Your Majesty," Hamilton told the Sultan one night, "the best thing would be for him to travel. A change of scene will change him. At his age, he needs to discover other countries, to see the world."

The Sultan did not hide his anxiety at this idea; he did not think that things had reached the point of such extreme measures. He shook his head.

"He can travel hereabouts, Sahib. He can go hunting, we can send him out with some of our people, or he can go to war."

"The best thing is for him to go to other countries, so that he can change his perspective, discover the world. It will change him."

"Who would he travel with?"

"I will travel with him, Your Majesty."

"And leave us?"

"We really must consult with London on a number of issues that concern Your Majesty, and find suitable solutions, and such things are not settled in the post, Your Majesty. They must be discussed directly so that we can make decisions." He smiled. "It would be best to have Your Majesty's representative at my side, and this time that is what Fanar will be!"

"You have really got a blessing in you, Sahib," exclaimed the Sultan. "You have become one of us—you know all our problems and all our concerns."

"This will be a chance for Fanar to see and learn."

After a brief hesitation the Sultan agreed, especially since there were several pending issues he had long been waiting to see resolved.

"We were afraid for him because of an infidel," Omair said when he heard of Fanar's trip, "and now they've taken him to the very den of unbelief."

Mudi fell ill when she heard that Fanar had left, but her father the Sultan told her firmly, almost rebukingly, that "you must know: Fanar is a man, not a woman. He's gone today but he will be back, and I don't want to hear another word about it."

When he bid Fanar goodbye, he told him, "Remember me to the English king, and tell him, 'My father sends you his regards, his very, very warm regards!' "

Hamilton would remember years later: "I had planned on traveling by boat, because it would give us plenty of time to talk, time for his fear and reservations to give way—time for us to become friends. I didn't want the whole, huge change to come as a shock to him. I wanted him to take it by degrees, to enjoy it, for it to leave an indelible impression in his mind and heart. Disembarking at the port, taking the train to London, would make it easier for him to swallow the bitter medicine. But no sooner did we put out to sea than Fanar got sick: his neck got out of shape and his eyes bugged out, and for part of the voyage I thought the boy was leaving us. I blamed myself, and was very down—those bedouin who always show so much goodness and courage are not quite as forbearing when faced with a death they regard as unnatural, and they're terribly skeptical about everything you tell them. They go mad, and don't regain their senses again until they smell blood. They must take revenge. I did everything I could, and we spent a week at Alexandria, until the prince had regained his health. I don't know how the Devil tricked me again, but I decided to continue our journey by sea. Perhaps that was the necessary idiocy! For as soon as we passed the Aegean Islands and headed west, the prince got like a tame cat. Was it homesickness? The difference in languages? The north wind that blows from the farthest regions, so unlike the desert winds? Something had happened, and after that escape, like flight, really, and his peculiar sickness, which neither the doctors on shipboard nor those in Alexandria could explain, he'd look at me with this pleading in his eyes: 'Don't leave me!'

"I had been waiting for that moment; it came, and I have never abandoned him since."

Fanar never spoke of his first trip to London. It wounded him, or at least made him uncomfortable, even years later. Despite Hamilton's encouragement and the smiles he met everywhere, he remained afraid. He was never at ease with the way people looked at him. They exchanged words and looks and smiles among themselves. He did not know whether to respond to their smiles in kind, or to answer their questions, especially those of old ladies, who caused him embarrassment he found it impossible to hide.

His uncle Omair, who was at first uneasy about the visit, no longer had anything to say against it in light of what came after. In later times, when people in Ain Fadda asked him how Fanar was doing, he shook his head and smiled sadly.

"My friends, human beings and their intentions are all open to Satan's designs. Since Khureybit joined hands with the infidels, and handed his children over to them, nothing has been right in this world."

They would repeat the question about Fanar and get an impetuous reply.

"Fanar, if God spares him, will come back to his uncles, because two-thirds of a boy are his uncles, as they say, and I don't think Fanar has forgotten the water of Ain Fadda. When God has entered a man's heart, no one can drive Him out."

Omair spoke this way because the Sultan had asked him explicitly, and for a fleeting moment angrily, to leave Fanar alone. When Fanar came home from his journey, and Omair once again came to stay in Mooran, the Sultan told him, "Listen, Omair, and remember: Fanar is our son, and is being raised our way and with our knowledge. If he grows up right, he will be one of us, and if he turns out bad, then we're responsible. If a man has something to say, and wants to teach it to others, he teaches it to his sons."

He paused, clearly angry.

"We don't need more headaches, Omair, we have enough as it is. Let every man do as he pleases."

Tahany remembered nothing of Fanar's visit to the land of the infidels except the blue prayer beads he brought back for her. She did not know whether they were a gift for her or for the Sheikha; it was said, in the beginning, that they were for Ummi Zahwa, and, later on, that the Sheikha had refused to touch them because they were unclean. Tahany insisted that he had presented them to her the day after he returned home, saying that they were genuine turquoise. He brought the Sheikha a gray shawl that she wore for years and years; Tahany would never forget it. When she lost the beads, she went into a deep depression, and Lulua said it was because of the value of the beads—she had, Lulua said, offered them for sale at one point.

Khazael delayed a few days after Fanar's homecoming before seeing his brother. He planned to spend a few extra days in Wadi Riha, near Mooran, on the pretext that his mediation between two quarreling sheikhs was still incomplete—despite the fact that the mediation, as people who knew said, had concluded the day before Fanar arrived home. Khazael commented on all the talk he'd heard about Fanar's journey, the wonders he had seen and things he had learned, with two gestures and one word: the gestures were a plopping sound with his tongue and a dismissive wave of his big hand, and the word was "Lies."

Nor had Mudi been interested in learning the details of Fanar's journey. She only wanted him back, and now he was back. She gazed at him, unbelieving, and while he tried to escape her stare and her efforts to make him talk about the sea voyage and the things he had seen, when tears rolled from her eyes, from both joy and sadness, he hugged her and asked her how she had been, and what was new at the Rawdh Palace and Ain Fadda.

Only the Sultan could not conceal his delight and wonder. He had several reasons to be delighted, and his wonder at Sahib and Fanar was enhanced. He listened to the details, hearing first from Hamilton how his son had been received in the English court, how parties and dinners were given in his honor wherever he went, of the gifts he received, the questions he and Hamilton were asked, mostly inquiries about His Majesty's health, the friendship His Britannic Majesty's government harbored for the Sultan of Mooran, and the hopes for cooperation between the two kingdoms; and having heard all this, he was overjoyed and really very excited. That same night he saw Hamilton off at the outer palace gate and asked Fanar to join him and tell him all about his journey "from the day you left Mooran until you came back, one day at a time." Fanar went through everything he had already heard from Hamilton earlier that evening, but in his own way, according to his own understanding. He spoke at length about the huge ship, the rainy gloom of London, the grandeur of the English palaces, and how the women there wore no veils. The Sultan was very pleased, and repeated the same words over and over again: "We're still weary, and they'll see; yes, the weariness is still there, and they will see."

The Sultan did not relax in his pleasure; his mind was racing: What should he do tomorrow? How would he deal with the others? Who were his friends today? Who were his enemies? Hamilton had given him much good news. He knew how to get it and preserve it. He spoke to Mahyoub.

"You must know, Mahyoub, that when a horse sits too long, it becomes a mule!"

Mahyoub nodded in expectant agreement.

"Now we're going to get revenge. There's no cause to fear for virtuous women, and horses will bear us or we'll leave them to be food for the vultures. You must prepare yourself and tell your family, because this time our trip will be a long one, Mahyoub, and may God bring us back victorious."

"Nahi, son of Farhan," said Talleh al-Oreifan, "His Majesty is making decisions and giving orders. Prepare your head, baldy. Now is our chance with the women." He paused to laugh. "If he's away long, friend, we'll be all set; he hears only what he wants to hear—are you listening, Nahi?"

"What are you saying?" laughed Nahi. Then in a different tone he added, "However long he's gone, Abu Jazi, the women won't forget or forgive. The best thing is to hope that he comes back victorious, because his mind will be only on his booty, whereas if he loses, he'll come back and start in on whoever's closest."

As winter drew to its end and signs of spring appeared, the Sultan launched one of his greatest campaigns, one from which he expected great things.

With the Sultan in that campaign were his uncle Dahaim and two of his sons, Khazael and Fanar. Sahib stayed on two weeks in Mooran handling urgent business, then joined the war party.

1o

ALL MOORAN TREMBLED: EVERYONE WAS AF-
fected by what was going on. Women were
possessed by fear, fear of starvation and fear
of losing their men, and said so out loud, but with the passage of time,
the determination on the war and then its coming, they fell silent.
Fathers left their young teenage sons with their mothers and sisters
out of fear for them, and because they did not trust the promises they
were given. These boys did more than anyone else to clean and oil the
new rifles and prepare the ammunition. They endlessly took apart and
reassembled the old weapons kept at home, and practiced with them;
some of the boys proved to be good shots. All this went on without
their fathers' knowledge or their mothers learning a thing, and some
of the boys got so worked up that they sought permission to take part
in the war.

The more knowing among the palace servants, who saw everything that went on, said confidently that "the Sheikha has opened her

vaults and got all her gold out and told Khureybit, 'This is your day, Abu Mansour—if you need gold, here is the gold; if you need weapons, you can get them with gold. Just give the order, and help yourself. The people are only waiting for a word to march under your banner.' And the Sultan didn't wait—he helped himself to all he could carry away, and bought enough weapons to load down a thousand camels!"

Those who knew the Sultan's moods and desires were sure that the Sheikha was involved, but they did not know how deeply. If he took Watfa with him on this campaign, and she became his favorite wife, then it must have been the Sheikha who imposed this condition. This rumor was given currency by three of the palace eunuchs, all Fadda's servants, who reported that their mistress was preparing to accompany the Sultan and was all ready to leave: she had ordered tents, all sorts of henna and incense, fifty pairs of young pigeons and all the cages she could lay her hands on, plus honey, so that everyone who visited her was sure that she was either expecting again, or preparing for a trip. The three eunuchs, unable to keep straight faces, said that their mistress showed her visitors the pigeons more proudly than she had ever shown them her jewels or new clothes. One of the three said that he had seen her stop at the birdcages and laugh aloud, just like a sick mare, and seemed utterly delighted!

But everything changed very suddenly, if silently, as something unexpected had happened: the Sultan had changed—in his behavior, the way he dressed, and in his relations with people. He offered smiles wherever he turned. He gave money openhandedly, and he distributed new weapons along with ammunition in exchange for old weapons, with no questions asked—to say nothing of his endless and unlimited promises.

The Souq al-Halal was wild with rumors that the price of camels would go up tenfold.

Some of the market brokers went further, saying that camel prices would go up twenty or thirty times; whoever owned a horse and was willing to sell, they said, would get rich.

So many other things happened or changed. The Wadi al-Faid campaign spawned a great deal of conflicting news, which was at times totally contradictory; in spite of the troops and weapons, it was rumored that the Sultan was thinking of canceling or postponing it—

then, abruptly, the drums of war sounded and his soldiers rushed to the front. Much later it was said that the Sultan was nearly killed: one night before the Battle of al-Huweiza, an assassination plot was uncovered. He himself executed five of the conspirators. It was said that one of his most important engagements, the Battle of the Fortress, was nearly lost, and might have settled the fate of the war, even the fate of the Sultanate, had it not been for the arrival of huge quantities of weapons and tough fighters. Those who knew of these fighters' arrival, or saw them, insisted that they alone engaged and defeated the enemy while the Sultan sought to reorganize his forces; they said that they withdrew after the battle, with no one knowing where they had come from or where they had gone.

Some of the transport and supply workers saw Sheikha Zahwa in a large caravan that appeared hastily on the scene. Sahib was with her. The caravan headed north and set up camp half a day's journey from the Sultan's own troops. Spectators said that the forces with the caravan turned the tide of the battle and decided the outcome. Three weeks later the troops went back west, and it was not known whether or not the Sheikha went with them; no one could define exactly the Sheikha's role in the battle.

Prince Khazael fell into an ambush, was taken prisoner and held in the Rafia Fortress. Negotiations for Khazael's release between Awayid al-Mishaan and the captors lasted three days, and the Sultan seemed pleased when he heard about them; he asked that negotiations with the captors be drawn out for as long as possible, and that readiness to meet their demands be expressed, until he was able to storm the fortress and free Khazael.

In this affair, too, the news and narratives conflicted. Most were convinced that the Sultan was more interested in winning the battle than in freeing the prisoners, Khazael included. Others said that a number of enemy soldiers came over to the Sultan, supposedly with Khazael, after he gave them money, which was what made it possible for him to occupy the fortress and free the prisoners. Those who did not like Khazael were positive that chance, and chance alone, had saved him, because the Sultan's orders in that regard had been very clear: "Destroy the fortress." When he was asked about the prisoners, he repeated: "Destroy the fortress."

Fanar was one of the detachment commanded by Uncle Dahaim. Their mission was to distract the enemy and to serve as the chief reserve force. The Sultan had told them to await further orders; he wanted to be able to call on them, to deal the final, lethal blow, so that the victory could be attributed to no one but him.

Calling out these troops was not enough for the Sultan. He moved his command post to a forward position and gave orders in person, and it was said that he had instructed Ibn Mishaan to show no mercy to any of the enemy who came his way. Some of his men overheard him addressing Ibn Mishaan.

"Kill them and move on," were his exact words. "We don't want prisoners."

When he signaled the reserve troops to advance all at once, with his uncle Dahaim at their head, they were ordered to parley with the people of al-Huweiza and advise them to surrender to the Sultan himself. During his march northward toward al-Huweiza he had some of his spies spread news of Awayid and his atrocities, to circulate the rumor that he would respect no one's safety unless they had surrendered to the Sultan. And indeed the Sultan accepted the surrender of many towns and settlements on his route.

Sahib spent most of the battle in the rear lines, now and then shuttling between the Sultan and Uncle Dahaim and the field commander, Ibn Mishaan, carrying messages, orders and ammunition. He wanted to take part in the battle despite his promise to the Sultan that he would stay in the rear, and this was confirmed when the command post was moved to a forward position. Hamilton not only sent the Sultan messengers to tell him of his wish to move, he actually did move. The Sultan heard that Sahib had moved to the front while he, the Sultan, was engineering sieges around several points leading to al-Huweiza, and flew into a rage. He sent Mahyoub and a unit of men to prevent Sahib from getting any closer than he had come, because he was worried about a counterattack and wanted Sahib to be able to move freely, to play a role beyond that of a foot soldier in order to do whatever he could with greater efficiency than His Majesty's soldiers; and he recalled how another Englishman, Fowler, had died just a few years before when he insisted on taking a direct part in the Battle of Rehaiba. The loss of Fowler was devastating, causing the Sultan such pain and grief that he did not leave his tent for several days. Now he did not want to lose Sahib as well, nor did he want to limit his role to that of a mere private carrying a rifle.

Hamilton gave in grudgingly to the Sultan's wish that he come no closer than he had already, though he yearned to join in the last battle, expected to take place any day now. He longed to live some perilous moments, as he put it to himself, and he wanted to witness the fall of al-Huweiza, and one rarely had such chances twice in a lifetime. And he was bored with the roles, seen by others as obscure, played at the rear. He wanted to prove his courage and skill, to be able to tell any man, now or in the future, that he had actually fought in a war. In an overheated moment he actually wished to be wounded, to receive a scar visible for life, a testimony to all who saw it.

Often he felt that the difference separating him from the bedouin could never be overcome. They not only perceived him as a foreigner, he made them nervous, and he saw in their smiles something that defied understanding or explanation, and this tormented him. Yes, they were friendly on the surface, and listened to him, and most were willing to eat with him, but under their stares he grinned, like a woman, almost, or a child, and some of them showed their aversion by staying far away from him, or by their silence, in spite of the friendliness he showed them and the many services he rendered them.

These attitudes tormented Hamilton, and made him feel foreign and expendable, unwanted and unloved. With this exposure to nature and turbulence, he felt that his body would not obey him, that it had mutinied and would not revert to his control again, especially after such a long time without a woman, and that only by violent action, no less violent than war, could he restore strength and discipline to his body.

The Sultan sensed, despite his overwork, that Sahib was surely going mad, exactly as had happened to Fowler, and so he took care to send him his uncle a day or two after Mahyoub came back. This is what the Sultan told his uncle:

"Just like a ram or a dog, Uncle, who is crazy with thirst, the man is wild and uncontrollable. I remember his countryman a few years ago—he thrashed and bucked, and we calmed him down: my good man, my friend, he lashed out like a bull, and then you know the rest." He rested a moment reflectively, then went on. "You must tell him, you must counsel him, Uncle, that we need him for bigger and better things."

"Trust in God, nephew, only the best will befall."

With Dahaim, Hamilton was unambiguous.

"A battle like this one only comes along once. It would be impos-

sible to write about it or record it for history without the chance to
see it firsthand, to take part in it."

"Sahib, they have sent us messengers saying, 'If you value life and
honor, lay down arms,' and that order is from His Majesty."

"Why doesn't the Sultan want me at his side, to witness the surrender of his enemies and the fall of al-Huweiza?"

"His Majesty says they are treacherous. They know you're their
enemy, and he's worried about their hot blood. One of them might
take it into his head to do something terrible."

Hamilton had not considered this. He said to himself that "the bedouin may rival foxes when it comes to trickery, but foxes leave no
trace behind them."

At last an agreement was reached, with some strain and moments
of anger and sullenness: Hamilton could advance, on condition that
he took no part in the fighting.

Long years later Hamilton wrote:

"The Sultan spent the evening of 2 May preparing to attack the city
and to capture its immense fort, issuing terse instructions as to how
his plan would be executed. His best troops had cut down the palm
trees in a small oasis nearby, and built ladders out of them, for scaling
walls. At the same time, well ropes were passed out to all the men in
the detachment assigned to climb, to dangle them from atop the walls
once they had achieved their first objective.

"The march began at midnight, on foot, and by sunrise the ropes
swung from the walls, allowing the infiltrators to silence the sleeping
guards forever. Before the garrison itself could shake off the conster-
nation that struck them in the dark, the fort was in the hands of the
Sultan's soldiers. Its defenders retreated to the mosque and secured
their position there while awaiting further developments.

"In the meantime, the Sultan's soldiers captured one of the city
gates, and Khureybit's soldiers surged in, firing and chanting their
battle cries to intensify the terror that gripped the inhabitants and convince the enemy that they had no hope of being saved.

"Khureybit's men took a number of the enemy prisoner and sent
them to their commander seeking his surrender, and telling him that
the Sultan would guarantee their forces' lives. They were to tell him
that any delay in surrendering would result in the blowing up of the
fort and the demolition of the city walls.

"There was no alternative to surrender, and thus al-Huweiza fell."

Long years later, the Sultan recalled:

"As God is my witness, my friends, in al-Huweiza I sent messengers to Sahib until there was no one left to send! I was in such a state until he gave in." And with a loud laugh: "That bunch, my friends, are different from you or me; if one of them is stubborn and says no, there's no dealing with him, and after all that Uncle Dahaim, God rest his soul, took charge and went through all sorts of give-and-take with him until he agreed to stay in al-Wajh. I told him, I'll send you a messenger every hour to give you the latest news. He watched everything from al-Wajh through binoculars, and we kept the messengers moving back and forth. When they surrendered, I sent for him, I told him, 'Come,' and he came with his people's prudence and wariness, afraid that some son of a bitch would get hot-blooded and try to settle a score with us, but God watched over us and everything went smoothly. Sahib stayed angry for a month or even two months, but then a few months later he left on a two-month trip, and by the time he came back, everything was fine again."

11

JUST A FEW MONTHS AFTER THE BATTLE OF AL-
Huweiza, Hamilton went back to Britain for
a long vacation. He needed a vacation badly;
he felt overburdened by the huge and incessant effort of the past three
years, and had fallen into a deep depression as a result of being frus-
trated and misunderstood. He felt unwanted by most of the people
around him, which made him feel that the mission he had devoted
himself to had been in vain. His wife, Dorothy, had unambiguous
motives for the trip: "I don't want our child to be born in this desolate
place, which gives one a certain ill feeling that never departs. I want
our child born in a normal place, in surroundings that won't give him
a complex against his father." Hamilton went along with his wife and
appeared to prepare himself for the trip, recalling his own childhood
in that remote place. His recollections were clouded and confused,
and very remote themselves, but they had left their mark on his life.
Now he was paying the price for his birth, as he said to himself when
he was feeling rueful.

The Sultan was not opposed to Hamilton's trip, and was quick to allow Fanar to go along, too. The Sultan had several reasons: After his victory, with al-Huweiza humbled, he was beset by a mass of problems and obstacles he would not be free of for some time. And he needed money, particularly the foreign aid he'd been promised. He had received one payment, but the rest had been delayed, and there was no one better able than Hamilton to persuade those people to pay up, perhaps even to increase the amount. This required inquiries and follow-up in London; the post took too long, and the envoys who came and made promises never kept their promises. Furthermore, he wanted to know how the outcome of the Battle of al-Huweiza had changed their policies. Had his standing improved? Would they agree to abandon some of their former allies, who were no longer useful or powerful in these new circumstances? Hamilton, who had once been so lucid, so decisive, now seemed befuddled and indecisive; so he had to consult with his superiors.

As to the Sultan's decision to let Fanar go with them—there were special reasons for that. On the third day after the Sultan's triumphal homecoming, with feasts and gift-giving on a scale unseen in long years, a messenger arrived from Ain Fadda with the news of Sheikh Awad's death. The Sultan was more alarmed than saddened by the news, coming at the time it did. He had to curtail the festivities and postpone his marriage to Shama, the widow of the emir of al-Huweiza, who had been killed in the battle.

The death of Fanar and Mudi's grandfather grieved the two to the point of calamity, of shock, as if they had expected him to live forever. Mudi's tears flowed, and she let them flow with no fear or concern for what anyone would think, and Fanar, who had returned from the Wadi al-Faid campaign refreshed and optimistic, now sank into a mournful silence. The Sultan sent his uncle Dahaim to Ain Fadda to offer condolences, accompanied by Fanar, who went unasked because he regarded this as a duty that would admit of no delay.

This visit to Ain Fadda came so many years after he had left, and in such sad circumstances, that Omair's grief was redoubled. He sent word that "the prince had come to accept condolences and receive the mourners," so Fanar had to prolong his stay time and again, as if his longing for this place had reasserted itself, or at least to receive those who had come to offer their sympathy.

Omair thought it right to declare himself the head of the family, and to declare his opposition to, or at least his opinion concerning everything that was going on; "Sahib" came in for his share of commentary and a good deal of mockery. Someone present reported to the Sultan what was happening in Ain Fadda and precisely what Omair was saying, and one of the relatives who had seen a meeting of locals added that three of Khureybit's enemies had either attended in person or sent representatives.

"When Omair went to Ain Fadda, we thought we could relax," the Sultan told his uncle Dahaim when he heard this. "When our boy Fanar came here, we thought. 'That's that.' But old habits never die, Uncle. Now we have to keep our eyes open, because Omair has ambitions, and evil intentions. I want Fanar back here yesterday! He'll never be safe with a wolf wandering among the sheep."

When Fanar recalled the events of his second visit to Britain, he felt that it was that visit that had made him grow up—it had been a crucial visit. His father told him about the events in Ain Fadda in an almost chiding tone, and made him suffer pangs of conscience.

"After God Himself," his father told him with a sad smile, "our hopes depend on you. You are to be the very sword we fight with. I am sure that you would never want to be in a place, or with people, where we were the subject of unacceptable talk."

The Sultan changed his tone, becoming perfectly paternal.

"Your mother's brother, my boy, is a suspicious and difficult man. He thinks it is his lot to have you, that you are his, as if he did not know that Fanar is his father's son, that blood is thicker than water. Your uncle has to clear these delusions out of his head, my boy, otherwise he will reap what he's sowing!"

The Sultan did not want Fanar to be overcome with remorse, especially at this time, and that was why Hamilton's suggestion came at just the right time. If Fanar set off on this long journey, he would surely forget, and everything would be fine by the time he came home again. His father spoke to him kindly.

"Sahib, my boy, asked if you would travel with him, and we said, 'As God wills.' What do you say?"

Within a few days the journey began.

The first visit had been unpleasant—almost like a chore. Fanar remembered it clearly, and now, after all he'd heard Hamilton say, he was prepared. His eagerness grew when he heard the news, circulating in whispers, of Khazael's captivity. It was alleged that Khazael had arranged it all himself, so the whole affair elicited more scorn than surprise, which moved the Sultan to anger. He threatened the direst consequences for anyone who had played a part in deceiving him. A small number of palace women were reported to have said that the Sheikha had, at about this time, begun to speak of Fanar in the most favorable and enthusiastic terms, which meant, to most people, that he would succeed his father as sultan. Mudi said that she had heard this from Tahany, and added that when some of the women asked the Sheikha about it jokingly, she smiled and replied, "Everything in its proper time."

When Uncle Dahaim heard of Fanar's intention to travel, he patted him on the back and said, "There's always good in what God wills." He added, in a different tone, "In our day, my boy, when we were your age, we used to drive our family mad until they finally allowed us to travel, and back then a journey was an ordeal! Not like now . . ."

He shook his head and then turned this way and that to make sure that no one but Fanar was listening.

"And it would be a good idea for you to be out of his way for a few months after that business in Ain Fadda!"

On his third day in London, Fanar stopped wearing his desert clothes, at Hamilton's request, but he was happy to do it. He did not want to appear to others a plaything they never tired of staring or smiling at. He felt even more liberated when Hamilton suggested more time in the countryside: "The English countryside is so lovely and peaceful. No one will bother us there; within a few days a visitor feels at home, he feels like a native. Just the opposite of London, which amuses itself and fights its boredom by staring at people, especially foreigners, with a snide smile." Fanar understood part of what Hamilton said, or at least understood it in his own way. The fuss that encircled him with every step he took in the street, in a restaurant, in the hotel lobby, frightened or at least embarrassed him. He had never seen anything like it before, and felt that he would never get used to it. And that was not all.

"You have to learn English," said Hamilton. "If you learn English, you'll have surpassed all of your brothers in something. The Sultan will be immensely surprised and pleased! Especially if you can take over interpreting between him and his foreign visitors."

Fanar's eyes widened in surprise and curiosity, and he answered timidly, "English is so hard. It can only be learned in a school."

Hamilton laughed and shook his head.

"Everything looks hard at first. Remember your first visit to London. You were afraid—every day you asked me several times when we were going back to Mooran. Now you're doing much better. Look at you in your European clothes!"

Fanar's eyes shone and he nodded in agreement.

"English looks hard at first, but if you give it a few hours each day it will be easier than you ever imagined."

"Outside of school?"

"You and I will establish our very own school." He laughed, looking at Fanar. "A school with one pupil, and just a few teachers. The teachers may be old men, or family members, or . . ." Hamilton went on to describe, very temptingly, how easy and important the language was, how this would all be in the countryside, through contact and daily life with a family. Hamilton would plan everything himself so that there would be no problem of any kind. Fanar would have to rely solely upon him for his simplest daily needs.

Fanar was to remember the two reasons he agreed to go as his wish to surpass his brothers, particularly Khazael, in something, and to surprise his father.

Fanar endured a long period of pining, of muddle and homesickness, in addition to illness and loss of interest in his studies. But they both persevered, thanks to Hamilton's extraordinary effort, the stability of their last two months together after Dorothy and the child left for Wales, and the return of his aides and bodyguards to Mooran, at Hamilton's request and with the consent of Fanar and the Sultan. He also chose a place less damp than the other places, all of which helped things to go more smoothly. Fanar was now able to converse with others and to express some of his thoughts. His sentences were rather simple and extremely short, but sufficed to say what he wished.

His greatest help was Hamilton's aunt, Miss Margot. The time he spent with her was the last and longest part of his sojourn. Miss Margot was a magnificent woman, and the days he spent as her guest were the happiest of his trip; not only did this middle-aged lady excel at oriental cookery, she knew how to talk, and how to make others talk. Fanar spent long days on end with her when Hamilton was off in London dealing with complex business and travel plans, as he explained rather apologetically.

Miss Margot was, to Fanar, a combination of schoolmistress,

mother and friend. He always remembered the days he spent with her in Oxford, and never tired of reminiscing about them even long years later. Hamilton's absences, which were very frequent in those two months, did not bother him or make him lonely. Miss Margot knew how to arrange a full program for each day, even when it rained; even, in his very last days, when it began to snow, she found things that kept both of them busy and happy.

Miss Margot had spent twenty years in Ceylon, first as a nurse, then as a head nurse, traveling from one part of the island to another to learn details of the way of life and the nature of the land. She had gained knowledge and expertise unavailable to many other people, and used it to write two books of which she was very proud, as they represented the essence of her ample experience and knowledge.

After leaving Ceylon of her own accord, she went to southern Africa for seven years, which yielded a third book. It was a less comprehensive book than her first two, but a far richer one from the standpoint of human experience, as she pointed out proudly. She was very careful in choosing the pages she read aloud to Fanar; she often had to stop to explain or comment, or to expand upon what lay behind some of the direct words, and although Fanar listened attentively, he was unable to grasp some of the larger meanings she alluded to, though he never tired of her reading or her explanations. She would lower her eyeglasses nearly to her mouth, and begin, often resorting to pausing and acting out passages, gesticulating and even rearranging the furniture.

A week before the end of the stay, while Hamilton was away, Miss Margot gave one of her books to Fanar, formally and majestically, reminding him of the philosophy of her book: if writing did not come from the heart, if it was solely the product of reading or contemplation, it would be of little importance; it would not be a true contribution. If it was not written today, it could be written some other day, whereas experience, human life, any person's life, was unique, even though there were millions of people, and worthy of being recorded, so that it might help us to see, in depth and detail, the meaning of life.

Fanar was utterly fascinated by all he saw and heard. For the first time in his life he had come to know a woman; while his grandmother loved and cared about him, she was a mass of blackness and confusion and even at times absence. Her flowing black garments and attentiveness to others, the nights so weighted with silence and the sound of the wind, made her present yet absent at the same time. On sleepless nights or party nights, when people talked or sang, or listened to others talk and sing, she paid more attention to the children's cries and sicknesses, the demands and opinions of the old men. Or else she busied herself with the cats, dogs and other animals. Fanar always remembered his grandmother on the move. She often fell asleep sitting by the hearth as she appeared to be following all the conversations in progress.

Miss Margot was a different sort of woman, for while she was no longer young, she reminded him of a colored bird. While he never dared gaze at her long or pay too close attention to her clothes or jewelry, her presence and aroma filled the room, so that whoever sat before her felt the intensity of her presence, indeed her dominance; felt, moreover, that she was his alone. When she spoke, she conjured things up and gave them a rough texture, almost as if they were being re-created. She spoke softly, looking directly into his eyes, moving her hands as if creating something, and she reminisced lovingly, as if living her memories over again.

Fanar often missed words that recurred in Miss Margot's conversation, but he understood the meaning from her gestures, from her excitement, and though that was enough for him, she was such a resolute and exacting woman, with regard equally to herself and others, that when she sensed some words had gone past him she paused to ask and explain. This was very much part of her teaching.

Years later Hamilton and His Highness the Prince were thinking back on that sojourn, and Hamilton said, "The woman that had the greatest influence on my life was Aunt Margot—more than my mother, or all my teachers put together. My mother saw our living in that remote place as a penance the Empire inflicted upon us, and impatiently counted the days and hours until the penance ended and we could go back to freedom, as she put it, meaning England. Aunt Margot was a different sort: she had gone to Ceylon completely of her own accord, and loved being there. She longed to know everything about the place, and lost no time in learning some of the local languages; she gets the credit for steering me toward the oriental languages. She always used to say, to herself as much as to anyone else, 'We must not be fooled by the surfaces we see. The East is deeper than it seems, and more dangerous than many think, and the history, traditions and myths enliven it as much as they hold it back, and impart to it the power to carry on, to resist, to renew itself. The first thing in understanding the East is to live there, not to treat it with rejection or aversion; to learn its languages, so that one knows how they think and express themselves. Language is the cornerstone of understanding, the first step in the dialogue.' "

Hamilton was silent for a moment, overtaken by the stream of thoughts that momentarily blocked his reminiscence; he did not want to be carried away by it.

"Because she lived for so many years outside of Britain," he went on in the same tone, "and had so much contact with foreigners, she became the finest language teacher. She knew how to teach, and the easiest things to begin with."

Fanar smiled, as if discovering that he had been the victim of a plot hatched by Hamilton and his aunt, and asked jokingly, "So that is why you chose her to teach me English."

"I chose her because she knew how to work with other peoples, and because she knows what kings, more than anyone else, need to learn."

Fanar laughed pleasantly, and when he fell silent looked deep into Hamilton's eyes. This was something he rarely did. If Hamilton feared anyone or anything, it was these stabbing, piercing looks, which suddenly flew at him, as he thought to himself, from those hard, dusty bedouin faces. They were looks not with the aim of seeing, but of slicing open the person opposite, to tear away any covering he wore, to deprive him of any possibility of lying. Hamilton withdrew his eyes and looked far off, then resumed speaking.

"Aunt Margot knew what foreigners needed to know about English, and she made the language delightful, living, responsive to their actual needs—in a word, a beloved language. She believed that the love of any people required, above all else, a love for its language, just as she loved the languages of the East, and made me love them, too, and wanted you to love English. That's the best way to learn a language."

Fanar felt a certain pride and ascendancy over his brothers, because he had traveled and seen the world and learned English, even though he had been, until the very end, too shy or reserved to speak it.

When he was compelled to use it, simple words and short phrases were the backbone of his speech. He furthermore avoided speaking English as much as possible while in Mooran, after the teasing he got, even from Uncle Omair, who repeated, along with the old men, that "Arabic is the language spoken by the dwellers of Paradise—English is spoken in Hell!" Omair also avoided saying whether or not he knew English himself, so that he did not have to change his opinion of it, and so that he would not have to feel bad if anyone learned that he knew it.

Fanar was not content with avoiding speaking English: he tried to outdo his brothers in perfecting his bedouin dialect, particularly Khazael, who claimed to be more fluent in that dialect than any bedouin! One of the Sultan's favorite pastimes was organizing contests involving desert poems and sayings, with his sons in attendance or even taking part, and Khazael made no secret of his skill; Fanar remembered a great deal from Ain Fadda, from its long nights, its endless tales, and what he had picked up in subsequent years, and he impressed people, too.

"I think, Abu Mansour," said Uncle Dahaim to the Sultan one evening, "that if a man does not learn when he's young, then he won't learn when he's old either."

The Sultan did not disagree, but kept his silence, so that his uncle might finish explaining what he wanted to say.

"And if he isn't suckled on his mother's milk, he'll be weaned off of it and his whole people."

"So?"

"That night when we were listening to Fanar talk about the sayings of Ain Fadda, he said some good things, some wonderful things. He's clever—he's very intelligent."

The Sultan laughed delightedly but said nothing.

"Living among the bedouin did him a huge amount of good, Abu Mansour. He learned a lot from them."

Hamilton, who attended the contests, and sometimes had to ask the meaning of certain words, played a silent, observant role. One night in Oxford he told Fanar, "It is better for a man not to show everything he knows, especially in front of rivals; furthermore, he should leave them a few things in which to distinguish themselves, for them to be proud of. It costs him nothing, and might give them the illusion of having won. When the time comes for the game to begin in earnest, we see who the real winner and the real loser are!"

Fanar was accustomed to being quiet and attentive when he was with Hamilton, or any of the adults of his family, especially his father. He said nothing. Hamilton felt sure that he was talking to himself, at that moment, more than he was talking to Fanar. He cleared his throat and spoke in a very polished tone.

"Khazael may know desert poetry and proverbs better than you, but that means nothing. There are far more important things, and those are what you must learn."

Fanar was silent, but knew, or more precisely felt. the meaning of Hamilton's words. For the first time, in the presence of another person, he felt fear and something like danger. If he had learned anything valuable in Ain Fadda, it was secrecy. One night his grandmother spoke to him after hearing something that had displeased her, sighing like a wounded or thirsty person.

"It took Halima, your mother, God rest her soul, for our people to swallow a stone, to say all, far and near, 'And they took us from them and they became our men, and they had to be quiet.' But our hope is in you, my boy, and by God's hand and by your hand everything will come right." She was silent a moment, then spoke in a low, almost conspiratorial tone. "This is just between us, my boy—a stone in a well. No one can see or hear us—if they knew, they'd kill us both!"

Now, in the twinkling of an eye, Fanar recalled his grandmother's words, and compared them with what he was hearing from Hamilton now. The world seemed to him a mass of clashing boulders, but with muted sound; inevitably, one boulder would smash all the rest, or like a mass of ghastly knives tearing into flesh, soundlessly, and in the dark, so that one knife would prevail over the others.

Hamilton's voice rose again, sharp and clear.

"You know something important, I don't know where you learned it, but you must preserve it: silence." He took a deep breath, and resumed a moment later, speaking as if to himself. "Silence is the weapon of the strong, not of the weak or cowardly—never forget that."

At certain moments, sometimes abruptly, in an instant briefer than a flash of lightning, a man may learn, discover or see something he had not grasped over time. Suddenly, it comes clear that he has been asleep or inattentive, or perhaps even good to the point of foolishness.

Now, from these few and indirect and even mysterious words, Fanar felt that he was the object of a bet, and the image of his grandmother filled his mind. He said sadly to himself, "If I want, I may learn from you, or else be food for the vultures. We shall see."

The battles of Wadi al-Faid and al-Huweiza had wrought great changes in Mooran, and Hamilton's return with Fanar after their long journey, and the Sultan's warm welcome and festivities along with them, also made for some unforeseen changes in the flow of events.

Mudi had waited impatiently during the months of the journey, and wept a great deal. She had much to say to Fanar when he arrived home; when she saw him, her tears mixed with her laughter and she could not even speak. She gazed at him for a long time and then pounced on him, able to use only her fist to express herself: she banged it on his shoulder, harder and harder. He shrieked with laughter, but Qatma reprimanded her.

"You'll hurt him, girl, you're hitting him on that shoulder!"

Mudi's eyes flew open wide in fear as she remembered his old wound.

"Are you really hurt?" she asked entreatingly.

Fanar only laughed even more loudly than before, but Qatma told him, "And you, sir, should be ashamed—you stayed away much too long!"

"You'll never go away again," said Mudi between her tears.

Tahany arrived at that moment, curious about what gifts he may have brought for her, saying, "The longer you stay away, the better the gifts you should bring back!" Then she said, "Now we're holding our aprons out, and you have to put something in them, even if it's only a stone!"

Mudi and Qatma went off to unpack Fanar's luggage and take the gifts out while Tahany brought Fanar up to date on what had been going on in his absence.

"While you were away, sir, you got three new brothers and five new sisters. After your father married Shama, he married Melahed's daughter. And he's been at it again with your uncle Omair. The Sheikha has kept you in her prayers. Your brother Khazael has taken another wife. Fadda is pregnant and ready to give birth any day now—Watfa, too."

"Would you leave him alone, girl, Tahany? That's enough—you're making him dizzy!" shrieked Mudi from the next room.

12

AWAYID AL-MISHAAN'S PERSONALITY WAS A
puzzle and provoked widely disparate senti-
ments in the minds and hearts of everyone
who knew or knew of him. The very name of this man, who in his
bulk and features resembled a shadow, hidden in his cloak as a drop of
water is hidden in a cloud, never addressed by anyone who did not
know him, gave fright to women and their children, even in their silence or sleep. In the men's councils, scarcely an evening passed without a discussion of his campaigns, his courage and his cruelty, along
with a discussion of his justice and his aversion to taking booty, which
he always gave out to his men, never touching a straw of it. Evidence
of his intelligence and boldness was mixed with fantasy and delusion,
for much of what was attributed to him had actually been done
by others, and the men competed with one another in telling the mi-
nutest details of his life, to show their knowledge of everything
about him. Even those who were not his soldiers, or had never even

laid eyes on him, spoke of him with a confidence that bordered on exaggeration.

This was not all that gave rise to puzzlement and contradiction in Awayid al-Mishaan's personality. His humility, the total lack of formality between him and the men under his command, the fact that they ate the same food and wore the same clothes, his respect for every one of his men, all set him apart from the other tribal sheikhs and military commanders, and especially from the men close to Khureybit.

The Sultan treated him differently from the way he treated others. While he made no effort to hide his admiration for him, from Awayid himself or from anyone else, he was very wary of him, the more so since one of the qualities Awayid possessed was the gift of silence. He hid behind his silence, so that neither his friends nor his enemies knew what he was thinking and what he would do next. On the few occasions during the campaigns for Wadi al-Faid and al-Huweiza when he said what ought to be done, he limited himself to briefly stated ideas and proposals.

A year and a few months after the Battle of al-Huweiza, the Sultan and Hamilton talked about Awayid for the first time; they had never discussed him in detail or at any length before. He had often been mentioned, especially when they were planning a campaign, but as long as he was absent from their camp at al-Beqaa, the talk about him was indirect and died away quickly, perhaps because the mystery that surrounded his person and personality obscured their opinion of him.

Awayid spent considerable time with the Sultan, or corresponded with him when they were apart, but the Sultan hardly noticed him, and the news or conversation he shared with him, and the contents of messengers' dispatches he shared, made him apprehensive, suspicious and even a little afraid.

When Awayid came to Mooran, which he visited once or twice a year, he mastered his doubts and was filled with warmth and friendliness, for he received more welcome and cordiality than any other of the other visiting sheikhs or generals. Not merely the forces the Sultan put at Awayid's disposal, but their quality, was a sign of the ruler's esteem, for they were different from other soldiers: they knew what they were fighting for. That is what they said, and that is what Awayid insisted upon. He shook with excitement as he said, "We are fighting in God's cause—to exalt the Truth!" He told his men with confidence that "you are like the first Muslims fighting for the triumph of Islam. Not for land, not for booty, or to please any person. If you win, you will prevail over the whole world, and those of you who die will have Paradise for his abode!"

With this as the aim of their war, Awayid's men had, in the eyes of most, unlimited drive, stamina and patience.

Early on, the Sultan appointed a number of aides, chosen by himself, to assist Awayid, but this failed, because the soldiers refused to obey them, so the Sultan was forced to allow Awayid to choose his own staff. Those who tried to compete with him, to rival his stature, whether out of personal ambition or because the Sultan egged them on, always ended up capitulating to him completely, with the result that the Sultan gave up interfering in Awayid's business.

It was not an easy thing for Hamilton to become friends with Awayid, in spite of his many various efforts, which he never gave up. He had run up against Awayid's wary bedouin nature, always fortified by silence and immense politeness, even at times a certain affected ignorance, and Awayid did not give in, though he did not stoop to ignoring Hamilton or treating him with hostility. Furthermore, there was a tacit agreement between the two men to avoid one another, which made Awayid, in Hamilton's eyes, even more important and indispensable, no matter how he might feel toward him.

Awayid had different ideas. He did not fear Hamilton, who was not hidden, but did fear Hamilton's influence over the Sultan, and said as much to his close friends.

"Beware your enemy once, but beware your friend a thousand times. It's not just a question of this Englishman—he's naked and bareheaded as far as we're concerned. I'm worried about the ones who wear turbans."

One night the Sultan sat with Uncle Dahaim and Hamilton. Awayid had left Mooran that day, and the Sultan had accompanied him as far as Wadi Riha on the pretext of wanting to see some of the new horses that had just come to market there. The Sultan spoke to the two, unasked, as if talking to himself.

"Ibn Mishaan mustn't leave unless he's satisfied. He is friends with Mugharrib." When he saw that they did not completely understand what he meant, he explained, "If he weren't on our side, we'd be in trouble, but the man's faith is strong, and we, with God as our witness, have not failed him."

"Abu Mansour, Awayid's faith is stronger than a rock. As long as he's with us, we'll be fine—we'll be victorious," said Dahaim. He took a deep breath and added, "But you should know: Awayid is more stubborn than a goat. His stubbornness can help us or hurt us. Keep an eye on it, Abu Mansour, and be ready."

Hamilton needed more information, and said, to prod them, "Awayid al-Mishaan is a tiresome man, and very suspect."

"Sahib," said the Sultan in a pained voice, "with Awayid it's like a woman and a little boy—he's not happy unless everything is his way, so you have to please him, and be on your guard from him."

That night the three of them agreed that at this stage they needed Awayid; they needed his presence and power. He would be given what he asked, but they would have to be cautious and watch him, for as Hamilton said, "A foolish friend is worse than a wise enemy."

Awayid returned to al-Beqaa with five horses from the Sultan, which had been chosen for him by the Sultan himself, and which the Sultan had insisted that he accept, these or at least some others. While it gave him pleasure to try and decline, in spite of the gifts and fanfare of his welcome in Mooran, he was deeply upset by the Sultan's relationship with Hamilton and feared what might come out of it. He remembered the first time he had ever seen Hamilton, years ago.

"Abu Mahjam," the Sultan had told him, "this man has come to us with the best intentions, and deluged us with water. He was the one who said, 'Dig here and you'll find water,' and we dug exactly where he pointed, and found water. I believe he's a fine man and means well."

Awayid had nodded, but remained unconvinced.

Uncle Dahaim had long been one of Awayid's closest friends and could talk to him differently from the Sultan, so he was the one who tried to persuade him that Sahib had come to Mooran not only for water, but to help people with medicine—for he had brought with him a large quantity of drugs—and even wanted to embrace Islam; God had given him that wish. Dahaim concluded by saying that "we need to help him, too, Awayid, for if he opens his heart and accepts Islam, God will reward us."

For a long while nothing changed. In every period of time the good aspects of the situation were paralleled by doubts and fears.

After the al-Huweiza campaign things became clearer. When the battle was over, Awayid told the Sultan, "Now, Abu Mansour, our carpet is spread, that we may tell everything that is on our minds."

The Sultan laughed richly.

"Yes, here is our carpet, Abu Mahjam—what's on your mind?"

"This man, Sahib, has his good and bad points, Abu Mansour. I see him racing around night and day, here and there, never stopping, never pausing. We don't know whether he's doing it all for God . . . or for someone else."

"Don't worry, trust in God, Abu Mahjam." The Sultan laughed to hide his embarrassment, and after reviewing mentally what possible things Awayid could be thinking of, he said firmly, "As God said in his perfect Scripture, Ibn Mishaan: 'Some assumptions are sin.' We bedouin never believe anything unless we see it with our own eyes, but believe me when I tell you that I have seen and made sure with my own eyes, and I know him well. And that is enough."

He took a deep breath.

"By God, by God, by God, Abu Mahjam, I have seen nothing but good come from that man, and everything he's done has been to our benefit." His tone of voice changed. "I was like you, Awayid. I used to say to myself, 'What does this man want from us?' But when we saw him, we were reassured. If you trust your brother Abu Mansour, and trust his judgment of others, then have no fear."

That ended the discussion.

Hamilton came back from his trip full of plans and dreams, all his energy and vitality restored, his melancholy dispelled, ready for a great project: to start a new era in Mooran.

He was not yet sure what this would require, and was almost afraid, what with the malaise of failure that pervaded London during his stay and the hesitating, doubtful questions they asked him there. The powers dealing with the "question of the East" were in the midst of an open and acrimonious struggle; every feuding party blamed the failure on the others, and cast doubt on the worth of any plan or its chances of success. Hamilton was forced time and again to prolong his stay in London in order to study and select among a great many files and proposals. Despite the studies and agreements in principle that had been reached, delays, second thoughts and revisions in some of the plans, plus a stricter attitude toward disbursing aid funds, dominated the issue. Not until his final week was he able to obtain results that he considered satisfactory.

They told him quite clearly that "those bedouin only know how to do one thing: to take money forever and do nothing in return. That's not all—they act purely in their own self-interest, and trust words spoken or promises given in the past, in exceptional circumstances, and they have no knowledge or appreciation for the changes that have taken place in the world. They pull these tattered papers from their old cloth purses and have no idea what is written on them, except for a few words translated for them by sailors or servants, and wave them in the face of the Empire, demanding that we keep promises. They are so wearying, unbearable really; some of our men came along, the Devil only knows why, to fill their heads with dreams and empty posturing, with the result that we have to contend with this cataract of problems, as if the Empire did not have enough to worry about!"

This was part of a long harangue he listened to at the Foreign Office in London.

In his final week, thanks to persistence that reached the point of desperation, they agreed that he might go back to Mooran and pay out the money that had been promised to the Sultan. It was also agreed that Hamilton would be given six months, a year at the outside, in which to present a comprehensive plan to reverse the sorry situation and formulate a viable plan for the new era.

It was Hamilton's second-to-last chance to build his kingdom on earth. London had borne the failures of others and was convinced that the problems needed to be dealt with by a fresh mind, and asked him to bear full responsibility.

Before, he had been a mere intermediary, contacting London through higher-ups, in direct touch with no one but the Sultan and his court. Now London spread all its maps out before him and asked him to take action.

Now he was ready to deal with anything, with anyone, without reservations or prejudice. He might rethink some of the concepts and plans, and meet with all of the clans without making commitments or even so much as a promise. He remembered his own first days in Mooran: they were happening again, but this time to the good, and with him in charge. The last time, he had sent in his reports and then occupied himself looking for archaeological ruins and drawing maps of the borders while waiting for a response. The response usually consisted of vague general expressions, which he contemplated in moments of anger or irritation during those hot oriental nights.

Now he could act differently and prove to London that he might succeed where others had failed. For this reason he had no trouble about leaving Dorothy behind in Britain and forgetting many of his convictions—his caprices, he called them—because he had decided, he said to himself, "to demand success of myself, and nothing but success."

He did not give the Sultan the money brought all at once; he gave him half and held back the other half, saying that the rest would be following soon. The Sultan, who only cared for the present day and the money in his hands, did not object. In an attempt to set out his view of the others, who had made promises they did not keep, he said, "I think, dear friend, that the people who came here did not convey what I said to our friends there—because our friends never forget." He paused and nodded. "Your going was essential, and has brought much good."

The Sultan's aim in speaking this way was to find out whether London had dropped its former allies, and whether he might resume his campaigns. These were his chief concerns. When it came to his need for money, he had found a partial solution in the spoils of his campaign, which helped him a great deal, and solved problems for him and his soldiers which would have been otherwise unsolvable. The rains that year were heavy, too, so that the Sultan and the rest of them had a feeling of security they hadn't had in years.

Hamilton spoke, not without sarcasm.

"The journey was tiring but it was unavoidable; renewing contacts with officials there and discussing all the issues is far different from writing letters and waiting for a response, to say nothing of the delays that involves, and the danger of their neglect and forgetfulness."

"That's the truth. One meeting eye-to-eye is worth a thousand letters."

His letters went, for the most part, to men who knew about the region only what they had learned from an atlas; no matter how diligent and serious they were, they could not appreciate how momentous their decisions were or how they should be implemented. They were simply employees committing their recommendations to paper. Hamilton took a deep breath and went on.

"The knowledgeable ones, who know the people and places and relationships, they are the only ones who understand, who can say what must be done at the right time."

The Sultan perceived that Sahib was digressing, he made an effort to bring him back.

"Our friends, God willing, are pleased with us?"

"Most certainly, Your Majesty. If they weren't, events should have gone very differently."

"But—and I don't want you to get angry, Sahib—they and our friends there are very tight with one another, and if they had pulled the reins in on them a little, things wouldn't have come out this way. They would have told them, 'Things will be like this—not like that.' "

Hamilton thought to himself that "these bedouin never forget what they want—they retreat just a bit, but only so that they can make a longer jump—like a toy that moves backward only to store the power to spring forward." He smiled and said aloud, "Back there, Your Majesty, they have a special regard for you. They see you as someone different from all the others. You'll see this for yourself."

They left it there.

Just a few weeks after Awayid al-Mishaan's visit to Mooran, someone came and said that Awayid was in a rage, and had asked Omair to stay with him in al-Beqaa when he found out that the Sultan had summoned two of his cousins to discuss the siege of that area with them.

As water muddies when a new stream opens into it, so their relations muddied and disrupted. The Sultan, who at the best of times hardly welcomed Omair's visits to other sheikhs, became wary and worried about this visit, especially when he heard what Omair had been saying about Sahib.

"Omair al-Awad is playing with his blood, Uncle," the Sultan told his uncle Dahaim, with Fanar listening. "And this game is not going to be a long one."

"Patience, Abu Mansour."

"We are patient, Uncle, but we don't want others to think us afraid or weak."

"Don't worry, Abu Mansour. You are well known, and people know what you are capable of."

"Our folk used to say—and they were right—'Recite the holy Sura of Ya Sin, but have a stone in your hand.' " He nodded sadly. "We want nothing from Omair, but he's gone too far, and if our advice fails, and sweet talk fails, then he should know that when medicine fails extreme measures are called for. We have held our peace until now, but no longer."

"It was just a phase and it's passing, Abu Mansour."

"It has lasted too long, Uncle."

"I hope to God we will not regret this."

Hamilton thought, "These bedouin only understand one thing: money. Money turns their heads, it makes them swifter and more obedient than water running downhill. It turns them into a mouth that only knows one word: yes. When they get money, they're like dogs with a bone—no one can go near them. They can't let go of it, but they don't know what to do with it. After they've turned it over in their hands hundreds of times, hiding it under their pillows, beside their hearts, they let it run through their fingers like water. They might buy a new rifle or take a new wife or give a banquet for people they know and others they don't, so they can overeat, only to prove that they can. Money can't solve their problems. It corrupts them. It transforms them into creatures useless for work or war. They have no scruple against fighting the giver of the money, even should he be a Sultan, because they imagine they're stronger than he is!"

He drew a deep breath as a flood of images passed by his mind's eye, thinking, "Even so, we have to placate them and meet their demands, no matter what we think of their actions."

Fanar followed the conversation closely, but only grew more tired and confused. Mudi had told him she was homesick for Ain Fadda and wanted him to go back with her. He made the excuse that "I got ill the last time I went to Ain Fadda. It would be better to put off the visit."

She gave him a very scolding look, and he laughed.

"Ain Fadda can come to us here—within a day or two we can have the whole crowd staying with us!"

In this way Fanar did not respond to Mudi's feelings or her request to go to Ain Fadda. Hamilton had told him, as their plane was landing in Cairo: "These next few years will be the most important years in the history of this region, perhaps in the life of every person. A man is going to have to be very shrewd to know how to choose his outlook, his friends and alliances—and to be in the right place at the right time."

13

MOORAN KNEW NO REST OR PEACE IN THE FOUR years that followed the Wadi al-Faid campaign. There was unceasing commotion in all four directions; the Sultan and his men paid visits to every place and every tribe, and promises and money were dispensed lavishly. Hopes mounted, raised by expectations and gossip. Military leaders and tribal sheikhs flocked to the capital city of Mooran, where they whiled away the time waiting for money and guns. The Sultan appointed provincial emirs and sent them away with money and promises to recruit people. The Sultan's paternal uncles and his sons were constantly away traveling. Now and then the Sultan remembered to marry into one of the tribes, to win its loyalty and the strong arms of its men. In a word: there was nothing and no one in Mooran untouched by the contagion that galvanized them.

Khazael felt, after his imprisonment at Rafia Fortress, a certain guilt and a great deal of bitterness, especially with the rumors going around the Rawdh Palace, which reached his ears, so he was sent out to the desert on a mission to defend the dignity of the state. This was his uncle Dahaim's suggestion, and his father concurred, with the advice that he be compassionate, and Dahaim reiterated this point when he saw him off on the campaign of al-Samra.

"You know, my boy, and God is my witness, that you are a lion. Your determination can shatter rocks, but I want you to listen and remember: In these times we want to please people so that they'll be with us. We do not want them rising against us. And I must tell you: Know when to watch and when to act. Know when to offer a date and when to offer a bullet. The last resort of all is anger. God keep you— may you come back safe and sound." Uncle Dahaim laughed lightly and added, "The rest, my boy, leave to us."

Between one battle and another, or sometimes during the course of a battle, Khazael summoned his father, or his father summoned him, generally to have him marry into a certain tribe whose loyalty was required. The Sultan heard reports that Khazael was learning well, that the people liked him, and that good fortune followed him wherever he went, so he sometimes took his son's advice, and sometimes sent him a verse of poetry suggesting that he should put aside what he was doing—something better awaited him somewhere else! Khazael always obeyed his father. He knew that the messengers, and spies in his own camp, told the Sultan everything, and this suited him perfectly, since these secret reports would prove to his father that he was the perfect man for this job.

While the campaign for al-Samra was in progress, the Sultan sent emissaries and messages to the rulers of surrounding areas, reassuring them, negotiating with them, exploring the topic of borders, water and grazing land. He wrote to friends, asking for loans, weapons and for their preparedness to fight alongside him, and had Hamilton travel here and there to follow up the messages, to negotiate and conclude agreements.

Awayid al-Mishaan had begun to spend as much time in Mooran as he spent in al-Beqaa. When the Sultan got news of Awayid's anger at him, because he was taking orders from infidels and did not want Islam to spread and conquer, he sent Uncle Dahaim to visit Awayid and bring him back to Mooran.

All through that visit and during his stay in Mooran, Awayid was in a state of religious fervor which often drove him into frenzies, swearing on the Koran, then melting into submissiveness and tears when the Sultan promised him that the banner of Islam would fly everywhere. Khureybit told Awayid that the only thing delaying him—for nothing could actually stop him—was his lack of money and guns, and his wait for precisely the right moment.

The Sultan noticed that Awayid avoided Hamilton. He assigned him several aides, and sought the help of two of his close friends: Anan Bassiuni and Rafet Sheikh al-Sagha. He asked them to attend to Awayid and be his closest and most trusted advisers. Whatever he and Dahaim were unable to learn would be discovered by these two, each in his own way. Anan was bursting with the right spirit: he wanted to reshape the whole world, and hated infidels and materialists. He dripped with bitterness for his failure in past battles. To Mooran he came, to offer his services to the Sultan, to accomplish here what he had failed to do at home in Egypt; to start anew from the desert, whence the faith had come in the first place.

Rafet Sheikh al-Sagha thought himself a unique man; surely he would be great, and the road to greatness, as the bad company he had kept—as he described them—had led him to believe, lay in the follies he had committed in confronting Syria's French occupiers. For the degree in medicine he had brought back from France alone did not suffice to get him what he wanted, with the result that he joined the battle. Imprisonment and the savagery of the French occupiers were new to him; the troops were so different from the people he had known as a student there. He decided upon exile, and while when he opened the atlas to choose his place of banishment he could not make up his mind whether to go back to France or to emigrate to Mooran, he was not slow, after choosing Mooran, to become one of Khureybit's men. He had many talents: not only could he practice medicine, he was quick-witted, a brilliant orator and told jokes well, and was conversant with the ways of royal courts. He came from a powerful and well-connected family; one of his ancestors had been the sheikh of al-Sagha, hence his name and his overriding sense of noble origins.

The Sultan asked these two men to attach themselves to Awayid al-Mishaan with the idea, despite his uneasiness, that "we ought to take people for what they are"; as long as Ibn Mishaan disliked and distrusted Hamilton, there was no need for there to be any direct friendship between them. The important thing was to keep the loyalty of both men, and to keep them apart, for if they were to come together, Ibn Mishaan might be seduced and get ambitious: Hamilton might see a possible ally in Awayid and exploit the situation. So this was the best option. It was imperative to gather all their strength to fight the final battle. Mooran was becoming the largest country in the region, and the strongest state. Reaching this point had meant placating many different parties, and using every available resource to achieve victory, but let history be the judge! Ibn Mishaan's detractors said that he had long ago "gone ablution crazy" from excess religious fervor, but the Sultan said that that was Ibn Mishaan's own business, between him and God. What concerned the Sultan was victory over his enemies in this world, and for that he needed money, men and guns.

Awayid was a child of fifty. When he loved, it was without reservation, and when he hated, his hate possessed him. He was stubborn to the point of unreason, and as easy as ripe fruit. Once he was convinced of something, he never budged, and when he trusted someone, it was hard for him to deal with informers or enemies. His relationships with Dahaim, Khureybit and the Rawdh Palace were generally based on his conviction that these men craved martyrdom more than they craved dominion, and that they alone were capable of establishing justice in this land so filled with evildoing. He had fought alongside them at Rehaiba and Quweiya at Rawdhat al-Mashti and Wadi al-Faid, and finally at al-Huweiza, and was sure of them. Dahaim's eyes glistened with tears as he prayed over the dead men, and Khureybit's voice boomed out from among the soldiers: "The winds of Paradise are blowing! Where are ye who seek it?" He was convinced of their religious faith. But the infidel—he did not know why he had come here or what he wanted—worried him, for Hamilton had as yet given no sign to indicate what his beliefs were. Dahaim assured Awayid that Hamilton was on the verge of converting to Islam, and that "we have to help him." Awayid said to himself, with bitter irony, that "these days we round people up and herd them to religion with a stick, and they run away, and this one comes from the ends of the earth and wants to be a Muslim? We don't know who to believe, but when dawn comes, we know—we'll see."

Hamilton watched all of this free of any commitment. He wanted to blend history and geography with a unique aim. He had read, at university, about the history of the peoples of this region, and the traits and traces this history had left on people, things and ideas; he had had the opportunity, on many occasions, to read reports, especially on his recent trip to London, comparing the old reports with the latest ones, and the vast difference between the peoples' desires and delusions, and what had actually been accomplished on the ground; he knew this desert well, and had ventured to cross it from one end to the other, something no one before him had ever dared to do. He knew everyone who held power here, or aspired to it, and everyone who wanted to go from one shore to the other—that is to say, those who wanted to pass through life quickly to reach death—and only after learning all this did he get a clear picture of what he had to do.

The whole scene seemed to him, despite its somberness and solidity, very shaky, full of rough edges and peril, but he was certain that he was the only one who could do something about it and reap results that no one else could.

Around this time he became far less utopian, far more practical, and put aside the pastimes that had occupied him during his long sojourn in the desert: scouring the sky to investigate the positions of the stars and the phases of the moon, to await and place confident bets on sighting the crescent moon, relying on his calculations, and his eyes, which were as yet untouched by trachoma.

Now that was all in the past. He no longer saw the stars suspended over him like lamps; they did not inspire him. He remembered the moon only when he saw it. He had become a "son of each day," as the bedouin say.

Not only the moon and stars deserted his memory; the bedouin fancy that had allowed him to believe most of what he was told was also gone. In his first days in Mooran he had delighted in listening to their conversations, full of miracles and bizarre occurrences. They always cited the names of the people who had actually witnessed these marvels; it was clear that these were people who had nothing better to do than wait for such events to recur. To persuade himself, to wait with them, he said to himself that "science has not yet found a way of explaining every earthly phenomenon." When he found this thought unworthy of his intellect and education, he said to himself, with a certainty that knew no doubt, that "it is impossible to understand any people without first understanding their legends and their mental frame of reference: What are their beliefs? How do they think? What are their ideas, their convictions, their rituals?"

Although most of his questions remained mere questions, he continued to assimilate himself into their ambience, "as a prelude to getting there," as he said when he was unable to get anywhere.

He was no longer affected by the overpowering flood of marvels and miracles and lies that grew every day and occupied evenings in the East. He was much more eager to apply his mind to solid, practical affairs.

Even Khureybit's ideas, his alliances and antagonisms, the things he said and the things he strove for, meant little to Hamilton now. He would study them again and recast them in a form compatible with the basic plan that had to be implemented. England herself had spread out the maps and told him, "You may redraw them." That was his basic mission, imposed on him by the real world; his thinking, his culture, and his deepest consciousness would influence the remaking of this region. Otherwise he would become a prisoner of the "tales of the East," as he put it to himself, for he could find no other word than this one, used by the bedouin themselves to describe useless and meaningless talk. They would say, with a movement of the hand, "Rubbish!"

"Furthermore, Awayid al-Mishaan is not my enemy, nor need he ever be. His feelings mean nothing to me. Does he curse me? Treat me contemptuously? I mustn't attach any importance to that, must not allow it to influence my plan, or what I consider basic and essential to achieving my goal."

Hamilton said to himself, in regard to this tempting image: "In the East, they forget, or never knew, what is fundamental. They understand only this moment and the obvious surface. The tent is a metaphor for their mentality—it embodies their archetypal reaction. It is a function of time; it has no continuity, no permanence. It is concerned only with the wind that rages today. They don't think of the winds that blew yesterday or those that will come tomorrow. Their thoughts and feelings are apt to change with the weather."

As soon as Hamilton had convinced himself of this, he was assailed by other images: "What really amazes me is that these simple bedouin, in spite of the superstitions and delusions that fill their heads, generally never forget what is essential for them. Khureybit, for example, takes me by surprise whenever we travel; wherever we go, he has his stories, poetry and desert sayings. I leave him and he goes off to the mosque to spend most of the night praying, and they tell me that he leaves one mosque and goes to another! He's always asking questions. He asks me about things that concern him, and he asks casually but he is really very deliberate, and despite my resolve not to give any explicit answer, to give myself the time to arrive at a solution, he's not satisfied with posing questions, he looks straight into my eyes to find out whether I'm lying. Those looks bother me, they weaken me, and usually compel me to say what I really think about what I really want to do. How do they inherit that way of looking at people—how do they learn it? Even small children, who aren't yet used to innocent obscenity, look at you that way, and when you lie, their eyes tell you, with that predatory look, 'You're lying.'

"I must dispense with so many of the burdens and notions that hampered me before, and be practical in everything. That's the best way, perhaps the only way, to establish a modern monarchy!"

That was not all; Hamilton wanted to go all the way. Khureybit's enemies, whom he had seen crossing this huge harsh ocean of sand, would have to contend with him. He had gone to them to negotiate over borders and water and grazing land. Sometimes he bargained in Khureybit's name, and sometimes Khureybit bargained on behalf of others, but it was always to test their convictions and potential actions, with a view to taking final decisions.

Khureybit was still very cautious about Hamilton's trips, and brilliantly shammed indifference to them and to his inability to prevent them or to find out what really went on during them; he pretended to be satisfied with what Sahib reported to him. What he could not learn directly he found out from his spies and what went on after Hamilton left. In the bedouin way, he was never hasty or irritable. What Hamilton did not say today he might say tomorrow, or might be told by one of his fellow travelers. If there was no one to pass along the news, it would be exposed by the enemies' actions and gifts, for no matter how skillful they were at hiding the money they'd been given, or distributing it secretly among their followers, they could not hide the horses. When new horses suddenly appeared, tossing their heads and neighing, Khureybit told his uncle, "They're baying like jackals, Uncle. We have to get them before they get us."

Very slyly and quietly, aiming to create a new situation, the Sultan chose a group of trusted men, men full of malice, fire and frenzy. In the second half of the lunar month, he sent them on short but strenuous missions in which weapons and regular troops could not help them: out to the borders, the caravan routes and oases, to act on their own.

"Whatever you can carry away will be yours alone, and rightfully yours," Dahaim told the groups of men before they set out. "All we want you to do is to frighten fearless people so that they are never able to sleep again."

Khureybit was a master at raids of this sort and had long used them. He knew what they accomplished. When a number of such raids had been staged with noise and terror, he proceeded to "bring in the law of the stick, executing all thieves and villains," showing a pretended reluctance due to the difficulty of this task, or an inability to go ahead with it. After a great deal of pressure and insistence and a meeting with the local chief, however, agreements were made easily.

Hamilton said to himself: "The bedouin never do something for nothing, and usually don't make you pay what you refused to at first. They hoard their knowledge and skills until you are desperately in need of them, and only then do they lay down their conditions. You have no choice but to go along with their conditions, and be grateful at the same time!

"Khureybit has something to do with what's going on at the borders; I'm sure of that though I have no proof. And here we are resorting to him alone to help us."

That was not all. The religious visionaries and fanatics were resurfacing and making themselves heard. Hamilton was, most of the time, unable to negotiate even with moderates, or even to establish a common language for dialogue, but now his mental state deteriorated and he felt close to physical collapse when he was surrounded by those angry stares; his ears were invaded by the clamor of all the unexpected arrivals, enveloped in dust, who wanted to be present. He did not know whether they were the Sultan's enemies or his allies, for they spared no one and nothing their words of provocation and threat, and once again he appealed to the Sultan, who sent his uncle or one of his sons with his men to soothe those men whose wants were not known.

In the face of the vigilance so prevalent in Mooran, especially in some of the sensitive border regions, the Sultan had never been more serene. He felt flooded by mildness and friendliness, and evidenced a certain humility no one had ever seen before. In his majlises and conversations he tended to stay off the subjects that interested most people, Hamilton among them, and even disappeared at times, to go hunting or to organize horse races or poetry contests.

In order for the cycle to be complete, the Sultan took care, in this period, to make use of Fanar as a messenger and mediator along with Hamilton. Fanar did whatever he was told with great thoroughness and skill, which deeply impressed the Sultan and Uncle Dahaim. It was at just this time, after Fanar took up his mission, that the Sultan realized, all of a sudden, it seemed, that he had not found a wife for Fanar.

The twenty years of Fanar's life had passed without attracting anyone's attention, not even that of the women of the Rawdh Palace, who had speculated solely on possible wives since his birth, shrilly suggesting that it should be so-and-so or such-a-one, never agreeing on who was the most suitable bride. Ummi Zahwa received him when he came from Ain Fadda to settle in Mooran, and asked several of her women how old he was, counted on her fingers and closed her eyes. When she opened them again, she looked at him closely to make sure. The plain fact is that she had forgotten. She did not remember again until during the Sultan's wedding or Khazael's, or the uncles'. She remembered his face, but she forgot the years, and that was that.

Tahany was even surer than the Sheikha that Fanar was still too young. When the Sultan married Farha, the Sheikha asked her to name off to her all of the Sultan's wives, and the names of his children and their ages. Tahany started in enthusiastically and named all the wives but three or four, whose omission the Sheikha did not notice. She began to name the children, but when she had come to the twelfth, she lost her patience, saying, "That's all I can do, my lady— I'm tempting Satan's evil eye!"

Tahany recalled the recent death of two of the children in the Rawdh Palace and did not want to remind the Sheikha, which is why she wanted her to stop.

"Don't believe what people say," said the Sheikha in a dignified but obstinate tone. "Life is given by God, and so is death."

Like Tahany and the Sheikha, Mudi thought Fanar too young to consider marrying. All her life her body had been a burden to her, so that she was a constant patient of the English lady doctor in Mooran.

Fanar had asked her to come with him when he made his first visit to Britain, to be examined by doctors there.

Lulua confided to several of the palace ladies that her mistress had a sister, and that this sister would be Fanar's bride, but that wedding plans had been delayed due to Fanar's youth.

Aunt Muzna talked of marriage more than anyone else, though she confined herself to the principle of it rather than names or details. "The important thing is for him to get married—it doesn't make any difference to whom," because she knew that her daughter Sheikha was the only one of marriageable age, and the girl likeliest to be selected as Fanar's wife. Omair's three daughters were still too small.

"My friends," said Omair testily when the subject came up, "just forget it. Fanar is too young! There's plenty of time!"

Muzna reminded him how old they had been when they were married.

"My dear, things were different in our day!" he answered her impatiently. When she turned sad and silent, he added, "Anyway, the important thing is that he should make the decision."

Everyone had his say, but Fanar did not know. The only time Aunt Muzna reminded him that he would have to get married, he looked at her in a way that frightened her and said, as if threatening to have nothing more to do with her, "I don't want to hear about this again!"

The Sultan, who had no difficulty making decisions for himself and others, was bewildered. Fanar was still a boy. All his years did not help him to determine how old he was. If he was well one summer, he would be ill that winter. His body was delicate, as slender as a stalk of sugar cane. There was sorrow in his eyes, and Omair was watching as a wolf does, ready to pounce when the shepherd dozes for even a second. Ummi Zahwa was eager for him to marry anyone, as if it were her own wedding she was looking forward to, but when the Sultan asked her who was the best match for Fanar, she answered cautiously.

"A girl, Abu Mansour, is unhappy if she gets a boy instead of a man. He might not want it, or he's cold, or he might fail—I don't think you want any of your sons to be unable to sleep with a woman!"

After much more thinking and wondering, with even Fadda and Uncle Dahaim joining in the search, Fanar agreed to marry.

"If it has to be," he told Dahaim, "I want my uncle Sanad's daughter."

Sanad lived in al-Mreija, where he grew palm trees that he loved more than anything else in the world. He had left Ain Fadda long ago, "because the people there think of the hereafter more than they think of this world." He said this angrily when he saw Ain Fadda's palm trees falling down and dying year after year as the result of neglect. Most of the people, in particular his father, spoke often of the trees in Paradise but never of the trees on their land, and people listened to him and nodded.

"I'm leaving," Sanad told his father, three brothers and a knot of people, after packing his bags and preparing his departure. "I am going to say something, so listen: I want nothing from this town. I have already got all my rights and all the inheritance I want." He looked at them sadly for a long time. "You'll be sorry." Then he spoke angrily. "If there was any good in Ain Fadda, or any living people, it's thanks to the palm trees, nothing else. If you abandon a palm tree, it dies. All you do is talk about Paradise and Hellfire, and in a few years there won't be one of you left—you'll have died or moved somewhere else."

Sheikh Awad listened abstractedly; he was hardly there. When the argument heated up, he got up crossly and spoke as if defending himself.

"I marvel at anyone whose afterlife will be in this world!"

Omair saw Sanad's action as some sort of fit, perhaps brought on by quarrels with women, and he spoke up sternly, almost angrily.

"Since the day God created the earth, Ain Fadda has been here in its place and just as it is now. If a man wants to plant, no one prevents him or opposes him, and if a man wants to worship his Lord, then his Lord will provide for him."

"You should know," replied Sanad testily, "that God is everywhere, not only in Ain Fadda." He laughed ironically. "Ain Fadda is just like any other place. It is not Mecca. It is not Jerusalem. And it is not Medina."

Sheikh Awad, now some distance away, shouted back angrily.

"Many came before you, Sanad, and are now gone—and Ain Fadda is none the poorer!"

The break between al-Mreija and Ain Fadda was not healed, nor between Sheikh Awad's sons, though his daughters stayed in touch with one another; and by virtue of this conduit, always open, Sarah often visited her brother in al-Mreija, always accompanied by Fanar. This was how Fanar met Zaina, who never left his mind. And this was why, when he was beleaguered by Uncle Dahaim, he said, "My uncle Sanad's daughter."

Uncle Dahaim was surprised, taken aback, and he looked around before asking, "Your uncle Sanad has a daughter? He has children?"

"I want Zaina."

"Zaina?"

"Yes, Zaina."

At that time the Sultan wanted to celebrate something, to express his power, to create a mood in Mooran, and this gave him his chance.

Everyone who saw the Sultan's festivities to mark this son's wedding became certain that the Sultan would name Fanar his successor. Those who missed the wedding, but heard about it, were also sure, and went so far as to say that the festivities were meant to celebrate the succession more than the wedding. What helped to persuade them was that Khazael did not attend; it was said that Fanar had personally gone to Khazael's encampment in al-Safra to invite him, and insisted on his coming, but to no avail.

The Sultan had never looked younger or stronger. Sahib was one of the prominent guests, and it was said that he gave the groom a silver-mounted rifle, with the humble disclaimer that it came not from him but from the king of England.

Lulua said that the Sheikha, Ummi Zahwa, had given the happy couple a huge amount of gold, and word got around that Uncle Dahaim was seen to dance for the first time. Watfa, who had been hoping for Fanar to marry her sister, insisted—according to Lulua—that her sister had married three months before Fanar.

The Sultan gave Fanar a seven-year-old thoroughbred horse, which Mahyoub said no one but His Majesty had ridden.

Mudi was ill from the time of the engagement up to the wedding, but the palace midwife caring for the princess showed up a few minutes before the actual wedding ceremony with a diamond necklace for the bride, from Mudi.

It was days before Mooran talked of anything but the shots that were fired, the perfumes lavished on the hands of men and women alike, the sweets and coins that were showered upon the children and the poor, and the sheep that were slaughtered for the feast.

14

L ATE THAT WINTER, AND IN THE EARLY SPRING, preparations in Mooran reached a climax. The Sultan gathered his family elders, the tribal leaders, religious sheikhs, merchants, social notables and some of his advisers in an atmosphere steeped in zealous enthusiasm, and told them all that the crimes and misdeeds of the sultan of Awali and the tribes loyal to him had reached a point where they could no longer be tolerated or ignored. If this were not corrected as soon as possible, then Mooran—its citizens and resources, its settled people and bedouin, old and young—would be exposed to grave dangers and terrible calamities. Khureybit told them that he had, himself, been patient and borne much from Ibn Madi, the sultan of Awali, in the hope that he would mend his ways, and because he only wanted peace and security for Mooran and its neighbors. He promised them that he would do absolutely everything within his power to keep Muslim blood from being shed, but Ibn Madi's insolence, his contempt for religion, his hostility toward the rights of Muslims and Islam, and his laxity in allowing the holy places to be mocked and violated, had now forced him to declare to the world, and to the elite of Mooran, that his patience was at an end.

The Sultan had acted as a rein in past years, holding back his men from advancing, finding dozens of excuses to do so. But this time he did not need their encouragement or this inflammable atmosphere. The tribal sheikhs, the clergy, the advisers and the military competed with each other in their eager affirmation that the situation had, indeed, gone as far as it could go; there was no question of ignoring it. Some went so far as to say angrily that they could not understand or forgive the Sultan's previous silence, or his barring them from punishing these enemies, thus depriving them of the chance to achieve martyrdom. Mooran had had more than it could take; its enemies had presumed too far. Had the Sultan not gathered them now to announce his decision, they would have made the same decision without him, and taken action to serve God and His Prophet!

The sheikhs gave their official sanction, the merchants gave their support, the advisers determined how the war would be presented at home and abroad, the military announced their readiness with immense pleasure and pride, and the town notables gave their blessing. They renewed their allegiance to the Sultan, praised his wisdom, and left it to him to act as he saw fit. All of them in the spacious, splendid tent—servants, guards, coffee servers, camel drivers, storytellers and eunuchs, the boys brought along by their fathers, the beggars at the edges of the pavilion, and the five blind men leading one another around, who attended every public celebration and funeral, and took part in deciding matters of peace and war—all were excited and deeply moved, and wanted to join the army, to be the first to wreak vengeance on the sultan of Awali.

Awayid al-Mishaan had refused to come to Mooran for eight months, and was angrier and more full of curses than ever before. He said openly, even to the very messengers of the Sultan, that he did not trust anyone anymore; he would act according to God's commandments, no matter what the Sultan said. Awayid did not come to Mooran this time until the Sultan's uncle Dahaim visited him and said that "everything is over—this is your day, Abu Mahjam," and when he was satisfied, he set off; but when he saw the throng, and heard the speeches, and felt the excitement that spread from body to body and from soul to soul, he chided himself for his misgivings and his lack of confidence in others. He wanted to attack the Sultan, to accuse him of weakness and collusion, but he watched and listened and kept quiet. The Sultan tried to rouse his fervor—he looked at Awayid several times as he spoke. He pointed to him when he alluded to his having prevented his men from attacking the borders with Awali. When every eye turned to look at him, Awayid spoke without raising his head.

"What we want is to raise the banner of Islam or martyrdom—as long as the Sultan is fighting for that, we're his!"

Ibn Mayyah spoke even more frankly.

"Khureybit, I have something to say, even though it may anger you: we were talking among ourselves, saying, 'Khureybit has traded in his courage for cowardice,' and before he came, we hoped for his coming. Now we find ourselves saying, 'Why didn't he stay where he was, far away from us?' If there is any provable indication that he is in the right, he will show it to us so that we may follow him. We are his own servants; and if you had no intention but to covet our death, well, no one dies before his time. As God is our witness, we have no wish but to die as martyrs, any death is better than the death we're dying now, and any job involving harm to Islam and Muslims is more than a job with the sultan of Awali and his children."

There were others who wanted to speak, for emotions were running high and the air was very tense, but Dahaim, who was seated beside the Sultan, now rose and tapped the ground with his stick.

"My friends . . ." He gazed sadly at their faces for a long time and finally went on. "So, not all that is known has been said."

He turned to the Sultan and looked at him, shaking his head, then turned back to the throng.

"This man, as God is my witness, has borne much. He has borne more than a mountain could bear, between the fire of his own heart and the fire of others." He pounded his stick twice on the ground in slow succession. "He has borne much from you, and from others. All he wants is to raise the banner of God and His Prophet. All he wants is your well-being. Now only one thing is required: that we all be of one heart, and one hand, that we march behind him. This is the hour, and this the day to prove our manhood. Either we will triumph, or fall as martyrs, and after that there is nothing more to say."

Silence and profound emotion had gripped the crowd.

"There's no time, my friends," said Ibn Mayyah. "Starting now is better than waiting until tomorrow or the next day."

"No one has any excuse not to," said Awayid al-Mishaan. "Let's put our trust in God and set out."

The Sultan's gaze moved from one face to the next. "God bless you all—may He make many more like you! I tell you, I see Paradise in the face of every one of you." He nodded repeatedly. "With the strength of your arms and your hearts and by the will of God, we will be victorious."

There was a moment of silence before one of the blind men spoke. "Khureybit, war starts easily, and in the end brings only sorrow. People of Mooran, if your enemy does not know, you must warn him—for the blood of Muslims will accuse him, in this world and the next!"

Heads turned toward the source of this voice, and an apprehensive silence fell. The Sultan spoke to his men in a voice audible to those nearby. "The seer, Hamad al-Shayeh, again?" He smiled ruefully and added, "Shayeh's sons never shut up—when all else fails, they try to smear everything with their shit!"

He turned around to see his guards and servants, to rebuke them with a look for having failed him, then said, "It's not your fault—it's the fault of whoever let him in here!"

The meeting was adjourned after the Sultan said, firmly, even sharply, "You will be our guests for supper this evening—we have much to discuss, for there is no time to be lost!"

None of this talk or these details meant a thing to Hamilton. He had agreed with the Sultan, after considerable delay and procrastination and fuss, that things could no longer go on as they were, that the time for action had come. Ibn Madi, the sultan of Awali, was not only annoying but now wholly intolerable. All their past efforts to make him behave like a reasonable ruler, as others did, had been to no avail.

There were a vast number of complicated issues and problems; as hard as Khureybit pushed for permission to attack Awali, and to seize it, or a part of it, Hamilton strained to understand the logic of it, and stalled and waited for the right moment, for Ibn Madi was no ordinary antagonist, or a ruler like the others; he was a real enemy, and while he castigated Hamilton, and any other English who visited him or met with him elsewhere, for their protection of Khureybit, or their cooperation with him, he was unable to persuade them to abandon him, or to act neutrally. He was always trying; he never missed an opportunity. He swore to them that, with the power and resources he commanded, he was the only man capable of giving them the results they wanted. But, like mules, they did not understand and so did nothing except according to their own wish and whims.

One night Khureybit's uncle told him, when they were talking about why the English had refused permission for them to advance on Awali, "Nephew, the English are like a woman . . ." He shook his head and smiled. The Sultan smiled politely but did not understand. "The sort of woman, Abu Mansour, for whom you must be hers alone, or else she'll belong to everyone."

He shook his head and went on in a different tone.

"With the English, nephew, either you are with them, with them and no one else, or they'll set the dogs on you—they'll crowd your door with a thousand and one enemies. The English, Abu Mansour— and we've known them for a long time—must have everything, or they know no peace and leave no one else in peace. This friend of yours, Sahib, was a torment to us. Every day found him in a different town with a different tribe, every day he came up with a different story—you hardly knew what was going on."

The Sultan shared his uncle's concern, and knew better than he that it was no longer a matter of wishes, or a few hundred voters, to decide what had to be done. The great powers had to be taken into consideration—some kind of understanding had to be reached, because they made the decisions. Not only his advisers said this, nor was the wish his own; it was a fact. For the English were on his northern and eastern borders, and now even his western border. They were the givers, and they were perfectly able to stop giving, or to change kings and countries.

Hamilton and other Englishmen who had come to Mooran spoke plainly. True, one hardly agreed with everything they said, but he could not argue with them or be hard on them. They were outspoken in saying what they wanted. At first this trait greatly annoyed the Sultan, and even roused his cruelty, but before long he began to admire it. He wanted to know exactly what they wanted so that he could decide whether or not he could help them. There were many others who did not understand this trait and hated it, and were driven to fits of rage from hearing things that they did not like.

Uncle Dahaim was of a different generation, and had been nurtured by different values, but now he saw the results, which led him to be like this with the Sultan.

Years before, he had considered Khureybit a hotheaded youth with only a strong body and courage too close to recklessness, but after putting him to the test in different circumstances, he changed his mind.

"Our people were always poor, Abu Mansour," he told him one night. "They said whatever was in their hearts. That's the reason we are the way we are now." He looked at Khureybit almost in awe. "What happened to us, nephew, is that we have lost our will. We aren't bedouin, but we're not settled. No one is afraid of our weapons or our raids, no one covets what little money we have, or takes any account of us."

The Sultan asked Fanar for his opinion, what he thought of Hamilton. No one knew how the boy had grown up so fast.

"The world, Father, is not only Mooran and its neighbors. The world is immense," Fanar answered. "This world is ruled by force. You know that the English, the Turks, the Russians, and the Germans, every one of these ruled the world and did as they pleased. Turkey used to be the most powerful country, but its time came and went. Then the Germans, the industrialists: makers of tires, cars, railroads, and everything else—people in love with science and power. The Russians, the same thing. Now the English. They have the fleets and the guns, they make the cars and aircraft, and they have so many countries that the sun never sets on them. We have to reach some kind of understanding with them—they are the most powerful nation, the most gifted."

Feeling weary and a little shamed for talking while his father listened, he went on in a new tone of voice.

"I have read some, and seen, Your Majesty. Britain is the greatest, the most powerful and important country in the world, and no one can oppose her or stand against her. You know that she has a fleet of hundreds of ships, thousands of ships—you have to see it to believe it."

The Sultan nodded quietly, his mind wandering. He was pondering many things, knowing that he should not take lightly the power, wealth and might that his son had seen with his own eyes. It was true that Fanar talked as all youths talk, and that Uncle Dahaim thought this of no importance—Dahaim thought that a few hundred swords and a like number of rifles could make all the difference, but the Sultan had to think for himself, take everything into consideration and make the right decision, especially in these circumstances.

When Khureybit had met recently with Hamilton, whom he had not seen in three whole months, he looked him directly in the eye and asked his question.

"You have to tell me, Sahib, your people over there, now that they know everything—do they want us, or someone else?"

Hamilton smiled sadly.

"Britain, Your Majesty, has placed all its weight and its confidence behind Your Majesty. You may be sure of that."

"Our patience is gone. We must act."

"That's why I'm here, to agree on that and make a decision, Your Majesty!"

They had several sessions, mostly between the two of them, and with immense care, patience and precision, they examined their maps, estimated what the campaign would require, selected the commanders and the routes they would use and agreed to attack Awali and seize it from Ibn Madi. One result of this was the meeting the Sultan had sought, and a wave of messengers was sent to a number of neighboring countries and friends, carrying letters describing, in great detail, the crimes and injuries Ibn Madi had committed, which Khureybit could no longer tolerate. When agreement was concluded on all of this, Dahaim spoke to the Sultan.

"Praise God—everything has come out well!"

"Now, Uncle," replied the Sultan with a smile, "we must tie up the old fox with a lion's rope, and be very careful, because if Ibn Madi sees that calamities are coming, that they're looming over his head, he'll try something desperate!" He shook his head and spoke, as if to himself. "This is our chance, Uncle. If we defeat Ibn Madi, we've won everything. If something different happens, the English will abandon us and find someone else. They're not like us or our camels, always patient and waiting."

In mid-spring, the battle for Awali began.

15

ONE OF THE MANY THINGS THEY HAD AGREED upon was that Hamilton would go to Ibn Madi, on the pretext of mediating or negotiating, with the Sultan's armies advancing slowly, so that Awali would be encircled by slow degrees, ultimately forcing Ibn Madi's surrender. In order for their plan to yield these results, they would have to strike ruthless blows in strategic places at the right times. These blows would be even more painful when struck by hardened, almost crazed men, who would order people from one place to another and from one life to another. "And the Sultan promises to protect the villages that surrender peacefully, and to lavish gifts upon them."

Khureybit knew his men and knew his enemies and had no need for plans and proposals, or for anyone to advise him. He had waited long years for this battle, and planned for it, and the skirmishes between Mooran and Awali of past years had taught him much. Travelers and his spies had told him a great deal about Ibn Madi's difficult situation: how he had become irksome to himself and everyone around him, particularly his English friends. His people were suffering, and complaining bitterly of the taxes and bribes they had to pay. It was said that he no longer got along with the people closest to him, not even his own sons.

At the suggestion that Hamilton should be there, with Ibn Madi himself, all Khureybit's bedouin caution was aroused, and it showed so clearly that Hamilton spoke to reassure him.

"It is better, Your Majesty, that I be with Ibn Madi. It will help me to understand how he thinks, what he wants, and how we should handle the situation. So that I can take whatever action is appropriate."

"That is the truth, Sahib," nodded the Sultan.

"And I may be able to discover his military plans, and get word to you of what you should do to defeat him."

"That is what we want—God protect you!"

"Surely the outcome will be as we wish it, Your Majesty."

"God willing. In your sight and in your presence we find all the blessings we want."

The Sultan was unable to forbid Hamilton from being there, and yet could not show his true feelings or make any dissenting remark; he could only wait and see how things turned out. He listened and said to himself, "As Fanar said, they only respect the strong, and keep their secrets to themselves. Let's make the best of it with them and see the good and the bad they have to offer. This is our country and our people, and we know best."

The plan to advance slowly and start a siege did nothing to reassure or encourage the Sultan—it troubled him. "The bedouin are impatient folk, and know how to raid. To put them under the command of others and tell them to wait, when they barely tolerate us when they're on their own land, among their own families and tribes—they won't understand, and they won't put up with it. And not only that: on top of tribulation, uncertainty? To say to them, 'Leave the cool while the weather is good, and sit and wait, and look at the sea and the mountain'? No, by God, that won't work with our men."

The Sultan consented that Hamilton be there with Ibn Madi because he could not oppose the idea, so planning the battle and plotting its course fell to him and the actual combatants. They would decide

what would happen on the battlefield, with no need of prior announcement or consultations with Hamilton.

Three days before the forces of Awayid and Ibn Mayyah moved,
the Sultan spoke to his uncle Dahaim.

"You know, Uncle, we only got the men's consent by getting their
hearts pounding and their breath short. Now we have to prepare
them, and that is no game." He took a long, sorrowing breath and
went on in a deep voice. "Awayid and Ibn Mayyah think it will be an
Arab footrace and maybe last a day or two—they do, Uncle. Ibn Madi
is not the emir of Quweiya and he is not the emir of Rehaiba, and he
is nothing like the emir of al-Huweiza. He has friends everywhere,
and to him a mistake is a blasphemy. If we don't eliminate him, he
may eliminate us, and go around tirelessly shouting, 'Look, ye faithful, on Khureybit and his cohorts.' The English have gone along with
this on one condition: that we take Awali with no one the wiser. If we
do it with a huge noise, God only knows how we'll pay for that."

Uncle Dahaim did not completely understand. He did not know
what he should do, or what was expected of him. Four days before,
and after the meeting everyone had attended, and the Sultan's dinner,
two meetings were held, both attended by Ibn Mishaan and Ibn
Mayyah as well as the Sultan's cousins and sons. In these meetings
they agreed upon the whole plan, and a Koran was brought so that all
might swear not to end the war and not to cease fighting until Awali
had been reconquered by Islam and Ibn Madi and his offspring had
been dispatched to Hell.

"After two or three days," his uncle said humbly, "the men will
march, nephew, and everything will be told then."

"Yes, Uncle, but I want you to spur them on, to tell them what
goes and what doesn't; and I want you to explain to them that this will
be a long job. It might last a month or two."

Very patiently, the Sultan explained to his uncle that the armies
would advance, but the decisive battle might not come for some time,
or might come unexpectedly, or be prone to other changes because
conditions in Mooran and the region in general were very delicate;
this battle would be unlike any other they had fought. He did not
want the English to let him down or to hold him to positions or commitments he would find it hard to defend.

That was not all. The Sultan asked his uncle to explain to Ibn

Mayyah and Awayid that the battle with Ibn Madi would be different from all previous battles, so they were not to take up any position without consulting him.

Dahaim, who understood this in his own way, realizing that the matter was more serious than he had previously thought, promised to spend the next three days with Awayid and Ibn Mayyah and to tell them everything. After a moment of thought he suggested that he take part in the campaign, "so that we can continue to pray over them, and so that we may always be in the right." The Sultan agreed enthusiastically to the promise and then the suggestion, and said that he would soon include him in the campaign, with plenty of soldiers.

No one seemed to think that Fadda would accompany the Sultan this time, unlike earlier times, in spite of the commotion behind the walls of the palace's main suite that grew more unsettled every day. The women, in the palace and the added-on wings, traded myriad conflicting stories as to which women would go along with the Sultan, but when a credible rumor stated that the Sheikha would accompany the Sultan, everyone was sure that neither Alanoud nor Fadda, nor any lesser-regarded wife, would go. There was a rumor—no one knew who started it—that the Sultan would marry anew before the campaign, to put an end to the contention among his women, and to please Ibn Mayyah. Watfa heard some of the rumors and reports but stayed ready to go, convinced that she alone would accompany the Sultan. She had sent her son, Mufarrih, to Ramaka, for she did not want to leave him alone. She sent him to stay with her mother, loaded down with gifts and advice, and entrusted the three girls to Lulua, who had previously told people that she would be going along with her mistress. Then, abruptly, because of the palace feuds and rivalries, she decided not to go, only to prove that the Sultan preferred no woman to Watfa!

That was not all; Tahany told everyone who asked her that the Sheikha had made some momentous decisions at the last minute, after brooding over it for three straight days. Tahany added, smiling, that Fanar would stay behind in Mooran, because Zaina was in her third month and seemed worried; this was the first sign of her pregnancy. Fanar was by her side, and after talking it over with the Sultan, they agreed that he would stay there. Tahany said that she had heard this from Zaina's maid. The maid had not said so explicitly, not in these exact words, but from what she'd heard she thought that this is what would happen.

Khazael was a frequent visitor at the Rawdh Palace at this time, and was lavish with the money and gifts he gave to most of those he visited to say goodbye. Everyone he spoke to, or who heard reports of what he said, gathered that he would be in the front lines of the attack, with the advance units. He sadly told his loved ones that the advance units of any battle, especially one such as the assault on Awali, were exposed to the greatest danger, though he added a little boastfully that "the most important commanders, the most courageous soldiers and best cavalry are usually in the front lines."

Mudi was, as usual, in poor health and ready to believe anything. When one of her servants told her that she'd heard the palace women saying that Fanar would stay behind, she was delighted and told everyone the news. When another woman declared that Fanar was not inferior to Khazael and should go with the vanguard of the army, she ran to her room and burst into sobs. When Fanar was asked about it, he smiled and nodded and said nothing, though when he was prodded for an answer, it was muttered and cryptic and could not be clearly understood.

The younger princes, even those who had begun in recent years or months to come near the Sultan's councils, began to prepare for the war. The Monday council, which the Sultan had not stopped, and which had not stopped him, was full, these days, of questions, messages and signals, all having to do with the war; the Sultan, who was extremely busy with visitors, delegations and messages he had to dispatch, was proud that he had managed to form regiments without the council's knowing or even suspecting a thing. These regiments were now loudly and insistently demanding to be deployed with the vanguards who would be sent in first.

Mooran had never experienced a mood of such optimism, but it was not unaccompanied by some worry and doubt and a certain measure of caution.

Talleh al-Oreifan was very dubious indeed, and worried about the Sultan's venture.

"For a few years now we've been peaceful," he told Nahi, "but the Sultan's blood has been restless. All we can do is run and fetch. Now if His Majesty is going to be gone a long time, God help us; if the women get lonely, life will get more interesting—we won't know who to flatter first."

"We know them, and we've learned, Abu Jazi. Don't worry!"

"He doesn't bet on them, my good man; they're an army, not just one or two!"

"So you say?"

"Not only that, each one of them is a squad. Every one of them has four or five servants, and they all give orders."

"His Majesty should have recruited them—if they'd ride into battle on camelback, he would surely win. An army of women would win the war the first day, because they lack arrogance!"

"This war is bigger and more dangerous, friend, and it may have been forced on us by the others. As long as the Sultan is alive, everything will be fine, but if he goes . . ." He laughed ironically and added in a whisper, "They're still young—they're still in their father's tent, but someday when they grow up—God help us."

"Don't worry, and don't be sad, Abu Jazi. As we say: A horse without reins is like a man without teeth."

The two men could come to no definitive conclusion.

Everything else in Mooran crackled like flames with change. The merchants who had done the most business now stopped selling in anticipation of higher prices; they foresaw a cutoff of supplies. Now that the campaign was under way, the Awali Road would be closed, and prices would soar. Horse and camel dealers were expecting a good year, and said that the years to come would be even better, but harbored some uneasiness and fear, because all the animals they'd bought would surely end up going with the campaign, and they would not be able to buy again. They would have to wait for new births or the arrival of new animals from elsewhere. Shopkeepers and those waiting for harvest had sold all they had to the campaign, and had no guarantee that new stock would come, or that they would be able to secure it in the future.

As in previous raids, but to a far greater extent, Mooran was obsessed with the salaries soldiers collected and the new arms and uniforms, though the women were occupied only with sorrow and solitude. The old men followed the news immersed in silent meditation, more confused than ever before: "The English do nothing for God. Ibn Madi was their man, someone who never told them 'No,' but they left him and told Khureybit, 'Get rid of this man and do whatever you like, and God knows that our friend Khureybit is either going to turn Christian, like them, or turn around and find no one following him. We have to keep our eyes and ears open—these days we are seeing things we never saw before.'"

Hamad al-Shayeh, or Hamad the Seer, as he was called in Mooran, received dozens of blows and pinches, while still in the Sultan's tent, from the guards, soldiers and the sheikhs's servants. Men who lagged behind the Sultan's procession said that they saw him, his clothes torn and bloody, his headcloth lost or stolen. It was said that his blind friends had been the first to turn on him and beat him; in fact, one bystander said that no sooner had the Sultan stood up, marking the end of the meeting, than the blind men attacked their friend. They screeched at him but he did not respond, and when they found him, they raised their fists along with their voices: "Take this, you bastard! Are you with Ibn Madi? Why don't you say something? Don't we know you're with Ibn Madi?" The shouts were lost in the general clamor, however. It was said that he was alone in the clearing near the grand tent, trying to find his headcloth and mend his clothes, when three of the Sultan's guards came along and dragged him off no one knew where.

Mooran never slept or knew any peace while the preparations were in progress. The Sultan was sighted more than once going to Wadi Riha, and his brothers and cousins were seen, joy and anticipation glowing on their faces. Gunfire was heard now and then, at odd hours of the day and night, and some of the more knowledgeable men said that the shots were being fired in farewell to units leaving for the front. It was said that the volleys of rifle fire they heard on Monday night from the direction of Wadi Riha had been to see off Prince Khazael, who was leaving with the advance units. Some of the youths said that the Sultan had been the first to shoot: he took up Khazael's rifle and loaded it himself, raised it to his shoulder and fired. Others said that the firing they heard very late that night, Monday, from the direction of Wadi Riha, signaled the execution of eight of Ibn Madi's men who had been seized the day before. Reports varied: some said that the men had been caught paying out money sent by Ibn Madi, some said that they had come to spy on the army's movements and to get an idea of its size and weaponry. Others said that they were poor merchants who had come to buy animals, and to support this version were their wallets, with such pitifully little money in them that the soldiers sneered at them, especially because some of the money was old and out of circulation. There was a report that Hamad al-Shayeh, who had not reappeared, and of whom nothing had been heard, was among those executed.

As the last week of March was drawing to a close, the town drumbeater came out to announce news to the people. He pounded the drum vigorously and shouted, "I am here, O God! You have no partner! Here I am!"

He rested a little, then resumed in a different voice: "Let those who are present convey this to the absent, people of Mooran! The Sultan says that today is your day, men. This is the day for men to march and grow rich, and never to regret—let those present tell those absent, people of Mooran!"

He pounded the drum loudly, then waited for the sound to die away, and Mubdar, who was marching beside him, began to recite:

> "Riders of fiery steeds,
> Don't let your hearts falter;
> The stronghold will fall in two days
> And your reward will be ample."

They were followed by formations of soldiers marching to Awali, one group led by Awayid al-Mishaan and the other by Ibn Mayyah. Khazael was in a third group that followed three days later. The Sultan's group, which included Fanar, departed three weeks late and was often delayed en route, for the Sultan took the longer, northern route and stopped frequently in villages and small settlements to accept pledges of support and allegiance from the residents and from people who had traveled from farther afield when they heard news of the Sultan's troops approaching.

The Awali War was hard to record or describe, because its three battles were extremely complex and confusing, the interests at stake were murky and convoluted, and reports of the war were highly contradictory. There were the discrepancies and conflicts of narrators, the shifting positions of the fighting forces, and the paucity of surviving eyewitnesses—no need to wonder why there were so few! History had become a huge assemblage of lies and fabrications, much as history is merely the history of the victors, from their own perspective, with a tendency to be kind to themselves, rich in chicanery and irony, recounting one episode in many very different ways—not always ascribable to evil intent or neglect, but to the injuries of time and disputed sources, the accumulation of small lies and the illusions that, in the end, created the single illusion of absolute truth, or the one truthful telling of an illusory history!

So Khureybit not only tarried in Mooran, he took the northern road to reach Awali, including many stops along the way to take pledges of loyalty, look in on his subjects' conditions and complete his preparations. A camel-mounted courier Dahaim sent to the Sultan three weeks before the Battle of al-Samha, carrying detailed information of Ibn Mayyah's intentions, reached Khureybit as he was at the waters of Ain Dama, with instructions to bring back a reply immediately. The Sultan, however, made the courier stay, and sent Dahaim no messenger of his own. This very secondary point was recorded in eleven different versions by one researcher, who was killed in mysterious circumstances one year after he wrote his history, but before it was published. None of his work could be reduplicated, because his papers disappeared, which by itself gave rise to much speculation. It was said that, during the investigation, the police gathered up the papers along with the murder weapons and the clothing stained with blood and fingerprints, though when they were asked for the papers, the police said that they had no interest in the papers, books or ideas of the murderer or the victim, because such matters were outside of their competence and meant nothing to them. They said that the books and papers had been sold, along with other objects, since they knew of no next of kin and no one had come forward to claim them. It was whispered that, two weeks before the murder, the researcher gave his manuscript to one of his friends to read and critique. When questioned, this friend said that he had returned the manuscript three days later because he could not read the writing. A third man, who knew both of them, said that the friend had given the manuscript, after just one day, to one of the Sultan's advisers. When it had been examined, a demand was made for immediate, decisive action, since those times called for the closing of ranks and firm determination, not the provocation of anxiety and disturbing the peace. The manuscript itself never turned up again, and no one knew whether it had been kept or destroyed.

As to how it became known that the researcher had compiled eleven versions of the courier's mission to Ain Dama: a relative of Ibn Mishaan, who knew the courier, and met him after the war, was one of those interviewed by the researcher, and told him everything he knew. The researcher smiled and said, "That's the eleventh version I've heard!"

Though the story seemed garbled, and perhaps suspect, the other versions were no less so. Mahyoub, chief of the Sultan's guards, said that the courier's message, which was verbal, made the Sultan so suspicious that he detained the messenger without officially telling him that he was under guard—he assigned three of his men to watch him and keep him from leaving the encampment. Anan Bassiuni, who had accompanied the Sultan on this campaign, claimed that only negligence was to blame for the Sultan's failure to respond to the message, since he had, at that time, many things on his mind, though he did not allude to what these may have been. Sheikh al-Sagha said he recalled hearing something about a message and a messenger from Dahaim, but nothing more. The Sultan blamed the forgetfulness of his scribe, Irfan al-Hijris; he had ordered him, from the very beginning, to remind him of important business or anything that bore remembering, "because a man's mind is not a ledger," but Ibn Hijris failed to remind the Sultan in Ain Dama. Irfan told some of his trusted relatives, including a lady cousin who spread the story, that the Sultan had forgotten on purpose; that Irfan had reminded him three times for three days running; that the Sultan had smiled and nodded, which Irfan interpreted as meaning that the matter was of no importance.

The most reliable and current version, at least at first, was Dahaim's. After the vanguards arrived at al-Safa, where they were to camp until Prince Khazael's men turned up or they received marching orders from the Sultan, Ibn Mayyah began to make hurried preparations for the march to al-Samha. Furthermore, he refused to listen to any other point of view, and with his close friends he threatened to destroy al-Samha utterly, and it was this desire of his that led to the deterioration of his relations with Dahaim, and moved Dahaim to stay in al-Safa. Ibn Mayyah did not hesitate, while discussing the resumption of the march and the plan they should follow, when Dahaim said:

"Forget it, my friend; the Sultan himself told me, his lips to my very ear: 'Not every day gives us the chance to get Ibn Madi—since we have the chance now, don't leave one stone upon another, and don't let anyone stand in your way, and don't listen to what anyone says!' "

As to what should have been done, and why it hadn't been, and who was responsible, the confusion of facts prevented any decisive settling of these points.

But before verdicts were given and the outcome weighed, there had to be an answer to the most basic question: what had happened?

Even this question, which should not have caused any great dissension, gave rise to the wildest discrepancies.

One of the Sultan's biographers, writing seven years after the Awali campaign, wrote: "The narrow-minded fanatic Ibn Mayyah, driven by vanity and ambition, did not submit to the Sultan's orders; he pounced blindly, as wild animals do, using the element of surprise to assault al-Samha. The outnumbered soldiers guarding it were taken unaware, and after a battle of only a few hours the defenders were routed, and those few remaining offered their surrender; but Ibn Mayyah ordered his soldiers to give chase to the fleeing enemy and kill them all, with no exceptions. The soldiers obeyed this order, and carried out the ghastly work, but when news reached His Majesty the Sultan, he flew into a rage and then became deeply sorrowful, and there were many witnesses to the copious tears that streamed into his beard. He dispatched his son Fanar urgently to put an end to Ibn Mayyah's massacres and atrocities."

One of Mooran's "historians" wrote of the Battle of al-Samha: "Then the soldiers of Mooran, whose presence was unsuspected, attacked, and the two sides fought their battle for several hours, with the resulting defeat of Ibn Mayyah's army, a number of whom had taken up positions in the nearby hills and began to rain bullets upon the marching fighters. This went on futilely for three days, after which the forces of Mooran poured into the city. Meanwhile, some of the native population opened fire on the army of Mooran, leading to a frightful massacre which stopped only with Ibn Mayyah's personal intervention. When the Sultan learned of the incident, he issued strict orders that innocent civilians should not be molested, and ordered that compensation be paid to all those who had lost a loved one, or whose property had been damaged, and formed a committee expressly to see to this noble cause."

A more recent researcher who came to Mooran with a number of motives, one of which was the writing of history, wrote of the battle that "the soldiers of Mooran entered al-Samha like a raging torrent, praying, singing and firing their rifles in the air, then began to fire them in the marketplaces as they moved about the city, killing a number of innocent people . . .

"There were a number of bedouin in the city, to say nothing of those who had entered with the army; these groups joined up by the dark of night, and it was a time of terror and panic. They banged on doors or broke them down and violated homes, subdued the residents and looted the houses, and committed murder in the course of their plunder."

Hamilton wrote about the Battle of al-Samha years later, working from his journals: "The Moorani army encountered little resistance, and when the army of Awali fled, thousands of townsfolk and chosen others fled with them. The soldiers of Mooran expelled the lagging soldiers and refugees, killed all of the deserters among them, and skirmished with the forces of Awali. Ibn Madi's soldiers fled in disarray across the wide, canyon-wracked mountains. Ibn Mayyah and the rest of his army slaughtered many of Awali's people and subjected the survivors to a rule of terror, killing all unbelievers, violating every house and every person."

Hamilton added that "this sufficed to spread alarm and panic."

Much later a neutral historian recounting the battle wrote that "the soldiers of Mooran captured the munitions dump in al-Samha and held it for three days while most residents fled; those staying behind were butchered by Ibn Mayyah's soldiers."

The researcher who came to Mooran and Awali to study and record the history and geography of the region wrote about the three days following the entry into the city: "When Ibn Mayyah entered, he ordered that all arms be confiscated and houses searched, so all residents were ordered out of their homes. The men and women were driven out and confined in a public park for three days, then released, and whoever wished to leave the city was permitted to do so."

The Battle of al-Samha was not, then, one of the numerous battles whose outcome would decide the fate of the war, or of Ibn Madi. It was both the beginning and the end.

Anyone who had doubted Khureybit's strength, or the possibility of raiding Awali, saw with their own eyes how his soldiers rushed

along with no one able to withstand them; even the scattered resistance they encountered was aimed only at slowing or distracting them,
to give Ibn Madi time to formulate a strategy. Anyone who had
thought the English would not allow Khureybit to advance now saw
their mistake, for it was the English who had asked Khureybit to raid
Awali, and what proved this even more firmly were the money and
weaponry that appeared, and the advisers who arrived every now and
then to train the men to use the new guns—none of this could have
happened without the consent and encouragement of the English. No
genius was required to perceive the reversal that had taken place, or
the change in people's sympathies and politics that took place with it.

After the Battle of al-Samha and what followed it, most people
agreed that "the best and safest way to watch goats butting horns is
from a distance."

Ibn Mayyah, who plunged headlong that way, as if to end the war
in its first days, wanted to be the sole victor. The Sultan also wanted
the war to end as soon as possible, but he too wanted to be sole victor,
and that was why he forgot to reply to his uncle's message and let the
war drag on for long months, to give him time to plan the postwar
scenario.

Foreign consuls reported to their capitals that Khureybit was advancing, that he alone was consolidating power at a time when all
others, especially Ibn Madi, were losing strength and retreating. The
foreign capitals wrote to their consuls to concentrate on two things:
establishing relationships, albeit cautious ones, with Sultan Khureybit, and winning his friendship, and doing their utmost to safeguard
the lives of their nationals and all foreign residents of Mooran. The
consuls shuddered at the bloodcurdling massacres and atrocities being
committed, but showed a lively interest in them, reporting the events
in great detail, with casualty statistics. They were warned by their
governments that these were an internal matter in which they could
not interfere; however, they were asked to monitor and relate back the
most accurate possible information, which might be of benefit in the
future.

Although the diplomatic reports were profoundly solicitous and
loaded with detail, the Dutch consul did not refrain from listing the
names of a number of the massacred families and the worth of plun-
dered goods. The consul based his account on an eyewitness report,

though he did not supply his witness's name. His government answered him that "this is how warfare goes on in the East. We urge you
to make strenuous inquiries and to be extremely careful in your deal-
ings with informers."

The name of Awayid al-Mishaan, used by mothers to terrorize their
children with the threat of that beast, now fell into disuse as the name
Ibn Mayyah replaced it on every tongue. Women extravagantly retold
the stories of what had befallen at al-Samha, which angered the men.
For that subject cast a pall over their love lives, or at least this is what
the men sensed in the women's conversations, though they masked
their anger in a sort of tentative courage, or a mixture of respect and
aversion.

Ibn Madi did not want to believe what had happened; his rage
mounted with every passing day, as did his curses and his fevered re-
deployment of his forces, his new attention to every small development, even what appeared in the *al-Zaman* newspaper; he spent hours
reading the articles and "rebuilding his zeal," as he put it, though he
sometimes used different words, or added other expressions or verses
of poetry. With increased intervention and his loss of confidence in
others, and his sense of their flagging enthusiasm, his mistakes multiplied and losses mounted, as did also his feelings of frustration and
disappointment.

Why was this? How had the change been so rapid and complete?
How had even fathers, relatives and the closest of friends, even among
adults, become enemies? Why had they changed? Why did they speak
when they should have been silent, and offer ideas and suggestions
reeking of cowardice, though they looked courageous? Even the bravest, who wanted to die, lacked sound enough reasons to give their
deaths motive or meaning.

While Ibn Madi found himself in this whirlpool of defeat and disappointment, of blunders and misunderstandings and even disguises,
what pained him most was that no one understood him, not even his
wife; he loved her and listened to her, but now found her siding with
others more often than with him. When his sons and advisers had
disagreements with him, they resorted to the emira, as he called his
wife, though some of them went so far as to call her queen; they used
primitive ploys and transparent ruses, stories circulated by servants
and cupbearers to fill her head, reasoning that when her head got full,

it would be emptied, and she had no one but her husband and children to pass the stories on to. Ibn Madi was a man in torment. He shouted and picked fights, and categorically refused to receive any of the mad-men dispatched to see him—he did not even know how they had come or who sent them. When he was able to see them, to use what power and shrewdness remained to him, to address them in such a way as to pass on a message, though perhaps not a pleasing one, he found her at the rear of the palace, or late at night, waiting to tell him stories, to tell him everything she knew, and to make demands. How had people persuaded her to do it for them? How had she believed them? At this point he rose up shouting, but ultimately saw that she was his only refuge and sanctuary.

Some of his servants said that he did nothing but bob his head one way and then the other. His head, according to Mufarrih, the one ser-vant who was never separated from him, was like a clock pendulum, never pausing or stopping. When he wanted a break, he changed the direction of movement, from nodding to shaking it side to side.

There were messages from his sons, field officers and provincial governors, even from tribal sheikhs, but he must have known who sent them before he opened them, for he often returned them or tore them up unread. He knew why they had sent them, what they wanted to tell him. He was afraid of his own power, as he was afraid of their weakness, and was careful to stay in this isolated region. If others did not obey him, if they did not understand, after all that had happened, and could no longer stand loyally by him, then he did not want to hear their words of fear and weakness; those he had known in other times, under other conditions, he did not want to see now, even via mes-sages, now that they had weakened and retreated. Not only that—they had acquired such prudence, such wisdom! He often wondered how in the world the weak, the craven and the defeated attained such wisdom—it was a weapon they unsheathed as if shitting on them-selves. He spread his legs apart and scratched himself and said, "Cow-ardly friends cause more defeats than enemies do."

Khureybit, on the other side, played the game with skill and au-thority. He struck and struck hard, always unexpectedly, and never let his adversary rest for a day. He constantly advanced, and not only forward—sometimes backward, to clear some positions, sometimes merely as a ploy, to confuse Ibn Madi more. This sort of playful illogic could be, in wartime, logical—a reasonable way to exhaust an enemy, especially if he were elderly and thought he knew everything. He always took the action least expected of him, using methods and resources no one suspected he possessed. He could recruit those closest to his enemy. He beckoned to them, he persuaded them with messages, gifts and promises conveyed by people he trusted or at least knew. It was not essential that the promises be sincere, it was only essential that his enemy's front collapse, that he attack from every angle, and only then, after reaching the positions he needed, he bargained from the point he had reached, not the point he had started from. The most devastating war that could be waged against old men was a war of nerves; for their nerve was all they possessed, having lost their strength and wealth. One needed only to aim blows at their sensitive points, their heads and testicles, and when the blows were hard, they worked. This sort of blow was unexpected, and highly destructive.

There was no day of respite in the long months of war, nor any two days that were alike; nor were any of the places alike.

Ibn Mayyah was speaking to Awayid one night, some months after the fall of al-Samha.

"Abu Mahjam, our story is dragging out—this Khureybit has the Almighty on one arm and Satan on the other!"

"A man never changes, my friend," smiled Awayid sadly. "As we used to say, you can splint a dog's tail for forty days, but it will still come out crooked."

"But we have no patience left. Our families, our homes, our children . . . if he doesn't march, we can march ourselves. If we don't move, we're lost!"

"Old men have long calendars, Abu Jazi, endless ones, and whether we wait for them or they wait for us, it's no easier to tell what they're thinking or what they want."

"Look," said Ibn Mayyah testily, "we thought we'd be spending a few days here. Do you remember that day at al-Samha, how we agreed that if we spent the summer here we'd march on to the farthest part of Awali? But you can see with your own eyes that the summer is over, and now comes winter and spring—God alone knows how many more springs. If we bring it up with him, he'll say, 'Patience is a virtue, and this Ibn Madi is something else again, but he's getting old, and if he makes it through the summer, he won't make it through the winter. Everything in its time.' "

Uncle Dahaim had for some time been so angry at the Sultan's failure to respond to his messages that he was like a different person. He met with the Sultan some two months after the Battle of al-Samha.

"Friend," said the Sultan, "this is war, and in war anything goes. We need both Ibn Mayyah and Awayid. You know them—between one prayer and the next they have to say a third prayer, and between one genuflection and the next they have to kneel a third time! You'd think they were giving advice to Almighty God, or reckoning their debt to him as being greater than mountains. As we said in Mooran, we have to take people for what they are. We left al-Samha to Ibn Mayyah; that's a debt, and we have to repay it, if not today then someday. Al-Samha—I swear it before God—exhausted every man's patience. Everyone is rubbing his head and saying, 'God help us.' Khureybit and his men arrived, and as we say, 'The repute of riches, not of poverty, prevails.' "

"May God will what's best," said Dahaim softly, then added in a slightly different tone, "All we want, Abu Mansour, is God's goodwill and our parents'."

When Uncle Dahaim wondered aloud (he did not actually ask) how and when the next battles would come, the Sultan replied that time was needed; they had to wait for the delivery of cannonballs and for damaged cannons to be repaired. He said that he had sent a request for ammunition and engineers to come and repair the weapons.

Fadda was not only keeping up with the Sultan, she never felt better, having given birth to a fourth son during this campaign. Although the Sultan had married again during one of his stops on the road, she had exulted after the Battle of al-Samha and insisted vehemently that the Sultan name the newborn Mansour. He hesitated, saddened by the memory, so that Fadda had to look away; finally, with the help of two of her lady relatives, she chose the name Fawaz, which, like Mansour, meant "victorious," and so it was.

Hamilton, who had spent long months at the court of Ibn Madi, clearly eager for Khureybit to achieve results that would satisfy both sides and end the fighting, fell silent and left when the mediation began. Now that Ibn Madi had left and been replaced by his son Muizz, Hamilton went to see Khureybit.

"They are ready to agree to any terms," he told the Sultan. "Redrawing the borders, including where they've lost territory, the establishment of friendly, neighborly relations, an end to the conflicts over water, and withdrawal of their demands."

Hamilton smiled and spoke as if to himself.

"All their demands are invalid. Ibn Madi and his family will have to leave for good, and leave to the nation all decisions regarding what will be best for the future of Awali."

The Sultan understood perfectly.

Only a few months later the Sultan made a futile appeal to Ibn Mayyah and Awayid. "If you want Fanar to take part in the battle, that will be fine with me; everything is in readiness, and the battle can begin anytime, so that we may be rid of the Madi clan, and raise the banner of Islam." He was quiet a moment, then looked at the two men contentedly and went on. "If we were to speak, to say a word, we might say too much, and find no way out of it, but a man must be prepared. War these days is different than before: we need cannons and ammunition, even airplanes, as you saw a few months back, when they shot at us from the sky."

He filled his chest with a deep breath, and spoke in a sharp, proud voice.

"Now, with God's blessing, everything is prepared, and if we do not march tomorrow, we'll march the day after. To whomever wishes to go with us, welcome, a hundred times welcome—and whoever doesn't is free to do as he likes."

The two had no other choice than to exaggerate their readiness; they would need very little time to prepare.

"So His Majesty's troops are enough, and more," said Uncle Dahaim, "only Abu Mansour forgets no one, and said, 'You're part of us,' and we'll never forget them, and he wants you to be with us."

The Sultan spoke somewhat angrily. "What I said was true, friend, only have mercy on your parents, don't press or embarrass anyone—God does not burden any soul with more than it can bear."

"We are ready, Your Majesty," said Awayid, "and, God willing, we'll acquit ourselves honorably."

"No one can prevent one of the faithful from waging jihad to serve God," said Ibn Mayyah.

This was how the Battle of Traifa, the last of the battles for Awali, was launched.

16

WHILE PREPARATIONS WERE UNDER WAY FOR THE Battle of Traifa, which would, it was assumed, be the last of the battles for Awali, as its course would determine the outcome of the war, disturbances broke out in the border region near al-Huweiza. Conflicting reports of the trouble led the Sultan to dispatch his son Khazael at the head of a fighting force to quell the disturbance and punish the insurgents, and he sent Ibn Mayyah and Uncle Dahaim along with him.

He counseled them all, in emphatic and angry language, mingled with unease, to be as tough as possible: "These things cannot be tolerated, and there is no need for niceties, especially at this time."

The Sultan was sure that the disturbances had come about at Ibn Madi's instigation, and that they were intended more to distract him and scatter his army than to pose an actual danger to the Sultan, but he purposely deputized Ibn Mayyah to accompany the troops heading there, because he wanted to be unencumbered for the main battle here, and did not want anyone to join him in reaping the fruits of victory.

"You will be the sultan in al-Huweiza," Khureybit told Khazael by way of parting advice. "You will give orders and make decisions, and all must obey you; you are above even my uncle Dahaim." He was silent for a few moments, thinking, then spoke coldly. "If Ibn Mayyah tries to take over, if he says 'Don't do this, do that,' break his neck. No one is indispensable to us—except the camels."

The Sultan spoke differently to his uncle Dahaim. "You know, Uncle, you have to keep the group in line. Ibn Mayyah always has to have his say, so just let him go on bothering people until he gets tired of it, or they get tired of it. God willing, within a month or two we'll all meet again in Mooran." He changed his tone. "Khazael has to learn how to govern. No matter how a man lives his life, it ends in death, and while now we're here, standing over him, saying 'Don't do this, do that,' tomorrow or someday he'll have to think for himself, and he'll need experience and discipline for that." Then he spoke warmly. "You'll be there, standing over him, so guide him. I told him to do nothing without your guidance and your knowledge. I believe things will go smoothly there. He was with us in al-Huweiza; he knows the land and the people, and they know and love him."

With Ibn Mayyah, he was yet another person. "When it comes to hardship, we have none but you, Abu Jazi, and I have chosen you only because of my trust in you and my reliance—after God—on you." He took a deep breath. "I'm worried, Abu Jazi, that the people there won't do a thing unless they're told that the Sultan and the whole army are in Awali. If you have something in mind to do, this is your day, and they can do nothing to resist you, and they're busy with Ibn Madi . . ." Again he adopted a different tone. "God keep you—what I want you to do is prove to them that we have a long arm, that our faith is in God, that nothing can prevent us from raising the banner of Islam. They must accept this and know their limits. Their sheikhs, their leaders who told them to rebel—I don't want you to spare one of them." He reverted to his first tone. "Khazael is your own son—guide and advise him."

The Sultan laughed and shook his head. "Sons, Abu Jazi, are hot-headed, and in a hurry, and you have to take them for what they are!"

Hamilton had asked the Sultan to send Khazael and Ibn Mayyah to al-Huweiza, but was more apprehensive than he, or at least this is what he led him to believe.

"Sometimes, Your Majesty, circumstances change at the very last minute, and this is borne out in the history of wars; how many tricks have deceived even the greatest commanders, and changed the course of wars and nations. In the case of Carthage, for example . . ."

He was about to embark upon a historical discourse, but the Sultan smiled and gave him a certain look. Hamilton swallowed and continued. "History teaches man important lessons, and makes him more aware and better able to do what he has to do." When he saw that the Sultan's mind was completely elsewhere, he added, in a new voice, "I know that these days things are different from the way they were ages ago, but I still think that the business in al-Huweiza will be dangerous, especially now, and it has to be settled decisively, and fast."

"God bless you," smiled the Sultan. "You all know history so much better than we bedouin do, but we bedouin—please do not take this amiss—but we know our own land and people best."

"Of course, Your Majesty."

"We know all about those al-Huweiza people. They said to themselves, 'Since the Sultan is so far away, we'll strike at his shadow, and if we don't get meat, we may get gravy.'" The Sultan's features changed dramatically, showing sternness. "But, with the will of Almighty God, and His help, we will break them, and their knives will be pointed back at their own hearts. We must break them and teach them a lesson, so that others will learn the lesson as well."

So began the second al-Huweiza campaign, along with final preparations for the Battle of Traifa. The Sultan appeared confident, but did not concern himself with the forces dispatched there. He concentrated on what he had to do here.

"If we succeed and survive here, the rest will be easy," the Sultan told Fanar in front of Hamilton because he wanted Hamilton to hear. "The head of the serpent is here, and we will crush it—then, you'll see, no one will raise his head again!"

The histories of the Battle of Traifa were all similar, almost as if they had been written by the same person. The battle came as a sort of crowning at the end of a long period of fighting, obstinacy and haggling, and in a certain sense ended even before it had begun. Some said that it ended the day of al-Samha; still others, better informed, said it had ended years before that. What had accumulated for a very long time, what the English had tried to create through any number of persons, was finally accomplished by Khureybit alone. While it may have represented an exception to their usual methods in the region, it justified them. Some friends had grown tiresome and fanatical on the subject of keeping old promises and standing against all other plans, since there were plenty of others ready and waiting to take on their own or other roles, but the only important thing was the result, and that is just what happened.

There were many details which may have differed from one account to the other, but no more crucially than in a description of a wedding or a horse race: the bridegroom, or horse, put the right foot before the left in entering or galloping; he seemed confident or solemn or nervous; he sweated, or not. All these details were secondary; the important thing is that the bridegroom wed and the horse won.

Khureybit entered Traifa the day after the flight of Muizz, the last of Awali's Madi princes; he had achieved victory. Fanar was by his side. They went and prayed in the town's great mosque, and gave a banquet for prominent citizens of the town. The first evening was spent reassuring the townspeople and diplomats. Khureybit said that he would leave it to the people of Awali to make whatever decisions they saw fit for themselves; he would be ready to obey and enforce whatever the Muslims agreed upon.

Khureybit could not believe his eyes. He stood among his soldiers and, in spite of his sternness and the gleam in his eye, glowed with delight as he returned the salutes of those who lined the way on both sides. He was in an almost narcotic state of rapture. He had never expected or even dreamed of this day, but it was a unique, living reality. He had been prepared for something much less than this, and had bargained untiringly with Ibn Madi, only to acknowledge him, and to agree only to his remaining in Mooran, and in spite of the gifts, money and humility, Ibn Madi never relented, refusing to send a single word of regard or congratulations.

Now Khureybit had entered the last city in Awali; one year before, Ibn Madi himself had been compelled to sail away into exile, and his son Muizz—who came as a solution to an unsolvable problem—had sailed away yesterday. He would never see Awali again. Khureybit's joy was almost too much for him. Tears rolled from his eyes as he looked with gratitude at the men around him, and his voice was husky: "Almighty God gives dominion to whom He wills, and honors whom He wills, and humbles whom He wills!"

Fanar and Hamilton reached the palace before the Sultan to see to the guards, security and accommodation he would need, but for themselves they had no wish to sleep at all this night. They were in an excited daze, almost a frenzy, which only grew when they stood on the balcony of al-Hazei Palace, watching the celebrations in the great plaza.

"Tonight is the conjunction of history, idealism and faith; only a madman would sleep tonight, because nothing like it will occur again in this lifetime."

"Mr. Hamilton, this is what we call here a 'Night of Power'!" replied Fanar, who was no less excited than Hamilton.

Late that night the Sultan returned to al-Hazei Palace after taking part in the dancing and shooting. He greeted everyone he saw and reminded Irfan al-Hijris to keep notes of everything, especially the names of the people who greeted him, so that he could send them gifts. He had him mark down Suweilem al-Theeb, the drummer, three times, for the poetry he recited, his stinging jokes about Ibn Madi, and his drumbeats, which did not cease all night long.

When the Sultan entered the palace, he found Fanar and Hamilton sitting up late, waiting for him. They chatted briefly, a few flattering and rapturous phrases, then in a moment of excitement, he asked everyone to come out onto the balcony, where they fired their guns repeatedly, and with every shot echoed back, "We will stay in your hearts until God removes us."

Khureybit's son Rakan came to him three times to tell him that his mother wanted him, that he must talk to her, but he did not turn to listen. He did see him, however, and embraced him, but did not hear what he said. When the boy insisted for the last time, because of Fadda's importuning, the exultant Sultan was listening, for the tenth time, to his servant Zain, whose name had been Ma'touq—"Emancipated"—until the Sultan renamed him, tell of how Muizz had left on a ship the night before, refusing to leave Traifa until they fired him a twenty-one-gun salute. When the Sultan heard this, he smiled broadly and asked, "Twenty-one what?" Matouq answered him: "Shots." "Shits?" said the Sultan. "Shots." "By God, he deserves them—not just twenty-one shits, but more." When Rakan begged him, during a lull, the men around the Sultan heard him say merrily, "That's enough, my boy, it isn't her turn tonight—it's another lady's."

Surviving witnesses of the Sultan's first night in Traifa said that he never slept or left al-Hazei Palace, or even its balconies. He moved from one balcony to another, and when he heard the call to dawn prayers in a moment of silence that had fallen, he spoke, in deep tones from his chest.

"I testify that there is no god but God, and that Muhammad is the prophet of God." He had suddenly changed, and said, as if giving an order, "Pray! Pray, ye servants of God!"

He and his men headed out. Hamilton, who stayed behind with a number of servants, said to himself: "How excellent, how convenient, that these sultans think themselves so great and powerful, that they enjoy this confidence, that they fear no man. They are courageous when they speak, and some day they will imagine that they actually fashion history; but history, fortunately, in our time, is made elsewhere, and in spite of its errors, and many do not err who read it, so it must be read only in certain places, especially the place where it was made. It is public property, and any strong man may claim it, just as any dreamer may also claim it, making use of the weakness or ignorance of others."

Although Hamilton kept his journal full, he counted it of little importance, especially at that time. He wanted to help shape the history of this region at a crucial time, or at least to help the makers of its history accomplish their mission, so he put off writing for the time being and gave his time to other things.

17

WITH THE FALL OF TRAIFA, THE PROBLEMS OF war gave way to the problems of peace. While it is true that there remained some pockets of resistance here and there, placing demands on the Sultan's time and resources, he was confident; and one night as he and Hamilton were talking of the future, he described these problems as resembling the shreds of meat that stayed in one's teeth, and added laughingly that "we bedouin have more than one toothpick—we have ten, and if the first doesn't work, we try the second, and so on until the mouth is like new!"

Awayid al-Mishaan was sent north on a campaign, and Fanar south on yet another. The point of both excursions was to root out what remained of support for Ibn Madi and give notice to all and sundry that a new nation had arisen, a nation whose power enabled it to subdue even the remotest areas and the strongest people. The Sultan particularly advised the leaders of the two campaigns to be firm and even, if necessary, harsh. He spoke to his son Fanar on the last night before the campaign set out.

"You're not like the others, my boy, you're educated, you understand things. You've traveled and seen the world. But I must tell you about our people: if you are gentle with them, they'll push you, and if you are tough with them, they'll be afraid and fall back. Wrath frightens fearless people. I don't want you to give anyone his way, because if you let these bedouin have their way, they'll get ambitious—they'll never be satisfied. Listen to the old before you listen to the young; listen to the sheikhs and to no one else. Never say 'No' and don't say 'Yes.' Keep your secrets to yourself; let no one know you or even guess at what's on your mind. Before you accept any community, let your friends infiltrate them and check them out, because the way is not secure. When you arrive there, let the earth tremble under your feet, and let there be no big man other than yourself, and never be ashamed or afraid, my boy."

He would have liked to say more, to talk longer, to sum up his experience for Fanar, who was leading his first military campaign, but felt confident that Fanar had grasped most of the lesson. He had tested him before, had long talks with him, and questioned, without Fanar's knowledge, the men who had accompanied him, learning that "Fanar is a real man, and intelligent—no need to worry about him." Even so, the Sultan chose his best men to go with him, the strongest and most courageous, and suggested to them that Fanar might be in need of their experience and their knowledge of the territory and people. He was sure, he said, that they would not disappoint him; and then concluded his talk with the most loyal men he was sending along on the campaign: "You know that life is the great teacher, and that man learns best from his own guile, but still the old teach the young, and he who knows teaches him who does not know. I don't need to tell you how highly I regard you all, how dear you are to me. God willing, upon your safe return, He will enable me to repay you!"

With Awayid al-Mishaan, the Sultan was bright and cocksure. "Abu Mahjam, a man recommends what he doesn't know, what he hasn't tried, and the north is all yours, its good things, its dwellings, and I don't think any man would destroy his wealth with his own hands!"

Ibn Mishaan looked at the Sultan questioningly.

"Awali is ours, Abu Mahjam, not Ibn Madi's or anyone else's. Its people are in our custody—they are not against us. Be forgiving on earth so that you will be forgiven in Heaven. We have no pity or mercy in our heart for the rebel, who bears arms or wants to fight the government. We will strike him, to discipline him and others. Others, the poor, who have no problem with us, are welcome—we can use them, and all we want from you, my friend, is for you to obey God and His prophet, and to come back to His Majesty safe and sound."

The Sultan paused a moment before adding pleasantly, "I tell myself this, Awayid, before I tell anyone else—don't think I don't! Now, we would like to ask you . . ."

Awayid al-Mishaan gazed at the Sultan warily before replying brusquely, "Yes, Your Majesty."

". . . to ask you, Abu Mahjam, before you go: Do you have anything to tell us? Do you want anything? What requests of yours have we neglected? What requests from you, your family, your people, or your men?"

"We want only your good health, Your Majesty; you are our main concern."

"Upon your return safe and sound, God keep you, the Awali campaign will be the stuff of tales and sayings told by the old to the young, passed on to grandchildren, and they'll tell of how Awayid al-Mishaan, Abu Mahjam, did this and did that. This is what man seeks in this world—nothing else is worth a thing!"

So Awayid al-Mishaan went out pleased, but regretting that he had, at one time, been mistaken about the Sultan—that he'd had doubts about him.

The thrill of victory turned the Sultan's head, filling him with faith and pride; his control over Awali's vast distances and prosperous cities, its people, so much more sophisticated and civilized than Mooran's, kept his mind working, too. In this age, when kingdoms were created and eliminated, when new maps of the region were being drawn, he knew that he was the only horse who could roam and vault, especially now that Ibn Madi was gone—the only one who could hold and justify others' faith in him.

Hamilton had spent years in Mooran and Awali, leaving only on short trips and then coming back again. One month after the end of the Awali War, he approached the Sultan seeking leave to travel.

"In other parts of the world, Your Majesty, vacations, yearly rests, even for military men, are considered essential, even sacred, just as work itself is essential and sacred; there they never put off or postpone their vacations, so I am entitled to ask Your Majesty for a vacation— after all these years."

The Sultan did not disagree. He wanted to know: how far could he get in the next few months?

He spoke to prolong their talk, in a friendly and familiar tone: "That's the truth, Sahib. As we say here: If you never go home, you'll never have children. You must go home and come back to us with your children and good news of more!"

"It's been years, Your Majesty, since I've seen my son, except in pictures," said Hamilton pleasantly. "If I don't go and show myself now, and tell him, 'Michael, I'm your father,' he'll forget me, and never recognize me in the future."

"No, no, we can't allow that." He smiled. "If God had willed you to become a Muslim, we would have married you off and made you stay here, but it's not in our hands. Almighty God has said, 'Thou givest as you like, but God gives whom He wills, and He is the most knowing of givers.'"

When silence fell after this friendly exchange, Hamilton spoke again. "I have been hoping, Your Majesty, that Fanar might come along with me on this trip, because he has many friends in Britain who miss him. And his visit would be useful, after all these years since he's been there."

"Blessings await us in future events, my auspicious friend," said the Sultan, whose merry mood had not left him. "Your word is enough for me, and you must promise to give my warm regards to all, especially His Majesty the King of the English, and tell him that he has good friends here who never stop asking about his health and happiness, and wish him all the very best."

Hamilton thanked the Sultan and assured him that the English followed events here with the greatest care, and that he would return soon, and with good news.

18

ONCE THE TROOPS SET OFF AND THE TUMULT OF celebrations died down, and with the onset of winter, Awali began to impress the Sultan and his men as an incomprehensible place. The people who had so hated Ibn Madi, and clamored with complaints against him, and made no secret of their bitterness, did not want that state of affairs to last, and voiced their happiness, mingled with wariness, when the war began to wind down. But now they were showing signs of exasperation and even unrest at the behavior of the Sultan's soldiers and officers. The soldiers, who had been afraid at first, watching the faces around them mistrustfully, soon felt confident and at ease, thus allowing them to respond to any problem and disagreement with force, and they were never slow to unsheathe their weapons, or to strike anyone who did not obey their wishes or orders. Disagreements in buying and selling, pleasantries and ambiguities of speech, and the frequent hawking of goods in song or chant, and other small customs of the

Awali people, in major cities and the smallest villages, forming traits and habits that children picked up from their elders, which got passed on from generation to generation—these were the things that roused and threatened the Sultan's men. Often in the town markets or in distant areas, there were incidents provoked by one side or the other. At first the incidents were brief, few and far between, and no one talked about them, but when there was an element of the obstinacy and uncompromising attitude the Sultan's men were known for in their demand that everything change—buying and selling, public behavior, even the way people looked at one another—the people showed an even stronger obstinacy and refusal to compromise. While such things were spontaneous and isolated and represented merely a reaction, they slowly became more common.

They became even more common after the posting of endless official directives informing the people of their religious obligations, such as praying publicly in the mosques at all the appointed prayer times, or facing punishment. Smoking was forbidden, and whoever was caught smoking was publicly flogged. Singing and games were to be forgotten, because the age of Ibn Madi was over and done with, and a new nation of faith had been founded.

Most people dismissed the stories they heard as rumors put about by Ibn Madi's men. Those who heard the stories from reliable friends said that it was only a whim, a fit of caprice such as often occurred at the beginning of new ages or with the arrival of newcomers, and soon died away. Some, who knew Khureybit's men best, said that "they think Mooran is the whole world—they certainly know nothing about Awali or anyplace else. They're bound to make mistakes, and then they'll regret it."

When the Sultan met with the merchants and social notables, and they alluded vaguely to some of what was going on, he smiled and replied in a manner they could not quite interpret, whose drift they could not quite agree upon. They noticed, however, that his features darkened and he seemed bothered, so they dropped the subject, leaving it for some other time, to some more congenial circumstance.

When they suggested what the proper relationship was between ruler and ruled in Awali, and quoted the Sultan's own words back to him, he assured them that he would honor every word he had given and every promise he had made. He asked for their cooperation and understanding, that it was all a matter of time. When they urgently asked him, in almost pleading tones, to set free some of Ibn Madi's employees, and the defending soldiers who had surrendered, he shouted for Ibn Hijris, who was always standing somewhere nearby, a notebook and pen in hand.

"Listen, Irfan, this is Monday. I want you to talk to the men and tell them 'the Sultan orders you, by Thursday at the very latest, to free every innocent man, everyone who didn't bear arms against us, who didn't steal or plunder—all must be released.' Are you listening, Ibn Hijris?"

He watched for the effect his words had on the faces and in the eyes of his visitors, and when he saw how delighted they were, he went on.

"On Thursday, I swear it myself, and the negligent can blame no one but themselves. Listen, Irfan, and tell the men this comes from me personally." He turned to the merchants and notables and said in a paternal voice, "I hope they'll be able to say Friday prayers with us, all together."

And they talked of other things.

For days on end the Sultan immersed himself in a routine of endless cares and problems. Ibn Madi, who had sailed away after losing the military contest, started other wars. The first was a war of provocation, using what forces he had, and public opinion, to exploit the atrocities in Awali: the killings, expulsions, destruction of whole neighborhoods and villages, robbery of homes and individuals. The refugees and fugitives put to good use the bedouin massacres in their reports of what was happening. What Khureybit's men did with regard to religion was talked about near and far, and stung the people. Sultan Khureybit seemed unafraid, or more precisely seemed sure of the military battle and its outcome, until he discovered that that battle had solved only a very few of his problems, and had, in fact, created problems of a new sort. He felt reassured that the echoes of most of the goings-on outside the country would not reach Awali or Mooran for a long time to come, after the worst was over and it was all in the past. There were so few means of contact from abroad, where the scandals and atrocities were published, and Awali had a single newspaper that was published twice a week; only the editor in chief of this paper was replaced, Ibn Madi having served in that capacity himself for a certain time. After he left, Ghaleb al-Dabbagh, one of Prince Muizz's men, took over, but when the prince fled, Ghaleb fled with him. With Khureybit's coming, Yunis Shaheen began running the newspaper, which published mostly poetry and official announcements.

Before long, however, the situation outside the country cost the Sultan more sleep than his domestic problems. He had thought his most crucial and worrisome battle was behind him, but now found that it was not over, and had shifted to beyond his borders. Just as he had sent troops to most of the areas north and south of Awali to mop up what was left of support for Ibn Madi, and to proclaim his new rule and impose the prestige of the state, he sent a number of his men to Ibn Madi himself. In these times of disturbances, confusion and shifting loyalties, it was easy for each adversary to spy on the other, to pass information, even about what went on behind locked bedroom doors. When the Sultan heard that Ibn Madi had sent his men to every leader, power and capital imaginable, and that newspapers abroad spoke of nothing but what was going on in Awali, he considered this deeply and chided himself for letting Hamilton leave—now the trip worried him.

The new war was not confined to print or speech. It was fought with money sent to people inside the country, to tribal chiefs and former military commanders, to merchants and the imams of mosques. It was in the difficulties people faced finding the things they needed once the markets had supplied the needs of the soldiers and the Sultan's campaigns, and in the problem of Khureybit's soldiers and the way they behaved. When a soldier beat Said al-Saqqaf for humming in the doorway of his shop one day, he shouted, in the middle of the market, "What is this? Are we slaves, or second-class citizens?" He shook his head sadly and added: "God forbid—there's no dealing with these people. You tell them, 'This is a bull,' and they say 'Milk it.' We tell them we're Muslims just like they are, and they sneer at us. There's no pleasing them, not if you fasted all year long. But they'll get theirs!"

On top of all these problems and the people's mounting resentment came the border war. Muizz was in a corner and thus compelled, in order to preserve the lives of his people, as he said, to forget the errors of the past, and force a battle, rather than having it forced upon him.

He was certain that, in the new circumstances, despite the hardships, he would do better. What did the English want? What did the French want? What did the tribes and the people and everybody in Awali want? He was ready to do it. He regretted leaving Traifa without a fight. He might have stayed and resisted, but his councillors, the same ones who had told his father that they had castrated the cattle and killed the horses of the Sultan, who always swarmed around him, tirelessly feuding and arguing among themselves, and being paid off by the English, listened, and then told him what to do.

Now he could think without the nagging of the bedouin and the cries of the refugees and fugitives, and make painstaking plans for the future. How was Khureybit better than he? Did people trust him any more than they trusted the sons of kings and monarchs who passed down the right to rule from father to son? And the bedouin—all they wanted was someone who saw that they got enough to eat each day. If the cities and merchants of Awali have made us forget the desert, he reasoned, then that mistake would have to be rectified; Khureybit would be fought with the same power that he used himself.

The border war had a beginning but no end; and he could start just as Khureybit had.

In this way, with the propaganda war, war of nerves and movement of money, the border war began. Khureybit was afraid of far-off places unknown to him, but not of the bedouin, who took a thousand bullets but used only ten, then came back to get thousands more bullets. What worried him were the faraway shots he could not hear yet, and, even more, the people who carried guns now, or who carried them and were not using them!

Had these been Khureybit's only worries, he would have relaxed, but the men of Mooran themselves, who had fought selflessly and with spirit, had changed: they complained and shouted, blaming the Sultan more than anyone else for not permitting them to suppress heresies, or to punish the people—the infidels!—who mocked them, and refused to do business with them.

The residents of Awali had shown great tolerance when the Sultan's forces first arrived, and were ready to welcome and cooperate with these newcomers, and stayed tolerant in the early days, but then changed. The cold water that flowed from their houses, the tender vegetables they offered, their bright conversational smiles, had all given way to an antipathy that verged on outright hostility, while a black sarcasm replaced the welcoming smiles, in addition to replies that were repeated by sellers, in bakeries, and in remote areas, at the seaside or at the edge of the desert: "Sold out! We haven't got a thing left—sorry about that." And the bedouin, the Sultan's men, and some who had come from remote regions for booty, for money, for war, or to raise the banner of Islam, found themselves surrounded by hostility, distrust, by silence steeped in suspicion and anger.

Because the Sultan's men had to face this every day, and they were the closest people to the Sultan, they told him about every incident, however trivial, over and over again, until he shouted angrily, "This is not Mooran, ye servants of God, and these are not our people! Try to understand them, and have some patience!"

The winter days elapsed and were succeeded by spring days, but spring that year was colder than it had been in years, and drier. The people of Awali and of Mooran tried to endure this winter, to wait for the coming spring and the fertility and ease it would bring, but spring's arrival was slow and feeble, and gave way to an early and intense summer, with a bad effect on the people's moods, behavior and even their minds. The city dwellers had said, when winter was drawing to an end, "Wait for spring—spring solves problems and soothes your cares." When spring came, they said, "Lord God, make this a year we can endure, and when it ends, may it take our troubles with it." When the summer came, searing and harsh, they became downcast and said behind closed doors, "God save us from great men." They shuffled around and kept close to home, seeing only relatives or people they knew well. The desert people, who were better able to bear the drought years, alleviated their suffering by coming in to the outskirts of the cities, or taking up positions along the commercial routes; there they obtained their daily bread by means of wiles, cruelty, and beggary, and managed to prolong their difficult lives.

After the assault of this troubled, torturous year, alms-givers stopped giving charity and the bedouin were no longer being offered work in the orchards, or digging trenches or carrying stones—not that these jobs had ever needed doing. The work had been offered so that the bedouin might do something in exchange for the food or money they were given. The people were no longer willing or able, because the bedouin saw themselves as part of the Sultan's men, and the givers had no extra money anymore.

It was a year unlike any other.

"Tell them, Yunis," the Sultan said to Yunis Shaheen, "that 'God blesses man with so much that he cannot reckon it.'" Yunis wrote it, but the blessings did not come.

Khureybit told his men, "We have been patient before; we've eaten locusts and endured, and we must endure this." He told them that God tested His servants, "and you are being tested now." They listened to him but turned and glanced all around, not knowing whether to agree with him or to do something else!

Before summer's end the Sultan detected on the horizon signs that buoyed his confidence and encouraged his optimism: the southern campaign did its job and came back, at least most of those taking part in it returned. Fanar seemed to all who saw him a new man: The sun had bronzed him and changed him completely. Not only his physical features but his manner had changed, and the way he looked at people and thought. The Sultan listened for a day and two nights to Fanar's detailed description of the campaign from the moment it set out until the moment of their return, often interrupting to ask questions or to marvel at the places and people described. He said to himself: "A day of war or a year of astrology; in war you carry your life in the palm of your hand and have no idea what the next hour will bring, so your nerves are taut and live and die every day." It seemed to him that having Fanar at his side, now that he was taller and more impressive than before, would be a great help.

News of the northern campaign was encouraging, but its mission was not yet accomplished. Ibn Mishaan, since his forces had set out, had become friendlier, and more eager to show the Sultan his zeal. The messengers he sent to keep the Sultan informed of troop movements and new developments, who often brought with them the choicest fruits or best horses they had found, also told His Majesty that he, Ibn Mishaan, had taken two wives during the campaign. These, he reasoned openly, were necessary to gain the trust of certain tribes. The messages and hints were clear: he was carrying out the Sultan's orders and winning people over instead of being cruel to them.

The Huweiza campaign had ended in three months, but there were still pockets of resistance, especially in the border region. These posed no serious threat but were extremely annoying: attackers moved with great speed from one place to another, which was a sign that they had

supporters in several regions and tribes, and their strategic proximity
to the border could lead to endless consequences and complications.

Khazael, after lengthy consultations with Uncle Dahaim and a letter to his father, decided to let Ibn Mayyah prosecute the campaign,
and headed for Mooran. He wanted to travel onward to Awali, but the
Sultan asked him to stay where he was, as he was not needed in Awali.

Also before summer's end, and much to the Sultan's relief, Hamilton returned.

This time, Hamilton came back by way of al-Huweiza, staying
there three days, then traveled on to Mooran. From there he sent a
discreet letter to the Sultan informing him of his arrival and saying
that he had much to discuss with him; did the Sultan prefer to stay in
Awali, or to come back to Mooran? He would make his own plans
accordingly, though Khazael, Uncle Dahaim and everyone else he
asked in Mooran assured him that the Sultan would be returning to
Mooran any day now.

When the Sultan received his letter, he talked to Fanar, with Rafet
Sheikh al-Sagha, Yunis Shaheen and Anan Bassiuni present; he
wanted them to hear.

"Since God first created the world, monarchs have never traveled
anywhere to receive messages, only, Fanar, look at your brother Khazael, God love him—we told him, hold that territory, consolidate
your position—but no!" The Sultan sighed as if in severe pain. "He
left al-Huweiza. We said, 'God willing, may this be for the best.' He
got to Mooran and said, 'I'm coming to you,' and we told him to stay
where he was. Now Sahib came today, and instead of sending him,
Khazael told him to ask me, 'Are you coming, or are you delayed?' For
how long can you teach a man and have him learn nothing?"

"Why not give him the benefit of the doubt, Your Majesty," said
Rafet Sheikh al-Sagha. "There could be so many things we aren't
aware of."

"But, Rafet Bey," said Anan sharply, "there are some things that
can't be overlooked. As His Majesty said, if anyone wants to meet the
Sultan, or give him a message, he has to go to His Majesty; and it
would be a grave error, as I see it, for it to be otherwise."

"But, men, are we facing an enemy here, or teaching our own how
to behave?" The Sultan sounded pained.

"The way I see it, Your Majesty," said Anan Bassiuni, "for several good reasons, you should summon Hamilton here, even if you had your mind made up to go back to Mooran."

The Sultan shook his head sadly and spoke to Fanar. "Send a letter, and tell them: Let Sahib come to us." He smiled sadly and added, "We must head back to Mooran, because we have been away too long, and long absences change people."

Fanar sent the letter, and the Sultan prepared for his return to Mooran; it was decided that he would stop in Ain Nabat and meet with Hamilton there.

He appointed governors for the cities and instructed them to keep him informed of everything that went on, and reminded them that he would be coming back to Awali soon.

19

THE SULTAN STAYED IN AIN NABAT FOR THREE days, waiting for Hamilton to arrive.

In those three days, with "the wind playing," as the Sultan put it, in view of Ain Nabat's high elevation and long way from the sea, and because it was the first height giving a view of Mooran, he felt greatly refreshed and revitalized. He was freed of his daily cares: he did not have to study documents or listen to endless complaints. He had time to prepare himself for what was to come. He wanted to reach an agreement with Hamilton on the remnants of the resistance, because if the resistance survived, it would be a knife in his back, but could be an opening to great new horizons for him if he could gain control over it. He had tried many times in the past to persuade Hamilton and others to do just that, even before he had thought about Awali, but they always refused—and not, in all cases, politely.

Now, in becoming master of Awali, he had taken a great step forward. They had seen his power for themselves, and he himself saw the emptiness of their talk about Ibn Madi, and their attachment to Ibn Madi, which did nothing to bar Khureybit from thinking of or even advancing into Awali, or at least some of its outer regions. They had abandoned Ibn Madi with appalling ease. Furthermore, the Sultan recalled what Hamilton had said only a few days before the fall of Traifa; he had said clearly that "there is no question of giving in; they must flee." Now a pact—yes, a pact—could do much, especially since Hamilton had become such a trusted friend, so in touch with the region and its people; and he was so different from anyone who had ever come before. They wanted the ruler as a friend, and the stronger the ruler and the bigger the land he ruled, the more successful they would be. What did they need with these little sheikhs who were capable of no good and could not prevent any evil? This is what the Sultan was thinking, and this is what he wanted to achieve; the tribal chiefs allied to him, and the soldiers they controlled, had recently begun to wonder, and then to ask aloud, "Where do we go now, and what will we do now?" Not only that, they were annoying him with their mounting demands as the battles waned and then ceased altogether. He was able to control them, to send them here and there, and ask for them to be patient and wait, but he would not be able to do so in the future.

"You must know, my boy," he told Fanar one night after they had returned home from the campaign, "that soldiers without a war to fight are a terrible worry. One day you can rule over them and the next day they want to rule themselves. We must find something for them to do, because if they stay here, in our faces, we'll get no end of trouble from them."

Now Hamilton was back, and within hours of his arrival, and in the bedouin way, the Sultan did not want to get serious or competitive too quickly: they talked of general matters, of people, of Traifa, with many questions about the well-being of each other's family and children. Neither balked at showing his feelings. They spoke of old times, of other talks they'd had, and old reminiscences. Hamilton told the Sultan that everyone sent their best regards, and described the acute interest he had detected abroad, the immense attention reserved for the latest news from Mooran and Awali; and he conveyed to His Majesty and Fanar warm regards from the British king and the British government.

A few hours after Hamilton's arrival in Ain Nabat, the British consul arrived from the direction of Traifa; it seemed that they had had an
appointment. The Sultan took an immediate dislike to this consul,
who had only been at this new posting for a few months. He was hard
to please, "not awfully refined," as Bassiuni said, kept recrossing his
legs whenever he got tired, right in the Sultan's presence, and never
once asked the Sultan, since their very first meeting, for permission to
smoke. He said that he could not wait, nor could he concentrate unless
he was smoking, especially "since our meetings will be long and will
deal with sensitive issues," he said with a smile, more by way of explanation than of seeking permission. The Sultan thought it unimportant
and told him to make himself at home, but soon guessed that the business was more important than he had at first thought, when the Sultan's soldiers, bodyguards, servants and advisers saw that the consul
never once stopped smoking.

Something else created a rift between the two: they could barely
understand one another. Dennis Eagleton spoke classical Arabic with
an Egyptian accent, and understood the Arabic of the desert only im-
perfectly. The Sultan spoke Arabic his own way, more or less as the
bedouin did, never imagining that there was any other Arabic. He had
once been shocked to hear Anan Bassiuni speaking with a visiting
Egyptian delegation in his native Egyptian dialect; he was greatly surprised and thought about it a great deal, as if this were some other
man, not the one he knew. The Sultan marveled less as the years
passed, and delegations from different parts of the world came to visit
Mooran.

This problem might have been easily solved, or might never have
come up at all, if Dennis had spoken English. They might have com-
municated through interpreters without any bother to the other, but
Dennis's insistence on using Arabic, his Arabic, meant that the Sultan
sometimes had to look to his advisers, especially Anan, to help him
understand what was being said. When the Sultan spoke, Dennis interrupted him to ask the meaning of some words, or to repeat some
of His Majesty's words, to make sure he had heard correctly.

If this had been all, there would have been no problem, but as it
was, the difficulty escalated to disagreement and even at times to confrontation. The Sultan became dubious and pessimistic about many of
the subjects of the last few months—promised financial support, arms

overdue for delivery, still-awaited replies to his letters, and other issues—when he saw that the consul was unconcerned or not suffi-
ciently interested in them.

What further complicated their relations were their vastly differing
priorities. What the Sultan considered essential and urgent, Dennis
regarded with casualness bordering on indifference, while with Dennis, on the other hand, a decision or clarification about the visit of
some British naval officer, or dealing with the relations between
Mooran and one of the little sheikhdoms, was of paramount importance. Not only did he put these issues first; in many cases he treated
them as his only concern, or the only ones meriting attention and
discussion. Other matters, which the Sultan wanted to discuss or explore, "we may discuss on my next visit," Dennis told him.

In spite of this, the Sultan held his temper, and even appeared
pleased, for the consul was his only means of contact, his only liaison,
after Hamilton had left. He did make his true feelings and opinions
known, at given moments, to some of his close associates, but these
feelings and opinions were meaningless in the face of need—of necessity. He had to remain calm and composed in order to get what he
wanted.

Dennis Eagleton's arrival that afternoon, however, changed everything. The Sultan acted as he did to create a favorable atmosphere for
confidential discussions with Hamilton, and thought the night the
best time for voicing their secrets and complaints, and to make crucial
decisions, as he had done so many times before, with Hamilton and
others, and he considered the consul's arrival an evil portent. "Those
two aren't safe together," he said to himself. "Their hearts are eaten up
with suspicion and jealousy. Neither is happy to see the other in a
position of strength, or both equal, and the nasal little consul won't
give Hamilton and me one night to talk and find out what's going on."

Even so, the Sultan was pleasant and hospitable, and gave no sign
of vexation; in fact, he behaved with exaggerated warmth and civility
so that Hamilton, and to a lesser extent Dennis, might enjoy a certain
degree of genuine kindness and concern. Because nights in Ain Nabat
tended to be cool compared to Traifa, thanks to the desert breezes that
brought mild and sometimes even chilly air, and due to the arduous
journey, their session was shorter than usual, contrary to the Sultan's
expectations, and his wishes, when he met with Hamilton. When

Dennis came, he was pleased that Hamilton and the Sultan preferred to sup early and then retire.

The Sultan had provided a private tent for each Englishman, but when supper was ended and the guests left, the two stayed up together for about an hour. This hour greatly disturbed the Sultan. "Sahib is our Sahib, our friend," he said to himself, "but this little blond shit must be a Jew, or very resourceful, otherwise he wouldn't have come at this time or on this day."

The Sultan was unsure whether to stay up and talk to "his men," as he had done previous nights, in order to relax and distract his mind, to feel good again, or to go off by himself to think things over: how to please Dennis, how to win back Hamilton. That "shit," as he called the consul, "like an office employee, always with his paper and pen so he won't forget," seemed, all the same, important and influential, because most of what he wanted and decided actually came to be, whether it related to arms deliveries or aid payments, and his coming here now also pointed to that importance. "He might even have come here to watch and instruct our Sahib."

He had a word with Mahyoub, with the moon above them round and fat as a ball.

"As long as the English are like sleeping hens, that's fine; we are Arabs, we can stay aloof and consider what's in our heads and our hearts."

"Whatever you say, Your Majesty."

"Tell the men that the Sultan is worried; let them come to me. Let Salman, al-Anaizi and Ibn Barquq provide supper for worried men, whose hearts are unquiet. Perhaps the merciful Lord will soothe them, and they'll be better than before."

Shortly after that the men, awaiting a signal from the Sultan, decided to do some singing and dancing. They withdrew to a distant spot, at the remotest end of the encampment, so that the guests might sleep in peace, as the Sultan wished, but the sound of their songs and shouts, their rifle shots, and a nostalgia that ignited suddenly, perhaps with the help of the moonlight filling the sky, and the sweet breezes wafting from the east, heavy with the scent of the desert, and memories, and the days of childhoods, all coalesced and seized them. The Sultan was inclined to be alone, or with only his closest men, but soon changed his mind, deciding that everyone should take part, that he should witness a night that he would never forget all his life, when he heard those voices lifted from the depths of their hearts echoing from the valleys, and because the tales told and scenes unfolding did not speak of old stories, or resound with events that belonged to the past, but with ones that were being invented that very night.

Hamilton, who had been in his bed for three hours or more, and could not sleep, and at a late hour saw from afar a throng of men swarming around the place, hesitated to barge in uninvited. When the Sultan heard this, he shouted, "Let Sahib join us—this is a night like no other!" He turned to Mahyoub and chuckled into his ear, "As they used to say: Let the starving eat; not every day is a feast."

That night, and for the following three days, the Sultan did his best to avoid any topic that might cause any discord or bring to the surface any difference of opinion. Moreover, he purposely did not ask Hamilton about the business he had alluded to in his letter. He had his men arrange a full program for the guests; he himself prepared a banquet on the first day, and a series of horse and camel races, with prizes. Fanar accompanied the guests on a hunting trip the next day, while the Sultan received a number of tribal leaders and hosted a banquet for them. It may have been his design that Hamilton and Dennis Eagleton not be among the guests, so that their presence would not be misinterpreted or the purpose of their visit misunderstood. On the third day, set aside for rest in preparation for the departure of the Sultan's retinue the following day, Hamilton suggested visiting a place near Ain Nabat—an important archaeological site, as he described it, a main stopping place on a trade route in ancient times. Dennis grudgingly agreed to go, but, before going, wanted to review with the Sultan the text of a treaty, to study and get a final go-ahead on it, and was counting on Hamilton's presence to aid him in this. The Sultan asked to postpone this piece of business, for in Traifa he had considered it premature, and he was not ready to sign it until he had returned to Mooran and learned all the latest goings-on, particularly after Hamilton's long visit.

When Anan reported that the consul had broached the topic with him, the Sultan was irritated.

"Just tell him, 'Among friends, papers have no meaning. Trust is far more important.'" He drew a deep breath. "And if he persists, tell him, 'Give us the documents and we'll read and study them, and we'll get back to you.'"

Hamilton seemed more interested in visiting the archaeological site than in engaging in any discussions, and made this clear to Dennis from the first night. He knew that the Sultan would not be open to the idea of discussing the treaty, because he was not in a position to make any conclusive decisions. He often thought and waited and lingered over doubts in matters far less weighty than signing a treaty.

Dennis asked Anan, whom the Sultan delegated to take the guests to the ruins, fully intending to be rude, and to be heard by the others, especially Hamilton, "What was His Royal Majesty's response to the accord and the proposal I gave him?"

"They are of great interest to His Majesty."

"And when will a decision be taken?"

"When His Majesty so orders."

"But when?"

"He's the one who'll decide."

"I gather from this reply that the subject will not be taken under study at this time or place."

"If it is unavoidable that action be taken, His Majesty will submit the text to us for study, and when it has been studied in Mooran, we will advise you of our response."

"So everything is being postponed."

Fanar was nearby, talking to Hamilton.

"Mr. Eagleton, this is not the time to discuss these matters." He paused to smile. "We will most assuredly find the proper time in which to study and decide upon it."

Dennis threw Hamilton a look of rebuke, almost of hatred. He was certain that Hamilton had something to do with the Sultan's inflexibility, or more precisely his refusal.

"Look, one studies the history of the past to understand the present; if we delay, the sun will spoil our trip, so let's get moving!" said Hamilton jovially.

Dennis had come from Traifa to meet Hamilton for the first time, and thought this very much the right time not only to hold successful talks but to achieve final results. This is what had led him to contact Hamilton and arrange to meet here, for he knew what close friends Hamilton was with the Sultan, and knew that he had come back from London laden with gifts. He had hoped that the two of them together could move the Sultan to give his consent where he had previously delayed or refused to give it.

Now he had found that Hamilton did not share his view, even that he was in collusion with the others, perhaps to thwart him or to show him to be weak and incompetent, and had no wish to go on with this futile game. He spoke to Anan.

"I beg you to convey to His Majesty my wish to return to Traifa."

"Don't you want to see these magnificent ruins, Eagleton?" asked Hamilton with subtle irony.

"Thank you, Hamilton, but I have much to do in Traifa."

After Dennis had left for Traifa, Hamilton told Fanar that "His Britannic Majesty's worst civil servants are the ones spoiled by books. They see everything in the light of what they have read, erroneously and maliciously, and instead of the world amending what they learned, they want to amend the world by imposing their learning upon it."

"There's just an animosity between him and this town," said Fanar lightly. "He didn't like it or want to understand it." He smiled. "God only knows whether the air of Traifa suits him any better!"

The Sultan, being informed of the consul's wish to leave, asked Anan and Mahyoub to escort him to al-Hilwa, and instructed them to do their utmost to soothe his anger, to please him and let him know that matters would take a positive turn very soon.

Because Hamilton had been in these parts before, he went with a number of men to have a look. He wrote in his journal: "When we reached the point, we took a tour of the area, and I went to explore part of the site and collect inscriptions here and there. Most of them dated back to the Thamudic era. I left the 'altar' for the valley to examine the eastern side of the stones, when we reached the site where two valleys meet at the base of the altar. Behind the western side of that site, after we headed east on a small narrow track on a slight tangent from the line of the altar stones, we found a solitary stone, which nature had hewn in the shape of a sphinx. What was really remarkable was that its broad face closely resembled that of the Sphinx in Egypt, as did the neck and body, which led me to think that the altar had been built here by the stone, so that people might offer sacrifices to one of the gods. I found that the sphinx's leg tapered in a lovely, graceful form, and bore an inscription seven or eight inches long. Unfortunately, the inscription was so badly eroded that it was impossible to trace it, or even to guess whether it was Thamudic or Nabatean. This was a most disagreeable fact, as I felt almost positive that we had discovered the altar that had given this region its name. As the hour was getting late, we headed back to the encampment, postponing the exploration of the rest of the area.

"During our outing we saw a number of odd-looking birds, but we lacked the gear to hunt them. I was unable to find out what kind of birds they were, or where they lived. They may have been some of those known as sisi birds; they do not in the least resemble bustards."

When Hamilton returned to the Sultan's encampment at sundown, it seemed to him that part of the camp had moved, for while the guards' tents were still in front and the Sultan's tent in the center beside Prince Fanar's and those of other guards and advisers, the land appeared empty, like an open marketplace or playing field.

Dennis Eagleton's unexpected visit and his irate departure left a certain bitterness in the Sultan's heart, for his friends, in sending such a person, perhaps even with instructions to act that way, had made a grave error. The great could not become small. He knew how to act and uphold his position: the Sultan of Mooran and Awali was not one of the coddled little sheikhs who could be treated this way.

The Sultan yearned for a long talk with Hamilton, and was eager to discuss "this little blond shit," but he was too diffident to begin, as he did not wish to show his eager impatience; he wanted Hamilton to broach the subject.

The Sultan was to spend a further day and two nights in Ain Nabat to meet with Ibn Mishaan, whom he had summoned, but instead he ordered a car to go on to Mooran, for he had been away a long time and missed the place very much, and there was nothing to slow him down, as there had been on his journey to Awali.

Hamilton sensed that the atmosphere of their last night in Ain Nabat was not quite right for embarking upon serious or complex discussions, so he described the nearby ruins and their significance, saying that civilizations had arisen from these very sites, and that he wanted to spend a few years, at some point, studying and writing about these ruins. The Sultan was spellbound by what he was hearing, openly showing amazement at the existence of the ruins and their proximity to his encampment, and the fact that he had not visited them. When Hamilton said that he wanted to take a few years to study the ruins, the Sultan declared that "if we are able to dispense with our heavier cares, Sahib, and have an untroubled mind, and if you wish, I will have my men pick up all these stones and idols and carry them wherever you like!"

Hamilton laughed heartily, and when he was through, he said, "History can't be carried around, Your Majesty. Anyone who wishes to study or write about it must go to it, freely, obediently; one of the historians' greatest mistakes is to strip history of its spirit, of the place where it transpired, of the people who were part of that history."

"Since that is your opinion, God keep you," said the Sultan pleasantly, "and the stones will stay in their place. As we say, 'A stone serves best in its place.' We will find the time for you, never fear."

Since the journey would begin before dawn, everyone went to bed early.

The next day, while the Sultan's retinue was being readied, Hamilton joked that "it might be better, Your Majesty, if I were to delay a little or take a different route, since my star and your guest's star aren't compatible; it's enough what's already gone on with the consul!"

The Sultan laughed when he remembered, and, looking into the distance, said, "If that's your opinion, I don't mind. When we get to Mooran, we'll have a good talk and everything will be fine."

20

THE SULTAN'S ARRIVAL AT MOORAN WAS MET BY fervor and festivities and surprises, especially in the Rawdh Palace; by delegations from every part of the Sultanate and the world. Khureybit, despite his longing to talk over all his important business, or at least the most important points of it, with Hamilton, was enthralled by the interest of these visiting foreign delegations, and had to postpone some of his business and focus his conversations and questions with Hamilton on what he should say to these delegations, and how he should treat them.

Furthermore, everything the Sultan saw seemed new, though he had seen all of this no more than a year ago.

His women in the palace: each of them seemed new, as though he had never seen her before. Their features, the movements of their eyes, their hair, even their perfumes and henna and the color of their clothes, their way of walking and the pealing of their voices, and still other things, were all new, as were some of their children.

The welcome, the way people were acting, and so much else was

new or had been created in his absence. The images intermingled and
often blurred, but he knew them and did not know them. In spite of
the convictions previously engraved in his mind, almost unalterably,
he now saw that he would have to rethink things. He said to himself
that "places and faces change and leave a man confused." He began to
remember his wives, his children, his bodyguards and servants, and
even imagined, seeing some of these faces, that he was seeing them
for the first time. "How odd," he said to himself, "that a man does not
see the nearest things to him. He has not enough distance from them,
and not enough time, to see them clearly."

He did not want to occupy himself with these matters but found
himself preoccupied with them anyway.

The women of the palace—wives, relatives, and even servants—
began to send him "messages of love and friendship," sometimes at
the instigation of visiting women friends, and at times they thought
propitious. His children had so grown during his absence that he had
to look at them very carefully to find the resemblance, the connection
between them, though most of the time he was bewildered, unable to
see it, and had to guess, thinking "from mare to mare." After scruti-
nizing the little face before him, and its laughing eyes, he would say to
himself, "This is Fadda's boy," or "This is Hafsa's boy," or "This one
is Alanoud's," and when he had settled whose son this was, he asked,
"What's your mother's name, my boy?"

As often as not he was wrong. When he guessed, he gathered the
child up in a hug and sometimes covered him in his cloak from fear of
the evil eye, the envy of his own eyes most of all, as he thought this
child the closest to him and most loved of them all.

The Sultan's daughters, who could not attend his majlis or even
come near it, coming out from behind their wall only from the west,
and even then with their nannies, were something of a mystery to
him. His sons, in spite of their mothers' lectures and the nannies' and
servants' instruction, were tough and arrogant, or so they usually
seemed to the Sultan. They were theatrical—they acted older than
their years. Even when they recited poetry, it felt like a boring school
recital. The girls were different: the way they laughed compelled their
father to laugh along with them. When they walked, or answered a
question, staring at him with their fingers in their mouths, he could
not keep from wondering, "Why haven't I got to know these creatures? Why haven't I been closer to them?"

The Sultan was discovering that the big world could not do without the small world, and without further delay, in an attempt to compensate for lost time and grow closer to his children, he decided to hold a majlis for the boys and one for the girls, and even thought of setting aside a whole day for each, but pressing business made him reconsider that idea.

In the Monday majlis, the old mixed with the young, gossip with petitions, poems with jokes, and if the Sultan had intended for this majlis to be a school for his children, he now discovered that they had already learned a great deal without this school. Most of them had grown big. While he had done his utmost to see that the majlis had a regular order, as it had before, his volume of work, the visiting delegations and other unending demands on his time, corresponding with his children began to overwhelm everything else, and he began to think of setting up a school within the palace. He would choose the best teachers, from among men he knew, whom he had tested before, to do the teaching in his place. He would pursue this Monday majlis, even if he were sometimes compelled to cut it short, but the school was still essential. He might suggest that the teachers use his own method of instruction, and help them out at first, perhaps even preparing some of the lessons, until a regular order was established and he could set his mind at rest.

Khazael occupied the northern section of the palace and had built a number of additional wings, which he enlarged again and again to accommodate his wives and numerous children, and all of the servants, administrators and guards they required. He chose a favorable moment in which to seek his father's permission to move to the new palace he had built, saying that he needed more room, and that there were others who needed this part of the palace. This request surprised the Sultan, and he did not respond to it. It was clear to him that he needed to rethink a great many things, and, moreover, he had to establish new traditions in the palace, and in his relationships with his children. "We must think to marry off every one of the boys who reaches maturity, and prepare him for marriage with gifts: a horse, a servant, and money. When he's married and has his first son, we'll have a banquet and let him move out to set up his own household, if he wants that, so he can become more self-reliant."

So the Sultan consented to Khazael's request, and within a few months Khazael had moved into the Ghadir Palace. The first to reap the benefits of the new traditions—which were reported from the Sultan's tongue in all sorts of different versions and interpreted in contradictory ways, with many mischievous servants and guards suggesting that the new privileges extended not only to sons but to daughters as well—the first to benefit was Fanar. One day in the second month of Jumada, in early spring, a week after Khazael had left, the Sultan summoned the family elders and a number of Mooran's elite to a splendid ceremony in which he presented Fanar with one of his best horses and announced to his guests that he had a new grandson. Fanar appeared embarrassed; he would have preferred this news to remain private, but now found himself the center of attention.

The women of the palace watched the proceedings from every direction and several vantage points, from the roofs and windows, but taking great care that the men should not see them. Some of them who lived comparatively far away either watched through binoculars or used their manservants or eunuchs as spies. The women noticed before any of the men that Khazael was absent, but before asking any questions they recalled his frequent absences from festivities in Fanar's honor, such as the day of Fanar's homecoming from his long journey or the day of the Battle of al-Huweiza. They knew that he had left the Rawdh Palace only days before the birth of Fanar's son.

Much as an offensive smell spreads, before the ceremony was over, and on the basis of no information whatever, rumors spread through the Rawdh Palace saying that this ceremony was not to mark the birth of the Sultan's new grandson, or to honor Fanar's becoming a father, but rather to name Fanar crown prince. What seemed to confirm this rumor, excluding all doubt or conjecture, was that Fanar had stood at the right hand of the Sultan while the delegations were received and seen off again, and Uncle Dahaim stood to his left.

What further strengthened the rumors was the presence of two of Fadda's sons, which suggested that Fadda herself knew just what the Sultan was intending and was going along with it, and as a sign of this had sent her oldest sons, for one thing, and was really behind Khazael's "expulsion" from the Rawdh Palace. What confirmed this and enhanced its meaning was that several of the Sultan's sons, some about the same age as Fadda's sons and some older, did not attend the ceremony, which meant that their mothers either did not know of the Sultan's decision or held other views.

Tahany moved from one spot to another to watch the ceremony, answering questions or curious looks with a bright, confident smile as if to meet the questions wordlessly with the answer that her being there was the Sheikha's doing, or with her approval. She never actually said so, but acted so as to give that impression, and to strengthen it spent most of her time watching the affair in the palace of the Sultan himself with Fadda. Three woman servants reported that the two women consulted in whispers constantly in spite of the presence of other women, and at one point even went off into an adjacent room together.

Surour, Ummi Zahwa's manservant, left the festivities twice to go to the western wing of the palace, and it was reported that the Sheikha spent five minutes alone with him. The second time, she told him to hurry back, and people who saw him said that after he whispered something to Mahyoub he left to go someplace—no one knew where.

Ummi Zahwa, who usually took pleasure, on such occasions, in passing through the men's majlis and greeting them, avoided doing so this time, keeping to her suite. This led people to say that her intention in doing this was to conceal the fact that she was behind everything that was happening, and they said she sent Tahany to visit Fadda and some of the Sultan's other wives, to watch and listen and then come back to report what she had heard.

The men attending the ceremony were oblivious to what was going on in the other parts of the palace, nor did they notice Khazael's absence. Those of them who did notice, very much later on, did not think it important or worth thinking about, because the ceremony involved Fanar and the new grandfather, and everyone in attendance besides them was secondary.

Those who knew more than others were reassured because they were aware that the Sultan had sent Khazael to meet with Ibn Mayyah near Zaafrana. It was said that the Sultan had summoned Ibn Mayyah to Mooran but he claimed that he could not leave al-Huweiza; the most he could do was to meet an envoy at its outskirts, so they settled on Zaafrana and decided that Khazael would be the envoy. This is why he was traveling instead of being present at the ceremony.

Omair was not at the Rawdh Palace, which was fine with the Sultan: he was with Ibn Mayyah. Someone came and told the Sultan that he had recruited a whole regiment from Ain Fadda and the surround-

ing areas, and had recently arrived in al-Huweiza. He did this a few
weeks after Khazael's return to Mooran, and some men who had been
there at that particular time said that Ibn Mayyah did nothing without
consulting Omair. This report was given credence by Dennis Eagleton's having asked the Sultan several times whether he trusted his
men, especially his commanders, in al-Huweiza and the border region
specifically. When the Sultan was taken aback by this question, and its
repetition, Dennis told him that he has solid information indicating
that there were forces hostile to Britain there, that they were inciting
the troops to widespread operations with the goal of fighting the English behind the al-Huweiza borders.

What worried the Sultan was why Omair would have chosen al-
Huweiza rather than Awali, why he would have chosen this particular
time and Ibn Mayyah rather than anyone else. This is what moved him
to send Khazael, to conciliate and reassure Ibn Mayyah and to tell him
about Omair as well. His worries grew with the growing number of
incidents at the border, and the threats and tensions they caused. Ibn
Madi used this state of affairs to stir up some of the Awali tribes and
send a number of ships full of volunteers. News from Awali promised
that the coming days would be difficult ones if the Sultan did not send
plenty of reinforcements, and quickly, especially to the front at Traifa.

Eagleton, who considered himself abandoned and thwarted by the
palace, could not give in or hold his peace. Reports reaching Mooran
confirmed that he had visited a number of Ibn Madi's men behind the
border and had given them money and made promises, and it was said
that he had asked them to incite their supporters and the general public in Awali against the new ruler. What lent credence to this was that
people had begun to talk openly with hostility and rejection, to demand freedom and self-rule for Awali, without referring to Ibn Madi.
Some of the mounting problems and calamities troubling the people
were natural, but the others were undoubtedly the doing of enemies.

Amid these developments and indirect messages, a few weeks after
the Sultan's return to Mooran, Eagleton, too, sent a draft of the treaty
to be signed by Great Britain and the State of Mooran. The offer of
financial aid was linked to agreement and ratification of this treaty.

When the commotion of the festivities died down and the visiting
delegations had gone home, the Sultan had a word with Hamilton. "A
lot happened here and there while you were away, God keep you, and

we said to ourselves, we shall do nothing until Sahib comes back. Now that you're back safe and sound, we must talk."

"I am at your service, Your Majesty," smiled Hamilton, "and listening with both ears."

"We need to talk . . . you, what's your advice?"

"On what topic, Your Majesty?"

"On all our topics!" The Sultan laughed and looked Hamilton straight in the eye, and in doing this told him, without words: "Let us put all niceties aside, and speak frankly." Hamilton understood the meaning of this look and smiled

"You know, Your Majesty, that ever since I arrived in your country and availed myself of your hospitality, my intention has been to play a positive role and to create goodwill between you and His Britannic Majesty's government. You know that I have no official capacity in which to make demands or decisions. Britain has her representatives. Regardless of what one thinks of Dennis Eagleton, only he is authorized to speak in the name of the government. I'm aware that some difficulties have come up between you and Britain's representative, but I don't know what service I can offer, or how I may be useful to Your Majesty."

Despite Hamilton's sincere tone, the Sultan remained unconvinced. "Listen, Sahib, I am telling you this, and no one else. We know many people, but we really know only you, and you are one of us more than you are one of them. You aren't like that little blond shit, and had it not been for our friendship with you and trust in you, everything would have gone very differently."

Hamilton laughed appreciatively at this candor and praise, and after a moment he asked feelingly, "What shall I do, Your Majesty?" When the Sultan looked at him in surprise, he changed his tone and added, "If you were to give me specific orders, what do you imagine, what would you like me to try and do to reach a satisfactory outcome?"

The question, for all its spontaneity, struck the Sultan as very tricky, even menacing. While no night had ever gone by without his pondering what he wanted, or dreamed of, now he was unable to formulate his thoughts or dreams into clear and defined demands. Moreover, he abruptly found that what he had thought to be resolved and finished was neither resolved nor finished. Al-Huweiza, which had been peaceful until just recently, was getting restless, or rather power centers there had begun to blur and intermingle, so that it was impossible to say how things would develop. Awali, which had been in the palm of his hand, and happy to be there, now boiled with provocation, as if its people wanted to bring the place down on his head. The side there which should have been an extension of his rule, and his access point to the outside world, had become an armed and fortified stronghold with the sole aim of aiding mutineers with arms and money to create problems.

As to the financial aid they had not given, and the arms that were supposed to have been delivered, not only had they delayed them; they had placed intolerable conditions on their use, so that he could not even consider agreeing. Above all, they had sent him that stupid diplomat, who was so much better at making enemies than making friends.

And what else?

Nothing at all had gone as he had imagined, or as he and Sahib had planned. This more than anything bewildered the Sultan and made him uneasy and pessimistic.

These thoughts and images flitted through his head while Hamilton's question stuck in his throat. He spoke glumly.

"You know that you've got us in a fix—you told us, 'Move ahead, we're with you, we'll give you everything: guns, money, men; only get rid of Ibn Madi, because we cannot endure him anymore.' As God is our witness, we want Awali, it was our ancestors' and it is ours, and it must come back to us, but a man can stretch out his feet only as far as his carpet reaches. You gave us a carpet with a beginning but no end, but once we were embroiled, you started to impose conditions on us: 'You can do this but not that,' and not only that, your people have begun to move against us, in the name of religion, with money and arms. Now who knows whether you are with us or against us?"

Hamilton was just as frank in his reply as the Sultan had been.

"I do not hide from you, Your Majesty, that it is in Britain's interests to build up in this region of the world a large and friendly state, because the only countries with which one can reach an understanding are large ones, and if it's possible to reach understandings with rival or hostile states, it is an even easier thing to reach understandings with friendly ones. All that's needed is to organize relations; and if Dennis Eagleton is unable to do that properly, he can be replaced. The question of money and arms can be easily resolved."

Hamilton wanted to go on, but saw that this kind of talk could get him into trouble. He smiled and nodded. There was an interval of silence. When the Sultan looked at him, he resumed.

"Nor would I conceal from you, Your Majesty, that information about this region is highly inconsistent and contradictory, so that I have been unable to convince our people there of certain conclusive things. All I have been able to do is come here, understand events and points of view, and go back there once more to try and make the right decisions." He paused, and his tone changed completely. "In these months, Your Majesty, I have been able to form a comprehensive idea of what is happening here, and if they were to ask me now, I would be able to give them a perfectly complete point of view which might be extremely useful to the decision-makers."

"So after learning everything, what do you think now?"

"That's a big question and a rather general one, Your Majesty. I cannot answer it in words."

Before the night was over, Hamilton and the Sultan agreed that the best, the essential way, was for Hamilton to go and take Fanar with him so that the boy might study all the crucial issues in London, with a view toward finding a suitable formula for the future.

Within a few days the two were ready, with a group of advisers and guards. The Sultan gazed now at one of them, now at the other, and warned them not to stay away too long.

The Sultan spent several evenings with Fanar, talking long hours on unnumbered subjects. He wanted him to grow up and use all of his experience and intelligence to find a solution.

21

MISS MARGOT HAD MOVED FROM OXFORD TO London, mainly to be near the British Museum Library. She was working on a new book, about Britain's role in conquering indigenous diseases in the Indian subcontinent, and had an insatiable need for documents. Her latest book, completed a few years since, had been a mixture of memoirs and impressions, with a good deal of research, focusing on the reciprocal influences of English and Indian cultures, with special attention to the influence on children's stories.

Fanar brought Miss Margot a number of gifts: three bolts of silk; a gold necklace with a bright topaz-hued stone; two cashmere wool shawls, one gray and the other fawn-colored; he had been sure to ask his men to buy a multicolored, locally made carpet like the one he had seen in her house before, which she had brought from Colombo, of which she was inordinately fond; three large goatskins; and an assortment of silver and pearl-studded ornaments.

He longed to bring her even more gifts, but the suddenness of the journey, which had been planned within just a few days, prevented him. He had furthermore decided to visit her in Oxford, "no matter how short the time is," as he said, "and spend several days with her." He was greatly surprised to learn that she was in London. Hamilton had told him many times that his aunt Margot sent him her regards but had forgotten to tell him that she had moved. Now that he knew, he was eager to visit her as soon as possible.

Miss Margot had not changed; it was as though the intervening years had lost their way and never found her. This was Fanar's impression in their first meeting; on the other hand, she refused to believe that the man before her was the same lad who had stayed two months with her just a few years ago. In all the time he had stayed with her, Fanar had never dared to look directly or scrutinizingly at her, but found himself doing so now. He even asked her to stand up and try on the two shawls so that he could tell whether they suited her! She held the necklace in her hands for a long time, gazing at it, and when she raised her face to his, she stammered, "I should have had a necklace like this one thirty or forty years ago." She sighed deeply.

"So many beautiful things, so many things we long for, come to us too late." She smiled sadly, but did not let her momentary gloom overwhelm her, and unrolled the carpet.

"Carpets reflect the psychology of peoples much better than the speeches of their leaders and politicians do," she observed, and produced a soft laugh, like the meow of a cat. "Forgive me—I wasn't referring to anyone in particular."

She paused and nodded. "One can best explore peoples, and know them most intimately, through their songs, their woven textiles, their children's stories . . ."

She would have liked to go on, but Hamilton broke in. "I forgot to tell you, Auntie, that His Highness the Prince was blessed with a handsome son a few weeks ago."

"I don't believe it—never, Hamilton!" They all laughed delightedly, and she added, in a different tone, "I'll never forgive you for not telling me about the prince's marriage before this!" She knit her brows. "Though in the East they perceive time passing, and think of it differently than we do." So that they would not misunderstand her, she added, in a new tone of voice, "I mean, they marry young, unlike the

British. It's only natural that those who marry young should have children young!"

She turned back to Fanar to ask him about his new life, about his new son, and why he had not brought his wife with him, though she did not let him reply to this, quickly answering on his behalf that a mother could not leave her baby in its first months; nor, Miss Margot continued, would it be seemly or safe for her to have brought along a nursing infant on such a long trip.

Although she generally presented her books to those who really deserved it, as she said to herself, and after they had passed the test of time, and sometimes after a long wait, she now got up and went to the bookcase at the front of the room and drew from it her latest book. She looked at the cover with her back to Fanar and Hamilton, and said, "If the old can do anything worthwhile for the young, for the future, it is to preserve what was entrusted to them by their fathers, for their children." She wanted them to understand more than the obvious meaning in these words, and when she turned toward them, she resumed, "I found, in writing this book, that the world we live in is very small, sometimes even too small. The stories told by grandmothers in Natal and Colombo are the very same as those told in the smallest English villages, with only one difference: the names of the people and places are not the same. The same stories are retold in Ahmedabad, and perhaps in your part of the world, in Nazareth and Bethlehem."

She sat down and looked at Fanar, then at Hamilton.

"There are differences between one place and another, and it is precisely these differences that give a place its uniqueness, its fragrance. This is what we must preserve, from one generation to the next. When all the countries of the world are just alike, and the differences have been erased, then humankind will have reached the end of a great era, which will necessarily pass away, exactly as happened with ancient civilizations, when the strongest civilization wiped out all the others."

Hamilton would have liked to correct this point of view, as he felt that the largely trivial information his aunt had collected for her book had inclined her to think this way, but did not think that it was worth arguing over, and anyway this was not the right time, so he changed the subject slightly.

"Auntie, if you had ever visited the ruins in Awali and Mooran, you would have seen some marvels!"

"Most assuredly. I must admit that."

When silence had fallen again, she held her book out to Fanar in both hands, looked at him and said, "When your son grows up and reads this book, he will find much that he recognizes from the stories and legends around him, and will remember, in this life, many of the generations that came before him."

Fanar said, not knowing how this idea came into his head, "When he grows up and reads it, perhaps he will write something similar—but about our land, of course!"

"He really should, I would love it," she answered firmly. "But if he doesn't, someone else will. The important thing is that the human legacy not be lost, that it not end in forgetfulness, compelling coming generations to start all over again from zero!"

At the end of this first visit Hamilton looked at Fanar but spoke to his aunt: "You must make it one of your chief priorities to visit Mooran and Awali, to write a new book!"

"Of course you will do it, Miss Margot. It would be a great honor to have you accept our invitation. You will so enjoy your visit!"

She laughed delightedly before answering. "I should love to go, but I may not before finishing my book." Then, as if correcting herself: "Or at least until I have most of it organized."

Fanar and Hamilton had much to do on most days; there was a nearly endless series of meetings, and the people taking part in them represented so many different ranks and professions that Fanar was astonished, even frightened: Foreign Office staffers, commissioned and retired military officers, professors, sailors, linguists and historians, cartographers and still others with unknown competences, because they did not announce them. In these very long meetings, no subject was left untouched or unexplored. Fanar followed the discussions closely but found that he was in dire need of Hamilton's assistance—to translate some terms and expressions, to ask about the historical places and events they alluded to. Hamilton was not only helpful but utterly indispensable, because this world was so wide and perilous, and Fanar needed more than mere help, he needed someone to stand by him.

"They know so much about Mooran," said Fanar to Hamilton at

the close of one of the meetings, as they strolled out into the air after long hours during which many maps, as wide as whole walls, had been unrolled, for several of those present to examine in turn. They debated, pointing with a long wand, how the countries of the region should be arranged!

Fanar had profited greatly from what he had learned in the six months he'd spent here years ago, but now saw that every day of his present stay was worth months, though he said nothing. He ascribed this to his being older, and able to understand everything, or almost everything, that was said to him; and also to the opportunity he now had to meet so many of those who had served, or at least visited, the region, and thus were knowledgeable. He was really amazed that the official in charge of the maps, who now and then was directed to fetch yet another map, with different colors and undulations from the last one and the next one, had never visited the region, and in fact had never been out of England! When Fanar voiced his surprise, the official looked at him and said something the prince would remember for years afterward.

"If one wishes to educate oneself, it isn't enough for him to travel round, in ships and on trains. One must travel in the world he wants, and with determination to discover it, to know it, and to be a part of it."

Fanar nodded earnestly, and the official went on lightly: "So many people travel and see nothing, sir, and others hold the earth in their hands, as God holds the globe in His, and see everything!"

The political talks differed essentially from the discussions of geography and history and languages. The men leading these talks were harder and more direct, and often seemed boorish: "What does the Sultan of Mooran want?" "How can he secure sources of financing?" "What's in it for us if we allow his juristiction to extend to this or that place?"

These were the questions they asked, looking him straight in the eye, wanting to know everything. They were not reluctant to ask about Omair and Ibn Mayyah and Awayid al-Mishaan. They wanted to know the tiniest details. They never hid their papers or showed any shame. Mr. Edmund Rickson said, in one of their talks, that "if we were to allow Mooran to annex some neighboring territories—no need to name them—what's in it for us?" Fanar did not know whether or not he was expected to reply to this question, and did not know what to say. His father had taught him to be firm, not to accept what others submitted to him—to bargain. But what answer could he give to this question, which was only one of dozens, just as there were dozens of men saying the same thing in different ways? He did not know how to answer, or how to behave with them.

They even had a copy of the treaty Dennis Eagleton had brought to Mooran. They produced it, marked up in red and green ink, and asked, "Does Mooran go along with this treaty?"

After these long and wearying discussions had ended, with Hamilton keeping to his role as translator, or at the most, clarifier of various terms or provisions, Fanar badly needed a change of scene. Hamilton was ever his help and support, thinking of what might be done to help him forget the day's discussions, to find faces to blot out his memory, in preparation for the next day.

In what was left of the day or night, they strolled around freely to see London's landmarks and visited parks or friends. On these walks and visits, Fanar recuperated, discovering that there was more to the world than maps and retired military officers. Nor could he sum up in words a stolidity like the steps of St. Paul's Cathedral. The world was so much broader and richer than those faces and hard words.

Six straight days of meetings and councils and maps, and the result was a few pages.

In the final meeting, two days before his return home, one Emerson at the Foreign Office spoke to Fanar: "Your Highness . . ." There was a long pause after this, and as the silence dragged on, those listening assumed that Mr. Emerson had changed his mind and would say nothing, or had decided to say something new or different. They waited, Fanar most eagerly of all, until Emerson resumed, "Your Highness . . ." He cleared his throat. "We have taken into consideration many of Mr. Hamilton's observations, and those of Mr. Dennis Eagleton, as indeed we have also had the honor of hearing your views; and we have, as a result, and after careful study, arrived at the wording of the treaty we wish you to take home with you to show to His Majesty the Sultan, so that he may study and endorse it."

The silence remained, and as there was no move to comment and inquire, he went on in the same tone.

"We have heeded His Majesty's view and studied the matter in all its aspects, and beg to have your response within two months from now."

Fanar was taken aback by this presentation of the treaty, or the justifications put forth for its acceptance, and said as much to Hamilton late that night, several hours after the session had come to a close.

"I don't need to tell you, Your Highness," Hamilton answered him, "how some of His Majesty's servants can be, especially those who served in Egypt and India. All they know how to do is give orders. They think of all people as paupers and beggars. This employee and his kind are the real problems of the Empire!" Hamilton shook his head. "If there is any danger to the Empire or to its friends, it is from them and their kind." There was a short silence. "But for now we have no choice. We have to listen to them, and may have to go along with them, because they are in charge."

Of all the things Fanar learned on this visit, the most important was never to answer yes or no. He recalled what his father had told him during their last campaign. He said to himself, "We must listen well, understand well, and act with as much force as we possibly can."

As he spoke these words, he found them wise and powerful, as if they alone could help him achieve the success he wanted.

Hamilton spent the last week visiting his wife; they were planning to go to Wales. He left, but came back in time to bid Fanar farewell; he had to stay on two or three weeks longer to deal with assorted business—the maps, the payment schedule, the new armaments promised to the Sultanate, including four or five aircraft—and to spend two additional vacation weeks with his wife and son.

They both spent the last evening with Miss Margot.

When Miss Margot talked, she delighted in being simple and direct, and to an even greater extent, wise. This was an English habit, as she liked to say smilingly.

"If I'm spared, if I'm able, even if I had never been invited, I may sell my necklaces and jewels to go," said Miss Margot when Fanar repeated his invitation for her to visit Mooran. She laughed and her eyes twinkled. "I love visiting the East, and this time it will be an East different from what I knew." She shook her head a few times and added, "Your East baffles me—it is such a strange mélange, and, though these words are so trite, such a crossroads of civilizations and religions, and thus unsettling to itself and others. It is like a pregnant woman whose time is past due, who doesn't know whether she will give birth to a prophet or a monster; will her fate follow the logic of history or geography, or try to be something else?"

She sighed despondently, and her voice sounded gravelly.

"Yes, this East truly baffles me; it is a mass of mystery and contradiction, to itself and to others as well. To the extent that it possesses gifts, and is blessed by circumstances, it is also slow and ponderous, and so lost as to seem a corpse needing nothing but a gravedigger. And yet it is full of surprises. As I used to tell Hamilton: this East, with all its civilizations and legends, with all its passions and manias, is capable of two things: either saving the world, or being the end of the world." She sighed again, sadly. "Your Highness, I don't want you to believe all you hear from a doddering old woman, a woman of a bygone era, but I still have strength to say a few words: the books I have written, whatever services I have rendered, the dreams that still fill my head, all of these persuade me that there is much in the East capable of movement and permanence, and that this is the secret of its existence. Without that, it would have perished long ago of the wars, epidemics and catastrophes which, had they befallen another people, would have wiped them out."

"All this talk about the East, about our land, before you visit us?" said Fanar pleasantly.

"Your Highness," she replied quickly, but silence fell, and her head and body trembled slightly, "perhaps my image of the East is better than the region is now, but it is still a storehouse of conflicting possibilities. As I said: it could be the beginning of a new world, or the end of this one."

"You are either very pessimistic or very optimistic, Miss Margot."

"Your Highness, it has nothing to do with optimism or pessimism; it has everything to do, before all else, with history, and will. You still have so much history; it is your inheritance, and perhaps you have no right to it—it may properly belong to your ancestors—but you have no trace of will, or the desire for will."

Miss Margot smoked very rarely, as a rule only when she was feeling either very festive or depressed, but now she opened the drawer of the little table to her side and took out a packet of cigarettes. She offered one to the prince, who declined with a smile, lit one and took two long puffs before resuming.

"I don't know what you want, or how you will get what you want, and I have no right to intrude into business that doesn't concern me. I don't like politics, either, in the common everyday sense, but I think that every people should cherish high ideals, which it fights for when necessary, ideals greater and more momentous for nations renowned in history, which had great roles in past ages, and I feel, without exactly knowing, that your country has a great mission to carry out."

Hamilton found the atmosphere had grown too solemn, and said, to lighten it, "That's why we're here, Auntie!"

"Here?" she asked ironically, and a moment later wondered out loud, "What can be done here?"

Because she knew so much, and had seen so much in her life, in the special places she had lived, she said as if to herself, "I don't like to get into other people's business, I don't like it any more than having other people get into my business, but if anything can be done, it should be done there."

She crushed out the cigarette irritably and looked at Fanar out of the corner of her eye, then smiled as she lifted her head, and spoke in an entirely different tone.

"As I told you before: I don't want you to fall under the influence of an old lady, as I'm sure you will not, but one's experience in this world should not be in vain; this is what I try to say through books."

"You must come to our East to write one of your important oriental books!" was Fanar's playful reply.

"If I live long enough to get to the East," she answered bitterly, "and I have the strength, and something to say, I will do it; not only that, there are many others who have the experience, and will live long enough, and have something to say, and they will, too!"

She looked at Hamilton and smiled, as if she meant him.

"You're the one who once told me that one man can never replace another," said Hamilton, "and that there is no people like another; so what you have done cannot be done by anyone else."

"You are still perfectly capable of being a conversational match for an old lady," she said softly, and laughed.

"We will be waiting for you there, Miss Margot," Fanar said. "I would be grateful if you were to let us know when the best time for you would be, so that we can prepare things properly; I don't think you will ever regret coming!"

They parted with a promise to be in close touch in the future, not like before. Miss Margot said neither yes nor no. She walked them to the door, and when they reached the street, she waved to them from the window. When silence had again fallen, she drew her cigarettes from the drawer, lit one and took one puff, then another, lost in thought.

22

THE SULTAN EXPECTED A GREAT DEAL OF FANAR. He waited a long impatient month for his return, and finally Fanar appeared, with news, promises, expectations—and nothing else. The money, the armaments, a commitment to stop funding his neighbors, especially Ibn Madi, and authorization for him to annex the border regions, all hinged on his accepting and signing the treaty. That meant that everything was postponed and endangered. What complicated things even more was that Dennis Eagleton was away on vacation, and Hamilton had further postponed his return. "These English communicate very clearly through their silence and absence," remarked Anan Bassiuni to the Sultan. "Otherwise, what does it mean, for someone to go away and not come back again?"

The treaty Fanar brought back differed only in a few details from one Dennis had put forth. It was as if they still considered the Sultan a puny ruler like the dozens of sheikhs and princes all around him, as if they could impose upon him conditions and restrictions to compel him to depend upon them in everything, small and large, in return for the aid and protection they offered. While he had, fifteen years ago, been forced to conclude a treaty that made him like one of the other sheikhs, at that time he did not control this same Mooran. Now he reigned not only over a bigger Mooran, but over al-Huweiza and Awali as well, and he was the only one who could speak in the name of this immense region; Why did they want him to remain small? Why did they deal with him this way?

Not only that, Mooran itself had begun to tremble. He had begun to detect hidden voices, to sense a mood which words or actions could not express, but which filled the atmosphere and the very atoms of the air.

His men, upon whom he depended for everything, had changed. Through silence or absence, they made him feel their restlessness and resentment. If the resentment had been directed against one another, or yet others, it would have been easy to understand the messages they sent from time to time. Ibn Mayyah and his forces at the border wanted to ruin his relations with all of his neighbors, and sabotage his friendships, especially with the English, in order to cut off his other options, so that he would eventually be forced to give them what they wanted.

Ibn Mishaan, in Awali, now collected women the way he collected horses; he wanted to subjugate the place by either peace or war. He took time to lecture the people and school them on the rituals of the hajj, the acts to omit so as not to render their ablutions invalid, and their prayers; and every few sentences he reminded all around him that, in the words of the Koran, "if kings enter a village, they corrupt it." They asked him who he was talking about—Ibn Madi or Khureybit—but he only looked this way, then that, and said, "To God, all kings are as alike as the teeth of a comb!"

Al-Huweiza, which has fallen as silent as a stone, now started to fidget and stir. Its borders, which had been quiet for years, unless he chose to stir them up, now lost their tranquility, and it was impossible to tell whether they were still his, and with him, or whether they had gone over to someone else.

As for Ibn Madi, who had been forced to pack his bags and take all his gold with him, and to sail away for good, he now almost decided to come back; his supporters raised their voices, their eyes were full of anger and mischief and their open defiance was everywhere. Commingled with their voices and defiance were the voices of others, announcing that they were going to be rescued, if not today, then tomorrow.

It was not enough that all humanity was against him; God Himself now seemed to be, too. The first year brought drought. It was a long, dark year for both animals and crops, and the people moaned with hunger. Livestock perished, the desert blew in to the very edges of the cities, bringing hunger and other menaces with it, and everything appeared to be on the brink of collapse and death. The ground shook and seemed ready to overturn. Ibn Madi sent money and volunteers, using want, misery and hunger to awaken those who were not yet awake, and to incite everyone far and near. Before long, all the newspapers of the world wondered "what kind of criminal the desert of Mooran had produced now," how long he would last, and why he shouldn't be done away with today?

It had taken everything in his power to persuade his men and the people of Mooran to wait and be patient; how could he convince others? Why should others wait? What were they waiting for?

Had matters gone no farther than that, he would have been patient, and the people would have been patient along with him, and endured, but no sooner did the famine year pass than the plague year came in. Old and young, the people died, and death did not stop at the gates of the Rawdh Palace, but went through them and invaded.

The palace midwife reassured Zaina, who had been ill since giving birth, that all first-time mothers suffered her symptoms, and that eating camel's liver and drinking fish oil would restore her health in no time. When her condition worsened, the English lady doctor was summoned, and announced firmly that it was progressing, and would continue to progress this way for several months; when the plague came, it took the sick and the well. Zaina's health declined, no medicine availed, and so it was that she left this world, leaving a nursing infant and a man bereaved for the second time.

The Sultan, who had been grooming Fanar to be his right hand, now saw him sunk in gloom from which he could not be saved, for with Zaina's death his sorrows over Ain Fadda were reawakened along with all the memories and scars of the past. Then Mudi fell ill and hung between life and death; no one knew whether she would survive, or follow those who had gone before her. Fanar did not need these new sorrows to become a different person; a few of them would have been sufficient for that.

The Sultan was trapped somewhere between anger and pity. One day he might fly into the most extreme rage, because he hated mourning in men—he thought it a weakness, and did not want his son to have a trace of it. The next day he might recall how Fanar suffered when his mother died, his long stay in Ain Fadda, and the sadness and scars it left upon him. Seeing Fanar like this now, going through the same thing, filled his heart with sorrow and pity, and he wondered why boys who lost their mothers became so weak? Where did all this sorrow come from?

Within a month of Fanar's trouble and isolation, Uncle Dahaim, too, died.

After a long evening and even longer debate on what to do about the famine, the hostility of friends, the condescension of foreigners and the harvest of death, Khureybit and Fanar decided that Uncle Dahaim should go back to al-Huweiza to set things right there, as Khazael had failed to do, to make a deal with Ibn Mayyah to get rid of Omair and his sort, and to give the Sultan another chance to cope with the disasters and put affairs back in order. They also decided that the Sultan should go to Awali and stay there long enough to get things back to normal.

At the end of that night, messengers arrived and informed the Sultan that Uncle Dahaim had left this life. The details were not important. He had vomited and felt skewers of fire piercing his chest, and shouted for help, but then calmed down, so that everyone felt relieved that his condition had improved, and that he only needed some sleep. Then he fell asleep and never woke up. None of these details changed anything, or caused mourning: now the Sultan was alone, and overwhelmed and overcome by feelings of loneliness.

Khazael was wandering like a stray camel between al-Huweiza and Mooran; no one knew exactly where. He sometimes stopped to rest at the home of one of his many wives, though generally no one knew which one, for he did not stay longer in one place or with one woman than he needed to hear the latest messages and send his direct replies.

Even the Sultan's wives at the Rawdh Palace were full of the nagging that grew out of fear and bitterness. They quarreled with the servants, the children and the nannies because they did not dare quarrel with one another. The women's and children's stories, once restricted by Talleh and Nahi al-Farhan, or other courtiers, were now far freer. They began to circulate in the form of complaints about errors and feuds that mounted so steeply that no one could stop them. If things went too far in this direction, the Sultan would hear about it, and there would be trouble.

The children waited longingly for Monday, when they would attend the Sultan's majlis. They put on their best clothes and perfumes, and competed to recite the poems and songs they learned from their nannies and tutors; each tried to distinguish himself from his brothers by reciting something new or unusual before anyone else, because he might have spent a week learning it. The children were transformed into instruments of complaint and feud. What could not be solved among themselves, or by involving their mothers and servants, turned up at the Monday majlis. The Sultan was at his most tolerant, and sometimes mediated their arguments, but sometimes got fed up and postponed the Monday majlis time and again, confident that his children stayed away from their classes in order to learn from him; the school he founded in the palace would have to do without him, because his children were diligent about their lessons! He later discovered that their school was in session only one or two days a week, and after that served as the school for the children of the servants and guards, which moved its overseers to suspend classes, so that the Sultan might find the time to receive the school overseers so they might explain to him how bad things were.

Even the servants and guards who were left, though they ate, slept and lived in the palace, were loud in their complaints because they were not getting their pay or any gifts. Others, who depended on their pay to feed, clothe and shelter themselves, complained and protested even more than the servants and guards, and some even asked to be sent to al-Huweiza and Awali. Those who had no choice but to stay stole from the palace and sold what they could in order to get by.

The Sultan could get money even in the worst times—he could dig it out of the earth or pick it out of the highest skies, according to those who were familiar with his talents—but now he was perplexed. All he could do was send messengers here and there: "A loan, a charitable loan, my friends, and in a few days it will be returned to you with a blessing." The messengers returned a few days later, either with small money bags that barely covered the palace's needs, or in silence, and in no hurry to meet the Sultan and be blamed for the failure of their mission: "Your ill-omened faces could dry up a brook!"

"Listen, Ibn Farhan," said Talleh al-Oreifan to Nahi with bitter irony, "try to find some little job here . . . here, before you mourn for the place and regret it."

"Abu Jazi, do you remember how he used to talk before he went to Awali? 'Good men, my own brothers and friends, who want both this world and the world to come, this is your day. Everything will come to him who marches with us, everything he desires: horses, camels, and booty.' A day came and went, and now you can see for yourself: 'Be patient, my good men, everyone will have his share, but you must be patient.' For month after month people have been waiting with their mouths open!"

"It's as I told you, Nahi, today is better than tomorrow; you might find some work in the Souq al-Halal, shepherding sheep or driving camels, and tomorrow you might not find it."

Mooran was able to resist or endure its hardships, sending its sons away to distant places to seek livelihoods, or to encourage them to use force against those competing for its resources. Mooran had done this through the ages, though most of her sons who traveled afar found themselves forced to come home again someday. Obscure motives brought them home. Despite the greenery, water, and abundant wealth of the towns they lived in, they felt suddenly beset by sorrows whose origin they could not understand, by glooms that chilled their buying and selling, their prosperity and tranquility, compelling them to think back on Mooran. Strange, even mad ideas contended in their minds. They must have been mad to leave Mooran, falsely swearing that they would never come back, because of the restrictions and hardships there. Though Mooran seemed to be gone, it slumbered in their depths, only to explode later on, with the same unreasoned force that had moved them to leave it, and it was this force that brought them home again.

Some who had left Mooran for the farthest points on earth, for Java and Sumatra, Zanzibar and Mombasa, had never imagined any other land than Mooran, or any place far away, and adventured as far as the

New World, seeking a new Mooran there, and, not finding it, or not being satisfied with an alternative Mooran, they stayed for a while, then left much of what they had built up, or hired agents to oversee it, and came home.

Something about the people of Mooran defied logic and understanding. They were a people still tautly bound to an umbilical cord. They roamed far away, and behaved for the most part as others did; they learned and lived but were always different from the others. This was a limiting rather than a defining character. Some learned well, and became an integral part of other places, but what made them proud deep inside was that they were from Mooran; had they not been from there, they would not have made such successes of themselves.

In years of famine and hardship, more than in years of plenty, Mooran's roaming citizens felt the longing to be among their own people, or to send them whatever they could.

It happened innumerable times. In easy times, when no famine threatened, when death reaped not and life was soft, grandmothers never tired of telling stories to make the children of their relatives appear when they were least expected, to save or help their families, who had sometimes completely forgotten about them, because so many others had traveled away and never been heard from again.

In this hard year Othman al-Olayan came home to Mooran. Othman had spent several years in Java. People who knew some of his life said that he had spent twelve years there; he had been a mere boy when his uncle took him there. According to the winter tales, God showed all His prosperity to Othman. After building his fortune, and trading in every business, he settled in Egypt. No one knew how long he had lived there, though those who loved Egypt said that he made all his money there, and whoever feared or disliked Egypt said that he had made his money elsewhere and did nothing in Egypt but marry one woman after another and enlist some Egyptians to look after his horses. His money, they said, was tied up in ships and in ventures in Basra, Gaza and Damascus—even, it was whispered, Manchester in Britain.

Whatever—the important thing is that one spring day Othman al-Olayan found himself in Balabac, weeping from homesickness for Mooran. People who knew him said that he had left Mooran when he was just fourteen, and others said he was only seven at the time. In a moment of anger and emotional turmoil, he decided to move back to Mooran. He had been gone thirty-two years; some of his enemies said he had been gone for forty. He was as secretive about his age as he was about how much money he had—especially in front of women.

So his decision to return came suddenly, and within a few weeks he had sold off his holdings in Egypt and elsewhere, though there were some who said that he had not sold a thing, but merely collected most of his debts, lengthened the term of others, put his agents in charge of them and left.

He came back to Mooran in search of his family. No one knew who he was, but because Mooran never forgot its children, and because in the Sultan's majlis foreigners met adventurers seeking family and friends, it was not long before Othman located his relatives.

After watching, listening and getting to know Mooran anew, he decided to put himself in the service of the Sultan.

The Sultan's relations with Ibn Olayan were obscure and very strange. It was as though each of them had been awaiting the other for a long time; and when they finally met, they became much more than friends. Some said Olayan's family was related to the Sultan's; others denied this, saying that the two families had only intermarried. Still others asserted that the relationship betwen the two men had nothing to do with blood or marriage, only with self-interest, and similarities in their age and outlook. They complemented one another, it was said; each needed what the other had.

Within a few months everything cleared up, as Othman al-Olayan knew trade and accounting, "and had money he wanted to put to work," according to Yunis Shaheen, "so he buttered the Sultan's pastry." These were Yunis's exact words, but he spoke them privately, and many years later, when Othman al-Olayan had reached the pinnacle of wealth and was the Sultan's adviser.

The stories and tidbits, and even the rumors about their relationship, and the matter of Othman's money and other affairs, were full of contradictions and conflicting versions due to the numerous narrators and their varying motives, so that it was impossible to establish the truth, or even a part of it.

After the drought year, and the plague, it seemed that the Sultan had made it through his worst days and his severest trials and hardships.

Around the time of Othman al-Olayan's return—two months after it, to be exact—Hamilton, too, came back, after a six-month absence. Dennis Eagleton stayed behind in Britain; there were conflicting reasons given for his staying there, but the most credible one was that he was having marital problems. His wife did not want to go back to Mooran, and threatened him with divorce if he forced her to go back. He loved her, so he asked the Foreign Office to keep him at home a little longer so he might work out this problem. The ministry permitted him to stay, and asked no further questions; not only that, they promptly decided to appoint a replacement for him. His successor was of a very different type in his behavior and speech; when he went to Mooran to pay his respects to the Sultan, he asked that they postpone any substantive discussion "until he'd had a chance to swot up on the files." He showed every eagerness to "cooperate and surmount our difficulties."

There was much speculation over how exactly Othman al-Olayan had managed to obtain money for the Sultan; everyone had his own widely divergent views, and there was no one in Mooran who had not reached an official verdict and proclaimed it. The merchants of Mooran and Awali, who were forced to pay fixed amounts based on their own wealth, did not know whether they were paying a tax or giving a loan or contributing to charity, because when they asked, they were told vaguely that it was something like charity or a loan, with solemn assurances that everything they gave would be paid back to them. Some of the Sultan's messengers added that "they would be paid back the loan, and more," which startled the more fanatical, who asserted that "we will accept no interest on our money," though the more easygoing said that it merely represented profit and there was nothing wrong with taking it. Their question was, "When would the repayment and the profit come?" Still others, who'd been slow to pay out their religious alms tax, considered that God was punishing His servants with drought and pestilence because they had not been generous in His cause, so they paid gladly. Others paid out of fear every envoy sent by Ibn Olayan was accompanied by soldiers of the Sultan, and looked all around them, as if appraising the assets of each man, or determining what they might help themselves to if he refused or hesitated to do as he was asked.

This is how the merchants understood or explained the money

taken from them. In any event, the amounts of money were not large, and were not enough for the Sultan to deal with the burdens of military campaigns and the demands of his soldiers, and to secure basic supplies. His expenditures had gone up, and people were saying that "this is just a cover for what Ibn Olayan is doing."

The palace servants, who looked on with eagle eyes and missed nothing, however small, though as a rule they held their peace, noticed that the Sheikha, who had kept isolated from everyone else for quite some time, now was more in evidence. It was said that she had, for the past few months, been worried about the plague, and so stayed in, particularly after the death of several of those living in the palace, either from dehydration or from drinking too much rose water; she had forbidden any of the servants from coming near her suite. It was said that she never once touched the food prepared for her by the palace kitchen. Tahany personally prepared all her meals.

Her appearance now was explained not only by the passing of the plague, but by the many private meetings between her and the Sultan, several of which were attended by Othman al-Olayan as well, and in the course of which she was persuaded to give the Sultan what money she had available to her.

Tahany said not a word when asked about it; she only smiled with a twinkle in her eye, to confuse her questioners.

What led people to think something had happened that involved the Sheikha was her own demeanor. She was more youthful, and had put away her black clothes in favor of gray ones. Much was made of this; it was said that the Sultan had asked her to do it, to motivate Fanar to get over his own sorrow; others said, with ironic smiles, that the familial bonds between the Sultan and the Olayan family, the subject of so much talk, were soon to be renewed—it was not an impossibility, they hinted broadly, that this was the topic of some of those private meetings. Others said that Olayan intended to return to the Sheikha, promptly and with interest, the loan she had given the Sultan, and that the Sultan had guaranteed this arrangement.

Citizens who had traveled and were acquanted with foreign lands, especially those who knew Egypt from living or visiting there—Mooran's travelers were renowned for their nosiness—said that Olayan was so rich that "there wasn't enough fire in the world to burn all his money," and that he saw his term loan to the Sultan—for it was certainly that, complete with witnesses and signed documents—as a mere business transaction. Just as he had once bankrolled many people and invested in businesses in Syria, Iraq, Bahrain and other places, he now expected to get back what he had put in. Perhaps the Sultan had put up his palaces and horses and collateral.

Some of the experienced travelers said, making no effort to hide their sarcasm, that Olayan was so cheap that "he would not piss to put out a fire," and so would not part with any of his money. He had, they said, urged the Sultan to contact Moorani expatriates abroad. Olayan provided their names and sent them letters full of sweet talk and promises by way of his relatives. The Sultan sealed these with his signet and sent, along with the letters, carefully selected henna and the choicest dates, even, it was said, a collection of fine carpets, shoes and cloaks, and his warmest and sincerest greetings. All this moved them to give him generous loans.

Thefts had become common in the Rawdh Palace, especially the theft of valuables, gold and precious stones, and Othman al-Olayan suggested that the Sultan set aside a large room in the palace, seal it with the strongest German locks, and assign his soldiers to guard it day and night. The Sultan agreed and did just that, and kept the key to the room—the only key—himself. Each of the Sultan's wives was asked to put her gold, jewels and money into a small box and lock it herself, so that all the boxes might be safeguarded in the room. The women were reluctant, but the rampant theft in the palace left them no choice.

There were radically different accounts of what happened next, after the gold and jewels were handed over. According to one version, the Sultan sold all of the gold in the markets of Haifa and Jaffa; according to another, Olayan took it all to India and sold it there. The best-informed people said that no final sale took place: the gold had all been deposited or pawned with Jewish goldsmiths and money changers in Baghdad, against commercial loans at interest.

In any case, the crises which nearly destroyed the Sultan ended, then began to reverse themselves. It happened slowly, with no lack of anxiety and doubt, to say nothing of unremitting rumors; then came camel traders with beasts laden with flour, tea, oil and sugar. The traders said they preferred to sell here rather than anywhere else, because they were assured good profits here, and there was no trouble or delay about payment, and that day the people began to feel a deep sense of security.

The traders arrived in late autumn and early winter, and there were early and copious rains that year: everyone was optimistic. People said aloud that "the hard days are over; we beseech God to end forever our sorrows and tribulations."

With the news of rain in Mooran came news of the heaviest rains in long years to fall on Awali. All the old men tried to remember the last time it had rained like this. Those who had sown late, from fear that this year would be like all the others, made desperate haste to plant, and with the sowing, buying, and selling, their songs and good humor now reappeared, but the Sultan's soldiers pretended not to hear.

"If this year ends well," the Sultan told Othman, "then the years to come will make the people forget their hardships; you'll see."

"They are over, Your Majesty," replied Othman, drawing a deep breath from his chest. "The seven lean years are over and the seven fat years have come in; we'll both see!"

"One fat year will do nicely—as for the rest, God provides."

"Don't worry, Your Majesty; God can open all the treasures of the world for you!"

Anan Bassiuni had been listening to this optimistic chat.

"May the Lord give us our daily bread," he laughed. "That is what we hope and pray for."

"Every puzzle has a solution," said the Sultan, looking far off. He looked up at the sky and almost bellowed, "God is all-powerful!"

23

THE SULTAN'S MEETINGS WITH HAMILTON WERE a mixture of exploration, inquiry and reprimand. After a long absence, which appeared to the Sultan incomprehensible and inexcusable, Hamilton wanted to know where he stood and what he should do. He was embarrassed and even sad at times, in his first days back, but soon regained his self-possession. They went on an outing, one warm winter day, to the brook at Ain Mileiha.

"You know, Your Majesty," said Hamilton, "that the people who make the decisions are there, and they must take many factors into consideration before making a final decision. The first day, they listened to us, and later the same day, or the next day, they received the delegation Ibn Madi sent. They listened to him and talked to him, then sent for His Majesty's ambassadors in the region to hear them out, too. Then they talked to the French and the Americans and other powers to reach some preliminary conclusions, all of which remained open to review, revision and further lobbying, and the second round of talks with each of the parties. In the end, as usual, negotiations were postponed to leave time for further study, or to await the most suitable time, or to allow conditions to be met."

They were walking along land whose vegetation was just sprouting from the early rains; the spring would be fruitful for the first time in years, not only due to the rains, but to the south winds rich with the smell of new rain to come. The Sultan had chosen this place and this time of day because they made him feel more able to take a comfortable stand. Prior to this he had always preferred nighttime. He remembered what Anan Bassiuni had said when they were thinking and talking about the future, about how the absence of Hamilton and Eagleton was no cause for reassurance. "All they give are promises, Your Majesty," Anan had said, "and the next day they've forgotten what they said the night before, just as the proverb says: 'Dawn annuls the promises of the night.' "

Hamilton guessed that the Sultan had chosen this place in order to be unobserved by others, so he decided to be candid; to share his thoughts and fears with him.

Despite the many scenes in Ain Milciha that might have invited questions or commentary, especially at this time, each man was absorbed in his inner world and estranged from the one around him. After a long silence Hamilton spoke.

"I don't want to remind you, Your Majesty, of the problems and hard times we have had to deal with these past few months; perhaps His Highness Prince Fanar has told you of some of what he has seen, but after he left, and a great many conferences and contacts with different parties, it seemed to me that there was no chance of success. Indeed, I was considering folding up my papers and doing one of two things: staying there, with no thought of returning here, or doing just the opposite."

This last sentence did not seem quite clear, especially since Hamilton accompanied it with a smile. The Sultan looked at him and waited uneasily. Hamilton spoke in a happy voice.

"That is, of course, if you consent to have me as your guest, and if my presence here is useful for you."

The Sultan laughed and looked far off, and Hamilton resumed his earlier tone.

"I don't deny, Your Majesty, that we achieved some measure of success, but not what we were seeking or hoping for. In spite of our efforts and our patience, I must concede that this is the most we were able to get." Now his tone was neutral. "This is what I personally was able to achieve; much is still tied up in the negotiations to be held here. I see that you have been sorely tried and have done all in your power to convince them to make further concessions."

In the next few hours, as they walked, squatted by the brook, or reclined on the sand, Hamilton explained to the Sultan that things now were very different from what they had been two or three years ago: "Now things are nearly finalized. It's only a question of a few finishing touches here and there, and signing the accords."

Despite the precision of his words, somehow the picture was not clear. The Sultanate's problems were innumerable and very complicated. The English were deeply implicated in these problems—more than that, the Sultan felt, they were behind them. Now he did not know how to bargain with them or come to terms with them.

"Sahib, I understand what you are saying," said the Sultan after they had discussed several topics. "And I am at your service, but I want you to enlighten me: your friends, do they still want us, or do they have other ideas now?"

"Of course they support you, Your Majesty."

"But it seems to me they have one foot on level ground and the other in the wilderness, Sahib."

Hamilton did not understand what this was supposed to mean, and asked, in his best bedouin dialect, "What, Your Majesty?"

"I'm saying: every time we get something done, you say, 'Take it slow,' and every time we make peace and say, 'We're agreed,' they say, 'Let us think about it,' as if they were obligated to someone else besides us."

Hamilton said nothing. He wanted the Sultan to go on, to say everything he had on his mind. Khureybit cleared his throat and went on, his clear voice rising from his chest.

"For years we demanded Ibn Madi's head, Sahib, and we were perfectly capable of taking it, but whenever we were ready, you stopped us, saying it wouldn't do. We nursed our pride and kept quiet. Time passed, you know how things went; you only agreed after an endless fuss." The Sultan turned to look Hamilton straight in the eye. "And that is not all. Now, if it were not for you and your assistance, Ibn Madi would not be able to do anything. We don't know whether to worry about him, and expel him, or let him go wherever he wants to go and do whatever he wants to do!"

Hamilton was very quick to react to this.

"I think the trouble with Ibn Madi is over, Your Majesty, and can be forgotten. But two things: first, that the Sultanate stay away from Britain's friends—that the Sultanate not bother or threaten them, or have designs on their territories. Second, that the accord between Britain and the Sultanate be ratified, and formally defined as a treaty." His tone of voice changed, as if he had casually remembered something. "I have not heard Your Majesty's views with regard to the treaty His Highness Prince Fanar brought."

After several weeks of meditation and preparation, and having sent some of his close advisers to al-Huweiza and Awali to report on conditions there and make painstaking inquiries into events, the Sultan thought things over and asked his allies their opinion of the treaty, what they thought he should do, and what conditions he should demand; then William Butler arrived at Traifa.

The Sultan had met Butler several times before; they were almost friends, or so at least the Sultan felt. This military man, a veteran of numerous wars, had lived in so many countries that he had acquired not only a bronzed complexion but many of those countries' traits, and a knack for communication. The Sultan recalled the freedom of his many discussions with Butler, the air of warmth, cordiality and energy the man exuded, and the successful outcome of those talks.

Now Butler was at Traifa, and was considering moving on to Mooran in order to meet the Sultan there, but as soon as the Sultan heard of Butler's presence, he sent him a messenger informing him of his plan to come to Awali, and suggesting that they meet at Ain Dama or Ain Nabat. He told the messenger—Anan Bassiuni—to have Butler confirm either site for their meeting.

Those who observed the meeting of the two men at Ain Nabat, where the Sultan arrived one day before his guest, said that such an encounter could only have occurred in the desert, between two authentic warriors.

Butler had arrived at Ain Dama by automobile by midafternoon, to refresh himself for the rest of the trip to Ain Nabat, a distance of about twenty kilometers, on horseback. He wanted to lead a procession worthy of a knight, and to enjoy the scenery as well, so he got ready to leave early the next morning. It was all arranged beforehand; the horses had been ready in Ain Dama for days, and a procession, including a trumpeter and drummer, soldiers, guards, courtiers, the consul and some of his employees.

Anan Bassiuni and others shuttled between Ain Dama and Ain Nabat in automobiles to settle last-minute details such as the site of the warriors' meeting and the timing of their arrival, the festivities and other shows of respect and hospitality.

One hundred meters from the hill, ranges of smaller hills spread out to form a pattern of wadis, and the ground spread out perfectly flat, so that the hill appeared almost like a throne overlooking the hills on one side, and the wadis and their smaller dry creekbeds. This was where Butler and the Sultan met.

The Sultan arrived at the hill a half hour before Butler, since Ain Nabat was only a few hundred meters away, and though the distance was negligible, he rode out on one of his finest thoroughbreds. As host, he wanted to be there before his guest.

Butler arrived at the appointed time, dismounting from his horse at a comfortable distance. He paused for a few moments to adjust his clothes and shady pith helmet, then strode with bold and purposeful steps toward the Sultan, who started toward Butler. They met halfway along the clearing, embraced, and pressed each other's hands while grasping the other's shoulder. The trumpet blared, the horses neighed, drumbeats sounded and a few shots were fired into the air.

It was a happy and affecting reunion, full of such unlimited welcome that it seemed like a scene from a play. Most of the details had already been settled and carefully prepared, but there was no acting or pretense in this scene. Those who saw this moment said that the two men were too great, too powerful for others' planning. The Sultan wanted to lead his guest to the end of the hill, walking through the rivers of blood where dozens of sheep were being slaughtered, with a great ram in the middle. Yunis Shaheen had suggested that it be slaughtered at the same time, so that the Sultan and his guest might walk through it all. This moment had been carefully planned by many especially selected people, because Butler had wanted to see the wadis and the Sultan agreed quickly and cordially. They stayed there longer than expected, so there were several mix-ups. The incense was lit too early, the drummers in back began drumming too soon, and the coffee pourers set to work while the Sultan and his guest were still far from the hill.

Butler and the Sultan got on well, and one or two sheep's heads were lopped off for their table after the delay and slackness of the slaughterers, though one of the horses broke loose suddenly and had to be caught; he might have shied at the sight of the slaughter or the color of the blood. Butler avoided the blood, walking around the carcasses, and the Sultan with him, though Mahyoub thought this a bad omen, and told the Sultan so among other things the next day. The guards and servants noticed such details and discussed them among themselves, then the talk spread to the rest of the entourage and reached the highest levels, it was said, though none of this changed or diminished the festivity of that warm winter noon in Ain Nabat, the place where the hills and the wadis met, which was also a breaking point between, or more properly a symbol of, Mooran and Awali. It was from this point that roads set out or converged.

Why had the Sultan chosen this specific place? Was there any meaning in this?

Historians were later perplexed by this detail, and found unnumbered interpretations for it. Not all of their reasoning can be examined, but they found it especially significant that this site was between Mooran and Awali and overlooked both mountains and valleys, which was understood to mean that the Sultan was ready and willing to be master of both.

And why had the Sultan come on his blackest steed? Was it a warning or admonition to Butler, or an expression of the delight he anticipated of this meeting? No one could be sure. The Sultan, in most of his battles and historic moments, entering a city or taking the surrender of a fallen commander, always rode the horse dearest to his heart: he rode Subha, because she gave him good luck.

Still, what had made Butler avoid walking on the blood of the butchered sheep? And the bolting of the horses, the premature lighting of incense—what was the meaning or interpretation here?

Was it chance or design that the Sultan's meeting with Butler concluded on a Monday? Some of the Sultan's guards, recalling similar instances, said that Khureybit had intended the meeting to be that very day. Of course, it was only a guess about something the Sultan had kept to himself; when he had sent word to Butler to meet him at Ain Nabat, he told Anan Bassiuni and a second messenger going the next day, with unusual firmness, so as to leave no room for ambiguity, that their meeting would be on Monday. Perhaps it was because this day was associated, in his memory, with what his grandmother used to say about the special luck of Mondays.

What underscored this interpretation was that the Sultan was happy to see the crescent moon, and when the moon was full, he saw it as a good omen. So it was with his meeting: the moon would be full in a day or two, which made some of his entourage happy to the point of giddiness. The Sultan himself joked with a number of his guards, spent more time with them than usual and warned them to be on alert: "This guest is dear to us, and this is Awali, not Mooran."

The first meetings were ceremonial. The Sultan and his guests exchanged visits filled with friendly chat and reminiscences in which other men joined in. On Tuesday they met in the great tent with only a few advisers, and Hamilton to interpret.

On this day more than one of them remarked that the sky was darkening, then the rain started falling, pounding more abundantly than they had ever seen before. It struck the great tent like stones as the men inside yowled like cats in a sack. Yunis Shaheen later reported that at one point Butler said, "No," and the Sultan replied, "You're killing me—I can't accept that." "That's it," said Butler, "I can't go on one more step with you." "You have taken half my kingdom," answered the Sultan, "and left me naked in front of my subjects. How can I receive people now and look them in the face?" Butler was about to reply to the Sultan but abruptly checked himself. Tears were streaming down the Sultan's face and into his beard, and he did not know how to stop them or what to do. Butler was as stolid as a boulder and determined to achieve the outcome that had been prepared. His map was unrolled on the table, and everyone took turns gazing at this dead, misunderstood, mysterious body, but suddenly Butler saw the Sultan's tears and anguish and perceived that Khureybit was about to leave the tent, get on his horse and order his men to follow him. At that moment, "a truly mad, weak moment," as Butler later described it, he was forced, or at any rate felt forced, to give in to some of the Sultan's demands, to please him.

Just as always happens in weak moments as well as in strong moments, although Butler had spoken in a clear, concise and final manner, he gripped the red pen in his hand which he used more for pointing than writing, and produced a sharp remark and Hamilton translated it. He addressed the Sultan rashly in this weak moment, and three advisers and five courtiers swore that they saw the tears on his cheeks, which he wiped away swiftly and angrily.

"Listen, and listen well, Your Majesty: anything I've taken from you in this place, I give you back here."

He motioned with the red pen. His gesture was broad, almost describing a full circle with the pen in front of him, drawing a balloon in red ink along what the Sultan took to be the borders of his Sultanate. Khureybit gazed at the large red circle and massaged his beard, then looked all around and spoke theatrically.

"Listen, Sahib . . ." He smiled sadly, tears still in his eyes and his beard. "By God, by God, by God, if we were not friends, and if I didn't only want this over with, I would never go along, but never mind . . ." His smile broadened. "And you should know, Sahib, that if you have cheated us this time, you will pay for it, as always happens with friends and partners."

That night the moon was full, and everything that had been seen was transformed, in the eye and the memory of all that had witnessed it, into something extraordinary; no one would ever forget what they had seen at Ain Nabat.

Some historians, visiting the region later, said that the winds blowing at that time of year were laden with pure, piercing aromas that deprived men of their reason, drugged them and affected all creatures, especially when the moon was full. Animals grew agitated and prone to fury.

An American mission visiting Ain Nabat many years later said that the planets exerted a special electromagnetic force there, especially during a full moon. They measured the distance between the hills and the opening of the wadi, and between the other openings; marked the watermarks, and flung down a rope tied to a metal weight to see how far it fell; and said that they would have to send all of the data to a laboratory to be analyzed. They could not explain some of the phenomena, and never spoke of it again.

24

HAMILTON HAD LEARNED OF THE DEATH OF Prince Fanar's wife toward the end of his stay in London, and the news desolated him. "Death," he said to himself, "is the perpetual, faithful guardian who never parts from a man, who never shirks his duty or tires of it. Fortunately, the bedouin aren't like us; we live our whole life in fear of death, even in our happiest moments, but they never think about it, no matter how close it comes to them. They're even eager to experience it, to take part in the eternal life that does not know death."

He tried to mitigate the shock with this explanation, but he was still sorry for Fanar, and at moments it all seemed terribly wrong, especially for a woman as young as a flower, as the Arabs said, and a young man in his prime, who wanted to start his life with vigor.

When he went to take his leave of Miss Margot, he told her the news, and she moaned.

"How strange they are—they're born, they marry, and then die, prematurely and in silence—why?"

Her question did not call for an answer, and he did not offer one. She went on as if talking to herself. "So much of the time one does not know what was wrong, and that may be the cruelest thing of all. And when you add silence to that confusion, there's nothing you can do to help them.

"Dear Hamilton, let me tell you something now: it's quite true that talking about one's cares can help one to forget, to give partial or temporary relief, but when he comes back to himself, his cares, death in particular, loom even larger, even become the only reality for him."

"Aunt, we are talking about what we know, how we live, which is something very specific to us," answered Hamilton. "Other people have their own ideas, their own ways of looking at these things."

"But death is still death. I have seen it myself dozens of times, hundreds of times, and it is always the same."

"But there are other ways, very different ways of seeing a single thing, including death." He took a deep breath and went on in a changed tone of voice. "Death, for us, is the end of everything—I don't want to offend your beliefs, or get into what you expect after death—but for them, life is only a phase, a crossing point from one condition to another. This gives them a certain strength and courage, the ability to face nature, poverty, sorrows and dozens of other calamities. Sometimes they enjoy their torments, rather as our monks do; they can delight in suffering because they hope for much after going through tribulations. They're like seamen, or men at war: when the ordeal is over, they're full of pride and boasting. It has passed into history, become a possession, and they go on with life, doubtless savoring it all the more."

She stood by the window and looked out at the street, possibly recalling how Fanar had waved goodbye to her.

"You can say what you please, but I still say that death is both friend and enemy; it puts an end to everything, and everything must have an end; it ends suffering, and, lastly, it ends waiting and hoping."

They talked of other things, to forget, and at the end of the visit, as he was putting on his overcoat and preparing to go out, she asked him, "I don't know whether it's appropriate for me to write him a few words of condolence, or whether you can tell him how very sorry I am to hear of his bereavement?"

"I will give him your condolences, Auntie, and mine as well."

"Please."

He asked for Fanar hours after arriving in Mooran but was told that Fanar was in the desert and might not be back for weeks. He asked the Sultan, who shook his head in grief.

"What happened while you were away, Sahib, would have been too much for mountains to bear, but men must bear up . . ." Hamilton waited and said nothing, and the Sultan sighed. "When a man sees another man's trouble, Sahib, his own diminishes, and, thanks be to God, Fanar is better than he was. He has held himself together, and told me, 'Father, I want to go hunting,' and I told him, 'Trust in God.' You know there's a lot of hunting now. If he shoots two or three bustards, chases some gazelles and rests by a brook to watch for grouse, he might forget. God willing, it won't take too much longer for the Fanar we know and love to come back to us."

But Fanar's hunt dragged, and because there were so many problems to deal with which could not be postponed, the Sultan and Hamilton set to work on them. Certain issues were postponed because the Sultan wanted Fanar with him when he was in Ain Nabat. When Butler asked about His Majesty's children, meaning Fanar most of all, for he had met him on his last visit to London, the Sultan answered him, looking at Hamilton.

"You know, Sahib, that if a country is not protected by its men here and there, it is lost. We told Khazael, 'You go here,' and we told Fanar, 'You go here,' and now they are both with their men, fighting, defending their country."

When Fanar came back from his hunting trip, Hamilton saw how far things had gone: when Fanar talked of the bustards and grouse, he spoke in an almost visionary way, as if this were the only topic in the world. He chose an opportune time to talk to the Sultan alone.

"I think, at the present time, that it is in Fanar's best interest to take a trip." When the Sultan gave him a curious, almost startled look, he added, "Fanar was not like this before, Your Majesty; this is the way he is trying to forget, to flee from problems." He nodded to emphasize his words. "If he goes on this way, he will reach a point where he's spending his whole life hiding behind animals and birds, so it would be better for us to find him another way. He has much to accomplish, and he must face up to his responsibilities."

The Sultan thought Hamilton's remarks wise, and spoke enthusiastically. "In place of the one who passed away, we can marry him to a thousand women, as long as he is with us and can communicate with us and say, 'My friends, you need help? Anything I can do?' But if he keeps to himself, we'll lose him, and God knows what would happen next."

"Very often, Your Majesty, shocks edify and mature a man, as long as the man faces them with reason and wisdom."

"What you say is true, you wise man."

"And I think that at this time, now that the accord has been finalized with His Majesty's government, you should do everything possible to obtain the recognition of foreign states; recognition means power for the Sultanate. It's part of the war. Fanar can play an important part in helping us win."

The Sultan intended to host a series of ceremonies for Fanar before his new journey, to express his power and victory, and to counter the claims and provocations of Ibn Madi, who had been tirelessly telling everyone that Khureybit had sold the whole country, not only Awali, to the English. Conditions had greatly improved, thanks to the arrival of provisions and the abundant rainfall, so the ceremonies and banquets were truly magnificent, and none of those attending could stop talking about them. This doing of the Sultan's was not the result of impulse or his famous hospitality alone, but of Hamilton's frequent assertion that "this country's status and power won't be noticed or realized unless the people see it, in its new and better state, with their own eyes."

The Sultan recalled how before he'd had to plead with people and borrow money from them to cover his essential needs; now he wanted to prove to all, far and near, friend and foe, that he had come through all his adversities still capable of everything. More than anything he wanted to eliminate whatever was left of Ibn Madi's power, so that he might turn his attention to domestic affairs and consolidate his position for good.

To this end he gave special priority to clergymen and the elders of the mosques, to orators who dwelled on the hereafter; these were influential people, especially among the bedouin, and he had to prove that he could do much for them. He had a word with Fanar, who had recovered some of his old self and was preparing to travel.

"These are our people and we know them. You will never see people who talk more about the hereafter, or have a greater love for this world. They want both this world and the next, but my feeling is that they know only this world. Look at the way they eat, and the way their eyes shine when the subject of women comes up. When they talk about food, they smack their lips and drool!" The Sultan laughed. "But we've got the medicine for them, my boy: money in the pocket, and a nightly reward for their faith!" He shook his head and added sarcastically: "If they multiply, that, too, is a blessing. They know dried muscat lemon candy from a lemon, and if they have the strength, they'll smack their lips!"

When all the celebrations and banquets in Mooran, Awali and al-Huweiza were over, and money and gifts given, Fanar and Hamilton set off and the Sultan prepared for what came next.

25

THE SULTAN INTENDED THAT ABDALLAH AL-Bakhit should take part in the delegation traveling with Fanar.

It was the first time in many years that the Sultan dared make such a decision, for Ibn Bakhit was not only an important man but an indispensable and irreplaceable one; irreplaceable by one man or ten. For this reason he was not allowed to get sick, to leave town or travel abroad. Even when he wanted to make the pilgrimage to Mecca, to prove to those who doubted his faith and piety that he was observant and God-fearing, the Sultan refused.

"Your pilgrimage would be invalid, Ibn Bakhit," laughed the Sultan. "You'd need a male escort!"

Bakhit moved his legs apart and made a slight gesture to indicate what was there. The Sultan laughed again.

"Sorry, that's no good—you'll have to wait until we all go together."

The Sultan had so many different reasons for his attachment to Abdallah al-Bakhit that everything that might have been said or speculated about them was probably true.

Whoever heard him speak to the Sultan and others of past Arab raids, with much detail and poetry, telling what had been said in and about the raids, said that Ibn Bakhit was the troubadour of raids, and that is why the Sultan loved him.

Those who heard Ibn Bakhit recite from memory, and recount what Abu Ali al-Qali had said in al-Amali, all said that the seven years he'd spent in El-Azhar University, and the beatings on the soles of the feet he got there, had helped him learn his lessons well!

Those fortunate enough to be included in the "Quarter," the Sultan's private council, who heard Ibn Bakhit's jokes, said he had learned nothing in Egypt but foulness and scandalous jokes. They said, furthermore, that the blind sheikh who taught him syntax and conjugations taught him about women as well. They went so far as to say that he had fallen out with the sheikh when the latter discovered that his young pupil had surpassed him in that art; that, in fact, he seduced Qatr El-Nada—Dewdrop—the sheikh's woman friend; that Qatr El-Nada, in fact, had wanted to seduce him herself. Their love affair lasted until Qatr El-Nada exposed Ibn Bakhit to the sheikh, who then expelled him.

Some admired Ibn Bakhit's knowledge of language and grammar, syntax and conjugations, and were ready to swear that when in Egypt he had never left El-Azhar except to go to the nearby mosques of Sayidna El-Hussein or Sitt Zainab; he'd spent his years there in the shadows of the mosque, like any other eminent and respected scholar, in order to learn his language perfectly.

Clergymen were not comfortable or friendly with Abdallah al-Bakhit, not because he was stupid or atheistic or heretical, but because he knew more than he ought, and could expose their lies and fabrications at whim. And not only that; he knew enough Koranic verses, traditions and prophetic stories to show what kind of people they were—how they stole and embezzled and seduced women—though he talked of these things only in a safe atmosphere, among trusted friends. Before starting in, he would turn like a fox to look far off, at the entrances and doors, and when reassured, he would smile at the faces close around him and fix his gaze with theirs.

"Ha, my friends, here we are and we know one another well. As we say, 'This place we know, our steps are light,' and if any but us hear what we have to say, we have nothing to say to him, but if there is, among us . . ."

He scrutinized his listeners to make sure that what he was about to say would never leave this room. Then he began, though he knew that what he said would travel; and before the evening was out, when the men were weak from laughter, he said, "There are no bones in the tongue, my friends, so be careful. The Prophet, peace be upon him, counseled us to exercise care."

The clergy heard most of the stories he told, though generally in versions altered to protect Abdallah al-Bakhit, but since no one could tell stories as he did, as he purposely embroidered and convoluted them, he resorted to inserting hard-to-remember names, or threw in verses of poetry, and he denied having anything to do with the story being circulated which was attributed to him. When people insisted, his mock-angry rejoinder was, "If you want, let's disprove them." They gave him questioning looks, which he answered with the same trace of anger: "I know a story like that, but it's different from yours; if you want, I'll tell it and you can judge!"

Sometimes they agreed to listen, though most of the time they did not want to, since the idea of yet more stories frightened them

Ibn Bakhit's closest friends said that the most remarkable thing about him was his voice: when he sang, it was impossible for anyone to remain unmoved. One of the Sultan's servants enthused that "Ibn Bakhit's singing can make sterile women get pregnant and pregnant women give birth, and the Sultan throw his headropes." The servant might have heard this said on one of those special nights when Ibn Bakhit sang and the Sultan was enraptured, and perhaps even threw his headropes.

People who did not like singing and never chanted unless reciting the Koran, loved the way Ibn Bakhit recited despite his Egyptian drawl and mispronunciations, arguing that "Ibn Bakhit articulates the letters clearly, without slurring them or speaking through his nose, as Egyptians do."

There was no end of stories about why Abdallah al-Bakhit had gone to Egypt in the first place, how many years he had spent there, and why he had come back. He had the same exasperated answer whenever the Sultan asked him why he had left: "What orphans get is a crime, Your Majesty!"

When the Sultan persisted in his question, Ibn Bakhit turned to address the others: "What need is there to ask? The Prophet, peace be upon him, said, 'Seek knowledge, even unto China.' So is it a crime if a poor slave manages to go to Egypt?"

The reply did not satisfy the Sultan, who looked skeptical, so Ibn Bakhit turned to him again.

"The truth is this, Your Majesty, and may it remain between the two of us. I went there to bring back a flock of sheep by way of El-Qantara and Gaza. I was to be the retailer. But Egypt can change you! The years came and went and I postponed leaving, until it was the will of the Almighty that the deal should fall through. Everyone there told me, 'Study! Learn a trade to avoid poverty.' But I didn't listen to them, and as you can plainly see, I came home without any sheep and without a trade; with only my clothes and my cloak!"

He laughed, and as he laughed, his features were transformed into an icon of mirth and movement.

"There was nothing I could do, no work I knew, so I thought, 'What is there besides work?' I looked here and there, and found nothing but—" He stopped abruptly, turned around again and again, feigning hesitation and fear, then added, in a different tone of voice, "Yes, found nothing but my tongue; and this is what I brought back with me."

Stories about his travels still multiplied and conflicted; people who loved him tended to see his Egyptian years as a blessing, "because he learned all the sciences, and anyone who doesn't believe it can just ask him!" People who hated or feared him or his tongue said that Egypt had taught him nothing but foulness, stupidity, impudent speech and hashish smoking; they cited the fact that he slept until noon, and his eyes—especially when he woke up—were as red as a rooster's comb. And despite his advanced years, he had never married!

When it came to what tribe and what place Abdallah al-Bakhit came from, Mooran, which never compromised when it came to lineage, made an exception. The first time he was asked directly, when he first attached himself to the Sultan's entourage, he said he was "Tamimi." That clear reply meant one of two things: either that his tribe was the Bani Tamim, which was fine; or else, as the bedouin saying ran, "Whoever's lost his lineage says, 'I am Tamimi.'" It was generally accepted that he was Tamimi; no one looked into his family background, and he never alluded to it.

Al-Ajrami was always ready to cause a commotion when he could find no one else to do so, but when he heard what Abdallah al-Bakhit was saying, or what was being said about him with regard to religion, he asked disapprovingly, "Ibn Bakhit, you say? You say he's Tamimi? Look, this is our Mooran, and you can quote me: I don't care if we went around the world, to India and Sind, to Egypt and back, we are talking about the faith of Muhammad, and no one has the right to talk about who or what he is. We are faithful, believing people and we know him, just as Meccans know the streets of Mecca best, and no one else should make it their business."

Ibn Bakhit heard about this and passed it on to the Sultan. "Al-Ajrami is the most trusted man in town; he never lies, and everyone likes him." When al-Ajrami heard what Ibn Bakhit and the Sultan were saying, he smiled and said, "Just as I told you, my friends, the people who know him, educated people, are all for him." He thought this a fitting reply. The Sultan send al-Ajrami several gifts to honor him, and Ibn Bakhit visited him three times in two weeks, and spent most of those visits listening and asking questions. The two became good friends, which Ibn Bakhit had never been with any of the other clergymen.

This was one side of Abdallah al-Bakhit. He was renowned among people far and near, and his fame was assured after a popular tale of the Wadi al-Faid campaign, at the time of the Battle of Huweiza. The Sultan had discovered an assassination plot and changed his body-guards, ordering them to be very watchful and careful. It so happened that Ibn Bakhit came the first day after that to see the Sultan, and the guards would not admit him.

"My boys," he told them in a fatherly tone, "I am Ibn Bakhit, and they call me Abu Badi. You must know me—if not all of you, then some of you. If you don't know Ibn Bakhit, Abu Badi, then you don't exist and neither does your Sultan!"

They looked angry and strode toward him.

"You must go see Mahyoub and ask him."

He laughed.

"Me, ask permission from Mahyoub? Are you crazy?" He laughed again and changed his tone. "My friends, it would be better for you to recognize your uncle. I am Abdallah al-Bakhit, and I'm afraid that if you don't recognize me, tomorrow you'll be sorry!"

The youngest and most excitable of the guards now shouted.

"Shut up and go see Mahyoub and have him give you the password or a piece of paper with his seal on it. If you stay here, we'll make you sorry."

"Listen, my boy," answered Ibn Bakhit with equal rage and calm, "I'm your father's age; you're a child. His Majesty wants people to protect him, not to isolate him. You tell Mahyoub that Uncle Abdallah, Abu Badi, is here."

"You must want a beating," said the chief guard. "You'd better get out now, or—"

"Abu Mansour!" shouted Abdallah al-Bakhit. "Protector of faith and the world, if you don't come, God's earth is wide—I'll go somewhere else and that will be that."

Everyone within earshot reported that the Sultan himself came out, and when he found what had happened between Ibn Bakhit and the guards, he made a remark that was often quoted later on. "If you don't know Ibn Bakhit, you don't know the Sultan; I want everyone of you to know him. No guard or doorman stands between me and Ibn Bakhit."

"That boy," Mahyoub said the next day, "still getting breast-fed, probably, who didn't know our sheikh, Abdallah al-Bakhit—I told him, 'Trust in God, boy, go get some sheep and find somewhere else to live, because we want people who know an enemy from a friend!' "

Ibn Bakhit had other private hobbies which only his friends knew about, mainly those who shared them: horses and tracking. Because he was still learning, and a little unsure of his horsemanship, especially with the military officers, tribal sheikhs and others who surrounded the Sultan, he denied knowing anything at all about horses, and even sneered at anyone who assumed he did!

He had come to know about tracking, because one day he discovered the protagonist of a story told at the Rawdh Palace, which confounded the whole palace. The Sultan had been gone for a year or more during the Wadi al-Faid campaign, and came home to find Yamama, one of his favorite concubines, was five months pregnant. The enraged Sultan threatened her, but when he tried to learn who was the fetus's father, Yamama wept and swore that she had had relations with no man. He went to great lengths to make her confess, but she would go no farther than saying she remembered a black demon entering into her as she was sleeping. She'd sensed that her belly was full, and when she awoke, terrified, she felt a black snake gliding out between her legs and sliding away. The snake looked at her for one moment, laughed, and slithered out of the room. This was the story she told the palace midwife, and it was the story the midwife told. The version Yamama told the Sultan was more detailed, and she told it with Ibn Bakhit present.

"I was sleeping, sir. I was in a very deep sleep and didn't see or feel anything except when my belly felt full—something had entered, and kept pushing until it went from here to here," and she indicated her thighs and up to her neck. "I was too afraid to cry out or even budge. I didn't move. After a little while I sensed that the thing wanted to go out, and I said to myself, 'Girl, let it out.' I let it go out, and didn't move until it was all the way out. I got up and lit a lamp, and saw a black monster at the door—may God never show you anything like it, sir—and that's when I knew that the demon had taken advantage of me."

Yamama stood by her story, changing only the most minor details.

"Yes, Your Majesty," said Ibn Bakhit to the Sultan with a wink, "when it's dark, demons go roaming and making merry unless we recite the Sura of Yassin."

A few days later Abdallah al-Bakhit identified the demon: Jadu, the Mecca-born African, the Sultan's executioner.

As to how Ibn Bakhit knew, there were at least three different stories:

The first alleged that he had brought a snake and asked Yamama to show him how it had entered her and how it came out; according to the second, Watfa's servant Lulua, who was friendly with Yamama until a recent quarrel, told Ibn Bakhit or the Sultan everything. The third story said that Ibn Bakhit had been silent on the subject for a week, until it was forgotten, or almost. He chose a moonless night to sprinkle some flour from the door of Yamama's room to the guards' quarters, though some of the servants got carried away and said he sprinkled a whole sackful. This was what led him to Jadu the African, because the footprints between Yamama's room and the place Jadu came from were perfectly clear.

In the next two days, after a new executioner was hired and the investigation of Yamama completed, but before she and Jadu were killed, a rumor started among the servants, frightening them, that

Abdallah al-Bakhit was not Tamimi but Murri, because no one but the Bani Murra were such capable trackers. He had falsified his background, the rumor had it, in collusion with the Sultan, so that they might find out what was going on in the palace. It was at about this time that several thefts were solved, months after they had taken place. The stolen goods were found in obvious places, to the general amazement.

A few months after this incident, while the Sultan and Ibn Bakhit were on a hunting trip, a new rumor, whose source and sponsors were unknown, circulated, saying that Ibn Bakhit had been a notorious pickpocket in Egypt, and spent five or six years in prison there. After serving his term he was expelled from Egypt and forbidden to come back. Here the rumors added that pickpockets were clever and cautious enough to choose their prey from simpletons and foreigners, and never erred; that could only be the result of education and training, just as with any other science. They concluded the story: Ibn Bakhit spent seven years in Egypt. He spent the early months learning pickpocketing and the next few months practicing it, until he was arrested and imprisoned, and when his prison term ended, he was deported, so he came to Mooran and joined the Sultan's retinue.

The stories told about Abdallah al-Bakhit were so ludicrous, and numerous, and contradictory, that Sheikh al-Sagha said, "If I write my memoirs someday, which is not unthinkable, I'm afraid that Abdallah al-Bakhit will get more space in it than the Sultan!" He added, after a pause, "If one escapes from these bedouin, it's hard for anyone to catch him!"

Anan Bassiuni, who considered that he had bedouin roots, saw in Abdallah al-Bakhit innate cleverness, typified in the best bedouin, and an ability to learn and acquire skills surpassing that of the fat, lazy young men found in cities, who never saw the moon unless it was full, and couldn't tell a snake from a rope.

The resulting warm and trusting relationship between Ibn Bakhit and Bassiuni were like those between two strangers from the same remote area of foreign land, and took on a cordiality and uniqueness it might not have had in some other place.

"I don't mean to flatter you," Anan Bassiuni told the Sultan one night, "nor do I wish to extol the men you depend upon; they have ability and confidence that make me proud to be one of them."

The Sultan was very pleased to hear this, and said, in his deepest voice, "What is it you're after? You shall have it!"

"I've known many people in my life," smiled Anan, "but Ibn Bakhits are very rare. Not only is he knowledgeable, he overflows with intelligence and humanity." He paused. "We Egyptians pride ourselves on our wit, but Ibn Bakhit is beyond any of us!"

Why had the Sultan made this difficult choice, to do without Abdallah al-Bakhit, to send him on a trip abroad that might be a long one? He had two aims in mind: to cheer up Fanar, first of all, and help him be himself again, particularly since he and Ibn Bakhit were more than friends; Ibn Bakhit might restore Fanar completely. As he himself had told the Sultan, "Believe it or not, Your Majesty, even stones move and have feelings when they're with Ibn Bakhit!"

The Sultan looked at him and smiled, and after inclining his head and looking askance to acknowledge the exaggeration, Anan went on, as if he had not heard: "You should ask the men. A few months ago, when we were in Ain Nabat, I heard, with my own ears, all of them say that the stones trembled, the horses bucked, and the brooks rose when I said 'Oof!'"

The Sultan laughed.

"Not only that, Your Majesty, in my time I made the deaf hear and the dead speak, and in Egypt I did the impossible!"

The Sultan knitted his brows and asked, in mock seriousness, "Is that all, Jesus son of Mary, or should I call you Moses son of . . ." He cackled and paused. "Really, Ibn Bakhit, what was Moses' father's name?"

Ibn Bakhit rolled his eyes like a cornered cat.

"Yes . . . Moses, son of . . . ?" They both laughed, and Abdallah al-Bakhit said in a conspiring tone, "It's better to stay away from the prophets, Your Majesty; they're too fussy. They won't stand for one word too much or too little!"

"You said it, Abu Badi."

The second reason the Sultan was sending Ibn Bakhit with Fanar was Omair: he wanted Ibn Bakhit to make Fanar forget Omair once and for all.

"He is my son, Abdallah," the Sultan counseled him. "I want him to be Sultan; I don't want him to end up droning, 'So say God and His prophet.' He needs to know what God and His prophet have said, but he has a thousand and one other things to take care of." He drew a quiet breath and paused. "But Omair and his kind only ruin a place and make people miserable, and their excuse is 'God and His prophet have said.' Here we know what we're doing; we don't need Omair and his kind ruling over us, and we don't want them treating us like cart horses, with blinders on our eyes and them yelling "Move!" "

Al-Bakhit did not need this sort of encouragement. He knew Omair's kind, and had been waiting for an opportunity to have his say about them. The Sultan knew Ibn Bakhit's thinking, and spoke to him with a smile.

"But be careful: don't bring up the subject of Omair. Talk about all of them, but don't mention him, because you know the saying: a boy is two-thirds his uncle. We don't want him to shy and throw us."

"You don't need to tell me, Your Majesty. Leave it to me and rest easy. As Suhaim says:

'She cradled me, closed her hand over me, her leg behind me
I swear by God that I saw her, and twenty more behind me.' "

The Sultan laughed delightedly, and his eyes twinkled.

"My boy, Abu Badi, it seems all you have is this 'behind'—are you afraid there's something behind this?"

Abdallah replied melodiously:

"If only I had met with a certain girl
To seek out our future family in ease."

The Sultan stroked his beard and thought.

"When you come back, we must marry you off—whether you want to or not, it's what we plan to do, we want to marry you, so that you can see what life is and put an end to your pain and sorrow."

Ibn Bakhit spoke, as if to himself:

"They give a sufferer a cure
And the price of the physic is illness."

A few days later the delegation left, to visit other lands and gain recognition for the new country emerging.

26

THE RAWDH PALACE WAS BUSIER THAN IT HAD ever been, receiving delegations and news from the provinces, and dealing with crises within its own walls.

Sultan Khureybit dispatched three of his oldest sons with a number of reliable men to see tribal chiefs, especially in the border areas, carrying gifts and invitations to visit Mooran. Within a few weeks the chiefs had flocked to Mooran with their families and attendants, and the city enjoyed an atmosphere of celebration and excitement it had not seen since the campaign of Wadi al-Faid. There were communal dances, races, contests and busy activity in the markets, where much of the Sultan's payments were spent buying provisions, convincing many that the hardships of recent years were now a thing of the past, even a distant memory.

The Sultan was at his best in the receptions and banquets attended by such crowds, and though Ibn Bakhit was absent and had left a certain void, there were others who animated the events with warmth and laughter. The Sultan ordered his men to do their utmost to make the guests feel welcome and to see to all their needs and desires. Even the horse stables, which the Sultan considered just as important and sacrosanct as the west wing of the palace, where only his closest friends were admitted, were opened up to guests. It was done grudgingly and gradually, but it was done. The master of the stables, Ibn Hanaihan, blamed the disappearance of some of the best and rarest horses on this move; when Ibn Mahyoub heard of the matter, he spoke testily to some of the guards, not caring if his words found their way to the Sultan.

"This is madness! We collected those horses with our hearts' blood, from all over creation, and put years and years into breeding and training them—and overnight they've sprouted wings and flown away!"

Othman al-Olayan was very optimistic; he assumed that the financial troubles had diminished or disappeared in the wake of the steady rains, rising foreign aid and the measures he himself had taken to increase revenues. He felt that matters left to the Sultan's whims or orders would inevitably lead to trouble; because "all merchants care about is their accounts: profit or loss. Yes, sometimes they give out of fear or ambition, but they expect something in return for their support, like anyone who sows seed. Whoever sows seed wants ten for one, but when the end of the year comes and the seed is on fallow ground, or birds have eaten it, they will surely wail and smite themselves and bellow, 'Friends, we are eating up our capital. We have lost everything, it's all gone, soon you'll see us go begging!'"

One night after the sheikhs of al-Huweiza had departed, Othman spoke to the Sultan.

"You know, Your Majesty, those bedouin are torn apart by greed: they're never satisfied. If they get used to this, God help us, we'll never be free of their jaws. Before they turn the world upside down on us, let's give them food and coffee and the same old talk we always gave them, because if we don't, and they think they have a right to this, we'll be no better than people who kill their own families . . ."

He would have gone on, but the Sultan laughed.

"Right now we need them, Othman. You can see for yourself that Ibn Madi and others are beckoning to them, sending them gifts and messengers and telling them, 'Come, take whatever you want, just take sides with us.'" He paused. "These days we have to be careful with them, because they've gotten more dangerous than jackals. They're casting their eyes all over, and listening and searching. If we're not totally with them, if we aren't generous with them and watchful of them, we'll end up like the ones we replaced: their hearts will be with us and their swords with someone else."

The Sultan sighed.

"And if I don't find those horses, Othman, we'll ride mules; these days your brother Abu Mansour doesn't want horses, he wants borders and obedience, and for people to be with us!"

"I'm with you, Your Majesty," replied Othman hastily, "but you should know: the eye sees far but the hand is short. I'm afraid that while we may have something in our hand today, tomorrow we won't."

"Trust in God, man."

"I trust Him, I trust Him," laughed Othman, and added cheerfully, "I just hope I'm not the only one!"

The Sultan was fairly confident that this round was nearing its end; after long discussions full of threats and shows of force, first with Hamilton, then with Butler, now everything had to be done to improve conditions and buy time, without formal announcement or consent, and to impose a new fait accompli without a confrontation or conflict.

Ibn Madi had a remnant of support in Awali, and could send in volunteers by ship to stir up some of the imams and tribal sheikhs, but once the treaty was signed, he was like an encircled cat, striking here and there, not to impose conditions or for physical gain, but to escape before the noose tightened and strangled him.

Ibn Olayan understood the Sultan's motives and the constraints that compelled him to make these moves, but could not comply with all his demands or please him. He told him, at the end of their discussion, "We may stretch our feet out as much as our carpet reaches, Your Majesty."

"Listen to me, Othman. You have traveled and seen much, but you should know: these days the carpet is like a flood: it rises and ebbs, and if we sink as much as we've risen, and rise as much as we've ebbed, we'll have nothing. You don't need to be told this."

The Sultan's thought, and the words he spoke, seemed to point to a certain meaning, but Othman did not see it. There was a long silence.

"What you say is true, Your Majesty, but this is a tricky world and

I am afraid things might get between us as they are between a fisherman and the fish: they give us space in order to grab us!"

"Trust in God, man, every problem has a solution."

And with the same solicitude he had shown the sheikhs of al-Huweiza, he now dealt with al-Ajrami and "the hereafter people," as he called them.

He wished Ibn Bakhit were with him now, especially in his meetings with al-Ajrami. Ibn Bakhit was able to play several roles, not just one, with the sheikh and others of his type. He helped his memory with chitchat, and offered evidence and arguments to support the Sultan's viewpoint; he could make him laugh, or impress him, and at times ask him innocent-seeming questions that were subtly sly, all of which was intended to make al-Ajrami look for "lucky Ibn Bakhit"—for *bakhit* meant "lucky"—as he affectionately called him.

In spite of the loss the Sultan felt in Ibn Bakhit's absence, he was not sorry, because the other sheikhs thought ill of "Haman," as they called him: he lay in ambush for them and shot down their lies. They did not want to be his enemies, yet they could not be his friends. They did not want to see or hear him; they wanted everyone to mind his own business.

"You know, my fine men," the Sultan told these sheikhs one night, "that jihad is not always fought with the blade of a sword. Jihad is also in speech, in deeds, and in one's own heart." He paused for a deep breath. "A sword by itself, seeking only booty, is not the sword of faith, and so is no different from the swords of rulers other than ourself.

"You," he went on in his earlier tone, "you men of wisdom and faith, you know and understand, and so you know that jihad in the soul is more important in people than jihad against foes."

He decided to leave it at this. The next day he had Mahyoub send gifts to the sheikhs, according to their respective eminence. Big sacks of rice and sugar, tins of fat, and sheep and horses were brought out of the palace to be distributed carefully under the watchful eyes—this was the Sultan's order—of Rafet Sheikh al-Sagha and Othman al-Olayan. Rafet wrote a heartfelt letter to accompany each gift, and the Sultan sealed each with his signet. Othman checked the final roster of deliveries and wrote "Approved," then affixed his signature. The gifts all reached the clergymen and imams of the mosques, who ascertained the value of the goods, read the letters, and experienced rare satisfaction.

While all this was in progress, the west wing of the palace was in a state of noisy chaos. In spite of the Sultan's concerns and overwork, the demands of both the mothers and children had mounted. They wanted banquets like the one given for Fanar, and a number of sons considered themselves of age, since the Sultan himself had sent them on business to visit tribal sheikhs. They had taken part in councils and danced the traditional *arda* with the adult men. This insistence came at a time of immense prosperity in the palaces, so that it seemed any demand was likely to be met, even welcomed. These new times were conducive to such demands and insistence upon them.

What made Fadda especially insistent was Khazael's absence in al-Huweiza. He had been gone a long time, and there were rumors; and then Fanar left.

She insisted that the Sultan have a banquet. With the consent of Ibn Hanaihan, chief of the palace's stablemen, she prepared a number of horses equal to the number of her male sons. While she knew the impossibility of his complying with what she wanted, she hoped that the Sultan would agree to have banquets for two or three of her sons, though Rakan was the only one of the sons Khureybit had sent to parley with a number of sheikhs.

Fadda was avid and unremitting, and worked deftly and secretly, but every one of the Sultan's wives was doing her utmost to achieve the same objective, or to frustrate Fadda's. Because palace tradition and the Sultan's views prevented the women from meeting or fighting, the servants, both men and women, did both of these on their behalf.

These months' battles in the west wing of the palace were so various and numerous that they affected everyone in one way or another, and everyone took sides. Even the Sultan, had his say, an oft-repeated one, after Mahyoub came to tell him that Ibn Oreifan and Ibn Farhan were asking an audience with him to discuss relieving them from further service; they had lost any semblance of authority or control as a result of the plots and feuds.

"God Almighty—God Almighty—are my own children and my prosperity my enemies?" He paused and spoke again, as if to himself. "We have prevailed over foreign and obscure peoples, and over our enemies, and against the closest people to us we can do nothing? We don't even know whether they're for or against us? Now a man must beware, and keep his eyes open!"

The Sultan was not slow to punish the servants severely: it was reported that the floggings began at dawn and were still going on well after noontime; a number of eunuchs were banished, in spite of protests, and Mayhoub came to the women with increasingly rough and impatient threats. All this, following the Sultan's outburst, served to calm the palace. Mollified, Oreifan and Nahi withdrew their resignations, and the Sultan promised them that he would be personally available to step in and put an end to the anarchy. It seemed that everyone had learned the lesson, but none of the women gave in or even let up. One of them might have begun before the other, and another might have started later, out of fear or an inclination to wait, but within a few weeks the palace was ablaze once again.

"Listen, Nahi," said Talleh al-Oreifan when Nahi refused to go back to work. He paused, almost forgetting that he had said a word to warn him, and after a long while began to talk to himself.

"Yes, he is a sultan—he commands and forbids, he says what goes and what doesn't—but all this is for us alone. As for the wives, God help us! They'll do whatever they can to hang on to him, and if two aren't enough for him . . ." He paused to laugh loudly, then asked, "Should I say it or not, Nahi?"

"Say it, Abu Jazi, look in your heart and proclaim!"

"Every one of them has her weapon: his Circassian girl is silky white, his Persian girl acts coy at night, his African girl dances like a sprite, his Arabian sings by candlelight, and his Georgian says, 'I'll find you somewhere nice and tight'!"

Nahi al-Farhan laughed until he nearly fell over.

"You're a poet, Abu Jazi!"

"By God, by God, by God, you can't live with these women without turning into a poet, or else you'd turn into a madman, or a sultan!"

Nahi backed up slightly and looked behind him, then looked at Talleh al-Oreifan seriously and asked, "You, Abu Jazi, what would you do if you were in his place?"

"Me?"

"Yes, you." He laughed. "Let us dream, my friend."

"If I were in his place, yes, if I were in his place, I'd have a Georgian night, then a Persian night, then a black-and-white night, with a Circassian or Turkish girl for good measure, and when I'd had my fill, I'd be a sleeping sultan!" He cackled. "Or I'd get like him: look right and go left, wink at one and sleep with another, and tell myself and everyone else that 'Only an infidel would reject God's gifts or not please His servants'!"

"And by the end of the night you'll have pleased one of them and infuriated a hundred!"

"Nahi, my friend, that kind of talk can cost you your head, but a man must say: if I were in his place, one of them would get covered, and rewarded with two or three children, thank God for that, but when a man goes mad no one can help him at all, there's only misery and death, fear and trembling; God save us from the calamities that are to come!"

The rumors and unrest in the palace were out of control, and could be ended only from within, and by one of the palace women, as long as the Sultan was too preoccupied to intervene.

Ummi Zahwa had not been in the palace for months, and much was made of her absence. Also, after switching to gray dresses she had gone back to wearing black. "Her love for Fanar," Tahany explained, "made her change styles." Lulua said, "Ibn Olayan has an army of women," and the palace midwife said that "a woman marries in order to give birth, even if it's to a goat—believe me." The Sultan said, "The Sheikha is a sheikha and will always be a sheikha."

Ummi Zahwa gathered most of the Sultan's wives to celebrate the day Turki, Watfa's son, was circumcised, although Watfa herself had invited only a few of them. Ummi Zahwa thumped the floor with her cane and said, "Girls—I have a few things to say!"

The general chatter and commotion did not die down, so Tahany, her voice as sharp as a bugle, shouted, "Be quiet and listen!"

When the noise continued unabated, the Sheikha pounded the floor with her cane and cried out, "She—she—she who listens, it will be far better for her!"

When silence fell so completely that the room felt empty, she went on.

"So Abu Mansour has given free rein, and all of you, like sheep, go running off as soon as the shepherd goes away. You remember that this palace is God's palace, and if any of you imagine that you're big, that you're in charge; if you say to yourselves, 'No one will cross me,' well, you're wrong. And not only that. If any of you wish to try us, and say 'I want things my way,' then we'll show you the way to the door. This is what I have to say, and it isn't just night gossip or women's talk. Just now I saw Abu Mansour, and with our heads together he told me, 'We don't want problems, we don't want headaches. Let every one of them look to her honor and raise her children.' That is all we have to say, and those of you who don't believe it will learn even better, the hard way."

These words fell on the women like rocks or hailstones. Fadda was the first to speak, to try to regain the initiative and change the mood of the gathering.

"You are tired, Auntie. You should rest."

"Listen, Fadda, you and everyone else," snapped Ummi Zahwa. "Abu Mansour said: 'I am tired of all their complaints. These women are too much. I have a thousand and one things on my mind, and they're all hanging on me and saying, 'This is my night, what about my children,' when I don't have any night or day either, nor do I favor any one of my children over another. To me they're all alike as grains of sand or drops of water. If any of these woman don't understand what I'm saying, and want to keep pushing, we know how to make her understand—and understand well!' "

The Sheikha looked all around, then shouted, "Tahany!"

Tahany squeezed through the crowd and came forward.

"Abu Mansour is dining with us this evening," said the Sheikha sharply, "and you sit here gossiping? God blacken your face! Now march in front of me!"

The anarchy might have passed away for a time and reappeared later on had it not been for a number of occurrences at the palace.

Lulua, Princess Watfa's servant, was found murdered near the stables with blue marks on her body. Some said that she had been tortured before being killed, perhaps because she had resisted the killer, or perhaps for some other reason. Others said that the marks were symptoms of poisoning, and some of the women whispered that the poison had been meant for Watfa, but by some strange chance, for unknown reasons, Lulua had taken the poison and died.

This incident might have passed without consequences, or with only limited consequences, had not related incidents befallen: the Sultan guessed that Fadda was behind the palace troubles, and wanted to punish her, and so stayed away from her rooms for weeks, residing instead in Watfa's suite. He did come and go to other suites some nights, but he was with Watfa the day Lulua was killed, and it was said that he had flattered Lulua and asked her if there was anything she wanted. Three maidservants said so. Then it was reported that the poison had been meant for the Sultan, not Watfa or Lulua. What further complicated matters was the fact that two eunuchs, Ghureifi and Tamam, who were close to Lulua, were slain three days later, in the palm groves in the extreme northwest of the city. People reported hearing gunshots late the night before, and there was a great deal of confusion over what exactly had happened. Of course, Ibn Madi's name was mentioned, as were others, which led the Sultan to head for Rehaiba to spend a few days, which turned into weeks. In the meantime, Ibn Bakhit returned.

With Ibn Bakhit's return, everyone in the palace remembered Yamama and her story, so there was no end of curiosity and whispering, particularly since the Sultan went back to the Rawdh Palace (and with him bustle and activity returned to the palace) to welcome the travelers and find out what had happened on their trip, which had ended up lasting about two and a half months and covering several countries.

A number of the Sultan's private guards said that the eastern half of the encampment had been set aside for His Majesty, to serve as his court, and a place for him to reside and sleep. This was said to be for security reasons, and because the Sultan was still angry and wanted to punish the whole palace. It was also said that the many projects that had piled up in this period made him decide to stay with his men.

Ummi Zahwa visited the Sultan in his majlis, and Tahany confided to some of her friends, rather uneasily, that the Sheikha had given him important news. When the friends tried to get details, she replied in a barely audible whisper that "seeing with one's own eyes was better than hearing." Mahyoub had long meetings for two days' running with Ibn Oreifan and Nahi. The servants who poured their coffee, or saw the men as they came out, said that they were all smiling broadly.

Everyone had been worried about Fanar, remembering how he'd looked when Zaina died, before he'd left, so they were surprised to see how healthy and vigorous he was. His sorrow had not completely left him, but at certain moments he seemed happy. He spent the first day back alone with his father; even Abdallah al-Bakhit was not with them. Two of the Sultan's guards said that the Sultan and Fanar, late that night, instead of retiring to the west wing of the palace, sent for Mudi to come to the Sultan's majlis on the east side, and that she spent an hour or more with them before leaving.

In the days that followed, Fanar went back to the west wing and received visitors. He seemed back to normal, though a little reserved. His answer to those who asked was that the visit had been useful and he had seen much. Qatma said that before long the prince would leave the palace for a residence of his own, and everyone who heard her say so put his own construction on this.

Hamilton was not among those who came back. The Sultan asked Fanar why and was told that the trip had been exhausting; it had been Hamilton's wish to spend two weeks with his family in Wales, and would delay no longer than that.

The only one still unaccounted for was Khazael.

"Don't worry," said the Sultan when asked what was new in al-Huweiza. "Everything is fine—Abu Mishael is there."

It seemed to most people that stability had come. This new era was different from times past; there were no surprises. The palace immersed itself in noise and whispers and waiting.

27

THE SULTAN WAS DELIGHTED TO SEE FANAR AND showered him with attention, but was still a little uneasy: "Sahib isn't letting our joy be complete. He has to see those people on his own and talk to them and gossip with them. When he's made his deal with them, he comes back here and says, 'This is what we're going to do.'" Even so, the Sultan did not look on Hamilton's delay as he had in past times, or with anger. He told Ibn Bakhit, who was telling him stories about his wondrous travels, and about how Sahib had improved with time. "Our Sahib, Abu Badi, is not as he was; this is a friend we can rely on!"

Ibn Bakhit tried to make him appreciate Sahib's importance, especially in England, how he behaved there, and how others looked upon him.

"He's a sheikh among his own kind," smiled the Sultan, "and if they hadn't wanted to please us, and didn't know our worth, they would have sent us people you wouldn't have given a coin for."

"As God is my witness, Your Majesty, he is a fine man, and a patient one." Ibn Bakhit laughed and smacked his lips. "After the parties
and the banquets and all the running around, Fanar said to the two of
us, 'Come on, if you aren't tired, let's go here and there. We owe it to
ourselves to have a look around, to have some fun and relaxation.'"

He paused a moment, remembering, then added: "He dragged us
everywhere! I think that Fanar now is better than he was before. You
can rely on him, and that's not only my opinion, it's Sahib's, too."

Hamilton was soon back. He seemed to think that a great deal had
been hanging on his return.

"My son," the Sultan counseled Fanar, "I don't want you to part
from him. He likes you, and you understand him. I want you to find
out what his big secret is, because the English can never come out and
tell you such things themselves unless they know . . ." He laughed.
"Let us try, and then we'll see if we got anywhere or not."

"Yes, Father," replied Fanar eagerly, "he's one of them, but he loves
Mooran just as it is . . ." He looked around and whispered, though he
seemed hesitant, "He told me everything. He said, 'Mooran could be
a bigger and more important country, but it has to know how to act,
how to be.'"

"Those words have a thousand and one meanings, my boy, and we
have to wait and see which meaning is the true one."

"Your Majesty," said Hamilton to the Sultan when they were alone,
"I would love to talk to you freely and tell you my thoughts and opinions on a number of issues, and hope that you have the time and inclination to hear them."

The Sultan gazed at him, wondering what this introduction might
be leading up to. Hamilton was wary of that look and went no further.

"My friend," said the Sultan, "we are always looking for advice. We
like it when people come and tell us what to do."

There was a short silence, as if Hamilton were not sure how to
begin.

"I don't want to speak as an Englishman but as a friend, and it has
nothing to do with justifying the treaty that is in effect. I want to talk
about thoughts and impressions of the future, and clear up a few
things—"

"And we want to listen to you," interrupted the Sultan.

"Before, things were so difficult and confused. It was hard for you,
for England and for me personally. I came here, Your Majesty, to be

useful, and because I think this region has a historic mission. We had many differences of opinion and had many arguments, because we had differing views about the role Mooran would play and what its future would be. Perhaps, Your Majesty, you remember how I went away for a time and even thought of secluding myself, of staying in England for good. I thought of giving up politics for some other line of work. I resisted, and overcame my misgivings, not allowing my personal feelings to affect my decision. All this was to reach a balance, a formula that accommodated what we wanted and what was possible."

The Sultan knew how to raise his voice above others', and how to be the sole speaker at times, especially when he was worried about the "madmen," as he called those who knew how to stir men up and move them to rage and violence. He also knew how to listen, how to make others do the talking.

"By God," he said to Hamilton, "I swear, for a long time I have wanted you to open your heart and speak freely . . ." He paused and added in a different tone, "As we used to say, your best friend is always the most truthful."

"Politics is not a matter of personal wishes," Hamilton went on, as if he had not heard, "nor of the ideas students learn at university. Politics is something else entirely: a struggle among powers, interests, ambitions and possibilities, which seems at times almost impossibly complex and convoluted, even hopelessly so, particularly where isolated and distant individuals, countries and even whole peoples are concerned."

He sighed and shook his head.

"There, in London, paths cross, Your Majesty, and where paths cross, one finds information, guesses and possibilities, and the men who do the debating and deciding. An outsider such as myself can only listen for echoes, to await developments, and anticipate collisions." He laughed bitterly. "To you I was hard to understand. Personally, I wanted only to escape when policy was being decided. By way of a web of complex and intermingled relations, you were demanding that I answer questions I could not answer, and that I take positions on issues I had nothing to do with. That embarrassed me and rendered me unable to answer or act. That is why I was silent and why I ran away."

He laughed again, but not the same way, and spoke triumphantly.

"Now, after all these years, I can speak my mind to Your Majesty on a number of issues, with more confidence, because what I say will be possible and can be implemented!"

The Sultan leaned toward him with a look of interest, and spoke, blazing with interest.

"Yes, by God, Sahib, let us leave the past behind us—that's all done and dead. What I want to talk about with you is the present and what comes after."

Hamilton threw the Sultan a provocative look, as if in answer to his gaze.

"The problem in the past, Your Majesty, was not Mooran or Ibn Madi or anyone else. For Britain the problem was much bigger and more complicated than that." He shook his head. "Great powers, Your Majesty, have so many ties and commitments, and so deal with others according to a logic very different from that employed by a country which has a single problem in one specific place and needs to deal with only that problem."

He cleared his throat and spoke in a refined tone.

"Now, of course, we cannot get into all the negotiations, though it must be pointed out that Britain was embarrassed and perplexed by its friends and enemies alike, because we did not know what action to take—whom to please and whom to anger. But now that everything is settled, we can talk, make agreements and get what we want."

It was in this meeting, with much maneuvering, connivance, and bad faith on both sides, that the Sultan understood he must furl up his flags of battle, raid and annexation. The principal players had reached agreement without the smaller players, leaving the small nothing to play with but wasted time; they might play without the knowledge of the principal players, but then only to record a few points or improve their positions. The Sultan also understood that Britain had other sons who played in yet other arenas, who had their own differences of opinion, which could put Britain as well as its friends in a plight.

While most of their discussion was obvious, not all of it was specific, and a great deal of effort and ingenuity was required to settle on details. After a long night of debate, inquiry, and exchange of ideas, the Sultan said, "No one is laying blame, Sahib, nor is anyone able to do everything he'd like, but you must know that your people did not deal with us fairly."

Khureybit shook his head and smiled sadly, perhaps reminiscing.

"Whenever they wanted anything of us, we told them, 'Fine, God bless you, whatever you want.' A year came, a year went, and when we met again, 'Come, friends, now it's time to do the things we decided upon,' but, as fate would have it, no one remembers. The ones we talked to, who had been here, turned into salt and dissolved; no one knew where they were now or why we never saw them again. So we began all over again; you know how it went."

After several days and nights of discussions and questions, in which Fanar usually participated, with some sessions also attended by Ibn Olayan, Yunis, Bassiuni and Sheikh al-Sagha, it became clear to the Sultan that he could no longer provoke Britain's friends, especially those on the borders of al-Huweiza; and he would have to set his internal affairs in order. In return, Britain promised him financial and political support, and Ibn Madi would belong to history.

This the Sultan knew; he had tacitly agreed to it with Butler after pretending to be angry at first, and saying that the British had tricked and abandoned him, just as they had tricked and abandoned Ibn Madi. He tried to remind Hamilton of the battle of Wadi al-Faid, how his forces had not held back; they might have continued their march and raised the banner of Islam had not Britain blocked his way. He was angry and pretended embarrassment too, for he did not know what to do or what to tell his troops, or his commanders, all of whom had borne so much and waited so long for the right moment to resume their march. Hamilton knew as well as the Sultan the futility of reopening this topic.

"As I mentioned to Your Majesty a few days ago," Hamilton said, with Fanar there and listening, "that matter was decided in London, and we haven't the right, or the ability, to change the outcome."

"It is not your fault, Sahib," said the Sultan sharply, "I don't mean you, I mean your people back there, because our people, the merchants of Mooran, agree to terms. At the end of the day, they say, our only condition is fairness." He paused before adding, sadly, "It's our fault. From the day we made peace with one another, from the first time we shook hands, we said, 'These are our terms, such and such'; only our goodness, and our trust in our friends, brought us to these entanglements, and now, 'Come, Khureybit, explain to the people, soothe them, tell them, Our People, the English, have dealt with us as you see, and we can say nothing!' "

"Your Majesty," said Hamilton in a deep voice, "I don't want to repeat in your hearing what I have said and done, in London, for this country which I love so much, of which I feel a part. If I did that I'd be a cheat. All I want is to please you."

The Sultan spoke sadly. "It isn't your fault at all, Sahib, and we are grateful for all your services and all the favors you've done—"

Hamilton did not let the Sultan finish, but cut in confidently. "The important thing, Your Majesty, at this delicate point in the balance of power between nations, is that the Sultanate be a strong and influential country; that is far preferable to being large and weak!" He nodded and spoke to himself. "Yes, to be a strong country, and ready to profit from international developments . . ." His tone changed. "Just as Mooran's fortunes have changed in past years, benefiting from developments in this region, this country will have other chances, and then many things can be reconsidered, Your Majesty.

"The important thing now, Your Majesty," he continued in his previous tone, "is that we all work to build a strong country, stronger than any other in the region. A strong country can impose its own terms. As you know, Your Majesty."

The Sultan seemed sad and thoughtful. He did not want to give in so easily, or make his consent explicit. He spoke as if to himself. "What you say is true, Sahib. All sorrows have a thousand solutions." He smiled, more at Fanar than at Hamilton, and added, "As we say:

> 'Had I put out the fire of conscience in my heart
> I would have wished he had appeared to me
> For all that is past and gone and lost
> Is now like the sound of wind in the dark night
> My only compensation is a memory, and my sorrow for them
> Wherever I go; but all troubles are followed by ease
> And all sorrows have a thousand solutions.'

"Yes, and I hope you are listening, Fanar: 'All troubles are followed by ease.' God is good."

The Sultan smiled as he chanted the verses, and looked fixedly at Fanar to help impart their meaning. Hamilton, too, smiled and nodded his head to show that he understood and was enjoying the poetry. There was a lengthy silence.

"The way I see it, Your Majesty," Hamilton then said, "the most important thing now is how to exert actual control over Awali, how it can be made into an organic part of Mooran, because the final elimination of Ibn Madi is linked to your ability to exert domestic control." After a pause his tone changed. "I allow myself to say, Your Majesty, insofar as I know your country extremely well, and I know al-Huweiza and Awali, that the basic problem is our winning over the people of Awali. The people there think of themselves as advanced, compared to Mooran and al-Huweiza. They are city people, and you know that controlling cities is much harder than controlling the desert folk."

"If the people there have nothing left to do with Ibn Madi, then it is up to us to deal with him and with Awali, Sahib—don't give it another thought."

"I'm not worried about you, Your Majesty. The whole outside world speaks now of nothing but Awali. Ibn Madi may be moving and making contacts, and Britain may have decided not to notice some of his movements and contacts, but still there are three fundamental problems: first, how to win over the people there; second, Britain is committed to solving the Ibn Madi problem, and will either abandon him completely or find some other appropriate action. And the last point is, how can the Sultanate return to their cages the small powers freed in order to help defeat her enemies? If these powers find no one to fight, they will turn on each other, and will fight and destroy before they can be destroyed or commit suicide!"

He nodded and looked intently at Fanar.

"I hope His Highness Prince Fanar understands this observation, how we can deal with the situation of Ibn Omair, Ibn Mishaan, Ibn Mayyah and others of that sort? I don't mean to provoke, and I mean no disrespect, but that sort of person represents a future threat to the Sultanate."

"They are our own people," said the Sultan, feeling challenged, "and we know them best. But what do you think of other people?"

For a moment Hamilton was nonplussed. He looked at Fanar before replying.

"As I told Your Majesty, as long as the Sultanate of Mooran abides by the treaty, and initiates no conflict with any of His Britannic Majesty's allies, every issue you raise will be met with all possible understanding and support."

After a series of long silences, with the Sultan looking convinced, though neither resigned nor approving, Hamilton carefully chose his moment to speak.

"We have a thinker we are very proud of, Your Majesty, who had a wise saying about building a nation and controlling people, and he had a solution for situations like Awali, if you would care to—"

The Sultan laughed like a child, and when he had sobered himself, said, "As I told you a few days ago, Sahib, we are seeking advice, and will reward it with a camel. Come on then—what did the learned man say?"

Hamilton smiled.

"He said, Your Majesty, 'Whoever seizes territories and wishes to keep them must always have two essential things in mind: the elimination of the previous ruling family, and the absence of substantial change in the laws or taxes of those territories; only in this way may two countries speedily become one.'"

The Sultan pressed his lips together and nodded, as if running Hamilton's words through his mind again.

"And on the same subject, Your Majesty, he also said, 'In the interest of holding new territories, the best and securest means is for the new ruler to establish his capital in the new territories; this decision will render his possession more secure.'"

In this meeting the Sultan recalled what Hamilton had said a second and a third time; it seemed to him that he knew this speech, only not so clearly, and that he applied some of these ideas though not all of them. He spoke to Hamilton softly, as if to himself. "That is what your man said. We have done it. We stayed in Awali for months and months, and told the people, 'Keep at your jobs, look after yourselves, good people; all we want is that you know a new state has arisen, and that Ibn Madi is gone forever.'"

He paused and added forcefully, "As you must know, Abu Mishael—our son Khazael—has spent months, if not a year, by now, in al-Huweiza, getting to know the people and living with them. We have not asked him to return, and he has not come!"

28

THE SULTAN WAS NOT SLOW TO SEE THE POSSI-
bilities of this era. The first thing he did was
to send some gifts to al-Ajrami: a golden
Koran he had recently received from India, a large quantity of rare
perfumes, a wonderful mare, and much talked about in recent weeks,
and a sumptuous wardrobe. And he did not forget to include a large
sum of money.

Al-Ajrami was surprised at the delivery of these gifts, and almost
suspicious of the Sultan's motives. He remembered what had happened to his predecessor, Muhammad al-Alqawi, a few years before.
For al-Alqawi had been deluged with gifts from the Sultan and was
murdered only days afterward on his way to dawn prayers. Despite
the Sultan's grief, there were persistent rumors that he had plotted the
murder. So despite Abdallah al-Bakhit's two visits in one week, his
doubts remained. The purpose of the first visit was to tell al-Ajrami
about everything he had seen and done on his journey, especially the

welfare of the Muslims in the countries he visited: the mosques he saw in Turkey, the call to prayer that sounded five times a day, people scurrying to prayer; how they prayed and prolonged their prayers, and their intense yearning to visit the holy places.

When Ibn Bakhit spoke, he knew how to excite the sheikh's surprise and sense of wonder; nor did he forget to relate some of the uncommon things that had happened to him here and there, and to dwell upon natural wonders: the cold, the summer rains, greenery as far as the eye could see, the wide rivers that surged along all year long. He nearly told him about the women in the streets and restaurants and everywhere else he visited; he nearly told him about the beauty he had seen: blond hair, pale complexions, bare arms and legs, and blue eyes whose like a man would never see except in Paradise. He nearly said all this, but checked himself. Then he mentioned the mission the Sultan had sent him on, and returned once more to the atmosphere of piety he had felt.

At the close of the first meeting, Ibn Bakhit said jokingly, "Dear Sheikh, someday you must visit those countries, because hearing about them is nothing compared to seeing them!"

"God forbid! God forbid, Ibn Bakhit, that you would send me, at the end of my days, to the abode of the infidels!"

"To increase your faith, dear Sheikh, to appreciate the grace of God we enjoy!"

"Leave me on my own land, Ibn Bakhit; if the eye strays, the heart may stray, too." He paused and spoke as if to himself. "God has fixed our mind and our faith."

Ibn Bakhit's second visit to Sheikh al-Ajrami came one day after a visit by a number of the Sultan's men, among them Ibn Olayan and Mahyoub. It seemed, from this visit and what preceded it, that the visit had a direct purpose. That is what al-Ajrami thought, and furthermore he began to mutter about this misgiving in the first hours before noon, for the news that he heard in the late morning that day, that a delegation from the palace would come to visit him, made him wonder and even worry. "What does Khureybit want? What do these gifts and this attention mean? Who would come, and what will happen?"

Just as had happened in many other instances, Othman al-Olayan whispered into Mahyoub's ear and winked at him, signaling him not to bring up the subject too quickly or directly; they would have to chat about a few general topics until the right moment, and then they would bring it up. Despite this agreement, barely had they drunk a cup of tea before Ibn Olayan laughed, and, once silence had fallen, spoke up. "If a man has a stone in his mouth, dear Sheikh, he cannot speak a word until he has spit it out."

Al-Ajrami's reply was both friendly and firm. "Yes, sir, as we say, the bearer of bad tidings is not to blame."

Al-Ajrami was ready for anything. His fiery disposition and his stubbornness made most people think him a hard person, but when he spoke, especially with enemies, he was not only harsh and mocking but inflammatory. Now, receiving the Sultan's men, he was confident that they had something to say, or something to demand, and he replied that way to reassure them, and to give himself a strong position if he wanted to resist.

"Shall I speak or you?" Olayan asked Mahyoub.

"Yes, respected sir," smiled Mahoub, to prepare al-Ajrami, "I must say, I wish all our tasks, all our demands, were like the present one from Abu Mishael!"

"Please proceed," said al-Ajrami sharply, with no trace of warmth this time.

Olayan rubbed his hands and spoke up. "His Majesty has asked us to come to you and offer you his compliments, to offer you his best wishes and wish you good health, and he has asked us to inform you that he wants to be part of your family—that he wants your daughter!"

This request took al-Ajrami by surprise. He looked around more than once at the men waiting to hear his answer, and fell silent. He had two unmarried daughters; the elder was forty years old or a little more, the child of his first wife, and she had not only despaired of marriage but had taken over the house and children, so that no one thought any more of asking for her hand. She was hurt and threatened whenever conversation turned, not only to the thought of her own marriage, but to anyone's marriage. The second daughter, from his second-to-last wife, was barely fourteen, and he still thought of her as a child, especially the way her beauty, features, and petite build reminded him of her mother. Did the Sultan want the older or the younger? Was either ready for marriage?

He came close to saying a single word to end the discussion; he almost said, "I have no daughters to marry off," but he thought of the consequences of that answer, and recalled the gifts he had recently been given, especially the mare that became the talk of Mooran after Mashhour, his middle son, rode her prancing through the markets of the city. Her unborn foals were already being discussed and bid upon, and men competed for the right to her first and second offspring. The sheikh scolded himself for acting hastily, especially with the money the Sultan had sent: he had given all of it to his oldest son, Mishael. And Mishael, who at first seemed angry because Mashhour had taken the mare, was quick to send the money with two merchants, who traveled to Egypt to buy him a flock of sheep, "and a few head of horses." Mishael sent a shepherd along to bring his animals back by way of Gaza.

The sheikh did not know how much time passed, how long he was silent, as these images and thoughts passed through his mind. He now lifted his eyes to his waiting guests and spoke plaintively.

"Give my warm regards to Abu Mansour, and tell him that Abu Mishael will visit him within two days. God willing, all will be well."

Mahyoub nearly asked for clarification, for something specific, because he wanted to report a clear-cut answer to the Sultan, but Olayan signaled him not to do so. It was preferable and more seemly to give the father a chance, not to refuse, but to justify his acceptance, to feel that he was free to say yes or no.

"The ancients, Abu Mishael," said Olayan as they were taking their leave, "used to say, 'A word spoken from the heart arrives in the heart; a word from the tongue is stopped by the ear.' God is our witness that our words have come from the heart." He smiled and glanced at Mahyoub. "And it isn't our word, Abu Mishael, it is His Majesty's. As I told you, we are only messengers, and we have done what we came to do!"

"Trust in God, my friend," said al-Ajrami, not allowing his gaze to settle anywhere.

Between the delegation's visit to al-Ajrami and its return, messengers informed the Sultan that al-Ajrami had two daughters, not one, as the palace midwife had reported when she was asked. They said that the elder of the sisters was old, but did not say whether she had been born before the flood that had devastated al-Arid, or a year later, but they mentioned that al-Ajrami had got married two or three years before the flood, that his first child had died, much to al-Ajrami's grief, and that the next baby was a girl; and this must be the one.

The Sultan lost no time. He sent investigators to question the midwife, Ummi Zahwa and other women, and when he was assured that al-Ajrami had two girls at home, he felt that he had blundered by not giving a name or being specific.

"That bitch Warida," he told his close friends, "thinks that the babies she delivered are the only people in the world! She has no idea that before Abraham there was Noah, and before Noah there was Adam." He shook his head sadly, then shouted, "Summon Ibn Bakhit! He'll write us an edict."

Abdallah al-Bakhit arrived with bloodshot eyes, stumbling slightly. He entered and greeted them, drowsily and quietly. The Sultan ordered coffee for him and asked pleasantly, "It seems, Abdallah, that you did not sleep well?"

"You kept us up until dawn," replied Abdallah testily, "then you went and slept, and we counted the stars! When we dozed off, you shouted, 'Where is so-and-so?! We were like wolves, with one eye open and the other idle or asleep."

"Bring coffee for Abu Badi!"

After several rounds of coffee Ibn Bakhit woke up completely, and the Sultan asked everyone then in the majlis to leave him alone with Ibn Bakhit.

"We have a problem, Abdallah," he said in a voice full of disquiet, "and you are the only one we can turn to!"

"Tell me, Your Majesty!"

Khureybit explained how he had sent Olayan, Mahyoub and some of his men to al-Ajrami to seek his daughter's hand; it was the chance of a lifetime for al-Ajrami to marry off his elder daughter, whose age was not known. Had she been born before the great al-Arid flood, or one or two years after it? The Sultan added that when he had proposed a marriage with a member of al-Ajrami's family, he had been thinking of the daughter Warida described to him, as she was young and beautiful.

Ibn Bakhit pretended to be defeated in most battles where the Sultan was his opponent, but now was his chance to play with the Sultan, to provoke him. He chanted:

"Beware of older women if they seek you in marriage
Her best half is that which is past.

"Oh, yes, that which is past, as Ibn Qataiba used to say in his *Book of Women,* but if you want my opinion, Your Majesty, an older and more experienced woman is preferable to a young one. A young woman doesn't let a man sleep, and you know that a sleepless man gets bloodshot eyes, and when they wake him before he's had adequate sleep, he just becomes a misery to himself and everyone else!"

"Shame on you, we called you here to give advice, and you offer only the vice!"

"I swear by God," said Ibn Bakhit solemnly, "that al-Ajrami, Abu Mishael, is dear to me, and when a friend is valued, so is his family. His elder daughter wants to get married—she wants a party. God created her the same way he created everybody else. It would be a shame for her to come into this world and leave it without knowing a man. Almighty God will judge the men of Mooran if they leave her to die unmarried."

"Listen, Ibn Bakhit: We have enough problems now, and don't want any more. We have sent for you because we need your cooperation, so no more humor, please. Be serious."

Ibn Bakhit laughed delightedly and said:

"If you ask me about women, I
Am an expert in women's things, a doctor
If a man's head is scarred or his money spent
He has no hope of their love
They see riches and reach for them
But O, to see them in their prime!"

The Sultan smiled.

"That's enough of that, Abdallah. Now we need a solution."

"Do you want Abu Moussa's solution or Amrou bin al-As's, Your Majesty?"

"I want al-Ajrami to stay one of us. If he says, 'The old one,' and I say 'No,' he'll never speak to me again, and I don't want that."

"So. Abu Mansour wants the young one?"

"Yes, my good man, this is what needs to be solved!"
"The poet said:

'Raindrops almost rend her skin
When her delicate skin is washed in water
Even if she wore a dress of pure roses
Her skin would shame the rose petals
The finest silk would bruise her
She would complain to her slaves of the weight of a jewel
Be very careful of her cheeks
Bruise them with no more than a blush.'"

"Listen, Abdallah, we've made a mistake by hauling you out of your bed, but by God if you keep giving us this poetry, and 'the poet said,' and God knows what else, you are going to marry the old daughter." The Sultan laughed. "Remember, before you went away, we told you in all seriousness that we were going to marry you off, whether you liked it or not? Now I'll tell al-Ajrami, 'Abu Mishael, people here want to marry off Ibn Bakhit and they heard you had a daughter his age, and he's too shy to talk to you. I don't want you to refuse, Abu Mishael; let's start the ceremony.'"

Abdallah tried to laugh, but his mouth would not oblige him. He realized that sultans could do anything, even force a person to get married. He shifted in his seat.

"Whatever Abu Mansour wants is what I will do," he said. "The Prophet, peace and blessings upon him, said, 'Amuse your hearts for hour after hour, because when hearts are tired, they go blind.' I hadn't even fallen asleep, Your Majesty, and that is the truth, when the muezzin began his call to prayer, and I said to myself, 'Sleep, you have an hour,' but the men came and said, 'Get up, get up and hurry, His Majesty wants you.' I got up and came, not knowing what was going on, and you, Your Majesty, without even a greeting, say, 'This is what I want,' and I was half asleep, and all that I could come up with was poetry and nonsense."

The Sultan called for more coffee.

Toward the end of their meeting, Abdallah al-Bakhit said, "Trust in God, Your Majesty, and you'll get what you want."

The next day, before Ibn Bakhit visited al-Ajrami, he asked Warida

and some of the other palace women about the name and age of the
girl, and whether she had any sisters. Warida was frightened and said
she knew only that Najma was old enough to marry. Then she remembered Hafiza and said that Hafiza was seven years old, or perhaps
younger. When Ummi Zahwa was asked, she replied through Surour:
"Al-Ajrami has only one daughter from his wife Moza, named
Najma, and she is the only one of marriageable age."

During the visit, which Ibn Bakhit did his best to make cordial, an
extension of his previous visit, he talked about all sorts of unrelated
subjects, and to reassure al-Ajrami, he chose a moment after a short
lull and said, "Do you remember, dear Sheikh, what Qais bin Duraih
said?"

Al-Ajrami shook his head.

> " 'If a man hides love from his conscience
> He will die knowing no conscience
> But God will speak, though the soul divulged nothing
> Of your secret, though questioners are many.'

"And Muslim ibn Qataiba said, 'Don't seek what you need from
one of three: not from the liar, because he makes things seem close
when they are far away, and far when they are near; not the simpleton,
because he'll harm you in his efforts to help. And stay away from a
man who owes something to others, because he'll make you his
collateral!' "

Al-Ajrami smiled because he thought what Ibn Bakhit was saying
was remarkable, and he knew that this visit had something to do with
yesterday's, so kept looking happy, expectant and somewhat quizzical. He wanted to know what the Sultan wanted. When he felt ready,
he spoke.

"Abdallah, I know that you're a learned man above all else, even
more than you are one of the Sultan's group. I have to tell you something I've never told anyone else. Our ancestors said: 'Keep the distance from a sultan that you would from a lion, because he'll haunt
you whether you obey or cross him.' Now I want to listen to you."

"You and I are the same, Abu Mishael . . . speak."

When Abu Mishael remained silent, Ibn Bakhit smiled, sighed and
spoke.

"Abu Mishael, we drag our capital around with us wherever we go, wherever we come—it's all we have . . ." He pointed to his head and his chest, and went on. "But this is not enough. We have to remember the times we live in. True, we don't want to become sultans, but we can't make enemies of sultans, because if a sultan wants to—"

"Abu Badi," said al-Ajrami testily, "this is not a question of Najma—Najma is his. I'm only afraid that someday soon the infidels will make it here and he'll tell me, 'Come, Abu Mishael, render an opinion,' and that's what I can do!"

Ibn Bakhit, who kept repeating Najma's name, in order to distinguish her from her elder sister, Naima, and her younger sister, Hafiza, seemed skeptical at his quick assent, and he got the names mixed up again. He spoke to get their conversation back on course.

"I must tell you, Abu Mishael. His Majesty told me, 'We wish to marry ourself into Sheikh al-Ajrami's family, we want to ask for the hand of his daughter Najma, the daughter of the late Moza.' I told him, 'May it be for the best, Your Majesty, may it be a happy and fruitful match, for good things are for good people, and good people are for good things.' "

"Is that all there is, Abdallah?"

"As far as I know, Abu Mishael, he wants to marry into your family, and that's everything."

"If that's all, then it's in God's hands. Najma is his. Destiny rules the world."

The huge celebrations for the Sultan's wedding were so splendid that no one could help but swap stories about them. The Sultan wanted the occasion to express the Sultanate's new power and luxury; he also wanted to teach the Rawdh Palace women a lesson. He wanted to show that the woman closest and dearest to him would be the meekest and most obedient. The Sultan also wanted to provoke Fanar, indirectly; to induce him into thinking that another marriage would be a very easy thing, something he had to consider, and carry out as soon as possible. To torment himself, to remain a widower at his age, to think that Zaina was the beginning and end of all creation, meant that his past life in Ain Fadda had been his ruin. The Sultan had to try his best to save the boy, but at the right time.

Olayan and Abdallah Bakhit both attended the wedding parties but left early, unnoticed by anyone. They were used to doing this when they felt in need of special "fuel" that they were especially used to in other places where they dined.

"What do you think of al-Ajrami's daughter?" Olayan asked Abdallah al-Bakhit.

Ibn Bakhit laughed loudly and shook his head.

"Does God allow this, Abu Badi?" Olayan went on. "We've gone to market and sold and bought, but we don't know what we've sold or bought!"

He tapped his glass against Ibn Bakhit's.

"You'll see, some day, when God judges us, he'll ask us 'What have you sold and what have you bought?' and sentence us to a thousand lashes, because we've never been lashed. He'll say, 'You asked for it, you bastards; whoever doesn't assist at the birth of a goat will get a kid!' You had no business selling a fish you hadn't caught yet!'"

Ibn Bakhit shook his head sadly, then lifted his eyes to Othman's.

"But your friend didn't let her be. She shouted at Warida, 'Come, my lady, this is the girl we wore ourselves out to get for His Majesty! What's she like? Tall, short, beautiful? Tell me!'"

"And?"

"She said much, my friend, and I understood from the two of them more or less what al-Mada'ini once said—I'll tell you what this old man said, quoting Umru al-Qais after sending a woman to see another woman on his behalf, for her to describe her to him, and she said, 'May you never be cursed, O King! Her hair is like the tail of triumphant horses; when she spreads it, you would think it bunches of grapes; beneath it, a forehead like a polished mirror, and underneath this forehead two lovely eyes that never knew force or constraint, white as the purest milk and black as the blackest night; and between them a nose like a polished sword blade, neither long nor short, flanked by rosy cheeks and pearly-white skin; a mouth like a slice of pomegranate with teeth like rows of pearls and a writhing and sweet tongue guided by a broad mind and a nimble wit; the softest lips with breath like honey; a slender neck, rounded upper arms as pure as pearl or coral, forearms and open palms, slender fingers like beaten silver; firm breasts and tapering curves leading to a full hip and buttocks prominent whether she sat or stood or slept. These are supported by thighs as round as her middle, curving legs, and slender feet as shapely as spearheads—God bless their smallness and shapeliness, their grace in carrying all above! There is more, O King, which I leave to your imagination.'"

Othman al-Olayan was able to grasp little of this torrent of speech, which Ibn Bakhit clearly seemed to have known by heart for long years and recited unnumbered times.

"Ibn Bakhit," he sighed, "God created you to bamboozle people by speaking neither good nor evil!"

"All this talk of mine and none of it pleased you?"

"We asked you, my friend, is she pretty? Is she worth all the trouble and heartache, or not?"

"Not!" cackled Ibn Bakhit, then added: "Look at al-Ajrami: he's black and African-looking, a flat-lipped midget; his nose is like a bell, his eyes are crooked as a street in the Jewish quarter. He looks like a grouse looking for water. We have not seen the mother, may she rest in peace, but she gave birth and said, 'Good riddance.' You can figure the rest out for yourself, learned man."

"You mean your description of her is worthless?"

"All poets are tempters. Instead of rejoicing in what God has created, they create images and descriptions, rejoice and get lost in them, and want us to rejoice with them. The result is that they have nothing to celebrate, but lose nothing in the effort!"

"You mean the Sultan is marrying a lamb tonight?"

"No, a fox."

29

THE SULTAN'S RETINUE HEADED FOR AWALI. HIS escort included Hamilton, al-Ajrami, Fanar, Abdallah al-Bakhit, a number of advisers, and Najma, accompanying the Sultan himself.

For the first time in years the Rawdh Palace throbbed less with jealousy and resentment than with fury. For the first time, the Sultan's wives joined in solidarity against a newcomer. It had been the custom, with previous marriages, to watch the bride closely in order to spot her faults, which, whether in her looks or comportment, were usually slight or negligible, or even invisible. There was always some woman who resisted, however, and took the part of this other who was entering the palace for the first time, if not due to conviction, for the most part, then in an attempt to lure another bird into one of the palace's feuding flocks. They cited her beauty, if she were beautiful, or her noble descent, if she could not claim beauty. They pointed out qualities the eye was slower to perceive: youth, a tender character, the clothes she wore or her perfume, which spread to scent the whole room; all this to make a few points.

Najma al-Ajrami united the whole palace in disapproval and rejection. Even before she arrived, and although people had sworn as late as two nights before the wedding that this marriage would not take place, she was being described in a simultaneously ridiculous and pitiable way. None of the Sultan's wives allowed herself to be troubled by the affair, since each considered herself far too elegant and elite to concern herself with this wedding, whose causes and motives were still muddy, but the ladies' servants took their places in circulating the news: "From the day Lulua died al-Ajrami's been the Sultan's shadow. He writes him charms and finds him philters, and between the two he oils and scents him, and now he trusts no one else; before he touches any food, the chef has to taste it, and he won't drink coffee unless it was brewed by Farhan al-Madloul. Not only that, no one knows where he sleeps anymore, or when! After al-Ajrami pestered him so much, he told him, 'I have the medicine for you.' And what is that medicine? This bony idol—no one would give a date pit for her—discarded by his last wife, this is the medicine." Another might add: "I swear to God, the boxes she brought with her are trash! Medicinal powders, oils, soot, she won't let anyone near them. You'd think she had gold and silk in them! And that's not all—she took them all with her, and her aunt was even more careful than she was when they carried the boxes, 'Be careful, watch out, don't drop them, go slow.' She was on top of them the whole time they packed and carried them." "Just as you say, and whoever wants to go back and find her place in the Rawdh Palace will find nothing, even a stone. Never! She took everything with her."

The rumors seemed to be confirmed when al-Ajrami accompanied the Sultan on his trip. It was his first time, and for the first time the Sultan took care to stay with him. This also explained the absence of the mare Fadda had freed, and prepared as a gift to her son Rakan in honor of his birthday, now that he had reached manhood. The Sultan took the mare without a second thought and sent it to al-Ajrami a few weeks before the wedding.

And so al-Ajrami's accompanying the Sultan was not due to their relationship by marriage which had come about only recently, as was rumored, but to the magical role he had begun to play with the Sultan from the time the Sultan was gripped by nightmares of murder or poisoning—to befall, according to some who heard al-Ajrami, within the palace, at the hand of some of his closest friends.

Fadda was the first of the Sultan's wives to feel insulted, and she felt the insult most keenly. She broadly hinted to all her servants and slaves that anything—anything at all—they knew about al-Ajrami should be spread around everywhere; a few days later the rest of the wives did the same. Even Watfa, who was afraid at first because of Lulua's murder, and then felt sad over being cut off from the Sultan, was not slow to tell her eunuchs and servants to get busy. As usual with the servants, they exaggerated a great deal, saying that al-Ajrami had been behind the killing of Lulua; their evidence was to say that he alone had benefited by what happened. On top of that, he'd refused to pray over the body of the deceased when asked to, with the excuse that "no one killed the departed; she killed herself."

As usual, Talleh al-Oreifan took charge of providing all the new bride's needs, once the Sultan gave her one of the three most luxurious suites built after Khazael moved out of the Rawdh Palace. The new situation in the palace was a surprise; it was usual for demands to mount at such times, and for violent conflicts to flourish, in order to create an atmosphere more to menace and confuse than to disturb the newcomer. This time things were different. When Irfan al-Hijris brought Talleh the Sultan's signed and sealed "edict," Talleh observed, "There's something you're not telling me, Irfan. I can see that al-Ajrami's daughter is different from His Majesty's other wives. 'Everything has to be perfect—instead of one of everything, she'll get two of everything, and do it all by yesterday.' What is going on?"

"You know better than I do, Abu Jazi, you've spent years in the palace. You know every little thing."

"I know about the big things, Irfan," was his ambiguous reply, "but these little things get past us."

"She is a sheikha and a daughter of sheikhs, Abu Jazi!"

Oreifan looked at him and smiled broadly and shook his head.

"Now I know the reason, and now that it's known, so much for surprise!"

The two were alluding to the fact that al-Ajrami had not prepared and did not remember when tribes and sheikhs were named!

Just as the Sultan used to put military forces in the vanguard of his retinue, he now used his wealth and messengers in their place. He tarried at several stops along the way and received a vast number of sheikhs, and spent considerable time at Ain Nabat. He did all this to give his advance men the time to prepare him fitting welcomes, and to see that the money and gifts had a chance to reach their recipients.

Abdallah al-Bakhit obeyed the Sultan's order: "I want you to follow him like his shadow, Abu Badi. If he forgets his prayers, or doesn't know which direction to face in, then help him." The Sultan smiled and brought his mouth close to Ibn Bakhit's ear and whispered:

"My prayer and submission to the Lord of Mankind
Count amidst the growth of countryside, as a single blossom."

Ibn Bakhit turned his head in surprise as he heard the Sultan begin to recite the verse; the Sultan stroked his shoulder and continued: "And, Abdallah, I want you to make it clear to him that he may know God and glorify Him, but we know Him, too, and glorify Him a hundred times more than he does!"

Ibn Bakhit, who might have played that role for a day or two, could not keep it up for weeks. Not only that, no matter how serious or pious he acted, the Sultan himself loved to relax with his closest men often, to listen to jokes, shout with laughter, and even tell stories about his experiences with women.

Now, on this long and plodding journey, because of al-Ajrami's presence, a new, sterner atmosphere prevailed, much to everyone's surprise. What caused equal surprise was that Najma was the wife who accompanied the Sultan. Had it been any other woman, or had al-Ajrami not been her father, Ibn Bakhit might have been able to get past this barrier of earnest piety and find a way to create a mood of gaiety to make the hardships of the journey more bearable.

"Do you know?" Olayan asked him when they were in Ain Nabat. When Othman only stared at him, he went on: "By God, if the people who named this place Ain Nabat—'Herb Brook'—had known that our sheikh was going to have fun here, they would have named it Dust Brook or Raven Brook!"

The Sultan took a short stroll with Hamilton and Fanar to relive some old memories. He heard the hearty laughter of Othman al-

Olayan and smiled, starting toward the two. When they were close enough to be heard, he asked them.

"Hah, my friends, I see you've left the group and gone off by yourselves. Ibn Bakhit must have had a hundred stories to tell!"

Ibn Bakhit assumed a serious demeanor when he saw al-Ajrami coming. "It was asked of Ubeidallah bin Abdallah bin Ataba bin Massoud, 'Do you compose your poetry with piety, grace and wisdom?' And he replied, 'A consumptive has to spit!' "

When al-Ajrami came up, he greeted them and looked in their faces to try and see whether what he had heard was the true subject of their conversation, or whether it had been said only for him to hear.

"What were you saying, Abdallah?" he asked Ibn Bakhit.

"Friend, I was just quoting Ubeidallah bin Abdallah—"

"Quote him again."

"It was asked of Ubeidallah bin Abdallah bin Ataba bin Massoud, 'Do you compose your poetry with piety, grace and wisdom?' And he said, 'A consumptive has to spit.' "

"Someone else said, Ibn Bakhit, 'Beware of song; it is the key to adultery.' "

"But dear sheikh, no one here is singing."

"I heard noise from a ways off, and said to myself, 'Go see what's going on,' and I got here as you were telling that story."

"You know, dear sheikh, that Omar bin Abdelaziz said, 'By God, I would pay a thousand dinars from the Muslims' treasury to discourse with Ubeidallah bin Abdallah bin Ataba bin Massoud.' He was asked, 'Do you say this in earnest?' He replied, 'Why wouldn't I? His counsel would be worth thousands and thousands of dinars to the Muslims' treasury. Such discourse constitutes instruction for the mind, refreshment for the heart, liberation from cares and broadening of culture.' "

"Ibn Bakhit may not be a sheikh, Your Majesty, but he's a sheikh-in-progress," al-Ajrami told the Sultan jokingly, or perhaps sarcastically. "He knows his history, but I think he remembers only the parts that serve his interests!"

"By God, dear sheikh, I thought you had a better opinion of me than that!"

"I have a fine opinion of you, Abdallah, I only want you to get better and better."

"As long as you stay with us on this long journey, and teach us, we are bound to learn and become even better." Ibn Bakhit laughed. "No matter what you heard about me before, now you can know me firsthand!"

Al-Ajrami nodded.

"I have heard much, Ibn Bakhit, but I always told them, 'My friends, there is no one like this Ibn Bakhit; he's a scholar and a fine man.' And now, on this journey, as God is my witness, I have been vindicated!"

"If we depended on Ibn Bakhit the way Omar bin Abdelaziz depended on Ibn Massoud," said Othman al-Olayan, to create a sprightly mood, "with his discourse worth a thousand dinars, all our money wouldn't be enough—he talks so much!"

"If I don't get my full fee in this world, I'll get it in the next," said Ibn Bakhit gaily. "Don't worry. In the meantime, your approval will do."

Abdallah al-Bakhit wanted to scream before leaving Ain Nabat, as did Olayan; so, perhaps, did the Sultan as well, but the heavy atmosphere forced Hamilton to leave it for three and four days at a time, accompanied by Fanar, to explore nearby ruins, giving him a chance, in the early part of the evening, to record what he had come up with. He spent the remainder of the evening listening to talk of religion and the law, or learning the names of various of his new acquaintances.

Anan Bassiuni had gone back and forth to Traifa more than once, in order to take part, with others, in distributing funds on behalf of the Sultan, and to prepare a fitting welcome for His Majesty. After arranging a few evenings, in which al-Ajrami was one of the most prominent speakers, he told Ibn Bakhit, as they were heading for bed, "Even at El-Azhar University itself they know how to smile and tell a joke—this man is such a pest! God love you, Abu Badi, for putting up with him this long."

"For me, sir, it's just a matter of days, and I'll go to God. What I wonder is, how do his own people stand him?"

"How are they supposed to stand him, Abu Mansour?"

"There is no beast so humble but Almighty God watches over it."

"God help the land while they are on it, and when they are buried beneath it!"

The celebrations in Awali were so moving and splendid that even al-Ajrami felt powerful and proud, for he was not merely the sheikh of Mooran and a confidant of the Sultan; he was the nation's religious authority. He summoned the clergy of Awali several times, to exchange ideas, and they left with the impression that "Sheikh al-Ajrami is a man we can reason with, because he's not only very learned, patient and long-suffering, but broad-minded." This appeared to please the Sultan very much. He asked al-Ajrami and their eminences the clergy to keep in touch and work together, and turned to other matters.

Awali for some time had remained uneasy and expectant, and prone to instability, but finally relaxed, thanks to heavy rains and ample financial aid. Ibn Madi's influence was on the wane; war had wearied the people, and hunger and death weakened them. The fighting parties meant nothing to them.

The poor of Awali were still poor or even poorer, for the war had deprived them of livelihoods. The rich, who were afraid at first, hid their wealth and pretended to have lost everything, even pretended to be poor. But things returned to normal, buying and selling resumed, the markets were full, the wealth of the rich reappeared, and the rich again bought and sold and grew richer than before, due mostly to money of uncertain origins.

Those who had been loyal to Ibn Madi, who had fought with him or in his name, after the defenses they had built collapsed, and leaders retreated, as Khureybit's forces advanced, vanished in the first weeks, though when the fighting died down they reappeared, only this time as vocal and enthusiastic supporters of Khureybit, which in fact they soon actually became. The marketplace remained the same marketplace, local leaders the same local leaders, and so the tribal sheikhs and the rich.

"Everything changes in this world, except for poverty and the poor," said some of the poor as they watched a nation vanish and another appear in its place. "Poverty stays the same, and the poor increase!" They did not know why all of this was happening, or why they stayed poor.

Ibn Mishaan wanted to go to Ain Nabat to join the Sultan or to be one of his horsemen, but time did not permit this, as he had been slow to arrange it and summon the necessary forces. It was agreed that he would be part of the Sultan's welcoming party in Traifa.

"The thing now is to win over the people," Hamilton told the Sultan, "to please them. Inner contentment will show itself outwardly, especially at such an awkward time. The people aren't bound to Ibn Madi, but to their own interests and security, and if you secure their interests, and the safety of their lives and property, the opportunities of this new situation are far greater than before, especially since Ibn Madi was such a tyrant and so hard on the people, to say nothing of the hardships of war and destruction."

The Sultan needed no lessons in theory. He wanted men; he wanted to accomplish something that could be seen by all the people. He had sent several messengers to Ibn Mishaan, telling him to act wisely and reasonably, to win the people's affection, more than to force their obedience. Ibn Mishaan understood perfectly, especially after seeing things for himself, and before long he was a new man.

"When we were in Egypt, Your Majesty," Ibn Bakhit told the Sultan, who had been talking about the change in Ibn Mishaan, "we learned a great deal from the Egyptians: the Shafi'i school of laws, and telling jokes."

"And what about someone who won't learn, Abdallah?" asked the Sultan pleasantly.

"Not here, Your Majesty."

"Yes, here, my good man."

"Kill him before your enemy gets the chance!"

When the Sultan finally met Ibn Mishaan for the first time in Traifa, he told him, "There is no place like Awali—the air, the water, the people . . ."

"What you can say about Awali," replied Ibn Mishaan firmly, "is that it is not Mooran. Here." He looked around furtively. "People here think; they're smart, and you can deal with them."

"You have forgotten the water of Mooran, Ibn Mishaan!"

"I will never forget it, Your Majesty, but a man should be aware of what's around him, and understand it."

"Well, I would hope that you have not forgotten to cultivate every town and tribe, Ibn Mishaan," smiled the Sultan, "and that your seed has taken root?"

Ibn Mishaan's response sounded pained. "The people here are their own, Your Majesty, and if you don't treat them like the salt of the earth, they don't know you!"

"Treat them well, fine, but they don't swallow all their salt!" replied Ibn Bakhit pleasantly.

"Salt, Ibn Bakhit, isn't like other things—one grain is enough."

The Sultan went off to welcome the notables, merchants, sheikhs, clergymen and tribal leaders just as he had done on his previous visit, only this time he went further and visited many more people, and prayed in several of the mosques, with al-Ajrami and most of his men at his side. He did not limit his visits to Traifa and its environs; they covered a much wider area until he had visited every town in Awali. When there was no alternative to spending a few days in a certain place, he sent for Fanar and a number of his men to go there in his stead. The visits generally came off with amiable talks, gifts, and questions about rains and the growing season. Irfan al-Hijris always stood beside the Sultan, always ready to write down anything he was asked to.

"Write, Irfan, and leave nothing out. When we get home, remind me, because these people's demands are very honest and deserving!"

One night when they were alone, he said to al-Ajrami: "Abu Mishael, you aren't just the sheikh of Mooran anymore—Awali is yours, too, and al-Huweiza! All the land that's the Sultan's is yours, too, Abu Mishael!"

Al-Ajrami seemed preoccupied with the weight and immensity of these responsibilities, but on the inside he was dancing with joy. Until very recently he'd had his doubts about the Sultan, and wished that they had not been so close, but when he came to see the Sultan's deep affection and admiration, he changed and felt more alive.

"May God give us strength, Abu Mansour, because these responsibilities take their toll in this world and the next."

"You must have noticed that the people in Awali are different from us. One must be patient, and take them for what they are." The Sultan laughed. "You should ask Ibn Mishaan how he was and how he is these days. The people of Awali, if we're nice to them, and keep an eye on them, and are generous with them, and praise them, they'll be with us and no one else—not with Ibn Madi or anyone else!"

"That's the truth, Abu Mansour, and many of them have told me the same thing."

"You know, dear sheikh, that the clergy are the pillars of the state and the faith, and if we try to please them and they respond, everything will be fine."

"Leave that to me, Abu Mansour," said al-Ajrami briskly, "and you'll have nothing to worry about!"

"God bless you, Abu Mishael—without you we could do nothing!" The Sultan then added, more quietly, "And if you need money to give to whomever, well, you know that's no problem; just let me know."

Al-Ajrami nodded but said nothing.

30

FOR FOUR MONTHS THE SULTAN AND HIS MEN knew no rest. Despite his exertions and re- lentless travel, the Sultan was pleased with the results; and not only him, but most of his advisers, all of whom were optimistic. Even al-Ajrami, who preferred to stay close by the Sultan, was even inseparable from him, went off on his own tours, promising to build mosques and improve the lot of the clergy. And while he had, at first, thought of money as a corrupter which the gov- ernment should not touch, he found that there were problems that could be solved only with money, and he told the Sultan.

"These people here," he told the Sultan one night, "are attached to customs they can't give up. They're superstitious and wretchedly poor. If we don't help them out, no one will. I think we ought to do something for them."

"Then it is done—only give the word, Abu Mishael."

"I myself, Your Majesty, don't have one coin. You find the money, and let the treasurer pay it out."

"However you wish, old man, you have great tasks, and there are people to do these little things; you give the orders, and there are people to carry them out!"

"It's in God's hands!"

One night the British consul arrived unexpectedly. The Sultan was betweel Ain Dara and Dureim, some distance from Traifa, where he had set up his encampment to rest after his long journey.

In spite of his mildness, and eagerness to be of help and conduct business as cordially as possible—unlike his predecessor, Eagleton—the consul, Ryan Smith, seemed that night to be a different person.

"His Majesty's Government, the Government of Great Britain, regretfully informs Your Majesty that it is compelled to review relations with your government, and may be compelled to take urgent action in the border regions after the dangerous and repeated hostilities in which Your Majesty's forces have engaged."

The Sultan was surprised by the visit, and even more so by the consul's dry and resolute tone. He had not known of these hostilities. He spoke informally to dispel Smith's anger.

"God keep you—this is the first we have heard of it. Can you supply us with details?"

"His Majesty's Government considers you directly responsible for the hostilities."

The Sultan had flown into rages over far less than this, but did not react to the consul's anger; he imagined that some incidents had taken place and not come to his attention.

"Every problem has a solution, my good man," he said to the consul. "Tell us what happened."

The consul grew angrier, feeling that the Sultan's disregard made him the object of mockery, for it was impossible that the news of al-Huweiza had not reached him, but this was always a bedouin ploy. They knew everything, but pretended to know nothing, in order to size up their adversary, to find an opening in his speech or strategies, so that they could attack. The consul knew this; he had seen it for himself, and so was certain that the Sultan was playing this game with him.

Hamilton and Fanar arrived, and for a few minutes the conversation was in English; the tension dissipated, and the atmosphere changed.

The consul apologized briefly, because His Majesty the Sultan had

had no word of the dangerous hostilities undertaken by the forces of Ibn Mayyah in the border region, aimed at caravans. These forces had advanced farther and farther; the whole world talked of nothing else. Britain and her allies may have stood by in the past, but now they could no longer be silent.

The Sultan seemed stunned at this news, and remained silent for some time, shaking his head, seeing three faces in his mind's eye: Khazael's horsey face, Ibn Mayyah's sharp face and long, wolvish nose, and Omair's face, which intermingled with the other two, fickle and indistinct.

His head bowed in thought, the Sultan said nothing; it was the custom that no one broke the silence without his leave. The silence annoyed the consul, who was convinced that the bedouin game was still being played against him, perhaps with a variation or two.

He said something to Hamilton in English, and Hamilton replied with a word or two, then the consul cleared his throat and addressed the Sultan: "I have come here, Your Majesty, to deliver a protest in the name of my government against these hostilities, and also to inform you that His Majesty's government reserves the right to respond with any measures it deems fit, including military force."

The Sultan's eyes opened wide. He looked at the men around him with a look of both rage and entreaty, seemingly unable to reply.

"My government," Ryan Smith continued, "has asked me to report back on the measures Your Majesty plans to take."

"May I, Your Majesty?" asked Hamilton.

"Sahib, you were with us from the very day we left Mooran," said the Sultan decisively, but sadly. "You know everything, and I swear to God that we heard nothing, received no word, but Ibn Mayyah, that dog, that son of a dog, wants to ruin everything between us and you—he must have started this."

"I can absolutely swear that the government of His Majesty the Sultan had no knowledge whatever of the incidents to which His Excellency the Consul has reference. If anything untoward has happened, it must be the work of local elements in that region, possibly as the result of provocation between the two sides. This is first; secondly, relations between these two governments are strong enough to withstand the incidents to which you refer, and there is no need for these relations to suffer the slightest tension or discord."

The Sultan appeared very relieved. He shifted several times in his seat as if trying to get closer to Hamilton, and his eyes were full of gratitude. He had wanted to say something like Hamilton was saying, but it might not have been as clear or as organized, and this is what he wanted to convey.

"As to future action," Hamilton went on, "I think it will be given priority in treating this issue. His Majesty will take decisive measures to punish the perpetrators, so that this does not happen ever again."

"Excellent, Sahib, that is what we had in mind and that is what we will do—today—yesterday, if possible!" said the Sultan briskly, then looked around and added, "We will make our move within a day or two. I will go to al-Huweiza myself. You look after these people, and give them my best regards. Tell them: 'His Majesty is taking a great interest in this; what has happened is no small matter, and he will not have it.' The future—well, as you said."

This stopping point between Ain Dara and Dureim, known for its hot springs which were beneficial for innumerable ailments, had been on al-Ajrami's mind since the outset of the journey. He was intermittently plagued by pains in his knees and hips which disabled him for days or weeks. Everyone told him, some from experience, to take "a couple of dips in those waters, and by the third you'll be completely cured; not only that, you'll be fresh and strong." Two old men who had visited the springs together told him that they had been paralyzed, suffering excruciating pains in the back and legs, and all their limbs, in fact, but the waters made them feel young again within a week. One of them told him that he even married again within a month!

The Sultan selected that place to please al-Ajrami, and because he badly needed to rest and consider his next more. Now, after this visit, he was not only worried but completely changed: sharp, angry, and secluded in his tent, uninterested in seeing anyone. Everyone could hear the curses he heaped on his men in al-Huweiza.

With these new developments, and the mood they created, al-Ajrami did not know whether to begin his cure or postpone it. He didn't like the heat of the water the first day he went; he rolled his clothes up to his knees and dangled his legs in the water, but when he tried to stand up, he slipped and fell on his right side, so that the pains that had bothered him now affected both his sides rather than only one.

After the first night, following the Sultan's first day of seclusion, Hamilton told Fanar that "with politics, Your Highness, there is no escape, no anger; you must confront every problem, no matter how terrible or difficult, and make decisions, no matter how painful they may be."

Fanar nodded in agreement. "Our politics is like our marriage customs or travel: we have to sleep on it, ask around for advice and wait for Thursday—the lucky day."

This thought attracted Hamilton, who felt surprise that he had not noticed this before; he asked Fanar all about the lucky days for weddings, journeys, war, for buying and selling, and spoke carefully, so as not to offend.

"Most ancient peoples have their beliefs, rituals and old stories. One never knows how they started, or what their real exact meanings are."

Before long the two men were summoned in to see the Sultan, to discuss issues with him.

After lengthy preliminaries and pleasantries, Hamilton spoke up. "I had been hoping, Your Majesty, that you would spend some time in Awali, but now it seems you will have to leave. I must mention that in the past four months, while you have been here, conditions have improved greatly. Perhaps, if you had been able to stay longer, Your Majesty might have been able to eliminate what remains of Ibn Madi's influence and support . . ."

The Sultan sighed like a hog and turned to Fanar as if to ask, wordlessly: "Have you seen your brother Khazael?"

"I think, Your Majesty, that we may best profit by what has happened if you stay, if Fanar should take care of the other matter on your behalf until you are through with the al-Huweiza business."

"I'm staying with my father," said Fanar fiercely. "How can he go and fight, go to al-Huweiza, while I'm here in luxury!"

The Sultan chuckled sadly and shook his head. There was a period of silence. "There is more to war, my boy, than guns, and what Sahib said hits the target."

"Will you go to al-Huweiza alone?"

"No, my boy. Many have already gone, and I may not go. I may send some men I trust. Your brother Khazael may suffice to put an end to their mischief." Again the Sultan chuckled. "Your uncle, boy—

what shall we do with him? How shall we deal with him? Are we so desperate that we have no way to reach an understanding with him, while he runs around like a madman?"

"The state, Father, is bigger than me or my uncle," said Fanar excitedly. "Omair must learn his limit, and not overstep it; and if he does, then no, by God, we won't have it, not from him or anyone else!"

That night they agreed that Fanar would deputize for the Sultan in Awali, with Hamilton and a number of advisers; that the Sultan would set out within two days, or three at the most, to deal with the problem in al-Huweiza.

"If the matter demands my presence in Britain to settle a few things, Your Majesty, I am ready to go; all I ask are orders, and a letter from Your Majesty setting out the details, and I will obtain the results you desire."

Sheikh al-Ajrami, in spite of his pains, still longed for his two or three dunkings in the mineral springs. When the Sultan told him that he should return to Mooran by automobile, he curled his lower lip, as if it were peeling off his face, which meant not only refusal but aversion.

The Sultan stalled for a day so that he might depart on a Wednesday. He took with him Najma and a large number of guards and attendants. Sheikh al-Ajrami chose the persons who would stay with him, and the camels he preferred, and moved his tent from its place to a spot nearer the mineral springs of Ain Dama.

31

EVERYTHING THAT HAD CHANGED SO DRASTI-
cally during the period the Sultan spent in
Awali—the harmony, or tacit truce that had
taken hold between his wives in the matter of Najma—fell apart
within a week of the Sultan's departure. Worse, the coexistence that
had always prevailed in the past now gave way to open hostility, to an
unending stream of rumors and accusations. The contentment, or silence, that characterized the relations between the women was replaced by provocation and an unhidden readiness to collide and fight.

Fadda, Rakan's mother, was depressed and humiliated at her failure
to persuade the Sultan to have a banquet to celebrate the boy's eigh-
teenth birthday. She had hired horses and singers for the occasion, and
it had already been rumored in the palace that Rakan's banquet in the
palace would be talked about for years and years. Not only that, she
had failed to be chosen as the wife who would accompany the Sultan
on the journey to Awali. It was not long before her depression and

humiliation turned into threats and violence; not a day passed without her inciting more slaves, eunuchs and servants, to reestablish control; she still occupied the central wing of the palace, and was the most important, as well as the best loved, of all the Sultan's wives. She was the mother of the oldest boy then living in the palace, and wanted to use any means possible to impose her will and make everyone subservient to her.

Rakan himself was almost afraid; for the past few weeks he had been dreading the very idea of attending and taking part in the men's majlis; he was so young and did not know what to say. In the space of one last day he changed completely: his soft, shy voice became loud, and his fear turned to menace, much to everyone's surprise. While Fadda's servants ascribed this fear to respect and good upbringing, and others to bashfulness, those who knew said that it was because Rakan had not learned to talk until very late, not until he was four or five. Why not was a subject of discord. People who liked Rakan said that the reason was his Somali nanny; he was so attached to her, and she had made very few other friends, that it took him a long time to learn Arabic. They said that he spoke Somali like a native, but when parted from her he forgot the language. People who hated Fadda, or resented her, had another view: when Rakan was slow to talk, even to mimic sounds, Fadda beat him cruelly. His reaction, so the story went, was to fast. She despaired of him, which led her to have another child, then a third, quickly, and make a special effort to teach them to talk, so that the Sultan would see that her children were not like their maternal uncle, God forbid, who was deaf. This was in response to the Sultan's command that she explain Rakan's condition, which deeply wounded her.

For some reason, then, Rakan was both the oldest and youngest of his brothers; perfectly silent, until his tongue came untied. It was said that a blind black man had cured him; after he spat in his throat seven times, Rakan spoke. His maternal uncles said that the silence of his early years would help him in later years, because he had learned much, and put all his energy into listening. Those who hated him said that his tongue was still tied—the genie whose job it was to control it was still present in his body, and despite the dizziness brought on him by the black magician's enchantment, the genie would periodically be lucid and reappear. As proof, they cited the bladder Rakan constantly carried around with him, which he often put to his lips when he was in pain or had a fit of coughing, to put the genie to sleep and free his tongue.

Now that the Sultan was gone, Prince Rakan, as the oldest son, was the master of the Rawdh Palace.

A few weeks after his father left, the palace was swept by rumors that something terrible had happened. There was general fear and apprehension, so Rakan ordered all guards to be on alert, and several suites in the palace were searched. It was whispered that the three men claiming to be fleeing Ibn Madi who had come some months before and whom the Sultan had promised to support and assist had been arrested for the attempted murder of Rakan. According to the rumors, it was the Sultan himself who was supposed to be assassinated, but his absence from the palace and his journey came off before the plan could be carried out, so they decided to kill Rakan. It was also rumored that the three men had several accomplices among the palace servants.

The story of the assassination plot, whose details were still unknown, changed the whole palace, Rakan especially.

He stood in the courtyard of the majlis with his special guards and a small crowd of slaves and eunuchs. The three men were stretched out on the ground, their hands bound behind their backs.

"Will you confess or not?" he shouted.

The men did not want to confess, or had nothing to confess. They looked at him and the men around him and made no sound, so he shouted more violently.

"You don't want to confess? Now we'll see!" He looked at his men resolutely and gave his order: "Beat them. Break their bones."

For three days the punishment was repeated. On the fourth day, the torture ceased; it was reported that the men had confessed. They were said to be more dead than alive, and unable to take any more beating. And it seemed that they had said only one thing: "When His Majesty the Sultan returns, we will tell everything." So they were thrown into the palace prison and kept under even heavier guard.

Two or three weeks later, a number of Fadda's relatives arrived: two of her brothers, their children, and some more distant family members, with men and guards, all of which required a reshuffle of the palace accommodations. They were put up in unoccupied suites or others reserved for security reasons. Although Dughaim al-Sarhud protested vigorously, on behalf of the others, the atmosphere of terror that ensued, together with the aggression and hard words, especially on the part of the new arrivals, who now surrounded Rakan like a wall, obliged nearly everyone to submit or at least keep their silence.

Ibn Oreifan was deeply worried, or, more precisely, apprehensive, about the calm and harmony brought about by the Sultan's marriage to al-Ajrami's daughter. After the three men were arrested, he spoke to Nahi.

"Listen, Nahi. They used to say, 'To break a man, put a woman over him; to break a woman, put a slave over her; if you want to get rid of slaves, stay away from them!' "

Nahi was troubled and annoyed. He did not know who to blame. He had decided to leave the palace, but his relationship with Ibn Oreifan, and the Sultan's promises, compelled him to stay. Now he did not know whether to watch and laugh or to pack his bags and leave.

"Abu Jazi," he told Ibn Oreifan, "so much has happened, and I don't believe we can keep out of it. All I see is that we wait for a moonless night and get out of here, because if this bunch starts in on one another now, soon they'll be looking for someone else to blame and attack, and there we'll be, and I'm afraid that will be the end of us."

"If there were only three or four of them, Nahi, who could be reasoned with, I would have told you, 'Come on, let's go,' but they are nothing but trouble. Perhaps nothing will happen unless they pick a fight; then we have to stand up to them, and they'll be on us like wolves. Let's stay out of it and laugh!"

"Abu Jazi, my good man, by God, if you hadn't kept me. I'd be in Egypt now, but my heart wouldn't let me leave my brother behind and go." Then he added sadly, "If you want my advice, we should let Sarhud have this whole mess, and get out of here without telling a soul!"

"But he's an old man; all he knows how to do is recite the Koran, Nahi—if we left him behind, they'd eat him like locusts." He laughed. "But you and I, Nahi, know people for what they are. They say something and an hour later they've forgotten it, where we never do anything but what's on our mind. We tell them, 'Don't worry, either today or tomorrow,' and if they leave us, things will be different in a day or two."

"I once told you, Abu Jazi, we are the only ones who'll lose. They know how to deal, and tomorrow they'll say, 'These Western sons of bitches are the problem, there's nothing among us to cause trouble.' And everything will be perfect again—all milk and honey!"

"No, Nahi, never—they're like scorpions. You're as safe as you can be as long as you don't go near them, because you know that if no one else is around, a scorpion will sting himself."

"Perhaps so, but time will tell. We'll see."

"Trust in God, man!"

If things had been limited to the men, they might have taken a violent and rapid course. Had the Sultan's other wives kept their distance, as spectators, Fadda might have been able to impose her will, but every woman was able to resist until the last, each in her own ingenious way.

The first woman to stand up to Fadda was her own relative, Alanoud.

This woman, whose presence had long filled the palace, suddenly vanished. She was with child, and in her third or fourth month she left the palace to go and stay with her family, and she returned seven months later cradling a baby on her chest. She had chosen a name by herself; she named him Jasser. Although the Sultan was delighted by the news of a new son, and even more so at the sight of him, Alanoud stayed in the palace less than a year, during which time she got pregnant and once again went back to her family. On this rather longer sojourn she gave birth to a girl and named her Alshema. After staying away for a few more months, she reappeared with her two children; she wanted to get pregnant and go back home again, but the Sultan was in al-Huweiza and showed so sign of returning soon. Alanoud gave no sign of leaving the palace. Fadda may have preferred that she leave and go as far away as possible, but was careful to stay friendly with her. The servants, however, both male and female, let nothing go as their masters wished; they gossiped and spread the latest rumors and items of news, many of which were received with promises of secrecy. They said that Alanoud had married the Sultan against her will, and was really in love with one of her relatives. As a result of all this, she decided to go home for a good long visit.

Much of what was said did indeed happen—much later and rather differently—but it did happen. Alanoud waited for the right moment to return these blows, and visited several times between the Wadi al-

Faid campaign and the Sultan's trips to numerous other places, but bore up. It was a confused period, and times conflicted—Alanoud's availability and the Sultan's. When she returned a few months later with a child, the wives began to repeat their servants' stories, especially after they visited her to welcome and bless the new baby. There was a question in the women's eyes: was this the Sultan's, or someone else's? Alanoud read their glances clearly but decided to wait for the right moment to reply.

32

ALTHOUGH THE RAWDH PALACE HAD BEEN REN-
ovated and enlarged, its central section was
still the sought-after home of its most
important residents, those most intimate with the Sultan. Because
Alanoud occupied the southern part of this section, considered the
most desirable part, and the Sultan had not asked her to move out of
it, which she did not do, despite her long absences, she remained—in
everyone's view, including her own—one of the Sultan's favorite
wives.

During the time of the "assassination" episode, Rakan stayed in this
suite at his mother's request. Not only that; he drove out its former
inhabitants, to the remotest western wing of the palace. This he did
on the pretext that the assassination plot would involve an assault on
the palace, focusing on his quarters, and so he needed a tighter guard.

At this point Alanoud came back, firmly expecting that her suite
had been vacated; when she saw what the situation was, the great ex-
plosion occurred.

She went by herself to the east end of the palace, and while she stayed by the wall, under the palm trees, she sent her slave, Ariman, and her son, Jasser, to summon Rakan. She stood trembling until he arrived, and then spoke with almost insulting directness.

"Listen, Rakan, you have one hour to restore my home just as it was before. If you don't, I am going to turn the world upside down on you and your mother both."

Rakan was taken by surprise, and resorted to trying to ask her to explain; he pretended not to understand what had happened. She stepped closer to him.

"You understand quite well what I've told you, and if there is any trouble, you asked for it, and you can just live with it!"

Witnesses to this scene, which lasted only a matter of minutes, said that both Alanoud and Rakan were trembling when it ended and silence fell. They said that both of them cursed, that neither listened to the other, and that they were totally at cross-purposes. Within an hour, however, or slightly more, the suite was restored to its condition of several months before. Rakan's guards left, and his possessions were removed. Fadda intervened and tried to prevent this, but Alanoud had her way.

"My master Rakan meant no harm," Fadda's servant Moza said. "He didn't want to upset his aunt. He told her, 'It will be as you wish,' and couldn't go back on his word." She sighed. "My dear Fadda was asleep; she didn't know what was going on. When she saw Alanoud, she told her, 'Do you know, my dear, Ibn Madi sent his men to the palace to kill us, but God spared us,' and Rakan, God keep him, said, 'We need men around us to protect us,' but he was afraid and said, 'We cannot attack my aunt,' I told him, 'If your Aunt Alanoud were here, she'd be the first one to agree; now that we're sure and secure, and your aunt is here, you should put things back as they were.' "

Alanoud spoke, wishing the others to hear: "This is my home and my children's, as the Sultan knows. No one may remove one stone of it. If the eunuchs try it again, their heads will be removed! I think this should be known."

News of this insult spread through the Rawdh Palace; it was a clear provocation, because Fadda had more eunuchs than servants, and most of them in the women's quarters. Some reported that the eunuchs were passing messages not only between Fadda and the Sultan, but that they had other tasks, but said nothing more.

This incident marked the beginning of the end of Fadda's high standing and her challenge.

Watfa was still deep in mourning at Lulua's death and the Sultan's absence, but now became communicative, and the other women listened to her. There was much that she did not say directly, but it came out by way of the servants that "Fadda is the one who killed Lulua; and then came this fortune-teller to ruin everything!" This is what one of the servants said, and Watfa too. What had happened was that a Gypsy fortune-teller had come and settled in a suite near Fadda, and put all of her sorcery to work: she provided the Sultan with restorative medicine, but it didn't work; she made love potions, but he wouldn't touch them; she prepared eye medicine, but it did no good. Finally, she told Fadda, "We have only potions to break bones," and prepared it for Watfa to drink, only Moza mistakenly said it was a love potion; Lulua drank it and died. This was the story told of Lulua's death, and what seemed to support it was that the fortune-teller left the palace the next day and was never seen or heard from again.

There were stories told of the adventures involving the central section of the palace and the many other wings, including the servants' and guards' quarters. The eunuchs were the main players of these tales, which were so numerous, varied and strange that most people didn't even believe them, and looked shocked and curious when they heard them.

Fadda did not respond to the stories, and did not appear at any dinners or parties. She spent so much of her time secluded in her suite that people wondered how she could stay there for weeks on end, unseen by anyone. Yet she was still able to respond, here and there, most of the time perfectly, and at the right moment. Watfa's servants got slapped so often that it was almost a daily occurrence. There was always a good reason for it: making faces, stealing, or meddling with the wives.

Even the days free of provocative incidents were not free of rumors, of noise or even gunshots in the dead of night. There were so many competing explanations for these incidents that in the end no one actually knew what had happened.

After three months of this hellishness, Mudi wrote to Fanar and subsequently packed her bags and prepared to leave. She did all this very quietly, but it did not remain a secret, and when the women crowded in to bid her farewell, Fadda was among them, but she was alone, intending to choose a time when no one else would be there. She did it impulsively, out of fear that Mudi would give the Sultan a picture of palace life that would damage her.

Fadda had never been friendlier. She expressed, with evident sorrow, her regret at Mudi's departure, and said that she would tell the Sultan about everything she had seen and heard, and that she had witnesses. She suggested that it would be better not to trouble the Sultan at this time, because he had enough on his mind; nor did she forget to give Mudi a valuable gift, which was graciously received, and a gift for Qatma, too.

A few hours before Mudi left, she had a word with Alanoud and one of her relatives, "God help anyone living in this palace—you either die or go mad!" She added, as if to herself, "I hope never to see the place again."

Alanoud smiled sadly. "Trust in God, my girl, this is Abu Mansour's palace, and when he comes back, everything will be as it was, or better."

"One can only hope, Aunt, only I don't think that will happen; the rottenness is too deep. God help us!"

"If I could ask one thing of you, Mudi," said Alanoud hopefully, "it would be that you tell His Majesty, 'You have been away too long; a palace is no good without its masters; it's not the same world without you.'" She, too, paused and spoke again, as if to herself: "And if he can come back just one day sooner, it will make a difference."

Only a few days separated Ummi Zahwa's return from al-Rehaiba after five months there, out of necessity, for her broken foot to heal, and the Sultan's return to Mooran.

The Sheikha arrived supported by a cane and Tahany's shoulder, looking tired and obese. No sooner had she settled into the Rawdh Palace than news and delegations started to arrive, to welcome her back and report on what had gone on in her absence. While she preferred to listen, to learn in complete detail all that had happened, she did appear affected and even angered by what she heard. Fadda was the first of the women to visit her, but such haste struck the Sheikha as unusual, and the visit was so full of love and flattery that her suspicions were aroused, so that she was inclined to give credence to what the other wives, whose visits came after Fadda's, and Tahany and the servants, told her.

"You know, Abu Mansour," the Sheikha told the Sultan, "that God tests His servants. I was intending to go back after a week or two, but the Lord has been working on me—he broke my foot but blessed me; 'I do believe that you are here, in Mooran, I don't think you're away,' I thought then. My mind is at rest, and I said: 'Until God frees her, and I'm better,' " She paused to take a deep breath. "You were absent, Your Majesty, and I was absent, and it seems now that these women need a halter and a stick, because what I've heard did not make me proud." She laughed sadly. "You have cares, Your Majesty, that would crush mountains, and I don't want to add to them, but, as they say, A man doesn't go far unless his house and women are secure."

She paused and shook her head several times.

"I don't want you to believe everything—I myself didn't believe everything—but we cannot ignore what has gone on during our absence." She shifted in her sitting position, drawing closer to him, and lowered her voice to a whisper. "You know, Abu Mansour, that if you leave those women to their own devices, God help us all! There's no controlling them, and the nicer you are to them, the more you want to avoid trouble, the more they take advantage of you and act up; and this is what's been happening. I want to tell you what went on here while we were gone."

The Sultan sighed and eventually spoke, in a sad tone. "What confusion for a man: both here and there. With his enemies, and among his own friends and household."

The Sultan did not wait to hear everything, or to check every fact and witness, but took action. He summoned eight of the eunuchs, five of the servants and nine of the slaves, and within a day ordered all of them executed. They were taken to the extreme western end of the palace compound, not far from the horse stables, tied to palm trees and to posts that had been put there for hitching camels, and shot. This took place the morning of the fifth day after the Sultan's homecoming, and they were buried in a mass grave.

Before that, he ordered his wives to assemble, and they came. It was the first time they had seen him since his return from his journey, and their many conflicting feelings were clear: desire, fear, and an eagerness to talk. Irfan al-Hijris recalled it many years later:

"An hour or more before morning prayers I was fast asleep—I didn't see him until he was looking me in the face. 'Get up, Irfan!' I got up, by God, and he said, 'Come on.' He walked and I walked behind him. We were alone in the majlis; no one was around but the guards, and they were at a good distance. He told me: 'You have one hour, Irfan. Leave no one sleeping. Empty the palace of everyone inside it. If anyone is afraid, tell her, "This is my job and it is Abu Mansour's order. I don't want one word out of you, not even 'Yes.' You can come back when it's over." If anyone says, "Don't hit me," give him a good slap, but only in the face. Say, "These are Abu Mansour's orders." Then come back to me here, in this place.' I did it, too. I went to his palace, and woke them up, shouting, 'All of you, you have one hour, it's the Sultan's order, no one can stay behind.' They got up. They were afraid, whether they believed what was happening or not. To make a long story short: one of them screams, 'I must see His Majesty.' Another screams, 'This is my house and my children's.' A third one says, 'Let His Majesty come in person.' Some children were amused, others were crying. Anyway, once they all got the idea, I told them, 'Whoever doesn't come voluntarily will be brought by force; my stick is ready.' I was the one doing the talking, but I could hardly believe it; it was as if it was someone else talking. But I could imagine Abu Mansour's eyes striking sparks, and they made me do the impossible. Within an hour the palace was empty. When I went back, the sun was just rising. Ibn Abbad and Abdallah al-Bakhit were with His Majesty. He gave me a slip of paper no bigger than the palm of my hand, with names written on it. He said, 'Take ten guards; bring these, and come back.' By God, I brought them like sheep. Abu Mansour looked them up and down, then said, 'Take them to the stables and wait.'

"An hour later he sent someone out: 'Tie them up and wait.' We tied them up. In less than an hour, I saw Judgment Day! Abu Mansour and all of his wives, and ten or more of his private guard. When they got there, he said, 'No one will forget this day as long as they live.' He whispered something to Mahyoub and turned to the women; he told them to stand by the western guard house. He spoke very firmly: 'I want you to get a good look.' In minutes it was over. They shot eight eunuchs, five servants, and nine slaves."

It all happened quickly and silently; there was no sound of breathing from the observers of the scene, who could not believe their eyes. Not far away was a ditch at whose edge camels were slaughtered; the corpses were thrown in there, then covered with dirt, and the episode was over.

The Sultan ordered all of his wives to assemble in the palace, in the

wing vacated by Fadda, Alanoud and Suheila, in the great hall down-
stairs, where he sometimes gave private banquets.

Long months afterward, Rafet Sheikh al-Sagha wrote in his memoirs: "Tuesday, the seventh of Rabi al-Thani last year, was a memo-
rable day in Mooran, a day of blood and fear; a day of death in the
Rawdh Palace. Trusted people have told me that the Sultan ordered
the execution of his twenty-two servants and slaves because of what
he had been told about mistakes they had made while he was away in
Awali. Of course, there was no way of checking the truth of the
charges against them, as no trial or investigation took place. In a matter of hours, those men were rounded up and shot. Apparently, the
Sultan's wives were present when the sentence was carried out, at his
own wish! Subsequently, I was told that the Sultan forced his wives to
swallow large quantities of salt and pepper, and invited them to lunch
at his table; when one of the wives refused, he ordered his private
guards to beat her. This led to sickly reactions, some of which I witnessed personally, bearing in mind that the English lady doctor in
charge of the palace women's health told me that while most of the
illnesses she had treated involved the stomach, she doubted that the
amounts of salt and pepper the Sultan was supposed to have forced
the women to ingest were actually the trouble. There were other
symptoms. There was something strange and cruel about their condition; it had something to do with the Sultan's behavior."

No one was absolutely sure what transpired that Tuesday. Reports
that did not make it out of the palace until a day or two later speedily
took on an infinite number of forms and versions. The report of the
assassination attempt against Rakan was said to be behind what happened. Those who held this view cited the three men's confessions; it
was said that they did not confess until after the Sultan promised them
safety, and then named the servants and slaves who had some connection with Ibn Madi, and these were then executed. It was said that the
matter was part of an even older affair, the murder of Lulua; that Watfa
or perhaps the Sultan had been the intended target. The Sultan struck
back to teach a lesson to those acting with them, especially in the palace. What lent credence to this story was that most of the eunuchs
executed had been Fadda's eunuchs, and the Sultan's order that her
part of the palace be vacated.

Besides these two stories were many others relating to highly suspect mistakes of a number of the Sultan's wives, or their servants and governesses. The stories were told in extreme secrecy in different versions, and made believable—at least some of them—by the hasty weddings arranged between some of the servants and governesses and a number of the male palace workers, especially since many births had taken place at Warida's hands. She was surprised to see black children born to white fathers and mothers, and vice versa. This led to the recollection anew of many of the stories that had nearly faded from memory among the vast ocean of incidents that never let up for a day in the Rawdh Palace.

As a rule, it was the servants and slaves who circulated news, but now they were struck dumb, and stayed that way for weeks, and in some cases months, unable to believe what had happened. Umi Zahwa's absence had been a long one, and she was nearly forgotten, but her return after a few months, with the events of that Tuesday, showed her to be strong enough and enough in control to inspire terror. For everyone was sure that she was behind all that had happened. When she walked through the palace or even looked at anyone, people trembled, even the Sultan's own wives. The cane she had used in her period of convalescence now accompanied her everywhere and she used it for everything, and with the passage of time it became part of her personality. Some of the servants went so far as to say that the very sound or sight of the stick struck people dumb.

Najma now occupied the central wing of the palace by herself. After a few weeks Fadda moved into the suite previously occupied by Khazael, and Alanoud settled in the wing formerly reserved for Najma. Suheila, who was childless, died a few weeks after that Tuesday—all sorts of stories were told about that.

The Sultan's children were punished. Their financial allocations were cut off, their horses taken away, and their weapons confiscated. They were sent back to the private school, and the Sultan gave stern instructions to al-Idrisi, the new teacher he had selected for his children: "The flesh is yours and the bone is ours, sir; do what you must and have no fear."

Silence settled in the Rawdh Palace, and it settled in for a long period of dark gloom until the next spate of new troubles and unthinkable occurrences.

33

WITH THE INFLOW OF MONEY, IBN OLAYAN WAS like a small child unable to hide his delight or even sit still. Every day he tried any number of times to talk to the Sultan privately about his plans and ideas for investing the money, but the Sultan was in another world: if he wasn't busy receiving tribal leaders, he was deep in conversation with religious sheikhs, with messengers or spies he sent here and there carrying messages or following up leads. When the Sultan did have time, or rather when he made the time, he reserved it to spend with Sahib. Ibn Olayan, his eyes sharp as a hawk's, wanted to know who each new visitor was, and tried to guess how much money they would get from the Sultan before a deal was struck with them. He felt that he was in a desperate race against time.

"You and I, Othman, we aren't going anywhere," the Sultan told him one day when he was being insistent. "If we don't talk today, we'll talk tomorrow. Right now, give us a chance to talk to people who are leaving town today or tomorrow."

"You and I aren't going anywhere, Your Majesty, but the money is!"

Othman said it sadly, and when the Sultan looked at him in surprise, he went on. "If we keep giving it away to everyone this way, with no accounting, we'll have nothing left."

"Trust in God, my friend; now we have all the money we need and more!"

Al-Ajrami stayed away four months, but after receiving the third envoy from the Sultan demanding his return, he went back, with an Iranian attendant, one of three who had come to Ain Dama for treatment and ended up looking after al-Ajrami and sick-nursing him for his entire stay.

Al-Ajrami seemed, to most people who saw him, stronger, plumper and younger than before. The cane he used to rely on seemed superfluous, but he kept it; he felt it had become a part of him. Even the Sultan, who was irritated by his prolonged absence, could not help from exclaiming, when he saw him, "Who is this? Abu Mishael? Are you you, or your son?"

Al-Ajrami guffawed delightedly.

"No one would believe this without seeing it! As soon as we finish our business, Abu Mishael, we'll spend a month or two of fun there so that we can look like you!"

"The old saying went, 'An Iranian's cloak has seventy-seven patches,'" Abdallah al-Bakhit told Olayan. "Well, this Iranian has seventy-seven medicines he used to re-create al-Ajrami! Now all of this 'Yes, sir!' and 'Yes, agha!' has turned his head, and who knows what else has changed about him."

"Don't be deceived, Ibn Bakhit," answered Olayan with a cackle, "and don't forget how they fatten the calf before the slaughter, and fatten chickens before selling them!"

Within a few weeks the Sultan had arranged everything. He smiled at Ibn Bakhit and asked, "Do you recall what we talked about a long time ago, Abdallah?" He did not give him time to recall, but laughed and said, "If you flee from it or fear it, it will surely follow you, just as death and life do; I have advised you and taken care of it."

Ibn Bakhit was apprehensive and then frightened; it seemed to him that the Sultan meant just what he said. He asked, in a quavering voice, "Yes, Your Majesty, but tell me just what it's all about?"

"What did you uncle tell you?"

"My uncle?"

"Listen, Abdallah, without going into all the details—that day Olayan and I were talking, we said that 'Abdallah must take this step.' Olayan told me, 'Leave it to me, Your Majesty, my daughter is ready.' I've told him we've put our faith in God, read the prayer and made our agreement final; and I've ordered Ibn Hijris and al-Oreifan to prepare everything."

For a few moments Abdallah al-Bakhit was stunned, unable to believe his ears; he kept repeating, hardly realizing what he was saying, "This doesn't make sense, my friends. I'm the last to know?" After a time he asked, "You swear this is the truth, Your Majesty?" The Sultan was delighted, seeing that he had landed a death blow on Ibn Bakhit, and spoke to end the discussion.

"We've given orders for you to get a little money, to outfit yourself and get yourself ready!" He waited no further to bellow, "Irfan! Ibn Hijris!"

Irfan came running.

"Have you got everything ready for your uncle Abdallah?"

"Everything is ready, Your Majesty!"

"Bring the money."

Irfan al-Hijris slipped away with the stealth of a cat. Abdallah al-Bakhit still thought the whole thing was a trap, or one of the Sultan's practical jokes; he had often played a part in his practical jokes before, and excelled at it. But to be the butt of such a good one! He hoped only for this nightmare to end and to get out of it safely, but when Ibn Hijris reappeared with a large pouch, which the Sultan took and then threw to him, Ibn Bakhit knew that this had gone beyond a joke and become something else, something very dangerous.

"I would like to appeal, Your Majesty," he asked submissively.

"My good man, it's too late," replied the Sultan impatiently. "You're getting married. Try to enjoy a few days of this life." His tone changed. "If you say one word, Abdallah, after we have given our word and agreed on everything, then we're through with you!"

"Just as you say, Your Majesty!" said Abdallah miserably, adding, almost to himself, "Everything goes in this world, except a man getting married without his consent—without his knowledge, even!"

"Abdallah, that is enough!"

Later on, when Ibn Bakhit understood, he agreed completely, and at times even looked pleased.

" 'I swear in my loudest voice, I am not mad,' " the Sultan recited a
few days afterward, " 'I have nothing but love for the unclaimed love-
less.' " He laughed and nodded triumphantly, and when he had
stopped laughing added, "Abdallah, I want you to visit al-Ajrami; if
he's tempted, let's find him a nice girl who'll give him some fine
children!"

Ibn Bakhit laughed loudly.

"I notice that your brilliant schemes, Your Majesty, all start with
weddings!"

"Let the people be happy and wish me a long life!"

"But al-Ajrami . . . I'm afraid, Your Majesty, that marriage will
distract him from contemplating God, or from the things you need
him to do!"

"Don't worry about that now. Go see him, and let God look after
the outcome."

During the first visit and their conversation about Ain Dama and
Ain Dara, Ibn Bakhit hinted, not without a suggestion of sarcasm,
that a man advancing in years needed a girl to look after him, to
strengthen his bones and give him confidence. He cited the example
of the Prophet and his followers. Al-Ajrami smiled in silence and listened carefully to Ibn Bakhit, but said neither yes nor no.

On the second visit, several days later, and with no preliminaries,
Ibn Bakhit recited this verse:

" 'If a man accepts from one who loves him,
He has not sinned; he has a reward:
God multiplies his blessings and lightens his burdens.' "

"So you're a poet today, Ibn Bakhit?" Al-Ajrami replied pleasantly.
Ibn Bakhit answered without hesitation:

"White skin to the edge of thick, smooth hair
Radiant day below and blackest night above."

Al-Ajrami had turned to stare at Abdallah al-Bakhit.

"Are you trying to say something, Abdallah?"

"Yes, yes, I am, sir, and not only that:

'I don't know whether you remember her
Or whether two or eight were praying;
As I prayed I turned my face toward her,
Away from the prayer place, seeking solace from her.' "

Al-Ajrami shook a warning finger but spoke jovially:

"If you go back to what you mentioned,
And find yourself nailed to the trunk of a tree."

Ibn Bakhit smiled but went on:

"Do you threaten me with murder to grieve me?
Murder to me is rest; death already decreed."

Al-Ajrami raised both his hands and spoke softly. "Enough, Ibn Bakhit, enough." He paused. "Either you are in love, or have some message for me!"

"You are wise, Abu Mishael: I am in love, *and* have a message for you."

"From whom?"

"From His Majesty."

"Let's have it. Let me hear it."

"I can't wait to, sir—here it is." He laughed and shook his head, looking in all directions to see that no one was eavesdropping.

Al-Ajrami, too, looked around, seeing now that this business required some care and seriousness, but when he thought Ibn Bakhit too slow to continue, he spoke sharply: "Come on—don't wear me to death!"

"Listen, Abu Mishael . . ." He looked around again, then went on. "A few days ago, after His Majesty saw you, and the good that Ain Dama did you, he told Olayan, 'Listen, Othman, both these men are dear to us, Abu Mishael and Ibn Bakhit, especially Abu Mishael; he has done much for us. Now, since he's young again, and strong as a horse, let's do something for him.' Olayan said, 'There is nothing like Moorani girls.' His Majesty said, 'I want two of your daughters, one for Abu Mishael and the other for Ibn Bakhit.' Olayan answered him, 'All you can find us are those two poisonous, powerless old men?' His

Majesty said, 'Those two are stronger than any teenagers, Othman; they are experienced, and still virile—don't be fooled by age and appearances.' That shut Olayan up—he didn't say a word. And His Majesty, without asking permission, just took over. On his behalf, Abu Mishael, he decided that one of Olayan's daughters would marry, and told me, 'Talk to Abu Mishael and see if he's interested; if he is, we'll take care of him; if not, fine, God keep him.'" He was quiet a moment. "Now I've told you all I know, Abu Mishael, and I don't know whether I'm wrong or right for having said as much as I have."

"Abu Mansour will get what he wants," said al-Ajrami with a broad smile.

34

THE WEST WING OF THE RAWDH PALACE HAD been shrouded in silence for months; it felt like a prison. There was little movement within, no demands made, and very few visitors after the dismissal of Dughaim al-Sarhud and his replacement by al-Oreifan. Some of the Sultan's wives had been shuffled around, and new additions built on the western side. The whole palace now changed, however: money had enlivened the place. The Sultan resumed paying allowances and ordered that cloth and sweets be distributed, and that some of the older wings of the palace be remodeled.

The movement, however, was different.

The Sheikha, who had seemed strong and domineering—so much of what happened in the palace had been attributed to her—who had created such an atmosphere of terror, was now herself a prisoner of that terror. It had been her intention to goad the Sultan, to provoke him to cruelty, but she had never imagined he would be so cruel as to order that many executions. She was actually sorry, and sympathized with most of the wives. She did not visit any of them, but sent Tahany to convey her good wishes, and took care to stay aware of everything all the Sultan's wives were up to. She said to herself, and then to Tahany, intending that Tahany should quote her, that "men are mad from birth, and cowardly, and fickle. They think they're strong and brave, but they don't know how to behave any more than children do. When they try to do something, God help us all, they wreck everything; they don't know what to do or what not to do!"

Thus Ummi Zahwa spent the whole winter secluded in her wing, coming out rarely, and then only to enjoy the sun and fresh air, approaching the men's majlis only two or three times, but without speaking or even greeting the men. Now that she felt more at ease, or because she could not take it any longer, she came out of her wing as serpents do: she hesitated with a fidget, then glided through all the palace wings as if inspecting them, speaking little except to ask questions, and returned speedily to her residence frightened or unable to readapt.

Alanoud, who was accustomed to spending the longest sojourns with her family, had not done so in all this period, and despite the old stories she was used to and the rumors that used to fly in the Rawdh Palace, which provoked in her no wish to respond or to vindicate herself, especially after her detractors had become victims like herself, she was content to send for her mother and two of her sisters. They came to visit her for a few months. Alanoud's mother visited Fadda several times. Fadda had almost visited Alanoud, but then changed her mind and postponed the visit, and then forgot about it altogether.

Alanoud passed a message to Fadda and Ummi Zahwa by saying to her mother: "In the Rawdh Palace you need sharp claws or you'll get eaten. If you aren't stronger than they are, they'll skin and eat you, and no one will even trouble to say grace!"

The Sheikha did not quite understand, but she nodded in agreement. The message did get to Fadda, who responded by way of Alanoud's mother: "What ruined us: the bastards, who know how to do nothing but gossip, who laughed and danced when we fought among ourselves." She smiled sadly. "But it isn't their fault; it's the fault of whoever quarreled for no reason, who used to feed them information . . ." She shook her head. "We're the crazy ones, we're the ones who told them to come and eat our flesh . . . and I think Alanoud knows exactly what I mean!"

With this kind of slow, wary inner movement, a new spirit began to pervade the palace, a spirit more cunning than courageous, but with a certain insistence and ability to resist. Even the youths and children, who had conflicting views and feelings about what had happened, were readier to speak up, or to accept what they saw, as animals respond to the least change, and were quick to adopt more aggressive views, thus partially showing the influence of their homes, mothers and siblings.

Nothing was heard from Najma, who occupied the central section of the palace, and no one but her aunt—her father's sister—visited her. She came many times, but none of her visits were accompanied by any change of behavior; furthermore, when there were rumors that she had died in childbirth, no one had the evidence to deny them, though all eyes were fixed on images of what might befall if they were true. Even Warida, who had supervised the birth, and stayed busy for hours, and on into the first days, had nothing clear to say one way or the other.

Sheikh al-Ajrami visited his daughter when he got home from his journey, and after she gave birth to her first child, a boy, he seemed to all who saw him a different person. This gave rise to very discreet and highly contradictory rumors, questioning whether this was in fact him! The servants made known their surprise, and thought, after the change they noticed, that perhaps they had not known him very well, that this was someone else, but at that point matters took a course unforeseen by the Rawdh Palace.

Ibn Oreifan asked Nahi, "Do you think, Ibn Farhan, that the palace is the palace, and the people are its people?"

"Nothing has changed, Abu Jazi."

"Everything has changed, Ibn Farhan." He laughed. "The shedding of blood, Nahi, renews the blood, renews the man!"

He shook his head in astonishment.

"What's strange is that so many things in this world never happen unless you really are afraid, or"—he smiled and shook his head before going on in a different voice—"or unless you have a mind or conscience, though it is clear that a mind or conscience in this palace—"

"You are talking to yourself, Abu Jazi; there is no room in this palace for minds or consciences!"

Within a month two of Olayan's daughters were engaged to al-Ajrami and al-Bakhit. This had come about despite large-scale fighting, weeping and threats to commit suicide, but in the end the betrothals took place, albeit with a few changes. Olayan's twenty-year-old middle daughter, who had been chosen as al-Ajrami's wife, was put aside in favor of her younger sister after all the fuss. This sad youngest daughter had spoken to her mother resignedly: "Give Ibn Bakhit to Madiha—I'll marry the old man!"

Her mother was shocked, and at first could not believe her ears, but then looked at Nahla differently: she considered her from her feet to the crown of her head, gazed at her carefully, especially in her eyes, to see whether or not she had meant exactly what she said, and when she saw that she was serious—clearly, even decisively so—she gave her own resigned reply.

"If you mean it, then save us from this scandal." She sighed hatefully. "It's all your father's nonsense. He gave his word to the Sultan and can't go back on it, as if the Sultan were God, Whom no one may disobey!"

In the Rawdh Palace there were highly secretive rumors that al-Ajrami was a sorcerer who could do anything, but another sorcerer came along and put a spell on him. This second one, who had come as a nurse, made it clear that he was a far greater magician than al-Ajrami—immeasurably greater.

After she heard all the details, Fadda had a word with Alanoud's mother. "You know, my dear, that a man who digs a ditch for his brother Muslim will fall into it himself!" She smiled. "He bewitched His Majesty, he got the Sultan to marry his daughter, thinking that he'll own the Sultan if he becomes his in-law, but someone stronger came along. Today you think all this is strange? God knows what will happen tomorrow."

Although al-Ajrami was saying nothing about his marriage, and complained that the Prophet and his followers always married very privately, in those days, all that had been needed to conclude a marriage was the husband, a representative of the wife, and two witnesses. Everyone in Mooran was talking about this marriage, especially since the two, Olayan and al-Ajrami, were not direct associates of the Sultan and had nothing to do with what had happened.

"Write, Irfan," Farhan said. "And if you don't write it, take my word for it: from the first day God created this world, there's been no room on a rubbish heap for two roosters. Now look—Olayan and al-Ajrami—which one is going to be closer to His Majesty? Abu Mansour is patient, he can stand it, but those two—neither of them can stand the other. You'll see."

Ibn Hijris licked his lips and then his pen, and pretended to write. "But tell me, Nahi, when roosters fight, what happens to the hens?"

Nahi al-Farhan laughed until he almost fell over on his back, and when he had stopped, answered, "Don't worry, my friend, hens know how to look after themselves; yes, they know that." He paused and smiled. "It isn't the top roosters, the fighting roosters, that matter—it's the praying roosters!"

Al-Ajrami considered a trip to Ain Dama or Ain Dara for his honeymoon; he felt the need to escape the stares and stories that surrounded him and to reexperience some of the good he had from his first visit, but his doctor, who followed him around like his shadow, would not permit it. According to any woman who knew Najma at all, everything had already been prepared for him: the special meals he needed, restorative potions, and certain perfumes that were generally hidden and brought out only for special occasions such as this.

A few days after the wedding, the Sultan asked al-Ajrami rather ambiguously about his "circumstances," and received a quick and crisp reply.

"In your presence, being in your sight, Your Majesty, we are doing wonderfully well—we could never be better!"

The Sultan's surprise and pleasure were clear. As he tried to express his feelings, al-Ajrami spoke up proudly. "I want to tell you, Your Majesty, about Ain Dama. A man must go to Ain Dama every year, but our excellent friend, with all he knows, has prepared everything." He laughed. "And those Iranians are something!"

The Sultan looked at him with intense curiosity.

"Yes, Your Majesty, they have real heads on their shoulders, and they don't miss anything!" He guffawed and looked over his own body. "But you have to obey them, Your Majesty, and if you do, they'll see that you beget fine children!"

They laughed merrily, but the Sultan then showed an interest in knowing everything: What did they do? How? For while these things were said only diffidently and reluctantly, they were being said nonetheless; and it seemed to the Sultan that al-Ajrami meant every word.

"I need to know more about these things, Abu Mishael," he said seriously.

"I'm ready anytime, Abu Mansour . . . and so is my friend, and he would love to do the same thing for His Majesty!"

A few days later, Hussein Motamadi was appointed an adviser at the Rawdh Palace. Irfan al-Hijris asked the Sultan, with al-Ajrami present, whether it was really necessary to make him an adviser, like the other advisers; the Sultan glanced at al-Ajrami, looked around more than once, finally ordering impatiently, "So, appoint him 'personal adviser'—that's enough!"

Rafet Sheikh al-Sagha had known before most of the others that Motamadi would be appointed the Sultan's "adviser for health affairs." "God give me patience," he muttered, sighing like a bull. He paused before adding, "God save us from the great!"

35

WITHIN BARELY FOUR MONTHS THE SULTAN RE-
ceived a letter from Hamilton. It was delivered by Anan Bassiuni, and contained a
request that Hamilton, along with Anan, head for London to hammer
out an agreement with the British government regarding neighboring
countries bound to Britain by treaty or special relationships. The Sultan had demanded that Anan find out exactly what Britain's policy
was toward Ibn Mayyah. The Sultan had received reliable information
that Mayyah had contacted the English, or the English had contacted
him, and he had proposed to them one of two solutions: since he was
master of al-Huweiza, and provided support for its tribes, he could
remain an enemy and engulf the whole region in flames, so that neither Britain nor its allies would have a moment of peace; or—this was
the second solution—they might support him, and independence for
al-Huweiza, in which case he would be their greatest friend, and do
anything they wanted.

The Sultan felt that the battle with Ibn Mayyah would be decisive, and that there was no need for haste, especially after learning of the new friendship between Ibn Mayyah and Ibn Madi, and discovering that huge sums of money had changed hands in the border regions. Several tribal chiefs had visited Ibn Mayyah, returning with anger and hard words that echoed all the way to Mooran, alleging that "Khureybit had gone in with the English and sold the country, that he no longer recognizes religion or the law—all his advisers are infidels!"

Khazael, who insisted on being the governor of the area and commander of its forces, had become a tool in Ibn Mayyah's hands. Khazael was courageous in battle, but not with his true enemies. He set off for the northern tribes, and instead of winning them over, he resorted to punishing even those who had not taken part in highway robbery or plundering caravans. As compliant as Ibn Mayyah pretended to be, he wanted to impose every possible problem and catastrophe on Khazael. The Sultan found out all the details of what had happened while in Mooran and decided to defer his attack. He had sent a number of messengers to Ibn Mayyah, asking him to come to Mooran, but he always had an excuse, either illness or an incipient attack; at the same time, Khazael was busily sending his close relatives, even his son, to others. He sent his brother to Ibn Mishaan in Awali, and sent innumerable messengers to tribal sheikhs with gifts.

Now the Sultan was convinced that something big was in store. He often felt that Britain had something to do with what was happening. When Awali was quiet, al-Huweiza started up. When Ibn Madi was inactive on one front, there was word of movement or impending movement on another front. In addition to Ibn Mayyah and Ibn Mishaan was "the finishing touch, Omair," as the Sultan referred to him; they were never inactive, and never to be trusted.

Al-Ajrami had been feeling strong and lively, but suffered a relapse of old age, and abruptly headed for Ain Dama. He decided to prolong his stay there, especially after his adviser, Motamadi, came across an Indian sorcerer on a visit to Mooran searching for life-prolonging herbs, who told him that the springs at Ain Dama were fully effectual only when the moon was full. The springs restored one's youth and sexual potency; he had learned that from some ancient Indian books. If a man spent six or seven months there, and used perfumes made from the essence of cloves mixed with musk, and a little fish oil, he would be able to marry and sire children until he was a hundred years old.

So al-Ajrami was not slow to quit Mooran for Ain Dama. When he had been gone a long time, the Sultan sent him two letters, the first inquiring after his health and well-being, with a suggestion that he was missed, that everyone in Mooran was asking for him and eagerly awaiting his return. Al-Ajrami responded by way of the same camel-back courier that he was in excellent health and sent his warm regards to everyone who was asking for him. He said that as soon as his cure was complete he would come back to Mooran. The second letter was slightly more explicit; the Sultan informed him that "some new business requires consultation," but since the moon was on the verge of its full phase, the courier returned with word that "we will be at your side very soon, as soon as our health allows us to bear the hardships of the journey."

When the courier returned with the second message, the Sultan told Ibn Bakhit that "in two answers, he told me all I needed to know." He paused before adding, almost to himself, "We wanted his help, but now it is he who needs our help."

"You want meat, but you get broth," smirked Ibn Bakhit.

"By God, Abdallah," replied the Sultan ironically, "all is confusion. We don't know who is with us and who is against us."

" 'And one of them said to Abu Bakr, "If a decision lies with one who will not pronounce it, and a weapon with one who will not use it, and money with one who will not spend it, then all is confusion." ' " Ibn Bakhit smiled. "I don't understand politics, Your Majesty, and I can give no real judgment on the man. I have noticed that most of those swarming around us are thieves and freeloaders, but I am sure that His Majesty knows his own men."

Then he declaimed:

> "O maker of the bow, oppress not the bow,
> Give it to the best archer;
> Give no task to less than an expert."

Anan Bassiuni spoke to Prince Fanar the day before he left: "His Majesty says, 'His Highness Prince Fanar must be patient; whatever he sees or hears from Ibn Mishaan, he must do and say nothing. There will be a time for everything.' "

Hamilton said, in the presence of Yunis Shaheen: "We sail tomorrow, Your Majesty. We'll go on to Cairo from Suez, and fly to London from there." He smiled. "How difficult these trips would be without ocean liners!"

"Before there were ocean liners, people managed to get from one place to another," said Yunis ambiguously.

"To England? To America?"

"The important thing is to go somewhere and come back with good news," smiled Fanar. "Whether you went by camel or ship."

"God 'teacheth man that which he knew not,' " said Anan Bassiuni.

36

IBN MAYYAH WAS THE ACTUAL RULER OF AL-
Huweiza and beyond; his rule was an accomplished fact, and the Sultan could not isolate
him or intrude in his affairs. To the same extent that he followed the
Sultan, he was independent of him. He demanded money, provisions
and ammunition, when they were slow in arriving, and sent no share
of the sheep or taxes he collected, "because war is war, Your Majesty."
He was filled with dreams, desires and whims; he wanted to conquer
the four corners of the world, but could barely manage the shortest
distances before encountering artillery manned by the British and
their infidel followers and Khureybit, who was like a wolf: he never
slept or missed anything, and was ready to attack at any moment.

Relations between the two were extremely delicate, at a point between peace and war; they were not friends, but not quite enemies.
When fighting broke out and the Sultan's reproach came, Ibn Mayyah
bellowed like a wounded man, "This is God's will decreed for us!" and
when things quieted down, it was Omair's turn to preach: "We have

borne arms solely to raise the banner of Islam, to fight innovation and kill infidels. Time has passed, but we have not changed; our weapons are in our hands. It is Khureybit that's changed. He has joined the English and turned against his own brothers, and wants us to do as he's done. No, by God, we will still fight and risk our lives, and win either victory or martyrdom. That's all we want. This is our conflict with Khureybit; you, people of reason and faith, come and judge—who is wronged, and who is in the wrong!"

After several tentative tries, Khureybit felt assured that war was coming, but he would have to prepare for it, and choose its hour, rather than having it chosen for him.

After envoys and gifts, and after living for a period in Awali, Ibn Mishaan "was now ready to talk," as Ibn Bakhit said, so the Sultan did not leave him.

One night as they sat around discussing their enemies' traits and how to deal with them, Ibn Bakhit told the Sultan, "Ibn Mayyah, Your Majesty, is what the Egyptians call 'crooked-straight'—he's an honest man, but with the brains of a bird, more stubborn than a sheikh's mule in a mountain pass. If he's with you, he'll go along with you; if he's against you, he'll go along with you. I should have told you my views years ago, but, Your Majesty, I was protecting him as a hen protects her eggs, and no one ever spoke against Ibn Mayyah. Time passed, the eggs hatched, the chicks stepped out, and now he sits on all of al-Huweiza. That's his story!"

"What do you think of Ibn Mishaan, Abdallah?"

"Ibn Mishaan, Your Majesty, has heard the music they make in Awali, and smelled and tasted their women, and come to know silk and darkness. He looks up and feels confused; he doesn't know whether to be with the Sultan or with Ibn Mayyah. He wants this life and the afterlife; he wants to be in two places at once."

He paused and took a deep breath, then added slyly: "Your Majesty, I don't judge people by what they say, but by what they don't say. I learn about a man when he talks and when he's silent, from how he cleans his teeth, what he says to the fellow who pours his coffee or pours water on his hands when he washes them. I know him by what jokes he laughs at and which side he sleeps on!" He laughed. "Take me for what I am, Your Majesty, and God willing I will not disappoint you."

"And?"

"And nothing but happy endings, Your Majesty."

"What do you suppose Ibn Mishaan wants?"

"I suppose, if I am not mistaken, that he wants the clover of Awali, the pomegranates of Traifa, and the women of Watfan!" He paused and smiled. "They tell me that he would not trade his Watfani woman for all the other women on earth—she's the one who advises him and makes the decisions!"

"Are these women from Watfan beautiful?"

"You know as much as I do, Your Majesty, but in Awali they say so."

"How can we get to this Watfani woman, Abdallah? How can we get her to help us with him?"

"That, Your Majesty, is what I do not know. You need a key: a sorcerer or reader of omens, a healer or fertile woman. When you've found his key, Ibn Mishaan is ours—he is nothing like Ibn Mayyah."

The Sultan laughed like a child.

"How do you know so much, Ibn Bakhit?" he asked.

"I keep my ears open!"

"No—tell me."

"The people of Mooran, Your Majesty, learn from sheep and camels, and say nothing. But don't think they know nothing—no, they know everything!"

"Do they know about me? Or talk about me?"

"That I do not know, Your Majesty—they talk privately."

The Sultan wanted to know what the people knew, but that could wait. He spoke again in a different tone: "Fine, and Omair, Abdallah?"

"Omair?" Ibn Bakhit spoke the name in surprise akin to contempt.

"Yes—Omair," repeated the Sultan.

"Ask Fahmy al-Zouni!"

"Fahmy al-Zouni? My veterinarian?"

"If you have an animal doctor, who's familiar with jackasses and dogs, he'd be the best expert to ask."

"God forgive you!" laughed the Sultan. "I swear, if your wickedness were divided up among everyone in Mooran, it would be enough to ruin the place."

"God keep you, Your Majesty." He paused. "Tomorrow or someday, all heads will be revealed and you'll see who's bald!"

When Hamilton returned, a month and a few days later, he was a different person: he was thinner, pale and drawn. The Sultan was taken aback by the sight, but said nothing, especially since Hamilton was apparently not ill.

Hamilton—perplexed and embarrassed as he never had been before—explained to the Sultan that Britain was principally concerned with the security of Mooran's neighbors, and with Ibn Mayyah or anyone else only insofar as they affected those states. As to financial aid, Britain was now in the grip of a severe fiscal crisis, but would nevertheless try to keep its promises and find the money. It might be paid out late or in installments, but in the end Britain would absolutely stand by its commitments.

The Sultan could grasp no more than this, not because Hamilton was disinclined to talk, as he sometimes was before, but because he lacked information, or was unsure of it, in addition to being tired and uneasy.

Two or three days later in Mooran, at a carefully chosen moment, Hamilton drew the Sultan aside. "After long thought, after investigation and now being convinced, I want to become a Muslim, I want to convert to Islam, to remain in your kingdom and live my whole life here. I will stay by your side, or in any place you assign to me. I hope you will consent to this."

The Sultan was flabbergasted; he could not believe his ears. He stared at Hamilton to see if he had been drinking or was otherwise not himself. When he appeared sober, as well as unhappy, he asked, "Are you sure, Sahib?"

"I am sure—with all my heart and spirit and will, Your Majesty."

The Sultan did not know how he had decided this so quickly; he shouted for al-Ajrami to be summoned without delay. Within minutes, in the presence of Olayan, Ibn Bakhit and three guards, Hamilton formally professed his Islam, repeating the two creeds after al-Ajrami. The Sultan warmly and feelingly gave his blessing to Hamilton's conversion, and so did al-Ajrami, Olayan, the guards and even Ibn Bakhit, but late that night when he and Othman al-Olayan were going back, recalling in silence the evening's events, Ibn Bakhit asked, with cunning innocence: "What do you think, Uncle—now that Sahib has become a Muslim, should he be circumcised or not?"

The question took Othman al-Olayan by surprise. He answered, "The important thing is the creed, Abdallah; that he say, 'There is no god but God; Muhammad is the prophet of God,' and follow Islamic teachings."

"That's your opinion?"

"As long as a sheikh has recognized his conversion, Abdallah, stay out of it!"

"The Islamic religion is unlike others," Abdallah replied slyly. "It is tolerant, openhearted and generous . . . may God let it triumph!"

37

HAMILTON RETURNED TO AWALI WITH A NEW name, Abdelsamad, and was known by no other name than that. He loved it and insisted upon it, and wanted everyone to use it. Al-Ajrami had suggested it and Hamilton went along; before going to bed that night he looked up *samad* in the dictionary and read the definition of the word: Abd al-Samad made him the slave, *abd* of the Lord; the Eternal; the Everlasting; the Solid: *al-samad*.

Upon arrival in Awali, he wrote in his journal:

"One must, even in a small state, act and assimilate according to the logic of the state and its interests; one is capable and valued insofar as he is ready and able to become one with this state; if he does the opposite, he must fail, if not immediately, then eventually.

"Empires, such as the British Empire, have logic and interests of such vastness, diversity and changeability, that those wishing to be their permanent clients, who are not their agents of influence—as no individual can influence an empire—must change their colors much as snakes shed their skin, in order to remain acceptable, to be given the right to voice an opinion (but not to impose an opinion).

"In the 'Oriental Conference' the Empire made a statement in conflict with everything it had said before, with its treaties and former commitments, because the circumstances, and the Empire's new interests, demanded it. I tried, of course, as did others, to bring up Britain's treaties and promises, to draw attention to all our previous statements, but what we said was too strange to those gentlemen's ears, and even annoying; they wanted us to get our blathering over with quickly so that important things could come under discussion.

"I understand, of course, the motives that brought on the change in policy, and what factors and considerations were involved, but I insist that something should remain unchanged, as a guide. This is the criticism I made in that meeting, and what left me feeling so bitter and let down.

"I am too old to start over again, to change the way I think or to find new friends; it is too late, but I can still reshuffle my priorities, the things I need to do. I might find a margin of success between what the Empire wants and what I can do, within my convictions and existing friendships. I will make use of the margin granted me to accomplish several things at the same time: I will stay in Mooran, help these people, who seem to me worthy of help and ready to do something, at least in the region. I will continue my archaeological and historical discoveries, not for my personal satisfaction, but to shed some light on an important but unknown region at the same time. I am certain that what I write about the region will be important, and may even become a source for future researchers.

"Now, more than ever before, I feel that my Aunt Margot was right. She used to say, first of all, 'You must go deep into a society to discover it and learn about it; and secondly, you have to approach it with earnestness and affection to reach its truths.' This is what called me to become a Muslim. To enter this religion, in spite of its rigors, may open up opportunities and horizons to me that no Western travelers or explorers ever had before. People here are afraid of the 'other,' and the 'other' is, more than anything else, another religion more than another person. This is what I believe, and what I will try to explore.

"I kept thinking, during the Oriental Conference, that Britain must be ready to help discover Mooran's wealth, but it seemed to me that this does not take any urgent priority, so that I agreed that there be other options.

"It is true that some things happen by chance, but still have their effect, opening horizons unimagined before. After the dinner party at which I met Mr. Stephen Sinclair, who was so eager to learn about the desert of Mooran, because he knew the Australian desert well, as he told me, our conversation turned to the likelihood of finding certain resources there. Sinclair went from being curious to being deeply interested. He was ready to send an exploration team, and asked me for support.

"I did not hesitate to offer my support; Americans seem to me more daring and farsighted, and there is no incompatibility of interests between America and Britain. The important thing is that the West should be here.

"I mentioned Sinclair to the Sultan, saying that he might help us out looking for water, gold and oil. He was delighted, and immediately asked me, 'How much will they pay?' I told him that question was a little premature, and that the sums we could demand would depend upon what their exploration turned up. He nodded and said, 'When will they know?' When I told him, 'A few years,' he was crushed. These people have no patience when it comes to money; they want it all now.

"Ibn Mayyah has become a threat, because Britain is taking new realities into consideration, without concerning itself with what others say, however 'historical' or logical it sounds. I emphasized to the Sultan the necessity of taking measures, not to the point of war, because settling the situation this way will lead to what they will consider a *fait accompli*. He nodded but gave me no firm answer.

"I cannot adapt comfortably to the demands of the new religion; furthermore, I seem, even to myself, to be a different person. I am slow to pronounce opinions and to think through to final results, or at least this is what I feel, especially when I pray with the others. Their stares pierce me through and unnerve me, and I perceive that they are unsure, unconvinced by my conversion.

"Awali is still far preferable to Mooran. People here are more understanding, and readier to deal with foreigners.

"Fanar amazes me. He is coming along with startling speed, and is ready to act, very quick to understand and react. If it were not for these constantly chattering advisers and the presentation of contradictory suggestions day after day, things would be much better. Even so, I must not clash with others, and make an effort, without realizing it, to see the need for giving priority to projects and relationships more important than others.

"I have brought a large supply of books, and ordered yet more; a book is one of the few things in this world that gathers men together, and makes him a better thinker.

"I will not be able to do any long-range planning, because I am under obligation to Sinclair, and his men will be here in a few weeks. I will have to have things ready for them, and accompany them to Mooran; I may even have to go along with them to some of the sites. So I must give myself a short holiday to sort things out."

Anan Bassiuni had noticed the profound change in Hamilton after his journey, and was told by the British consul that "Hamilton does not represent the official policy of His Britannic Majesty's Government. He has his own views, some of which may be unacceptable." The consul smiled scornfully. He decided that the man's ambitions were meeting with disaster and would crumple completely, especially when this became clear to His Majesty the Sultan, and when he saw the results for himself. Anan Bassiuni, who had been optimistic, was dealt a terrible blow by the news that Hamilton had converted to Islam, taken the name Abdelsamad, was letting his beard grow, and generally behaving like the most deeply pious man anyone had ever seen. He said to himself: "He bested you as an infidel, he bested you as a Muslim, and now he's one of the Companions of the Prophet?" He thought of Abu Sufyan.

He asked the British consul about Hamilton's conversion, but the apathetic reply was that "we don't get involved in such personal affairs."

"Don't worry, market people!" said Shemran al-Oteibi in the Souq al-Halal. "The English have become Muslims, and tomorrow or some day your children will have blue eyes; whoever doesn't believe it, go ask al-Ajrami."

The topic continued to arouse sarcasm, curiosity and awe, until subsequent events wiped it from their memories.

38

ONCE AGAIN, TIMES WERE CHANGING.

Just as Khureybit had done in the campaigns at Wadi al-Faid and later in al-Huweiza and Awali, he now sent for his relatives and brothers-in-law and his closest advisers. Some of them had moved away, because of mistakes made or the bad treatment they had received, or because others had pushed them aside.

As soon as they arrived, they were all called into a meeting and addressed by the Sultan.

"You all know, my good friends, that for more than thirty years we have been galloping from place to place; in all this time we have known no rest, nor have we even closed our eyes. With help from God, however, and from you, we have founded this kingdom, and said to ourself that future generations, and those who had worked so hard, should be able to rest. For even Almighty God created the world in six days, and rested on the seventh. But we have among us a group of people who have worked tirelessly and taken no rest. We take people for what they are and tell them, 'Almighty God offers; so help yourselves. We must be satisfied, and praise and thank Him.' We tell them, 'God reward you, friends, and give you long life,' but they never listened to us or understood. Now, what it has taken us thirty or forty years to build, what was achieved only with the people's toil, they seek to destroy."

His features were sorrowful and angry. He gazed at his listeners to see the effect of his words, and when he saw how silent they were, how cautious and frightened, he went on.

"My friends, I have been patient and tolerant, and said to myself, 'Endure, Khureybit, some day they will appreciate you.' But day after day, as we held our peace and stayed patient, they got worse. You know, my friends, that every man, even if he were as big as a camel, reaches a point where he must say, 'I can take no more; I can bear no more than I have already borne.'"

He sighed sadly, then his tone changed completely.

"Our people used to say, 'Whoever takes your advice is under your protection.' I, as God is my witness, have known sleepless nights, and have sent for you only to ask your advice and say what was on my mind." He lowered his voice, almost to a whisper, and went on sadly. "It occurred to me, my friends, I say it candidly, to leave and not come back, and you would have had to look among yourselves for some other leader than me."

He choked slightly on the last word, and let roll a tear he could not hold back. There was a pitiless atmosphere of strain and sadness over the gathering. Within moments, in spite of the many and diverse reactions among the many listeners, a single hidden impulse surged through the gathering, uniting them into a single bloc with no beginning or end.

The silence was brief, but seemed to those present long and oppressive. The Sultan put an end to it, speaking without raising his head.

"God burdens no soul beyond its limit, and I—I say it proudly, and with Almighty God as my witness—have done my duty and done what I can, and have never sought, not for a single day, any praise or thanks. If you wish me to resign, to spend the rest of my days on this earth devoted to the service of my Lord, Whom it is my only wish to please, I will be grateful to you. This is the whole story; it would be most gracious of you, God bless you all. This is what has been on my mind, and what I wanted to say to you."

Some of the elderly men exchanged glances, provocative and determined glances, full of the desire for confrontation. When no one else spoke, al-Ajrami stood up.

"Listen, Abu Mansour—and I want everyone to listen." He looked around at everyone, almost angrily. "It is we who pledged our obedience to you, and entrusted you with your authority, with the lives of our people; their honor and integrity are your responsibility in this world and the next. The shepherd may not leave his sheep, and a leader may not put aside his authority."

His tone changed.

"We, Abu Mansour, and God is our witness, know the weariness, trouble and hatred you have endured. I know, better than anyone else, that you bear upon your shoulders burdens that mountains could not bear. And I know that people don't know that, and don't appreciate it, but some day they will."

He reverted to his original tone.

"That is why I do not want to hear you pronounce the word 'resign,' or the word 'leave.' Not only that, I speak for all those present when I say that we will not allow it, because we still stand by the oath that we swore, that was witnessed by God and His Prophet, and we won't stand for anything else!"

Al-Ajrami was able to express what he thought clearly, and the thoughts of most of the men, but these were not the thoughts of all; for those who alternated talking after him were a mixture of excited and angry men, or surprised and stunned men, who resorted to shouting or weeping. Some of the bolder ones drew their weapons. There were chuckles and even songs heard, but on the whole it was an agitated buzz that started up abruptly, in which no actual words were discernible and no meaning evident. There was no sign of what should be done.

Waqiyan al-Darri, one of the Sultan's paternal uncles, who came to Mooran only rarely, preferring to stay far away with his falcons, was surprised at what he heard.

"Listen, Khureybit, if this is our fathers' and grandfathers' kingdoms you're ready to throw away in a moment of anger, or because you don't like what someone said, then swords will decide between us." He turned eagerly, as if wanting those around him to draw their swords, and added, between clenched teeth, "So listen well: before we go after Ibn Mayyah and take up arms against him, we will take them up against you, if you keep up this empty talk."

The Sultan laughed nervously and raised his eyes.

"My friends," he said bitterly, nodding and changing his tone of voice, "by God, by God, by God, I have spent long years licking my wounds in silence; thinking to myself that things would change; that these are our friends and must be borne; but it only got worse."

"Listen, Abu Mansour," said al-Ajrami, to change the mood, "a man's conscience can be neglectful; we sit in the shade and gab, we hunt, and if we earn two coins, we run out and marry, leaving all the burdens for you to bear . . ."

"The hardship is not the point, Abu Mishael," replied the Sultan almost irritably. "If it were a question of hard work, I wouldn't have said a thing, but it's a question of . . ." He laughed and looked at the two or three men nearest to him. "Brothers, the very closest people, who see and know everything, you heard them saying, 'Khureybit has left the faith, and forgotten what jihad is.' They said, 'Khureybit has sold the country.' It was never-ending. We were between two walls of flame: our brothers and our enemies! But at the same time, it was, 'Please, Khureybit,' and 'We want something, Khureybit,' 'Do this, Khureybit,' 'Don't do that, Khureybit,' until we no longer knew who was with us and who was against us!"

Waqiyan spoke sharply.

"Listen, Khureybit, you are speaking the truth. We didn't make you our leader until you showed you already were one. They were always saying how things should go and idly gossiping, but you could never find them when anything needed to be done. If you get one of them, though, the rest of them will get the point!"

"My friend, we have no wish to kill or strike anyone. We want people to understand us and work with us." This was the Sultan's reply.

Tarrad al-Mejoul, one of the Sultan's brothers-in-law, and a cousin of Fadda's, spoke up. "Friends, I have something to say and I want you all to hear it. A few days ago we had a visit from some men sent by Ibn Mayyah, and after some small talk, they brought out their gold and said, 'The whole place is with us; Khureybit is finished. We've come to you because you're dear to us, and we want to make a deal with you. If we rise up against Khureybit, you stick with us; if you're too afraid, or disagree with us, don't be with Khureybit, stay neutral—not with him or with us—and this gold will be yours.'"

Waqiyan al-Darri, who had stretched his neck out like a stork, asked, "And what did you say?"

Tarrad laughed and looked around at the men listening to him, then looked at Waqiyan al-Darri. "Us? What was our reply?" He turned all around, searching and called out. "Where are you, Ayid?"

Ayid raised his head.

"Tell them what our reply was."

"Our Tarrad told them, 'By God, by God, if you were not our guests,'" said Ayid uneasily, "'if you had not eaten bread and salt with us, not one of you would leave here alive.'"

"And then, Tarrad?" asked Waqiyan.

"I can't tell you every small thing that happened, Uncle. They said, 'The English!' They said, 'Islam!' They said, 'Khureybit is unjust, a tyrant.' In a word, I told them, 'This has gone too far. I may be a sheikh, and able, until now, to protect you, but no longer. You had better leave.' Not only that, I told them, 'Tell Ibn Mayyah that we are with Khureybit; we will be the first to take up arms against you, if you do not end all this and become loyal again.' I told them, 'Spare us your talk; return to your senses. As we used to say, "A bad sultan, or eternal discord." You are sowers of discord, and the people are with Khureybit!'"

"They've told me so much about you for so long, Tarrad," said Waqiyan al-Darri, "and everyone speaks well of you. They say you're a good man—that there's no one like you!"

The Sultan spoke up again to get back to the subject.

"There have been hundreds of such incidents, my friends, and many such even worse. That is why I do not want to face my Maker alone on Judgment Day, and as Tarrad said, 'A bad sultan, or eternal discord.'" He laughed and nodded. "Ibn Mayyah calls me a bad sultan and says that I've sold the country; but every one of you knows me well. If I have a fault, it is that I am too lenient. I'm too tolerant. I always say, 'We live for today; God forgive everything in the past.' But if someone has something in mind, or has ambitions, or treasonous ideas, he had better find a tent or a cloak in which to hide!"

His tone of voice changed completely.

"To get back to what I was saying, friends. I am alone, and tired, I have borne your troubles for years and years, and I don't say this to reassure you, no, by God, but a man is only flesh and blood. This can only go on for so long."

There was silence. He went on sadly.

"I want you, my friends, to look around and find someone else." He smiled and added quickly, "I will be the first to give my aid and loyalty to whomever you choose."

He almost went on, but Waqiyan al-Darri stood up, his face flushed, showing anger and aversion.

"Never! Do you hear me, Khureybit?" He pounded the ground with the blade of his sword. "We are not leaving this place until we find a way of helping you, of lightening your burden, so you can put anything else out of your head. Don't say another word! Everything will be as it was before."

"We are men of faith, men of the divine law, and know what is permissible and what is not, and now I am going to say what is on my mind."

"Before you speak, Abu Mishael," interrupted the Sultan, "I would like to hear some of the men who have not spoken."

Those who had not yet spoken, evidenced any opinion, or otherwise participated, now exchanged glances among themselves and the others and looked very nervous. Although any of them might have spoken, at length, too, and very eloquently, they were utterly at a loss. Some shrank down or looked away, as if they had nothing to do with these proceedings and wanted someone else to speak what was on his mind. They were not cowardly, or unaware of what should be said and done, but in this throng, in this charged atmosphere, they had become a peculiar species, deprived of their wits and the ability to express themselves, and, when compelled to speak, appeared foolish and even laughable.

The Sultan's words hung in the air, menacing them all. None of them wished to speak first, so al-Ajrami again came forward.

"These are our people," he proclaimed to the Sultan and the rest of the meeting, "and I can speak for them, if I may speak briefly—"

"Is that agreeable to you?" asked the Sultan, interrupting him again.

Their voices accumulated like children's stones, thick, fast and cha-
otic, but all in agreement. The Sultan laughed and looked at al-
Ajrami.

"Proceed, Abu Mishael."

"I could say, Your Majesty, 'We live for today, God forgive everything in the past'; and I don't want to say who has been negligent and
who not. We live for today." He drew a breath and looked around
him. "Yes, we live for today. The first thing we'll do is swear our oath
of loyalty anew; nothing less, whether you like it or not, Sultan. Your
authority demands it; otherwise God will reckon it against you in this
world and the next. You must agree to this before us all!"

The Sultan nodded several times and smiled, then looked around
and spoke hesitantly.

"I agree—on condition."

"Let us speak on, Abu Mansour, and then you may say and do what
you like."

"Just as you say, Abu Mishael," laughed the Sultan.

"After we swear our loyalty, Your Majesty, every man present must
bear his responsibilities and get busy; he must say, 'I am present, Your
Majesty,' and not only that—he must make up for past negligence and
see that the mistakes of the past are not repeated."

He laughed and looked around and spoke sadly.

"Friends, we have been a great trial to this man; he has struggled
from place to place, and now, if we want to help him, we must lighten
his burden, without his asking. We know what is expected of us. If we
were to leave him, to say, 'Go, you and your God, and fight; we'll stay
here,' why then he might take that two or three times, but a man has
his limits. He's not a rock. He's not made of iron. He needs our help."

Just as their voices had rung out, with warmth and assertiveness, to
demand that he stay on, they now announced their readiness to help
him.

"As our sheikh said, and the Sultan," said Waqiyan, shaking his finger warningly in their faces, "if any of you care to go your own way,
or talk against us, you'll have no one to blame but yourselves!"

The Sultan spoke comfortingly: "I have no desire to tell you, my
friends, how hard we have labored, and how things are with us; that
would only embarrass me. I always say to myself, 'Khureybit, this is
your duty—if a man wants to ride a camel, he needs to build higher

doorways.' but, as God is our witness, we have labored, but we can take only so much, and need the help of every one of you!"

The meeting, which went on for long hours, was not supposed to have been attended by advisers, not even Hamilton, Bassiuni or Rafet Sheikh al-Sagha, though Abdallah al-Bakhit attended it briefly, only to leave on an urgent summons which he had arranged beforehand. In this meeting everything that needed to be said was said, and the Sultan left it, as he had so many others before it, in triumph.

A few days later he reviewed the outcome of the meeting with his advisers and a number of his guards.

"You won't be angry if we say something?" Ibn Bakhit asked him.

"Our problem, Abdallah," answered the Sultan miserably, "is that people don't say anything anymore. That's what frightens me." He sighed. "When they talk, you know what they're thinking, what they want. Please say whatever you like."

Abdallah al-Bakhit chanted:

> "Before and behind you are varieties of desire
> No matter which way you roam."

"Our friend Abdallah is an optimist," remarked Rafet Sheikh al-Sagha. "He thinks the Romans are behind him. What if you told him that they were everywhere else, too?"

"Trust in God, Abu Habib, and keep your eyes open."

"The important thing about a meeting like that one," said Hamilton, "is that every man have a chance to speak, to state his point of view. That way each can consider himself the Sultan's political consultant and commentator on the rebels' views—but will all of them who were here keep their promises?"

The Sultan laughed.

"Sahib, what our people have to say is important, but what's more important is to look into their eyes, because eyes reveal—they say everything." He guffawed. "I looked at every one of them, I looked at them all. I wanted to know whether what they were saying was true or not, but, God is our witness, they were speaking from the heart."

Hamilton would write in his memoirs: "Among other things, it is no easy thing to judge the way these people think or act. The principal thing for me now is to gather facts, to watch their movements and pay especially careful attention to the way they react. The bedouin seem very friendly but excel at concealing their true feelings and reactions. They are like waterskins, for they fill up to a certain point, as much as they can stand, but beyond that burst and say what they think.

"The Sultan's recent meeting, preceded by a good many gifts and banquets, and notable for a great deal of play-acting, according to the facts as reported to me, would seem to indicate that these people have all sorts of ways of reaching an understanding. Words, no matter how persuasive, aren't enough, nor is friendship, no matter how exaggeratedly it is paraded. They have ways of probing found nowhere else, or at least understand one another in highly secret ways. I don't mean to reduce the thing to a heap of magic symbols, but, even so, they have other ways. When a man will believe only what he can see, he is bound to make grave mistakes.

"On the subject of practical facts, the Sultan was able, with surpassing skill, to win the first battle. I do not know what course things will take from now on, but in any case, every man left that meeting feeling a victor. The strange thing is that, as I understand, they came back only with words and personal gifts, but nonetheless they were pleased and content, but made no further demands or had no further ambitions. There are so many things in desert life that make one stop and think.

"Another fascinating thing is that the clergy, no matter what else one might think of them, are extremely important men. They have no power or soldiers, nor are they capable of influencing others directly, but they have unusual powers of oratory and casuistry, to say nothing of their insolence; it is this insolence that renders them capable of judging others.

"In this desert, tribal solidarity, blood kinship and ties of marriage represent the true scheme of life. Here they feel that blood relations are the mainsprings that control and animate everything else. I wasn't surprised that many men I met in Mooran and Awali, immediately upon discovering some tie of kinship between them, no matter how distant, become inseparable friends, as if they shared some unheard-of discovery.

"What does blood mean in this desert? What does kinship mean?

"I must make time, in the future, to study this fascinating phenomenon, not because it is something extraordinary but because it is a phenomenon so characteristic of this primitive society. Does it exist in other societies?"

The Sultan did not let this victory pass without putting it to use; he assigned each of his men a duty, either to recruit men, circulate propaganda, or otherwise prepare for the conclusive battle. He sent a number of his sons and relatives bearing gifts to the tribal sheikhs and replaced some of the provincial governors. Al-Ajrami dispatched a number of clergymen to sojourn in the desert. Less than three months after the first meeting, the Sultan convened a second meeting in Mooran, and this time it was not limited to the clergy and men he knew firsthand; he invited a large number of tribal leaders, prominent citizens and merchants; he invited Ibn Mishaan, Ibn Mayyah and Omair, and some of their supporters.

Those who attended the second meeting, or knew about it, said that Mooran had never seen anything like it; those who were close to the Rawdh Palace said that the palace, from the days it was built and first inhabited by the Sultan, had never held such a massive or eminent assemblage of men.

Ibn Mayyah was the only one not to show up. He pleaded illness and sent two of his relatives. Ibn Mishaan came, with a large contingent of bodyguards and advisers. Omair arrived one whole week early, and it was clear from his contacts and speech, and his general boldness, that matters would not proceed smoothly. Fanar, who was in Mooran, was told what his uncle Omair was saying, and appeared embarrassed, then angry, and asked his father to see personally that Omair was "disciplined."

The Sultan smiled and said, before a large number of his men: "No, my boy, Omair will always be your uncle." He then asked Fanar to come closer, and whispered in his ear. "We want him to talk as much as he wants. The more he talks and rants, the better we'll know what's on his mind. What's more, I think you should go and see him."

After brief hesitation, Fanar obeyed. Despite the anger and indifference of the early part of the meeting, as it progressed, Omair made a reckless attempt to persuade Fanar to abandon his father. His pretext had once been that Khureybit had sold himself and his country to the English, and still later that Khureybit had abandoned jihad and made peace with infidels, thus becoming an infidel himself. Fanar gave no serious thought to convincing his uncle; he was much more interested in discovering what Omair and the others wanted. He came with this goal, recalling one of Hamilton's precepts, that "a ruler should not be afraid of plots if his people are contented, but if he is hated and feels the hostility of his people, he should be afraid of everyone and everything."

The meeting ended inconclusively, but Fanar was able, after a long scolding, to absorb part of Omair's wrath, then fill him with uncertainty about Ibn Mayyah's intentions; while he did not succeed at driving a wedge between them, he left suspicion akin to fear in Omair's heart by alluding to the existence of letters between Ibn Mayyah and the English, which had been intercepted by the Sultan. Fanar also indicated that he understood his uncle's thinking, especially from the religious point of view. The two men reminisced sadly about Sheikh Awad and Ain Fadda, and wished that things had taken a different course.

Then came the banquets, receptions and conferences with sheikhs and notables that preceded the public meetings; gifts were given, and promises mounted and grew as the day of the meeting approached; the welcome, solicitude and attendants all created a thunder that rolled across Mooran from end to end. Many had taken part in this great effort, especially the Sultan's relatives and male in-laws, but Khazael was the busiest and best able to work with those sheikhs; even those who seemed unenthusiastic and aloof, or who took refuge in silence or generalities which did not amount to consent, no sooner arrived at the Ghadir Palace than, before or after lunch or dinner, they met in brief sessions with him and came out more convinced, and readier to confront the "mutineers and troublemakers."

When these meetings were over with, the Sultan told Khazael glowingly, "I must tell you, my boy, that the job you did amazed me." He guffawed and went on in a different tone of voice. "You have peculiarities, even though you are my son and I've known you all your life. You are unpredictable. You sleep as winter snakes hibernate; nothing can wake you. Then you do a month's work in one day!" He paused. "So—what's the story?"

Khazael laughed. It came out like a neigh.

"They are all our friends, sir," was his humble answer. "We know them well, and we have done them a good many favors."

"But they listen to you, and hear your views."

"Money, sir, helps loosen them up, and when they're loosened up, it all happens: hearts open, ears listen, and a man gets what he wants!"

How the meetings proceeded, what Ibn Mishaan, Omair and the others said, how the Sultan and al-Ajrami answered them; how Waqiyan al-Darri drew his sword and made threats, and Tarrad al-Mejoul and others told of Ibn Mayyah's attempts to create dissension, how the Sultan brandished a sheaf of papers, which he said were letters Ibn Mayyah had written to the English—all of this was retold with wonderment at the Sultan's eloquence, and with a great deal of mockery at what Ibn Mishaan and one of Ibn Mayyah's relatives said.

In short, what transpired in the meetings was the implementation of what had already been decided, and in spite of the accusations and angry speeches, everything had been known in advance. The final meeting concluded with a moving speech by the Sultan, at the end of which he said:

"You will never find any hatred in our hearts for anyone. In our eyes every man is a good and worthy person. We are people of faith, and as to what we defend, Almighty God, in His perfect scripture, condemned dissension even more strongly than murder. We want everyone to look carefully and weigh every step before he takes it. Before you all I say, 'God have mercy upon the past, but if a man turns against his people, he has only himself to blame'; no one is great or immune if he tramples his loyalty, and you, friends, are our witnesses."

Rafet Sheikh al-Sagha attended these meetings and recorded a number of the remarks, but what most caught his attention was the health of most of the other attendees. He was to write, in his health memoirs, that "malnutrition is very much in evidence, as can be seen from the emaciation and jaundiced eyes. Except for a very limited number of those present, the overwhelming majority of attendees show signs of malnutrition, not to mention chronic diseases in almost every case. There is a strikingly large number of men blind in one eye, or deaf. There is a huge incidence of premature senility. Those with chest ailments and hernia, who suffer from glandular defects, are in the clear majority, or so it must be, from the way they walk, talk and breathe, from their complexion; they are afflicted. It may be due to poverty in addition to lack of nutrients and necessary salts, rather than to their upbringing, as I was told when I asked people about it. The diabetics make themselves known: they can be singled out without the slightest difficulty.

"There are many other diseases, and I will follow closely the symptoms and conditions for the study which I . . ."

Hamilton followed the Mooran meetings from afar but did not appear, and most of those present did not even know of his existence. When he learned most of the details, he commented to Fanar one night, "Let me confess to something very basic, Your Highness."

Fanar opened his eyes to hear this confession, and listened with his gaze directed far away.

"I'm sure that His Majesty the Sultan has never read or even heard of *The Prince,* but he has been able to personify a great many of the fundamental laws attained by 'His Highness the Prince.' That book could have been about him!" He paused and looked directly at Fanar. "He can perceive the experiences of others, to grasp them, and to bestow them from his soul and the soul of the place where he resides. That is how he achieves his fabulous successes!"

"We have spent long days in Mooran, thank you very much," replied Fanar brusquely, "and have no idea what has been going on in Awali during our absence. We must excuse ourselves and get out of here. We have a thousand and one things to do."

"With the Sultan's permission," smiled Hamilton.

"Or with Ibn Mishaan's," said Fanar sarcastically.

39

THERE IS ONLY ONE MORE BLOW TO STRIKE,
which must be the last; then the circle will
close and it will all be done," Hamilton said
to himself when the Sultan had finished up his business.

The Sultan himself, despite his power and confidence, seemed in
no hurry. Furthermore, every so often he was revisited by bitter
doubts: "These English; they're never satisfied, and just as they are
never straight with us, they may not be straight with Ibn Mayyah,
otherwise where does the money come from that they send all over
creation? Where does their power come from?" Not only that, they
had recently stopped or delayed payment of the agreed-upon sums of
money. They wanted to embarrass him, to press him hard. They demanded an end to the border incidents, and alluded, though not in the
least explicitly, to his weakness and hesitancy in putting a stop to
them, though it was they who were funding them—or so he was becoming more and more convinced.

Khazael never for a single day stopped asking, "When will we move, Your Majesty?" He wanted vengeance upon Ibn Mayyah, who had deceived him so many times. The Sultan listened and nodded his head, and usually said nothing, but once said:

"Everything in its time, my boy. The four hardest things in this world are war, treason, farewells, and death. War begins, but you never know when or how it will end. You may prepare yourself well and not let your enemy confuse you, and he may not know where your next blow is coming from, but the war can still devour you before it devours your enemy. It starts simple but multiplies and grows, and that is why you must prepare for it well, my boy, otherwise you will be annihilated.

"Treason, my boy, comes at you from the most unexpected person. The one you most trusted betrays you. This is not only difficult for you, it undermines your strength, so you must keep your eyes open— sleep as wolves do.

"As to farewells, they are little deaths, but when true death comes, Khazael, my boy, no one can put it off."

Al-Ajrami, who had never once spoken of military affairs, was now more interested in them than the actual combatants were. After leading the conscription and propaganda drives, someone came with news of his brother-in-law's death; how he had been murdered in mysterious circumstances, and nothing whatever was known of the killer. What happened to him was that Ibn Mayyah had sent him a brief message: "I am after you; time is long. Let Khureybit protect you." He kept this message secret for a certain time, but fear began to stalk him night and day, causing his mental state to deteriorate, and that could not be hidden from those around him, least of all the Sultan.

"I think, Abu Mishael, that you aren't yourself today," the Sultan remarked to al-Ajrami one day when he was showing unusual watchfulness over who was coming in and going out. He smiled and added, "Is anything wrong? Are you feeling fine?"

"I'm fine, Your Majesty, just preoccupied."

"You have no right not to tell me about it, Abu Mishael."

"Never mind, Your Majesty."

"The mind," said Ibn Bakhit in mock seriousness, "gets rest and relief only from prayer, supplication and litanies!"

"Should we worry," asked the Sultan in the same gentle mockery, "that we may have alienated Motamadi from you?"

"My friends," al-Ajrami said in exasperation, pausing only an instant before adding, "the world is not always with us."

"In Iraq, they say, 'The Arabs are always with music!' "

The Sultan opened his eyes. He suspected that these two men knew something he didn't.

"Is everything all right, Abu Mishael?" he asked worriedly. "Speak."

Now al-Ajrami told how Ibn Mayyah had sent him messengers and letters, and how every letter contained more threats than the one before. He had not wanted to upset himself or anyone else with these threats, but recently they had become serious.

"And you know, Abu Mishael, that a man who has something in mind to do doesn't carry a drum with him, or announce it from a minaret!"

From then on al-Ajrami was accompanied, wherever he went, whether to pass through or to stay, by a group of heavily armed guards, which prompted a great deal of gossip and mockery.

Shemran al-Oteibi, the sage of Mooran, and the virtual sheikh of the Souq al-Halal, told the market people, "Don't worry about a thing, because your security is in good hands, and your commerce is guaranteed, as long as al-Ajrami is leading His Majesty's soldiers!"

Ibn Bakhit had much to say about it; he was full of mockery in this particular period, especially since al-Ajrami's household was known to be unquiet, which may have been the true cause of his weakness and worry. Ibn Bakhit knew most of the details of those domestic troubles, though he had no one with whom to share and discuss them. Some weeks after the soldiers had been detailed to protect al-Ajrami, he told the Sultan glowingly that "Ibn Mayyah is farther from al-Ajrami than the earth is from the sky, Your Majesty. He should be worried about the people around him—about the person on the pillow next to him! That's what his problem is."

The Sultan understood, and laughed.

Al-Ajrami was not the only one who seemed changed. Olayan, too, seemed a different man. He had handled the financial angle of the first meeting, found justification for the outflow of cash and gifts, and stayed friendly and close to the Sultan, but the second meeting gave him second thoughts and endless embarrassment. Up until the few days just before the final meeting, the Sultan alone controlled disbursements; he alone gave out all gifts of cash and goods, and when Khazael began taking part, Olayan lost his temper.

"It doesn't concern you, Othman," the Sultan told him in a friendly but firm voice. "If they should look around later on and be unhappy with what they got, it would be on you. This way I am responsible."

"Where is the money coming from, Your Majesty?"

"Have you no money now?"

"I have, Your Majesty, but a paper from your hand or Khazael's, and it's gone! God rest your father's soul."

"We know what your resources are, Othman, and will spend no more than you have. Trust in God and have no fear."

"Fear? I'm not afraid, Your Majesty, only when the money stops, I stop, and everyone will be running around looking for money and not finding it. When you fail, you'll be shamed—you won't be able to look in people's faces!"

These last words seemed harsher than Othman meant them to, but that was how they came to his tongue.

The Sultan addressed him firmly, with no trace of friendship.

"It is none of your affair. Pay. That's all."

The Sultan expected financial troubles soon, but was not waiting idly for them to befall. He had sent out a number of envoys with gifts to seek loans, which he received in greater numbers than he had expected. He kept the loan funds in reserve to surprise Olayan, and to help him with the hard challenges he would face in his final battle with Ibn Mayyah.

40

ONCE AGAIN IT WAS RUMORED THAT THE Sheikha had taken out all her gold plate, as she had done at the time of the Battle of Wadi al-Faid. It was said that al-Ajrami had given the Sultan huge sums of money. The loans he received from neighboring countries, and from the merchants of Mooran and Awali, were enormous. Fanar had done more than anyone else to secure these loans, and there was a persistent rumor that Sahib had been able to get his hands on great quantities of gold, in the form of loans and bullion, from companies seeking to extract gold from Mooran and Awali.

None of these efforts and precautions persuaded Olayan, and he took no part in them. As the time of the second meeting approached, and the money available to him began to vanish as rainwater vanishes into the sand, he was not allowed to visit the palace, and seemed nervous and upset. He constantly sent indirect messages to the Sultan. After once being inseparable from the palace, watching its visitors and checking out their relationship with the Sultan, and trying, as much as possible, to block gift-giving and prevent extravagance, things had reached a point where, with Khazael having gone beyond the limits he had set and considered reasonable, he refused to go to the palace and sent verbal messages to the Sultan with Irfan al-Hijris, all or at least some of which he expected to be delivered.

"Tell His Majesty," he told Irfan sternly, " 'there's very little money left; perhaps enough for today but not for tomorrow.' " He sighed like a bull. "And tell him, 'Show mercy to us on the earth, that you may be shown mercy in Heaven!' "

Olayan smiled sadly, looked all around and then almost screeched: "And if I keep on receiving these little papers stamped 'Pay to the bearer,' then one of these days I'm going to lose my patience and tell everyone who brings me a paper: 'Boil it, boy, and drink the broth, because His Majesty is bankrupt, and shitting out of an empty ass!' "

He saw that he had, in a moment of excitement, spoken unacceptably, and shook his head.

"Keep it between us, what I said, Irfan. Don't tell His Majesty. Tell him," he added sadly, "that the money is running out, our moneybags are flat. He must close his hand."

Olayan was silent a moment before adding angrily, "And I have no idea where we got this curse, whose greed is never satisfied, named Khazael . . ." He changed his tone of voice. "Tell His Majesty, spend what you want, but spare us this devil Khazael!"

While the Sultan had intervened, at first, to put an end to Khazael's extravagances, and later on to lend unexpected support to Olayan's finance ministry, things did not go back to normal, and relations between Olayan and the Sultan were not mended until much later. There was another reason no one mentioned out loud: the English firm which had come to him recommended by a friend of Olayan's, an Indian trader, in order to explore for gold in Mooran, to determine whether there were any other resources worth exploiting, and which promised to offer several loans if anything was found. They traveled from one end of Mooran to the other, and Othman al-Olayan had great expectations, but the company, once its explorations were complete, had nothing good to report, and said it would cover its losses, but left Mooran not completely dissatisfied, having left behind a small company, with a very limited staff, to continue the search for oil.

When the Sultan gave a huge banquet in the Rawdh Palace to celebrate three of his sons' reaching their majority, Rakan showed up uninvited, reckoning that he had become a man in every sense of the
word, without a banquet. The other two sons were Jazi the son of
Johara and Darri the son of Watfa. It seemed to Othman al-Olayan
that these celebrations would cost him dearly, so he asked leave to
travel to Awali, "as His Highness Prince Fanar has asked me to come,
to put his finances in order," but he had another, more important reason: to discuss with Hamilton the matter of "these English who don't
know how to work."

The Sultan consented to the journey, and said jokingly to Ibn Bakhit that "your uncle, Abdallah, doesn't want to join us out of fear of
opening his moneybags and inviting others."

"Leave my uncle to his worries," laughed Ibn Bakhit. "He never
sleeps at night."

The Sultan's eyes widened in surprise, and Ibn Bakhit added: "But
it is your intentions that matter." He laughed, then added in a different
tone, "My uncle, Your Majesty, has been slain by ambition. He cannot
sleep from fear of neglecting his money. When he counts it or looks at
it, he shrieks with laughter. And my other uncle cannot sleep because
fear is killing him. He thinks that if he dozes off, Ibn Mayyah will
come along and drag him out of his bed!" He laughed and nodded.
"They've asked me, Your Majesty, to sleep enough for both of them.
But never, Your Majesty, will you find anything better than the drummer in this world, the flutist in the next, no money to worry about,
no ghosts to pursue!" He nodded and laughed. "I should have stayed
by myself, Your Majesty, and borne it, me and my wife; but, as God
is my witness, there is no girl on earth like Olayan's daughter. She
says, 'Look after your money, guardian of Hell.' He can't rest! You
never know quite what she means."

The celebrations at the Rawdh Palace were tantamount to a rehabil-
itation, and a show of force and self-confidence. Fadda and Watfa
wanted the celebrations to threaten the other wives, and to create a
new social order in the palace, but the Sultan, in his own way, ordered
a different course: Ibn Oreifan had a word with the singers Fadda had
brought.

"Go to the Souq al-Halal—you might find someone who needs to
celebrate his son's circumcision, or someone who's marrying off his

mother or uncle. If you can't get them to hire you, go drum and pipe over the souls of departed Muslims! Here's the money Umm Rakan promised you!"

The members of the musical troupe were taken aback, and at first thought this was a joke or misunderstanding due to the difference in dialects, but when Ibn Oreifan insisted that they leave, saying that the party was canceled, and yet they saw all the preparations around them, all they could do was exchange glances and smile. Told about the Souq al-Halal, about the circumcisions and weddings, they thought that the festivities had been relocated there. They found nothing going on there, so scoffed, packed up their instruments and went back to Awali, saying that "Mooran is ignorant of music and can't dance, and doesn't deserve to have a single person living there."

Shemran al-Oteibi learned some of the details of what went on, and cried:

"Listen, market people!
'If the man of the house has a tambourine and snaps his fingers,
Everyone living in the house will dance!' "

Ibn Bakhit knew a great deal but could say nothing, especially in these circumstances; he was tied down on all sides. The Sultan himself was very busy and distracted by his involvement in desert poetry. When his first son came, he gave him his father's name, Badi, and was completely taken up with him. The Sultan sent him a gift and some verses of poetry he had composed himself; he did that to surprise him, and as a gesture to the mother of the newborn. After all, he saw Abdallah every day and had no need of communicating with him in this indirect way.

Months of conscription passed, of commotion and waiting, during which the Sultan tried to determine that the English would not take sides with Ibn Mayyah, or use Ibn Mayyah as a card to play against him. He was also trying to plan his battle; he sent Ibn Mishaan gifts and spies, and several messengers with promises to make him ruler of any region if he broke with Ibn Mayyah. Omair, on the other hand, was "a raging bull—no one, even God Himself, can handle him." In spite of the messages and religious rulings, and all his promises, all

Omair knew was, "The English are infidels, and anyone who coop-
erates with them is an infidel."

Olayan had spent more than three months in Awali, and achieved
some notable results in terms of righting some financial matters, but
came back depressed. He had been strict and stingy ever since the Sultan first put him in charge of financial affairs, and wanted, once more,
to expose the troubles facing the Sultanate. He drew attention especially to the lack of rain and the likelihood that this would, as a con-
sequence, be a hard year. Part of the pessimism dogging him, of
course, stemmed from the failure of the gold company. He had given
it much thought, and had even considered becoming a partner, against
the company's advice, through his friend the Indian trader, that he
limit himself to a small percentage as a fee.

There was a small gathering of men at al-Ajrami's house, at which
the Sultan said, after Olayan had revived his memories: "We have had
worse years, Othman, the stuff of stories and legends, but our people,
every one of them, came through with the patience and endurance of
a camel! Don't worry." He smiled and nodded. "In the words of the
Prophet, peace upon him, 'Believe in blessings and you will find
them.' Our sheikh here, Abu Mishael, knows how things used to be,
and Ibn Bakhit here, knows our history: what happened in this or that
year, and how, afterward, everything was right again, how people
lived on and had children. We must be patient, trust in God, and be of
good cheer."

"And the Lord God has said," replied Olayan in bitter haste, " 'Only
hear, O my servant, and I am with you,' and the Prophet, peace be
upon him, said, 'I do not fear poverty for my people, but poor
government.' "

Ibn Bakhit moaned, as if to himself. "Oh, this money, which
comes between friends, which ruins homes and brings wars!" He
laughed. "I'm not worried—I have no horses to give, and no money!"

"All the horses in Mooran are at your service, and yours for the
asking!" Khazael interrupted smilingly.

"I'll keep the fine steed I've got," was Ibn Bakhit's vague answer.

Al-Ajrami spoke, as host: "Trust in God, friends. It's not an order,
but I'm telling you, come along now, dinner is served!"

41

Years of plenty came slowly and serenely to the desert, and while the people welcomed them with relief, they never talked about them too loudly or confidently: they were afraid of themselves more than anything. "The evil eye never rests one day in its vigilant envy; it is always looking for the right moment to destroy everything." This had happened uncounted times in Mooran and al-Huweiza. No sooner did early rains come and people foresee a year in which they would not go hungry, than the markets started to bustle, and the pitch of buying and selling rose, in the expectation that buyers would be able to pay after selling their harvest of figs and barley or once their flocks returned from the desert, having eaten hugely and gotten fat, so the sellers agreed to wait. Then a pitiless invasion of locusts would move in and take over. Or an epidemic would come to claim most of the people or animals. The people could only look at one another in sorrow, and the sellers looked at buyers quizzically, to see looks of apology. Solutions were sometimes found, somehow, on some terms, to salvage what could be salvaged, as the catastrophe left no room for haggling or pressure.

There was nothing slow or serene about the arrival of drought years; they were strong and violent and heralded, from the first, by a warning hidden from no one. The dark winds, which were the powerful cold and dry winds, not only killed the livestock and drove away all clouds, or scattered them as dust scatters, but came early in the year, burying the last of the harvests, drying out the brooks, and bringing the people to despair. They did not know whether to sow or to move away or to attack and kill one another. Although they instinctively knew the signs of a drought year, they were eager to deceive themselves, and pretended, for one another, to be optimistic and confident. When the winter was half over and there was no hope left at all, then their anger mounted and overpowered all their other emotions, and took a long time to let up or fade away. It gave way to depression and despair, and a great deal happened between the beginning of their anger, the settling in of despair, and the descent of their sorrow.

The old men, strong men and rich men were the best able to give life in the desert, clear paths, and control over them, in good years, while the youngest and the lowest in social order were best able to understand these paths and comply with them—but the hard years changed everything: the rich, powerful and old men lost their control and cunning, and became less able to persuade and govern. The younger and lower-class men grew more vicious and violent, less prone to understand and obey. They seemed readier to overturn ideas, social arrangements and relationships that had seemed permanent and steadfast. Older men who perceived this defiance early on, and saw how it might go beyond any limit, generally grew readier to accept it and adapt to it.

Towns, cities and even villages, using their wiles and instincts passed down from generation to generation, were better able to bear the drought than the desert was. In a mysterious way, inhabitants of settled places had learned to put some things off in corners, or far from use, if they did not need them, then forgot them until these things became important or valuable in drought years; then they rediscovered and retrieved them to help face the hard years. City people, for longer than anyone could remember, had developed habits that were part of their lives, making it easier for them to adapt to and trick fate.

It was different in the desert, where, as soon as the ground hardened, the flocks grew thin and before long began to drop dead. Their
owners were quick to slaughter them, or to sell them for whatever
they could get, but this only gained them a few days, or, at the most,
a few weeks, after which they would be destitute and exposed as the
bare desert itself, or a tree which lost its leaves with the first cold
blasts.

City dwellers were readier and better able to encounter such years,
but the bedouin, despite their cunning and the mystery that surrounded their lives, quickly became like the trees that lost their leaves;
for that matter, exactly like poplar trees, tall in stature, thin and bare,
always agitated and trembling.

When the signs of anger appeared, people were apprehensive and
afraid; and this is what happened that year. With the onset of "the year
of resolution and prohibition," as it became known from being called
so in Khureybit's meeting, people began to fear hard days.

"We told him," said Othman al-Olayan to Ibn Bakhit testily,
"'Enough of this confusion, extravagance and money craze; a bright
coin will save a black day, but there is no life for someone who
meets . . .'" He paused long enough to draw a deep breath. "And now
it's, 'Come here, Othman'; 'See to this, Othman'; 'We need money,
Othman.' Even if I were the Prophet Joseph, there's nothing I could
do!"

"Don't worry, man," said Ibn Bakhit with a trace of sarcasm, "His
Majesty will fix everything!"

"Oh, of course. Irfan al-Hijris is engraving him pieces of paper, and
he puts his seal on them, and they send them to Olayan. 'Come, Othman, we need money.'"

Suddenly he shouted, "Tell me, Abdallah, where is this money
going to come from? Where am I supposed to find it?"

"I don't know any more than you do. God keep you."

"No, every day and every hour your head is beside his. You talk
and you chitchat. You have to tell him, 'This can't go on, Your Majesty, this is extravagance and ungodliness.'"

Abdallah al-Bakhit laughed. "If I were in your place, guardian of
the treasury, I'd lose the key, or disappear, and if neither trick worked,
I'd pretend to be dead!"

Othman al-Olayan bellowed like a muezzin. "I've already done
everything, Abdallah, and more, but nothing does any good!"

"Then you must simply be patient; God is with the patient." He paused and said sadly, "Me, I'm in your debt, I'll tell him everything, but whoever won't obey has no say, especially if he's like me: broke, and is no hero—no Antar bin Shaddad, and has no troops."

"Pray over him. Tell him. May God make it easy for you. If cupping doesn't work, we'll heat up the cautery irons. And if neither way works, we'll pack up and leave. Mecca has a God to protect her!"

42

WHEN IBN MISHAAN CAME BACK FROM AWALI, HE had all the men and money he needed, and awaited only the right moment to act, and to make known the position he had taken—not the one Omair or Ibn Mayyah wanted, nor Khureybit. This black year had unsettled and changed him. The signs of drought were clear at the start of the year, and the men of his clan grew curious and quizzical. He realized that he had been able to keep in control in past years because they had not been as harsh, and no good years were in sight, especially as most of his men came back from Awali rich; now he was on his guard. When he received a letter from Ibn Mayyah asking to meet with him in al-Jamra, "because things have reached a point no one can tolerate for another moment," he consented.

In al-Jamra they reviewed everything: the victories that had been won through courage and sacrifices. The banner of Islam would be raised only by their exertions; they had been the first to act, then

Omair joined in. None of the drought years of the past had been as hard or cruel as this one, for the "mujahideen" had been able to wrest the spoils of war from the infidels. Now they needed to begin again.

"We can set this nation right only by going back to the beginning," said Omair, who arrived at al-Jamra several days later. "Our only option is jihad. We can no longer be patient or silent, because the people are with us as much as we are with them."

"Remember, Awayid," said Ibn Mayyah, "how we used to be able to tell someone to die, and he'd die; now when we say to one of our men, 'Take this horse to water,' he takes her, but as if you had killed his father." He drew a deep breath. "The people are tired, Awayid. They are tired of hunger and infidels. They may obey us today, but you don't know what will happen tomorrow if we are hard on them."

At al-Jamra an agreement was reached to mobilize the whole desert. And in the middle of the spring it happened.

Some people observed that "Khureybit will be the last of his kind. He came in a drought year and will go in a drought year." Others said: "This is like no other year that ever was. If Khureybit survives it, he will live a hundred years, but most likely he'll flee."

Ibn Madi's men who had come from Awali to al-Huweiza said out loud that "Khureybit was helped and built up by the English. If it weren't for them, he would never have reached Awali or stayed there one day. Now they have abandoned him and he is going to pay the price, and settle accounts—not just his own, either. If you swallow needles, you shit awls. You'll see." Everything they said reached Ibn Mayyah's men.

The men of the desert heard it all but were in no need of edicts or persuasion, especially this year; nature alone would determine what would or would not be. When movement began and its echoes reverberated, the conviction spread that Khureybit would lose the fight and be forced out. Many people were even making bets, and said aloud, "The English have no friends. They'll abandon him today just as they abandoned someone else yesterday."

Khureybit's historian wrote, years later, that "the British plan succeeded in making Khureybit's position finer than a hair and sharper than a sword . . . every part of his country was full of the spirit of vengeance against him. Ibn Mayyah led the rebels, and the spirit of zeal had fired up the clans and tribes with common ground: the demand for a declaration of jihad. The cry was echoed in every part of the land. More rumors were planted than before: Khureybit had sold himself to the English, and had to be removed from power."

A neutral historian wrote, "Khureybit's situation was convulsed, but nonetheless British diplomacy saw in it the only effective power with which they could cooperate." And so attempts to reach an agreement were still possible, on condition that a treaty be fastidiously worded and all conditions agreed upon.

Khureybit would not allow the rebellion to come to him. He called in his city-based and clerical supporters, made use of whatever friendships or feuds that he could, some of which he had helped to create in the first place, and headed into the desert before the desert headed for him.

Ibn Bakhit was following it all in the greatest detail, and knew even the deepest secrets. "Your Majesty," he said, "hear me; you may not listen, but I must speak."

The Sultan smiled, and Ibn Bakhit took courage and went on. "Those English are godless. They'll take sides with whomever is left standing. They are with you, and not with you. If you listen to these consuls and talk of treaties, you will lose. But if you meet them only halfway, and tell them, 'This will do; this will not do,' they'll understand you much better." He shook his head and added sadly: "We told you, Your Majesty: Ibn Mishaan. The Watfani woman. Carrot and stick. The people advising you only know one word: sword."

Ibn Bakhit relaxed for a moment, seemingly undecided as to whether he should go on in the same tone, or some other.

"We have done everything possible, Abdallah—as you know."

"I do know, Your Majesty, but Ibn Mishaan is not Omair or Ibn Mayyah."

"Don't be misled. The mongrel is the greyhound's brother, and now you see them gathering."

"I think, Your Majesty," said al-Ajrami loftily, but with a trace of fear, "that appointing him ruler of al-Huweiza will be a fresh infusion of blood for Muslims, because death is staring Ibn Mayyah in the face, and he is running away. He worries me on your account!"

"Don't worry, Abu Mishael," said the king with angry irony. "When death comes, no one can turn it back!"

"The important thing is fresh blood for the Muslims."

"I have no problem with Muslim blood, dear sheikh, but Ibn Mayyah has things besides God on his mind, and wants more than al-Huweiza."

The Sultan decided not to listen, and set out for the desert, to find his enemies before they found him, and initiated the fight. He was sure that the English would, as Ibn Bakhit said, take sides with whomever was left standing, so that any concession he made would only lead to greater concessions, and any attempt at peace or concilia-tion would lead to defeat.

At the beginning of the battle he concentrated his attacks on Ibn Mishaan, because he was the weakest and most hesitant. After a few engagements he was able to open a breach and widen it, forcing the surrender of Ibn Mishaan, against whom some tribal groups had also mutinied.

Khureybit asked Khazael to distract or divert Ibn Mayyah, which led to a series of attacks and retreats by both sides. Messengers and messages went back and forth, as did promises and plots, and when the Sultan's victory over Ibn Mishaan was complete, he went out to meet Ibn Mayyah. One man's obstinacy clashed with the other's, and the ferocity that burst out from every quarter made the battle a long one. By the time the great summer of that cruel year began, it seemed that both sides had tired, and faced total ruin if they kept it up, and so the fighting tapered off and then died out, and one wait followed another.

The Sultan did not want to lose time. He sent Anan Bassiuni to the English over the border, and to Ibn Madi as well; and in these parleys everything was solved.

When the battles resumed in mid-autumn, the Sultan made a mas-sive assault to finish off Ibn Mayyah, and some of his soldiers said that the instructions given them were brief: "We want no prisoners." The blood shed in the sands of al-Huweiza, at al-Basima to be precise, nourished some very green trees, according to travelers leaving al-Huweiza from that border post, and might never have stopped flow-ing had not the word got around that Ibn Mayyah had been killed. The truth was that he had been gravely wounded and transported to the rear; when the Sultan heard this, he was so delighted that he could not sleep for one moment, and never stopped pacing around and ask-ing questions all night long. He told Ibn Bakhit, who was passing the night with him, "By God, by God, after I have defeated Ibn Mayyah,

I will teach him a lesson in front of the whole world!" He smiled and added confidently: "With death comes rest, but I'm not going to let him die, if we live, you'll see!"

Although Ibn Mayyah was defeated and wounded, "the Sultan insisted that he present himself, so he was brought on a stretcher of palm leaves to the tent prepared for the Sultan. He was in perilous condition and unable to speak. The Sultan discerned in his eyes the condition he had seen in one of his best army commanders, and was filled with pain. There was a brief silence, during which a terrible and fearful rage contorted his face," and then "the wounded man was transported to his house in al-Ruweifa, and the Sultan asked his own physician to treat him." He wanted him alive, and wanted to know how bad the wound was. He was told, and when Ibn Mayyah's relatives, including two of his wives, came a few days later to seek pardon, the Sultan was kind to them.

"Tell Abu Jazi I have no quarrel with him. I give my pardon, and may God pardon all of what is past."

Omair was so tall that he seemed like a giraffe to people seeing him from afar. His neck was the first thing they saw, and when he got closer, they saw his teeth. He was an energetic and restless man who never was still. The Sultan's guards arrested him as he was returning, at the head of a small contingent, to Ibn Mayyah's encampment. He tried to resist, to do something, but his resistance ended when he sensed that the men in front of him, whose guns were drawn, understood one thing, killing, and nothing but killing, better than they might understand any words he might utter. So he decided to surrender.

When he arrived at the Sultan's encampment and met the monarch's gaze, the Sultan asked him, "Well, Omair?"

"Nothing has changed, Khureybit," he said mockingly.

"That means you are not afraid?"

"Who is afraid of the truth?"

"Don't put on this manly front, Omair. It is better for you to ask for mercy, so that we can make a new beginning."

"Every day is a new beginning, because every day has five prayers, until God reclaims what is His."

"Omair, you are an adult, and an intelligent one. It is better for your blood not to be on us; you would be sorry and so would we!"

"Listen, Khureybit, and may others hear, too: life is taken away by

Him who gives it. We are mere travelers in this world. Don't be fooled; today you may have won and think you are strong, but Almighty God is stronger. We were with you, and today we are a nation, and the talk is of jihad, and jihad never ends until Judgment Day. But I am your prisoner today, and you can do what you please."

Khureybit did not prolong the conversation, but sent Omair to Awali.

"Tell Fanar there is a thousand-year-old fort in Ain Dama," the Sultan instructed Omair's escorts, "built by a caliph for rebels. That is where Omair will stay until he repents or dies!"

And he sent Awayid al-Mishaan to Mooran, to the Rawdh Palace prison. He left Ibn Mayyah alone, telling his men, al-Ajrami, Ibn Bakhit and others present: "If I arrest Ibn Mayyah and he dies in my custody, they'll say, 'Khureybit killed him,' but if he dies among his wives, in his own land, I'll be in the clear, with nothing to do with his death!"

The first winter rains came, and troubles seemed at an end. The Sultan went back to Mooran, where news of his victories had preceded him, and where the outdoors had a different look from the year before, or so it seemed, in addition to the shifted balance as a result of the many who had died or fled, the sorrows that occupied and plagued their homes, and the unquiet, unceasing question in Mooran, Awali and al-Huweiza: what would the next day bring?

Al-Ajrami seemed as happy as a child, and asked Mahyoub, emphasizing that the Sultan was not to be informed, for more guards, "because in these last wars, Abu Shibel, many vendettas were kindled, and one must be wary." With the Sultan, he was more direct.

"Remember, Your Majesty, it was my view from the first that the only thing they understand is the sword. Especially Ibn Mayyah. Indulgence only encourages them and risks everything!"

Othman al-Olayan's complaints never let up for a day, and while he was as tough, watchful and grasping as ever with all expenses, he seemed almost gleeful after the battles had ended, because they had brought in such fabulous booty, and the Sultan's share was more than expected.

"War is no game, Abdallah," he remarked to Ibn Bakhit as they surveyed the riches. "It is impossible to know how terrible it is." He shook his head. "But your Lord has made peace and protected it, and starting today, we must think differently."

The Sultan had not been absent long from the Rawdh Palace, but it held many surprises for him: Three new babies had been born, and Fadda and Alanoud had made peace. The Sheikha had mediated, along with five of the Sultan's sons, two of whom were Fadda's, and who were waiting, with horses, for the celebrations. Fadda had not protested when her singing party had been canceled, but insisted that it go ahead this time. The Sultan was delighted because of his victories, and the celebrations were more in honor of them than of the boys' coming of age.

When Talleh al-Oreifan saw the musicians from Awali coming into the Rawdh Palace with their instruments, and took note of their general demeanor and style, he had a word with Nahi al-Farhan.

"Listen, Ibn Farhan, starting today, both of us had better learn to become drummers or pipers, otherwise we're lost. Tomorrow they'll tell us, 'You're good for nothing here—we'll find you some work in the marketplace.'"

Nahi laughed.

"From your mouth to Heaven's gate, man. As long as God is pleased with us, we'll be saved."

"After today, I don't think anyone is going to be saved. The Sultan has become the champion rider, ruler of the land and sea, and you know that you can't save a man from victory or defeat!"

"Let's keep an eye on the drummers and pipers; God is good, and then we'll decide whether to become like them or to get out of here."

"You said it, Nahi; we shall see."

Waqiyan al-Darri, who received well-wishers at the Sultan's side, had never felt more magnificent. For the first time, he wore a pistol beside the sword at his waist. The pistol had been a gift from Sheikh al-Ajrami. When the right moment came, he seized the opportunity to say to the Sultan: "A high commander must have ten qualities: the generosity of a rooster, the tenderness of a hen, the courage of a lion, the daring of a . . . what now, Waqiyan? The daring of a . . . Oh, Satan be cursed for making a man forget . . ."

He had forgotten the other qualities, but to hide his forgetfulness, he swept on excitedly, pounding the ground with his sword: "In short, just look at Abu Mansour to see the rest!"

Ibn Bakhit stood by, watching and listening, and feeling that the place was getting too small for him: everyone who entered praised the Sultan and extolled his wisdom and gallantry. Most of them commended the Sultan's policy on Ibn Mayyah, how he had forgiven him and let him be even though he had been one of the Sultan's worst and wickedest enemies. No one mentioned how Ibn Mayyah had lost two of his sons, dozens of his friends and hundreds of his soldiers, in addition to the serious wound he had suffered.

Two months passed, during which the celebrations in the Rawdh Palace never stopped. The musical troupe from Awali gave several performances in the palace: for the boys' having reached manhood, the military victories, and the birth of a new son to the Sultan, who was named Nasr, or Victory. Fadda tried to persuade the Sultan to have a party to celebrate her new pregnancy, but he only aimed a look at her and made a gesture with his hand that made her ashamed, and she kept quiet. The troupe was brought, very cautiously and secretly, to al-Ajrami's house, to help celebrate the Prophet's birthday, which coincided with the three-month birthday of the son born to him of Olayan's daughter. He had named the baby Khureybit, after the Sultan.

Ibn Bakhit went to the party, and spoke to the Sultan about it the next day. "Everywhere you look, Your Majesty, you see those drummers and pipers. Can they be trusted? People are saying that they should trust God and get out of here before they cause a scandal!"

The Sultan's eyes were wide in surprise. He was quiet a moment and then spoke, as if to himself. "By God, that's the truth, Abdallah. They should leave." He then added in a distressed tone. "God's curse on women, from Eve on down! They are all Potiphar's wives, and bring nothing but troubles and catastrophes. God help us!"

Before the third month was up, there was news from Mooran: Ibn Mayyah had left al-Ruweifa, but no one knew where he had gone.

"God help us," said the Sultan when he was told.

"You know, Uncle, a wolf is at his fiercest when he is wounded," Ibn Bakhit told Othman al-Olayan. "What's past is one thing, but what's coming is something completely different. As His Majesty said, God help us!"

"Do you think there will be another war now?" asked Othman, as a child might ask.

"If it will come, it will come, but this time we'll see who's going to be devoured, and who'll be left!"

"May God give us good news." He said it hatefully. "If a man stays away, he keeps a cool head, but how did this happen? How did we lose all the joy, all the love and luxury, and come to this misery and poverty?"

Ibn Bakhit laughed, to soothe Ibn Olayan, and said, "Trust in God, Uncle, for things may once again be as they were."

The Sultan was feeling robust and confident. He remembered something his uncle Dahaim had told him years before: "Listen well, Abu Mansour: never go near a wounded man, an oppressed man or a madman until you've counted to one thousand; all these want to get their due before meeting their Maker."

So he was more careful now than ever before, especially since so many people were talking about the parties and gifts, and the English; how Ibn Mishaan, Omair and Ibn Mayyah were right in what they said. Piety and faith, even common morality, seemed to have become relics of the past!

When Mr. Miller wrote to him asking him to meet with Ibn Madi, to discuss everything for once and for all, to draw borders and agree upon them, the Sultan was quick to accept.

Ibn Bakhit went along with the Sultan, and told the story of Saqifa Bani Sa'eda, and the arbitration between Ali and Moawiyah, as if he wanted to memorize every word. He said slyly to Othman, al-Olayan:

"A man must be very careful, but he was like a camel: he wants it but he doesn't want it. When he met with Ibn Madi, he was blue, like the wind, but in an hour he relaxed, and told me, 'Ibn Madi said, "God forgive the past, we are men of today, leave the past, forget it; let us begin anew today."' He gave a shout of laughter and added ironically, 'Is any place stranger than this world? Every day you see and hear something new, and grow a new heart.'

"This Englishman, who was afraid, not knowing how to act for fear of offending one or the other, looked out of place. Khureybit was talking with Ibn Madi, and Ibn Madi was shouting, 'Coffee!' and then 'Tea!' and then 'Coffee!' again, and all the time they were deep in conversation. And they reached an agreement."

"Let them agree until all this is over!" snapped Olayan.

Ibn Mayyah had escaped from al-Ruweifa and gathered a good number of men. He wanted a decisive battle, and got it, but it was his ruin: he and his men fought courageously, and won some victories, but Khureybit had planned with Ibn Madi and the English to leave him an open rear line his forces might infiltrate, and when they did, it was all over.

Khureybit's historian wrote: "Ibn Mayyah's forces were encircled, and he had two options: a battle, or defeat. The Sultan, in personal command of his forces, took away the first option by launching a surprise attack with armored cars equipped with machine guns, which had the last word. Ibn Mayyah was defeated seeking refuge with the English, who took him away on the deck of a military cruiser, but the Sultan vigorously demanded that the English turn over him and his comrades, and they consented, sending him in an aircraft to His Majesty's tents."

A neutral historian wrote: "Ibn Madi invoked the granting of refuge to combatants, but the British did not share his view, and surrendered him to Sultan Khureybit."

There were uncounted contradictory versions of what happened next, and there was a long wait until the truth came out. Ibn Mishaan and a number of his men, in particular his close relatives, were put in the Rawdh Palace prison and stayed there until the death of Ibn Mishaan, which occurred within a year of his imprisonment. After that the rest were transferred to Mooran Prison, and there they stayed. His kinsmen's houses, and the villages they lived in, were leveled, and the large numbers of horses and camels they had owned were confiscated.

Ibn Mayyah was given a tent not far from the Sultan's and stayed there alone for several days. During those days the biggest festivities the desert had seen in long years were celebrated; he was meant to hear and see them in order to see how happy the Sultan was at this victory. Some of the Sultan's servants said that Ibn Mayyah did not eat a thing in that time, and took only water. Food was put at the opening of his tent, but within moments he would refuse it, without touching it.

He was taken back to Mooran blindfolded and with his headropes taken away, and it was said that he looked emaciated and exhausted, as if he had not slept for nights. He nearly fell when he was hoisted into the car that took him away, and one of the guards said that he never uttered a single word during the journey.

Ibn Mayyah was put in a solitary cell in the Rawdh Palace prison, where the Sultan's physician visited him several times during the first week. When he continued to refuse food, the physician had to treat him. Within a month of his imprisonment he died. One of al-Ajrami's relatives insisted—he whispered it to his friends—that the guards had "helped" him to die quickly.

Nothing was left of al-Ruweifa, once a prosperous town whose beautiful gardens were proverbial, except ruins to speak of the people who had once lived there. The families had been driven out of their homes. There was no agreement over the number of men and boys held captive in Khureybit's prisons, because they were not kept all in one place, and many of them died or grew up in the prisons.

Omair stayed in the Ain Dama fort for many years, and though he went blind, the Sultan never pardoned him. In his years in the fort and afterward, until he died long afterward, all of his organs and limbs grew skinny, weak or useless except one, which remained strong: his tongue. It never rested or stopped. Many of those who heard Omair, or were told what he said, declared that if danger loomed one day, it would be because of what Omair said—what he wanted people to know.

Once again, Mooran began to come alive, without the horsemen which had filled its life for such a long time.

"Mooran is patient," Shemran al-Oteibi told a crowd of men. "She conceives and bears, but never forgets. Not only that, she never hurries. Today Mooran may be a certain way, but no one knows what will happen tomorrow or the next day."

He shook his head and added, almost to himself:

"Blood, my friends, brings blood. You'll see."

About the Author

Dr. Abdelrahman Munif was born in Jordan circa 1933 into a trading family of Saudi Arabian origin. He was stripped of his Saudi citizenship for political reasons. He earned a license in law from Baghdad and Cairo universities and a Ph.D. in oil economics from the University of Belgrade. He served as director of planning in the Syrian Oil Company and later as director of crude-oil marketing. In Baghdad he was editor in chief of *Al-Naft wal Tanmiya* (Oil and Development), a monthly periodical. He now devotes his time to writing fiction. Munif resides in Damascus, Syria.

Variations on Night and Day is the third novel of his *Cities of Salt* trilogy; the previous novel, *The Trench,* is also available from Pantheon; the first, *Cities of Salt,* is available from Vintage International. Among his other novels are *Sharq al-Mutawasit* (East of the Mediterranean); *Heen Tarakna al-Jisr* (When We Left the Bridge); and *Alam Bila Kharait* (A World Without Maps), cowritten with Jabra Ibrahim Jabra.

About the Translator

Peter Theroux was born in Boston in 1956 and was educated at Harvard University and the American University of Cairo. He has lived and traveled in Iraq, Syria, and Saudi Arabia. He is the translator of *Cities of Salt* and *The Trench* and is the author of two books: *The Strange Disappearance of Imam Moussa Sadr* and *Sandstorms: Days and Nights in Arabia.* He resides in Long Beach, California.